Straight to the White House

House

Amerigo Merenda

Dedication

I would like to dedicate this book to my parents, Albert and Carmelina Merenda who as immigrants, arriving into the United States in the 1920's, raised eight children. My parents like millions of immigrants, worked very hard to achieve the American dream. They were my rock. To my brother Joseph and six sisters, Lena, Adeline, Yolanda, Julie, Mary, and Roberta, I thank you for your love of family. And to my children, John and Marly and their mother, Merilyn, thank you. And ultimately to my wife Joanne, thank you for your quiet and steady encouragement.

Chapter 1

Eric was a child who loved to get up early in the morning and think about what he wanted to do for fun and he managed to accomplish this more than not. He had friends who he called at this time; friends who shared his time clock- early risers were usually hard to find. After a bowl of Cheerios he would leave home and allow for the day to take shape. Not too far from his home was a wooded area that he gravitated to and where he enjoyed the solitude of being totally enclosed by trees and all the animal life that surrounded him. On this particular day he heard noise that sounded like leaves and twigs being stirred by someone walking ; quietly he gazed through the brush not to be noticed. It was a boy he didn't recognize so he kept still and just observed his movement approaching in his direct pathway. When their eyes glanced at each other it was like no other experience he had ever known and he was confused by what he felt. They both froze in their tracks as if statues posing for an artist. Eric was the first to speak. "Hi, my name is Eric. I heard you coming toward me; thought you were a friend who sometimes meets me to hang out together. Sometimes we sneak up on each other." The boy stared at Eric, somewhat startled but realized that Eric was no one to fear from the tone of his voice. He had a knife in a leather clip attached to his belt. Eric had a pocket knife but was impressed by the more appealing style of what he saw on this stranger. " I just moved here and wanted to explore these woods. Do you live nearby?" The conversation began and would lead to an amazing friendship that would open new emotions and trepidations for these two youngsters. They were eleven years old in 1958 and the world they knew was quietly evolving; family traditions, religious faith, and baseball were dominant themes in both of their lives. Eisenhower was president and America appeared to quietly and steadily progress in a decade that was stable and predictable.

Eric and Jim would begin a relationship that was based on shared interests and common beliefs. Both were Roman Catholics who attended St. Mary's church in upstate, Oswego, New York. Sunday mass was a regular habit and Eric was an alter boy who realized at one point that he may want to be a priest; he did however have mixed feelings even though his mind was leading in that direction. Jim on the other hand was an athlete who loved sports and was quite talented in high school and intercollegiate baseball; however he loved to follow political events and would gravitate toward history and political science.

Their childhood culture was surrounded by strong family ties and traditional values. Personal feelings were privately maintained; their futures seemed fairly predictable for their generation and could only be threatened by unconventional and unexpected behavior or events. The instant they met was ingrained in their memory; both knew something was present but as eleven year olds, could not understand their emotions nor where they would lead. Several years later after the high school prom which both attended with two female classmates who were childhood friends, they partied on the shores of Lake Ontario where a raging fire was built and where their dates would share intimate embraces on blankets covering large and small stones beneath their excited bodies. Whatever it was they felt with these two excited females would not take them the distance. Their inhibitions blocked natural instincts and sexual prowess; the girls were somewhat confused by the sexual disconnect that followed. All four peered into the blazing fire that generated a warmth in the night chill. Maybe the intimacy shared was not private enough for more activity to continue. Instead they stared at the fire and it satisfied them enough from saying a word. The crackling sound of flames and crashing waves on shore were enough to distract their natural impulses. Their silence was only broken by crackling flames that warmed their bodies but left their desires void. The girls were not inclined to stop but picked up some unexpected message displayed by Jim and Eric. Neither one of these young men took advantage of an opportunity for expressing their sexuality with a woman. Eight years later, Jim would marry his college sweetheart and Eric would follow his chosen path to priesthood. They would maintain distant friendships where infrequent letters would reveal their childhood innocence and the adult desires of two grown men.

Chapter 2

Eric graduated from Cornell University at the top of his class; the year was 1968. Several offers were received post graduation; all were declined. His intelligence was complimented by his good looks and Eric noticed women looking at him with more interest on many occasions. Eric however decided to embrace a non material world vocation, very different from the corporate/material professions of his peers. Eric had prayed about the decision to be a priest for over a year. On Good Friday his mother handed him an envelope; an appointment for an interview with Monsignor Quaid at St. Michael's Jesuit Seminary was inside. In order to be accepted for the seminary, Eric's interview had to be completed within a week of receiving the notice. He immediately called and scheduled a day and time for the interview with Monseigneur Quaid. Upon arriving at the seminary, Eric noticed the architecture of the buildings; it certainly appeared like a place for prayer and reflection. The driveway entrance was a city block long and lined with large Elm trees that draped over the road. Even without their leaves, their majesty was magnificent. Eric always loved trees and woods so he found these surroundings very attractive and comfortable. This he thought was a good sign. He parked in front of an old stone edifice that was the first building in the complex, St. Michael's Hall. When he walked inside there was an aromatic smell that he found very pleasing. The secretary at the desk looked up and saw Eric standing before her. He wore a dark blue suit, white shirt and tie. She was an older woman but she could not stop staring. Monseigneur Quaid opened the door of his office and greeted Eric with a friendly handshake. "Good afternoon Eric. Please come in and have a seat." Eric heard an accent in his speech. This priest was from Ireland with his brogue in tact. Since Eric was also half Irish, he was feeling more comfortable. Monsignor Quaid did not waste any time with small talk. After staring at Eric for a moment, and looking at his transcript he got very direct. "You are too good looking to be a priest. Are you sure you're in the right place? This is not going to be easy for a man like you." The smile on Monsignor Quaid did not alter Eric's discomfort. "Eric, I see you were valedictorian of your class. That's quite an honor. Why the priesthood Eric?" Apparently, Eric thought, intelligent men who are also handsome are suspect. "Well

Monsignor, this is a decision that was not hastefully made. My ambitions are not found in a material world. I prefer the spiritual." Eric was sure that he responded with conviction. "Would you call yourself an extrovert Eric?" This priest, Eric felt, had prejudged Eric based upon subjective feelings. Maybe monsignor was trying to unnerve him, to break him down. Was this a tactic? It was understandable that candidates have to be critically vetted in order to avoid wasting time and resources. After all this is a serious endeavor. "No, I am not an extrovert. I am however quite the opposite and prefer quiet surroundings most of the time. I do not have many close friends because I am mostly interested in my studies. I am not preoccupied with socialization as are most of my peers." Monsignor smiled and told Eric how his appointment was almost certain but that he had to ask questions that maybe difficult but are nevertheless necessary. After almost an hour with Monsignor Quaid, Eric was told that he would be accepted and that he could begin in the fall term. When Eric left he noticed several young men talking outside of the building. They looked at Eric not knowing he would be joining them in a few months.

Beginning seminary training during the following autumn was exactly what he imagined.. There were moments when he felt his decision was a mistake. He shared this feeling with other men but all agreed that it was something to be expected and most agreed to continue forward. One evening when classes and prayers were completed, the student seminarians gathered around the television to watch the 7th game of the world series when Msg. Quaid entered the room. All stood out of respect but were shocked and disappointed as Msg. Quaid walked over to the television, turned it off and without a word, left the room. This was obviously one of many "tests" of fortitude and will that would determine the staying power of priestly candidates; one by one they quietly left the parlor and moved to their rooms in retreat. Not a word was spoken. The next morning one candidate did leave before morning prayers. He left a note for Eric which read: Like you, I love baseball. The only difference is that I apparently love the seventh game of the world series more than the priesthood. I'm fortunate this happened so soon so that I can move forward with my life. My team at least won. Wish you well. John

Eric smiled and was sympathetic with the sentiments expressed but he apparently realized at that moment that he was going the distance. Nothing would stop him. He shared this story in a letter to Jim. In a response letter, Jim suggested they rendezvous one evening for a beer at a local tavern. Before leaving to meet Jim, Eric had an afternoon prayer seminar where Msg. Quaid led a discussion of meaningful prayer for seminarians who will on many occasions be faced with all sorts of temptations and moments of doubt where the absence of the holy spirit may leave one vulnerable to sins of the flesh. The discussion was very open, mature and relevant to issues that will confront all priests throughout their vocation. He was moved by the gravity of Msg. Quaid's advice which was to pray and move away from temptation when it was consuming ones mind and body. In essence, "leave the scene of the crime"; don't capitulate. While driving to meet Jim, Eric could not stop thinking about what was discussed with fellow seminarians and Msg. Quaid. He was shaking with fear and had to pull off the road and pause for silent prayer; he almost turned around to return to the seminary but once he allowed himself to think this through, he realized more and more what he would have to face. Why not now? Why reject a feeling without exploring it further. It would be worse to suppress or even repress sexual desires before surrendering to God's plan for him. Suddenly he felt a surge of energy and his composure returned. He remembered reading Victor Hugo's LES MISERABLES where a priest leaned on prayer and meditation when his mind was moving in a direction he was trying to avoid. He regained his balance and began to think of his sexuality in ways that were acceptable but also disturbing to him because he thought he was attracted to men but realized that maybe he was also attracted to women. With his peers he had discussed men who left the priesthood because they fell in love and wanted to marry and have children. Eric was really confused partially because he had not been with a woman or man for that matter. At age 22 he was grasping for his identity and thought the priesthood was a good place to start because he would place himself in a quasi solitary environment. Time alone was important for processing; he wanted to take control of his life. He knew he had to determine his sexual orientation before he could feel comfortable in his skin. He was concerned about Jim and feared their friendship could be compromised if he was not sure of his behavior when they were together.

Jim was sitting at the bar having a beer when Eric entered THE CHART ROOM. Jim was hungry and ordered a hamburg when Eric joined him. They decided to sit at a table overlooking the river view where they could have a meal along with private conversation. Jim appeared to have gained weight and looked much more mature and handsome than his appearance just six months earlier. They looked at each other, smiled and embraced warmly. Jim immediately wanted to know how the seminary was working for Eric. Their eyes locked and Jim revealed that he missed Eric and wanted to let him know his thoughts were confused since he met a few attractive women on campus. "What exactly do you mean Jim?" Jim didn't hesitate to respond. "I think you know what I mean Eric. Haven't we had this mutual feeling since our childhood? That's why I'm confused. What should we do?" Just then Eric looked into Jim's eyes and said. "What do you want to do? What do you think is best to do? I have these confused feelings too but I am about to become a priest. We were both raised in the Church and have to think before we leap into a relationship that can unravel our lives." Then Jim responded. "What about our happiness, our love for one another? Should we deny our feelings?" Eric was about to get up and leave, but instead, reached for Jim's hand, held it gently and said: :"I love you as a good friend, but only as a friend. Surely you can understand that. Our friendship and love can grow over time and our lives will be different. I will be married to the Church and you to some beautiful woman. You get laid regularly and I get to just think about it." They both laughed uncontrollably until the waitress brought them their juicy hamburgs. Jim began to tell Eric about his girlfriend from college and how she gave him goosebumps with her beauty and charm. He showed Eric a photo of Connie and Eric agreed that she was a very attractive young woman. He was almost relieved by Jim's new love because it distracted them from their focus on each other. Eric saw excitement in Jim's portrayal of Connie and realized that maybe it's normal for men to have loving feelings for another man without any sexual relationship. Could that be or were they both kidding themselves. Eric knew he had to be patient and allow their relationship to evolve without any expectations one way or the other. When they left the pub, they gave each other a warm embrace that seemed innocent and comforting. After all they were friends. Their religion, education, discipline and professional growth would lead them to their separate paths. They agreed to see each other whenever possible. When they left the CHART ROOM, they had advanced their relationship to a mature understanding of each others needs and wants.

Chapter 3

A month later, Eric left for home to visit his parents for the weekend. During an afternoon of shopping he met a woman he recognized from high school. She was two years younger, very attractive and would be teaching English beginning in the fall. Eric was 6 feet tall, had a good frame with dark brown hair, handsome and a good dresser. She had no hesitation in introducing herself outside of a pharmacy in the mall. Eric found her very attractive with her blond hair, blue eyes and beautiful smile. "Hi! Are you Eric?" Her smile was so pleasing and made her voice sound melodic. He often wondered if he would ever have feelings like this with a woman and was pleased with himself. "Yes, I am. I'm sorry but I can't remember your name but do know we went to high school together." She appeared pleased that she apparently made an impression. They both had bags filled with purchases and were walking toward their cars when Michelle asked: "Do you have time for a cup of coffee? There's a nice place just down the road on the right." Eric smiled, paused and reluctantly said. "Sure, why not. I'll meet you there in a few minutes." Eric was two years away from his ordination; better take advantage of every moment just in case his feelings changed. He realized situations presented themselves and anticipated occasions where he could test his commitment. His refusal would have been a sign of weakness and even rude.

In the local diner, they found a booth where they could sit facing each other. She ordered tea and Eric the same. She was not aware of Eric's future and rather than have her ask, he informed her of his future plans after completing his seminary schooling. "That's wonderful. What led you in that direction?" Her stare pierced through Eric and he was caught off guard; his response required some pondering and processing; he did not want to appear unsure or unworthy. "It's a first step on my journey to the papacy." She enjoyed his humor and wanted to hear more. "Seriously, that is a lifestyle that many men would find a real challenge. Was this something you planned for some time?" Eric knew he was experiencing one of many more tests that would make him question his judgment and determination. This was one he did not expect so soon but was looking forward to the challenge. "Being a priest is certainly a commitment but there are also many rewards that come with it. Serving a spiritual community will expand my appreciation and understanding of Christ's mission." Eric did not want to dominate the discussion. He wanted to hear more of her outlook on life and future plans. So he stopped and turned the conversation over to her. "Actually I would like to know what an attractive young woman, who just graduated from college will be doing with her life. You said something about teaching English. Is that correct?" Michelle's smile showed her beautiful teeth. Eric was feeling something he never found time for before and was surprised with himself. His sheltered life of retreating from social interaction was being altered by this sudden and unexpected encounter. He was enjoying her company and replayed Michelle's earlier comment. "Was this something you planned for some time." Those words hit a nerve deep within his soul and he never realized he would have a reality check so soon. Once he realized his uncertainty, Eric took a deep breath and allowed the moment to pass without too much notice. He was relieved when Michelle explained her new position as a high school English teacher. Her instincts noticed that Eric was unsettled by their brief exchange and she had enough sensitivity and compassion to refrain from probing too far. She lead her discussion into a new realm of public service and how both teacher and priest would both play similar roles. Eric was impressed with her finesse and marveled at the ease in which she transitioned their conversation. Her tactful demeanor was even more attractive so his ultimate mood was still one of finding her very appealing. This was truly a test he was not prepared for and realized that meeting with Michelle would only act to undermine his thinking and comfort level. Eric looked at his watch and suddenly remembered his obligation to his parents and sister Mary. He felt that Michelle knew what he was about to say and do and felt bad because what he was about to say was not completely true. "You'll have to forgive me Michelle but I have to leave. I promised my parents and sister that I would be home an hour ago. You will be an outstanding teacher." He took her hand and lightly squeezed a warm goodby. Before he could let go, Michelle stood and reached toward his shoulder and made contact to indicate her affection. "Eric, please notify me when your ordination will take place. I would like to attend if possible. Can non catholics attend?" Nothing she said diminished Eric's attraction to her. He felt trapped in a wonderful sort of way. "Of course. I will call you when the date is set."

Michelle wrote a telephone number down on a small piece of scrap paper from her purse and handed it to Eric. Was it her way of holding on to a moment in time. Eric wondered as he walked to his car.

Chapter 4

The drive to St. Michael's Seminary on Sunday afternoon was a four hour drive which allowed Eric time to reflect on two people in his life that he now could say had made his life more meaningful and emotional. One a man, Jim, who was a childhood friend from 5th grade through high school and the other a woman, Michelle who he just recently met and who made him question his whereabouts and vocation. This was a healthy conundrum for Eric and he realized the importance of resolving it but also realized that he wanted to complete his mission of becoming a priest before investigating his sexuality. He instinctively knew there was something wrong so he prayed that somehow he would resolve his uncertainties in due course but had to live out his life, one stage at a time. For now being a priest was primary. Eric knew he could focus and was thankful that his sexual habits were not knowingly problematic. His mind drifted to one evening when he was in 9th grade. He and Jim went to a movie and Jim invited him over to his home afterward for some ice cream and junk food. Jim's parents were away for the weekend and his older sister was in college far from home so there were no obstacles to inhibit social secrets and Eric did have a feeling something was about to happen. Jim appeared in his bathrobe with nothing on underneath. He asked Eric if he wanted to get more comfortable and Eric reluctantly agreed but did not undress underneath. When Jim thought it was time to initiate a move, he tried to hold Eric's hand. Eric complied but his mind was racing. Soon they were kissing passionately and Jim's hand made a move toward Eric's groin but Eric moved away. Jim persisted and Eric stood up and said. "I'm not ready for this." Jim insisted on moving toward Eric and overpowered him and performed sexual gestures while Eric unsuccessfully resisted due to Jim's strength. When they were finished Eric had tears in his eyes and he wasn't sure what he felt, disgust, disappointment, maybe both. Jim looked at him and said. "That was great; our first time. Did you wonder when this was going to happen?" Eric turned away and went to get his clothes which Jim had practically torn off his body. He was actually bruised from the encounter and thought that his resistance was not filled with enough determination. What did this mean? He left Jim's house without a word while Jim was trying to explain that nothing was wrong. He was sorry and pleaded with Eric to stay and talk it out. Eric hesitated walking away. He wanted an explanation; some reason for what just happened. He turned to Jim and said. "Why did you do that to me? Couldn't you tell that I was resisting you and uncomfortable? I don't know if I have the same feelings that you have. Can't you respect me and be more of a friend." Jim felt terrible because he really liked Eric. The last thing he wanted was to lose a good friend over something that he really could not understand without experience. Jim thought that unless he acted out his sexual desires and feelings, he would never know whether he was homosexual or heterosexual. "How are we supposed to know these things unless we try for ourselves. I have this strong urge and I have been attracted to you since we met in the woods. I think I am this way. Call it what you want. I thought you were too." Eric listened and could see that Jim was sincere in his explanation but that didn't change anything. He knew his uncertainty but could not offer enough resistance; for the time being he was confused about his sexuality. "Jim, you have been my friend for many years but I don't know myself as well as you seem to know yourself. Can you understand that and respect my feelings?" Jim left the room and returned fully dressed. "Come on, I'll drive you home. We can talk on the way."

The discussion with Jim revealed some concerns that Eric raised. "What if some of our friends suspect something between us. That would destroy our entire life. Think of that and maybe you will have second thoughts about how to react when these thoughts overpower you again. My parents would be so ashamed of me. Yours too." Jim did not respond but he did listen to every word. Whenever he was silent it usually meant that he understood and would not offer any challenge. Because he was a star athlete, he did not seem to see a problem. Students would not expect him to be queer; in fact Eric was also able to conceal any social concerns for similar reasons. Both came across as masculine and this is what bothered Eric. How could this even be a problem? Eric and Jim were not feminine in their behavior; both were quite opposite in fact. Neither seemed to fit the part. Eric raised this question with Jim. "Are you attracted to girls? There must be some hot ones in school that you find attractive. Any interests there?" Jim responded with: "Oh yeah. There are a few that I would like to see naked." Eric quickly responded: "So why me? Why me? I don't understand"

As Eric pulled into the parking lot of the seminary he realized that Jim was too shy to even ask a girl for a date but had to release his sexual drive some how so he became Jim's target. This realization did not change Eric's uncertainties about his sexuality. What happened with Jim caused him to feel terror; he could not trace the reason for this feeling but he felt it was real, not imagined.

Chapter 5

Seminary life was mentally and spiritually rigorous. Every day presented challenges especially from the dialogues of Socrates on Truth. For Socrates to surrender his life for his beliefs and values was a powerful example of personal strength and character. Socrates' old age was irrelevant. Eric was only 22 years old. His sacrifice may have appeared different but inner truth and "knowing thyself" were very important. Eric had to know his own truth. Other seminarians were also struggling with their personal shortcomings and they had several important conversations among themselves, all encouraged by their professors who were mostly priests and knew the meaning of sacrificing pleasures of the flesh. Several men already decided to leave after concluding they could not honestly cope with the strains of sacrifice required for the priesthood. Celibacy was not for them and they were grateful when they recognized their inner self; it did require a great deal of verbal and intellectual exchange where emotional integrity had to be displayed at all costs. For whatever reason, Eric maintained his firm belief that his life was that of a celibate and therefore priesthood was a vocation he could live with and suffer through without too much anguish. There were 28 men in his seminary class when he began, 14 remained. These 14 men continued to question each other with the blessings of their Jesuit teachers who maintained a rigorous mental and spiritual routine where no stone was left unturned. Philosophy, psychology, history and theology were assimilated with God's footprint. Greek rationalism did provide a logical blend of spiritual and intellectual reasoning that allowed Eric to reconcile the spirituality found in religion with the rational component of Greek philosophy. His inner strength was fortified by Father Hall whose pastoral guidance was exemplary. He told Eric that his decision to be a priest was made when many years ago, his girlfriend's father asked him when and if he planned on an engagement for his daughter. At that moment, Robert Hall decided to be a priest. Father Hall told Eric. "The point being that one never knows what triggers a momentous decision. You will find your compass one day and point to your future decision with confidence." Eric had to ask. "What if I change my mind later and decide to leave for whatever reason? How do I live with that? Isn't that failure on my part?" Professor

Father Hall looked at Eric with piercing eyes. "No Eric that is not failure. That is life with all its uncertainties. If and when that happens, you will have found that your compass has directed you toward a different goal." Eric felt like a massive weight had been removed from his shoulders. He felt he could now move forward without too much trepidation. He found comfort and peace in those words from his mentor. He wasn't trapped. Finally he could celebrate his life decision, knowing he still had options. Father Hall, Jesuit scholar, was also rector of St. Mary's Parish in Oswego where Eric was raised. He taught once a week at the seminary and Eric was comforted by his wisdom, friendship and mentoring.

Seminary life was not a walk in the park. Eric was schooled by some of the best minds within the Catholic intellectual community. There were days when he wanted to give up especially when he received a letter from Michelle. He felt a strong tug on his heart strings but was fortified by her words of encouragement. "We are where we are for a reason. Let's make the best out of our decisions and pray for the best outcome." She continued to inform Eric of the challenges involved in teaching high school English but knew that she would succeed because she enjoyed her classes and students. A few of the boys had to be advised of proper classroom decorum; apparently they were turned on by her natural beauty and charm. Eric found that he was most successful when he could focus on his mission and tried to detach himself more and more from the outside world. For that reason he did not respond to Michelle's letter hoping that her attraction would diminish with time and space.

Eric wanted to read about priests who questioned authority because he had many questions that were not resolved within the church. Copernicus for example questioned the understanding held by church leaders who believed the earth was the center of the universe. Galileo would confirm the fallacy of this belief using the telescope but in so doing was threatened with excommunication and imprisonment. Luther questioned many fundamental church practices and printed them for all to read in German and as a result was pursued by church authorities unsuccessfully. John Calvin questioned fundamental beliefs concerning scripture and introduced his predestination theology. The list of priests who questioned church doctrines is quite extensive and Eric found it disturbing. Where was the intellectual and spiritual integrity? He sensed that his Jesuit professors and mentors silently agreed with him but decided to take the long view; that is over time the church will be forced to change when truth in biblical scripture is revisited. Christianity and democracy will evolve under the free exchange of ideas. Eric wasn't so sure of this but decided to wait it out and work from the inside.

Prayer was offered as a means to an end. Prayer would silently and slowly make inroads that would unravel historical inaccuracies by religious scholars. Eric wanted to be a priest who was prepared for the intellectual challenges facing the Roman Catholic Church. Issues such as celibacy, birth control, divorce, pedophile priests and homosexuality were not being addressed to his satisfaction. He was correct in feeling that his mentality was far ahead of his time.

Chapter 6

A year passed and seminary culture was gradually absorbed by Eric and thirteen other men who survived the onslaught of spiritual meditation and study. He felt as though he had reached the point of no return one very early Sunday when he led morning prayers. Something seemed to click and he felt a surge of confidence overwhelm him. A spiritual breakthrough. Faith in the trinity was being discussed. How could God have three entities? Eric remembered his catholic school education when Sister Eileen explained the trinity to fifth graders. She used a clever scientific concept: water. "Water", Sister Eileen explained, "has three forms, liquid, ice and vapor. God is like water. He also has three forms, God the father who created all life and matter, who is eternal, God the son who came to life on Earth in order to experience our needs, weaknesses and strengths and who ultimately sacrificed his life for our salvation and God the holy ghost who lives as our spiritual guide and whose capacity for our eternal life is paramount." At the time Eric found this explanation very easy to understand; her reference to water just made sense so Eric shared this with his peers. Simplicity. There were however questions raised among seminarians who studied fundamental issues. Two seminarians came from divorced families. They were conflicted about divorce and annulment. The church's distinction was not satisfying these young men whose families were severely disrupted by painful memories. Apparently their parents divorced because they were forced to marry due to pregnancy. Love was not involved so both parents after three years wanted to divorce and could not remarry in a catholic church. This was upsetting because the new brides wanted and always dreamed of being married in their church. Because children were involved, the church would not grant annulments. The animosity of the parents over this family crisis was apparently passed along to their sons. Eric was surprised that personal experiences of this nature would not discourage these men from ever considering priesthood. Their explanation was, time heals and we must move on.

The 1960's introduced a new issue for Catholics with the discovery of birth control pills. Woman were now free of the constraints of their traditional sexuality. It was liberating and the results were revolutionary.

Women could now take control of their bodies like never before. The church was historically out of sync with science and technology so now birth control became another controversy for Catholics. Eric rejected the church on many issues and this was added to the list. He knew he would be confronted with questions from future parishioners and had to think of reasonable explanations for women to accept in order to maintain their faith. Sexual relations between husbands and wives was in Eric's mind filled with enough emotions and by adding spiritual anxiety to the act of sexual love and passion did not make sense. Leave people alone. Stay out of their bedrooms. There were moments like this when Eric did have doubts about his future role; he did not want to resort to church laws that were contrary to his views, especially personal issues. Eric was realizing more and more that he was up against a massive challenge. Birth control, divorce, abortion, and the fact that Roman Catholic priests could not marry and have a family were all very problematic for Eric. He had however this strong spiritual urge to move forward; all the problems would be part of his mission. Eric also had another issue, that of homosexuality. He questioned his own sexuality and believed that heterosexual and homosexual men and women were all God's children. When Eric pondered all these lifestyles and life choices he had difficulty reconciling his decision to move forward. Skepticism was becoming his obsession. When this happened, he prayed for hours. Eric also practiced meditation which he learned from one of his seminarian colleagues who was from India. He taught Eric the gift of meditation and more than any other mental routine, meditation went beyond prayer. He also discovered that Jesus learned meditation from Buddhist priests when he journeyed East to India during his late twenties. Yes Jesus was schooled by Hindu and Buddhist holy men who imparted their spiritual intelligence that combined with his own inner strengths allowed him to evolve into a Man-God being. Meditation made Eric stronger and wiser. Problems melted away and inner peace filled his spiritual body. This gave him hope and optimism that he could fulfill his obligation to complete holy orders.

Chapter 7

The day of reckoning was approaching. Eric would be ordained in eighteen months. He still had time to bail out but his mind was prepared for challenges that were constantly emerging. Failure to pursue his goal was now viewed as an unacceptable option. He would become Father Eric O'Reilly if all went well. The priests and scholars who became his mentors were truly men with gifted intellectual personalities. One individual, a philosophy teacher made a big impression on Eric. He was not an ordained priest but was retained by the seminary because of his brilliance and ethical intellect. He was in fact a man who apparently chose solitude without priesthood. On one occasion during a beautiful spring afternoon, Eric made a point of meeting with his professor in his office adjacent to the library. The history of Jesuit catholic scholars, both as priests and men of intellect was known throughout educational institutions. This philosophy teacher was someone who was born a catholic on his mother's side ; his father was Jewish. When Eric opened the door to his office, he was warmly greeted by Thomas Dreyfus, a man of sixty years of age but who looked forty something. "Eric, so good that you could make it. Please make yourself comfortable." The office was filled with books and papers, but was amazingly neat in appearance. Dreyfus was born in New York City but moved upstate during his college years and fell in love with the charm and laid back lifestyle shared by communities surrounding the finger lakes. He was well groomed and words flowed from his conversation with cheer and reservation. He was a big Yankee fan and he and Eric shared this in common. It was so important for Eric to have this meeting because he had a gut feeling that many of his questions would be answered with candor and integrity. "I appreciate your time because there are several issues and questions that I am sure you have heard before." As much as Eric loved baseball, he could not afford any time discussing relief pitching or batting averages. Dreyfus got right into the reasons for Eric's concerns and requests. "Well it is important for you to open your mind to all issues; after all this is a major life decision and vocation. Where do we start?" Eric looked puzzled, only because he wanted to ask him a question about his work. "Well I often wondered why a man of your stature decided to teach and work with church officials for the purpose of training priests. How did that happen?" Dreyfus smiled because he thought it strange their discussion was beginning with his life, not Eric's. But he understood the question and realized right away that Eric's question was reasonable; he too would want to know if he was Eric. How did he end up here? Dreyfus stared at Eric. "I'm pleased you asked me this because I often wonder about that myself. Let us however agree as gentlemen, that words shared between us be personal and private because I am sure our discussion will go there." Eric's heart was missing a few beats; he realized that everything was going to be shared with this man and he felt relieved and knew it was right. "Professor Dreyfus, I have tremendous respect for you and appreciate all that you have done for my intellectual growth. Now that we are about to share our personal lives, you can rest assured that our exchange will be totally respected and private." Now that the ground rules were established, Eric felt at ease. He had never been to therapy before but if he had the experience, he would want it to feel like this. He knew how important this was for him but strangely he felt that Dreyfus felt the same way. Was he reading this correctly? He had to be careful not to overreach. Being inquisitive for the right reasons were within the boundaries of personal discussions; were boundaries going to expand beyond that?

Dreyfus then led with: "You know Eric, I must tell you that you are one of the most gifted and interesting students I've had in my career. And that goes back awhile. I say this for several reasons. First your intellectual capacity led me to believe this, but upon reading your papers, I have also seen a deeper side of your mentality. You seem to be hiding something that is bothering you. Am I off the mark on this or what." Eric was pleasantly shocked. This man read him like a book. There was no hiding himself from this man of wisdom and he knew it. Eric never imagined or realized that he projected an image that was detectable but apparently something clicked and Dreyfus picked up on it. Dreyfus did not want to avoid Eric's earlier questions so he hesitated and said. " Eric, why don't I answer your question about my life first. You may have concluded correctly that I am not married and I might add, there are several reasons. First of all the woman who almost became my wife decided upon another lifestyle; she became a nun. We are still friends and it was her decision to refrain from the secular world in favor of the spiritual that made me wonder about my own true core. She was a transformational peer." Eric asked. "Do you have any regrets?" His response. "There are usually always some regrets but time has a way of healing emotional love. It is best not to dwell; one must move on. There is one thing I want you to know from the start and this is important. I have chosen a life of study, teaching and research. It consumes me. But if I had married my love, I would have been happy in that place too. It just didn't happen." Dreyfus paused. "There is one other point that may be important for me to place before you. I am not a homosexual. I think you may be thinking that so I just wanted to make that clear, not that it matters." Eric did not expect to get to this crossroad so soon. "You know Eric, what makes you attractive is your intelligence and timidity. It's a beautiful combination. Many young men have too much bravado and little discretion and humility. I don't see that in you. Am I wrong?" These personal comments and observations were pleasing for Eric. Dreyfus used the word timid to describe Eric. What did he mean by this? Eric wondered. Dreyfus stared silently at Eric; he wanted a response but Eric appeared to be lost for words. "Well I might as well be up front with you because the sooner I discover my inner soul and self the better. I sometimes am torn between two worlds: the world of men and the world of women." Dreyfus nodded as if to suggest he understood. "Continue Eric." "Well it revolves around an experience that goes back to my childhood; I was about ten years old when I first discovered this attraction to a boy my age. We became good friends throughout our school days together and there was one intimate episode in high school unsolicited by me. We are still friends; he has a girl friend and I discovered that I am also attracted to women; I seemed to have blossomed in this area later than most males. But I feel confused and uncertain about my sexuality." Eric felt relieved that he had "confessed" even if Dreyfus wasn't a priest. "Well Eric, Freud would not be concerned with your sexuality for this reason, and by the way, neither am I. Sexual behavior has many taboos attached to it, unwarranted taboos. If you were a homosexual, you would know, the signs are strong and compelling. You also are attracted to women. Is there someone in particular?" Eric had intentionally not thought of Michelle; it was a conscious attempt to reinforce a celibate mentality crucial at this juncture. "Well I met this women shortly after I entered the seminary. She has written me several letters but I decided to move away from the temptation. I did not want any hurt feelings. She's really attractive in so many ways, but I think I'm over it." Dreyfus once again gave Eric that staring look. "Have you officially ended this relationship? Closure is important. Before you can move on it would be a good idea to allow yourself the opportunity to tell her your decision in person." Eric had plans to do just that; now he knew he had to carry through and see Michelle. "Tell me Eric, what attracted you to the priesthood?" Dreyfus changed the subject. It was as though he went far enough and realized that for Eric, it would be best to allow him to process his situation and allow him to arrive at a solution concerning his personal life sooner or later. "When I was in elementary school or maybe more so in junior high, I found that I loved the silence experienced in church. I concluded that silence produced a gentleness throughout the congregation which appealed to me. Gradually the spirit would move me as well, but I think the solitude was more a part of what I was looking for. You seem to have found this in your life as well. Would you agree?" Dreyfus was impressed with Eric's perception. "Yes totally agree. Most people, men in particular, do not understand or appreciate this side of humanity." What Eric wanted to know was how did Dreyfus tolerate his life choice. " Is it difficult? Is it lonely existence?" Dreyfus answered these questions for Eric. "Having a full and rich life for me has many facets. First I try my best to surround myself with men and women who are interesting, intelligent and intellectual. I share the most interesting exchanges with my colleagues who are also my friends. My life is full Eric; I enjoy every day because I have learned to appreciate what most men would call non essentials. I am not living in mainstream America nor will you if you pursue the priesthood." Eric was satisfied with that explanation. But he wanted to know about intimacy. So he asked directly. "What about your feelings, passions, intimacy? Are they part of your life as well?" Dreyfus smiled. "Of course, all of them are important. I am not a monk , if that's what you're wondering Eric. For me, my life is rich and complete. I will leave it at that." He smiled again. "When someone lives a life surrounded by conventional, traditional, family centered behavior, those who live outside that sphere have chosen what's right for them." Eric understood and thought,it doesn't matter what others think; it's your life, live it. "Professor Dreyfus, there are other questions about church doctrine and policies that I question. Divorce, birth control, celibacy and priests who violate their sacred trust, especially sexual predators who have molested young boys. It's all swept under the rug. You know what I mean." Dreyfus stared at Eric. "There are problems, no question about it. Funny thing is, nuns seem to be more open minded than many priests. They get it. Old male priests don't. It's just a matter of time before all these evil episodes are exposed to the public. And as attitudes and mentality evolve, there will be a storm of public outrage. You will have to wait it out Eric because if you want to be a priest in the 1970's and beyond, you will have to silently and discretely work for change. This can happen when you counsel parishioners; here is where you can work on changing complacent social norms that are unfortunately evolving too slowly. Just be careful not to rock the boat." Eric was bothered by what he heard. He was disappointed in fact. "You mean to tell me that I have to overlook church maladies and intolerance?" Dreyfus lit up his pipe and walked to the window overlooking the rolling hills of the finger lakes. "You know Eric, I find inner peace by meditation, nature , reading, discussion and gardening. You will have to find your methods for escape from the worldly decadence that surrounds us. Don't get too far ahead of yourself. Work for change in little ways and you will survive the onslaught of religious hypocrisy. Otherwise these issues can and will consume you." It was difficult for Eric to listen to what he had believed was true. Truth is unvarnished. Eric felt he was subjecting himself to a enormous task. Dreyfus seemed to sense Eric's confusion and dismay. "If you're looking for certainties Eric, there are none. You have to make your own reality based upon the choices you make and your values. Remember, existentialists believe that our choices lead us to our reality. You have to choose." Eric almost regretted this session with Dreyfus. It unraveled him. He was back to square one. Dreyfus even sensed this. "Eric, if you're confused and disappointed, you're normal. The priesthood is filled with such moments. Get use to it."

Chapter 8

When Eric returned to his room, he was emotionally drained. His disciplined mind led him to kneel next to his bed and pray as he had done so many times before. He asked God how he got into this state of mind. It was not what he expected at this stage of his training. Things were expected to get easier as one approaches the finality of seminary training. He continued to pray and was distracted by an unopened letter from Michelle. He thought of what Dreyfus said about closure. He reached for the letter and could smell her scent as he opened it and read:

"Dear Eric, It has been some time since we communicated; I hope you are well and that your training is leading you to where you want to be. It must be difficult for you for different reasons. But I must confess that I miss you."

Eric dropped the letter. He could not read on. But his desire for closure was on his mind so he picked up the letter and continued.

"Eric, even though we are heading in different directions I want you to know how much I respect you and know that you feel a calling for something that most men avoid. I want you to know that you have made me move closer to my spirituality. For that I want to thank you. Maybe our paths will cross in the future even though I understand that it is something that you may want to avoid. I will pray for us to move forward for the right reasons. Peace and love, Michelle.

Eric was really confused and his eyes filled with tears of emotional uncertainty. He returned to prayer for calm and solace. "Lord help me to know myself. Lead me to what is right and positive for all those who will know me. I want to be genuine and sincere with my motives. Guide me with your holy spirit so that truth will manifest itself. I pray in your holy name, Amen." Eric laid on his bed and could feel the emotional calm slowly ease into his body and soul. When he awoke several hours later he felt refreshed and more determined to continue with his spiritual path. Something told him that he could not control his future but he could control the present. Moment by moment, hour by hour, day by day, until he could grasp a life that would be filled with unknown personal and professional events. He was willing to continue moving in the direction leading to his ordination as a Roman Catholic priest.

Chapter 9

Eric was looking forward to his weekend where he would spend some time with his parents and box some books that he wanted to include in his research library. It was nice to be home and when he entered the front door, his mother greeted him with a big hug. She was a warm and loving woman who adored her children with every ounce of her body. Eric noticed a look of concern when she handed him his mail from the Selective Service. Eric was dumbfounded when reading that he was drafted into the army, but he was not shocked because there was a war in Vietnam. His lottery number was 17, so his chance for active duty was fairly certain. His mother began to cry when he told her. It was all so sudden. Eric was surprisingly calm and thought why should he be excused from serving his country. He had no qualms; it was just the timing that bothered him. He had to report for a physical within two weeks. He decided to call Monsignor Quaid and inform him of his status and concluded that he did not want any special favors that would excuse him from his responsibility. He would explain his belief to Monsignor Quaid that military service was not something he wanted to avoid at the expense of some other recruit. He would not excuse himself if and when duty called so at that very moment Eric decided to call the seminary and speak with Monsignor Quaid. He used the phone in the upstairs hallway so his mom would not hear his conversation. Knowing Eric's determination, Monsignor reluctantly agreed, and told Eric that he would place him on a deferred list and that he could continue his seminary training without interruption when he returned. Eric was glad that he called right away to settle any uncertainty. He told Monsignor that he would not return to the seminary on Monday. He kept his conversation private because he knew his mother in particular would be upset. If he passed his physical exam, he would most likely be assigned to active duty after boot camp and any subsequent military training. Being a college graduate might allow him some options. For whatever reason, Eric felt relieved. He wasn't certain why, but he knew his feelings must have significance. Eric now had some time to spend at home with his family and he made sure he did just that. He looked forward to being home and enjoying good meals with his parents and sister.. Eric's father had served in the army and when Eric relayed the news to his father he informed Eric of his experiences in the army and tried to hide his anxiety from his son. It was shortly afterward that the telephone rang. Eric answered. It was Michelle. She was home for the weekend and Eric informed her of his current status. They agreed to meet after church on Sunday. His emotions were mixed and he did not know what to expect from Michelle.

When he met her after mass on Sunday, he was totally caught off guard. She was such a beautiful woman and when he saw her face up close it was like something happened inside him that he never experienced before. There was a vibrant attraction between them. Two attractive people, one a beautiful woman, the other a handsome man. She extended her hand and he gracefully held it with feeling. He stared at her and smiled. "How are you. You look so beautiful." Eric's reservations seemed to evaporate under his new circumstances. He felt liberated and she responded with warmth and a very friendly smile. "I have a week before my army physical. My life has changed over night and I cannot explain my feelings one way or the other. Maybe fate has taken over so that I no longer have to think for myself and plan my future. It's being done by forces beyond my control." Eric thought he was giving Michelle permission to allow for something more than just a handshake. He felt reckless in a sense. He was released from solitary confinement. Maybe he thought it was a fear of going into the army and maybe to Vietnam. All these thoughts raced through him. He was not his typical self and Michelle sensed his uncertainty. But her cool calm demeanor came through; it appeared that she understood his anxiety when she took a step forward to let him be close enough to smell her scent. It was at that moment when he kissed her on the cheek. It seemed so natural for him and wonderful at the same time; he imagined how he had refrained from such splendor on earlier occasions. Almost on cue she responded. "We must get to know one another. Is that compatible with your unfamiliar status?" Maybe she was right. He was in unfamiliar territory and uncertainty granted him a taste of personal liberty. Was his life so disciplined that he left no room for life without familiarity? Eric was impressed with her intuitive sensitivity. They held hands and conversed for several hours. Eric crossed a threshold and his insides were churning with desire under control. They embraced and kissed passionately and he opened up with his emotions. He never experienced a love emotion

like this before and he told her so. Michelle just listened. She sensed that
Eric had to release his extenuating circumstances before he could muster
his sense of reality. Eric realized what she was doing by listening. He felt
he was unraveling and moving into one of many empty spaces in his life.
Michelle was nurturing him with tenderness by allowing him to reveal
his inner emotions. Eric sensed a comfort zone. "Thank you Michelle for
your understanding and genuine concern for my situation." Eric knew
that fate had in some significant way changed his life. When they kissed
good bye, Eric realized there were other options. Michelle maintained
her poise throughout. Eric sensed she was a very special woman for
that alone. The few words she communicated indicated her maturity
for loving someone for the right reasons. "Eric we must not allow our
intimacy to determine a future that both of us are not sure of. That would
be a mistake. We must allow two forces to work here. Fate and our own
choices or decisions. They will unfold before us if we are patient." Eric felt
that Michelle was allowing their future to be free from untenable forces.
And she was right. Her intuitive feminine wisdom released Eric from his
preoccupation with priesthood; maybe Eric thought, God had other plans
for him.

Chapter 10

The week with his parents was special. His mother in particular conveyed her feelings with Eric and his consideration for her anxiety demonstrated his compassion and love for her. Eric did not try to escape from his mother's grasp; he knew she needed to be with him for several reasons. He was her first born child and their connection was strong. She would not admit it, but Eric felt her puzzlement and then her acceptance of his decision to be a priest. As time passed she felt a spiritual exuberance for her son and it made her a better Catholic. So now that Eric could possibly be called to military service during an unpopular war, his mother was totally unprepared for her son's radical change of plans; she was terrified and Eric innocently caused this to happen. The following day they sat on their screened front porch, both seated on a rocking love seat, with tea and grahm crackers. Eric's mother rested her hand on his; he could see tears rolling down her cheeks. She looked at him and cried; no words were necessary. Her cry pierced Eric's emotions until he too teared up. They hugged each other in total silence and allowed the moment to pass. Then she looked at Eric and said. "Maybe you could be a chaplain in the army." Eric looked into her eyes that were red with tears. She was waiting for a response but Eric just held her hands and looked on toward the lawn where autumn was making itself apparent with the change of colors on Maples that lined their street. He had lived his entire life at his home on Bronson street where he shared good times with his friends and neighbors. Eric's parents often had neighbors over for backyard gatherings which he recalled when he noticed his neighbors in their yards enjoying this beautiful autumn day in upstate New York. It was just then that his father drove into the driveway. He had taken liberty with his work hours so he could spend some time with his son. He joined them on the porch and could see his wife's face had suffered from tears of uncertainty. She knew her husband wanted to say something to Eric so she removed herself from her son's side. "I have to get dinner ready." She poured her husband a cup of tea and walked away.

Eric's father sipped his tea and looked out toward the street. Not being an emotional man, Eric was surprised at what happened. His father said that the war in Vietnam was escalating and that he was concerned about comments made by Walter Kronkite who had recently toured Vietnam. The most revered and trusted television journalist in America said that our mission there was untenable; victory was not imminent. He was suggesting a policy that was interpreted by many that a orderly withdrawal should be considered. Then he looked at Eric and said. "We cannot win this war. President Eisenhower warned us years ago not to entangle ourselves in a land war in southeast Asia. And now my only son may soon be heading for that quagmire. The protesters are right. This war is a mistake." He then turned toward Eric with watery eyes. "I am concerned for you and fear the worst." His eyes were tearing and Eric and his father stood and hugged silently; Eric could feel his father's anguish through his arms and back. The muscles in his fathers body were quivering with emotion. He had lost a brother in WWII so he personally experienced the tragedy of wartime loss. What he was about to say really shocked Eric. "If you want to ship out to Canada, I will support you." Eric was caught off guard by that comment. He never even thought of that option. He knew deep inside that he could not follow through with it. Somehow he felt that his parents had discussed this option but he decided not to go there. After a prolonged moment of silence that allowed his father's tears to fade, he said: "Dad, everything will work out for the best. Please don't worry. I love and respect you so much; I could not live with myself if I refused to serve with others who also have reasons not to step up but do." His father was moved by his son's words of conviction. His fears however were undiminished. From the kitchen they smelled a delicious pot roast simmering in a cast iron pot. The comfort of that smell seemed to neutralize their emotional discomfort. Eric placed his arm around his father as they walked into the kitchen. "Come on dad, I'm hungry. Want a beer with dinner?" He realized that his parents must have exchanged their emotions with one another. Strange as it seemed, their distress brought relief and comfort to Eric; he felt their love more than ever. In two days he was informed that his physical exam was passed without incident; a week later he received another letter informing him to report to Fort Hamilton for basic training in ten days. He realized he should also inform Michelle about his future military obligations and use time remaining for learning more about their relationship.

Chapter 11

Eric's emotions were building. He didn't know what his true feelings were about his military obligations. He was at a crossroads that had several pathways pulling on him for different reasons. He had to sort things out and knew Michelle could help him do just that. She was so level headed and calm; he loved being around her. Here he was about two years away from being ordained a Roman Catholic priest and looking forward to it only to be diverted by a war 10,000 miles away. Then due to the interruption he has an opportunity to be with a beautiful woman who has completely taken him by surprise and now he looks to her for guidance and direction. Then his parents, especially his father suggested draft dodging to Canada. Not a totally irrational idea. There's also a feeling of liberation from prearranged plans; sort of the feeling one has when he wants to run away from it all, pure and simple; he felt wanderlust. Travel would provide space and some time for reflection which Eric felt he really needed at this point. Not the kind of travel he had in mind . The only travel he would be experiencing would be through military orders. For some unknown feeling, he felt that Michelle could help him sort things out. When he met her the following day, she had just arrived from school. He marveled at how beautiful she looked and wondered how her high school seniors, especially young men, reacted toward her as their teacher. Eric wore a blue denim shirt with jeans and looked handsome with his sun glasses. When she got into his car, they embraced and kissed passionately. Wow! He felt such desire when he pressed her shapely body against his. The chemistry was there; they both knew it and embraced it. They paused and stared into each others eyes. It was at that moment he observed tears dripping from Michelle's eyes. No words were exchanged for an extended moment. Eric was waiting for her to speak but true to her personality, silence prevailed. Actually words were not necessary. It was obvious what she felt. Her embrace expressed her feelings. She pressed Eric close to her body. Throughout this euphoric and emotional moment, Eric whispered , "What's going to happen to us?" He didn't say, "I love you". He didn't have to. She knew it and so did he. They remained closely entwined and could feel their desires increase by the minute. Eric however knew he would have to maintain more composure and she responded to him reluctantly. "I know words are difficult Michelle, but I would like you to share your thoughts with me. We know what our feelings are; let's take it to the next level for the time being." Michelle smiled and just rested her head on Eric's chest. Without looking at Eric she said: "What would you like this to be? You must have so much going through your mind. Neither one of us expected this." That's for sure. Eric never thought he would be in this situation. Fate has a way of altering life plans. When we have little control over our lives, what's the best advice one should follow? Michelle finally spoke. Her timely wisdom surfaced with these words. "When one is uncertain, it's best to do nothing." How perfect was that advice. "Do Nothing". Yes Eric thought. Why do we have to disappoint ourselves even more than we are? Why can't we just go forward and allow the unknown mysteries in our lives to unfold? Why do we have to even attempt to ruin the moment by trying to control a future that lies beyond our grasp? Eric was amazed at how such an emotional moment could be relieved by rational and logical thoughts. He looked into her eyes. They felt their connection was strong and was leading them to a point of no return. They both wanted to be in the moment; nothing else mattered. The clock was running. They arranged a long weekend together where they could frolic in the joys of youthful and fervent love.

Chapter 12

The Adirondacks explode with color come October. Eric and Michelle rented a cottage on a mountain lake deep within the Adirondack park. It was quiet, remote and yet had all the conveniences of living without much hardship. Eric thought this is what a honeymoon must be like; if not it should be. Here there are no distractions. Hiking trails and a clear lake where the water was refreshing and getting cooler with each autumn day. It was Michelle who wanted to swim and Eric followed her toward the lake. She looked like a model in her two piece suit. Eric gazed at her knee deep in water. She submerged into the refreshing lake and swam about ten yards. He followed her and she reached out to him where they embraced passionately. She whispered, "Let's take off our suits." She tossed hers toward the shallows and Eric did the same. This was a first for Eric at age 24 and he thought he really didn't miss anything because Michelle was worth waiting for. Her breasts were large and firm and he pressed them toward his body. She was all over him when he penetrated her body for the very first time. She winced with pleasure and pain. "That is a first for me." He laughed and shared that it was his first as well. Their bodies were as close as two bodies could be and he could feel his release deep within her. He thought about what could happen but she did not concern herself. When they pulled apart their hearts were still throbbing from the rush and cool water.. It was the most wonderful feeling he ever experienced. They gathered their suits and ran for the towels to embrace themselves with warmth. Inside the cabin their lovemaking continued until they fell asleep before a roaring fire. They remained clutching each other for several hours and did not want to alter their mood or circumstance. As time passed their stomachs growled with a ravenous appetite. Michelle proved to be adept with her culinary skills. She had brought enough for the weekend and they feasted on chicken, red potatoes, and a delicious salad. Eric packed some cold beer; they both admitted how relaxed they felt with each other. It was beautiful to feel so alive with joy and love. Eric did not want this to end but his thoughts were projected into the not too distant future. Michelle could sense that he was preoccupied. "Be in the moment. I want you all to myself. Nothing else matters right now." She moved closer to him and they continued where they left off until sleep consumed them through the dark quiet night. Sleep was the only escape from their sexual desire for one another. When morning light arrived, their bodies had not separated throughout the entire night. Eric separated himself quietly and retreated to a comfortable chair where he could enjoy his reading during early morning hours. He had brought some literature he hadn't completed on Descartes who provided him with his philosophical stimulation. "I think therefore I am." That said it all and so precisely. Eric now realized without too much reservation that priesthood would have to be deferred, maybe forever. How could anything replace his love for Michelle. There was no going back so he thought. The idea of being a celibate was now a very distant thought. If he did have any reservations they were not apparent, at least at this moment in time. Life isn't always this perfect. He knew his faith was still there, not diminished by his love for Michelle. "When you're not sure, do nothing." Those words had so many applications. His thoughts always provided him with exciting possibilities; he knew there was something in his future that would allow him to use his intellectual and spiritual personalities. Life will provide him with the experiences that deliver him to that unknown future one day. Just be. Don't force life, allow life instead to take its course. Michelle taught him that, and she was so right. Preoccupation with the unknown was getting in the way of allowing life to happen without attachments and expectations. Eric began to realize that even God's plan for him would not be revealed until he was ready. You know when you're ready. At this point in his life Eric realized he had to allow life to be, by not getting in the way. His mind was his most important asset and he realized that with constant and rigorous development of his intellect, life experiences will sharpen his ability to see God's plan for him. His first sexual encounter with a woman helped to release him from his past presumptions. He looked at Michelle sleeping and thought how she had brought him to a different level of cognition and realized how important this was for his growth. The intimacy shared with Michelle relieved him, liberated him, and even brought him closer to God. Had he not had this wonderful experience with Michelle he would have been denied advancing and elevating his life to a beautiful time and place. He realized that without Michelle this would never have been possible at this point in time. He waited until he was 24 to be with a woman and it was a beautiful experience for him. The intensity was even greater than he imagined; maybe it was because he would be leaving soon into an unknown future. His thoughts now reverted to prayer. Eric's training and discipline at the seminary always brought him to spiritual meditation. He was so thankful to God for the gift of sexual love. It was strange how he merged the two forces, sex and love. The combination was intense. He wondered how these two emotions could be appreciated if separated. Now Eric thought he was thinking like a priest instead of a typical male. But it did make him perceive his experience with Michelle as genuine love. Then he briefly thought he was feeling catholic guilt. But no, that wasn't true at all. He had experienced genuine love and on his first experience with a woman. He had a strong feeling that his connection with Michelle was unique; he learned so much about himself and how events can open your life to unexpected and accelerated growth and realization. It was strange and frightening; it would soon end and he would be off and moving into another unknown. Michelle seemed to realize this as well. They both shared their sexual love for the first time, much later than most men and women. "When you're not sure, do nothing." She was placing all of this in the context of their life situations. Attachment to one another was not something that would work for them. She knew that and now he realized her wisdom. Love shouldn't be an attachment to someone; being in love should be attachment free. This is what Michelle was conveying; just be, without being attached. This was an important lesson to learn because it would make separating much easier for both of them. That was a major reality check. Who knows what the future holds? Let it go. How much control do we really have?

Chapter 13

Their return drive from the mountain retreat allowed them more time to discuss life and share dreams. Michelle listened more than Eric. Apparently she sensed his fear and anxiety now that he was drafted during wartime. The news coming home from Vietnam was not positive. Over 45,000 troops were killed and thousands were deployed each month replacing those whose one year tour ended. Many came home in body bags leading to protests on many college campuses. Eric was definitely concerned and wondered how far away events control ones life. He thought about his father who was a soldier during WWII and who was drafted in 1942 at age 18. The difference was stark. We were attacked at Pearl Harbor on December 7, 1941 by the Japanese. The war in Vietnam was quite different. It was part of a fear shared by the United States that communism would spread throughout southeast Asia. American forces filled the void left by the French after their defeat at Dien Bien Fu. The Cold War was now being fought with deadly force and the United States was sucked in for reasons that many thought were justified. Like many Americans, Eric did not know who was right but he did know that he could be a casualty; that's what he feared and so did Michelle even though she maintained her silence. It's as if they both realized their uncertain future was not worth discussing because nothing positive seemed possible so why go there. Suddenly Eric imagined a more favorable outlook so he asked Michelle: "What if we met during different circumstances, without a war that squirmed between us." Michelle was silent again. Momentarily she offered her insight. "You're wishful thinking; without this war we probably would not have met and made passionate love all weekend. So maybe in one way we should be thankful that we met and loved each other while we had the chance. This time together would never have occurred. We must not talk about what ifs." Eric was caught off guard and thought Michelle was being dramatic. He merely wanted to imagine their life under different circumstances. Michelle did not want to go there. Maybe he thought her reaction was a defense mechanism at work protecting her vulnerability. If so he could understand. However he would have liked to hear her say something that indicated a future together, but Michelle did not want to go there either.

Don't men and women have these discussions at some point, especially after intimacy. But Michelle was true to her psychological tendency to refrain from having a discussion of a future that was too remote and uncertain and even painful. Eric backed off and allowed silence to be broken by music from the radio. His emotions were confused. As hard as he tried to understand, there was something rubbing him the wrong way. After some time passed, Eric, who had not stopped thinking about how detached Michelle could be, realized that all he wanted was tender loving care. That's all he wanted. Was this too much to expect from the woman he loved and who loved him. He then tried to think as Michelle would think and concluded that her outlook was more mature and less stressful. He reached over and touched her hand and she held his firmly. Michelle could communicate without words; he realized that he should on more occasion mimic her style because it generated more compassion and mutual respect without words that can confuse and mislead.. "I wish I could be as stoic and detached as you. I understand your reluctance to discuss our situation because of all of the things that can go wrong. It would be meaningless." Michelle looked at Eric and said, " please pull over so I can talk to you while your not driving." Eric found a rest stop a few miles ahead and did as she requested. He turned off the engine and she looked at him with such intensity that made him feel uncomfortable. "Look at me. Do these eyes tell you anything? Did all that beautiful lovemaking tell you anything? Answer me!" He reached out to her and held her close while she cried on his shoulder. "Eric, actions speak louder than words. You know how much I love you. Totally, truly. Is that what you wanted to hear?" Eric held her close and kissed her tearful cheeks. No more words were necessary. He got what he wanted. They hugged for about twenty more minutes when Eric resumed the drive home. He held her hand the entire way.

Chapter 14

After Eric passed his army physical he received notification to report to Fort Hamilton for basic training. A bus would transport draftees from Elmira, to Fort Hamilton, on October 14, 1970. Eric's mom was very emotional and his dad kept his silence but there was fear in his disposition. His only son was probably going to Vietnam. Michelle was there as well and she saw emotional turmoil firsthand that left her feeling sick to her stomach. Eric's sister was crying as well; she had just read about young men who lived a stones throw from their home who were killed in action and whose bodies had just returned to their family for burial. The war by this time was growing more unpopular as the death toll kept increasing. Eric hugged his parents and sister. He told his parents that he would be fine and not to worry. Michelle drove Eric to Ithaca. He chose to depart from Ithaca because he wanted to visit his alma mater at Cornell and drive through the beautiful campus above Cayuga Lake. Their two hour ride was filled with silence as they just held each others hand. Words were absent and understandably so. As they drove through college town and around the student union, Eric finally broke his silence. He looked at Michelle who was stone faced with eyes filling with tears. "Destiny has taken over our lives. Pray for me and know that I will be thinking of you every waking hour. Please when you can, visit my parents and sister and try your best to keep them in good spirits. More than anything else I want to thank you for your love and friendship. You have changed my life more than you will ever know." They embraced and Michelle was holding him close until the last moment. "I love what we have and don't want it to end. Please be careful." They approached the bus depot where Eric boarded the bus, turned and blew her a kiss.

When the draftees arrived at Fort Hamilton they were greeted by their drill master, Sergeant Tobal, who was five feet eleven inches of pure muscle. His African American swagger was what Eric imagined, expected, and enjoyed. To be insulted so quickly was however not expected but Sergeant Tobal did not want to give any false impressions of what was in store. "Get your asses in building 22 so I can kick your ass where no one can see me. Run you mother fuckers. Welcome to the Army." The men moved quickly and it wasn't a pretty picture. They were falling over one another out of fear of this sergeant who was barking out orders and insults simultaneously. Once inside they were assigned lockers , bunks, fatigues, underwear, toiletries and told to line up outside quickly as he would be anxiously waiting. The recruits were fumbling with their clothing when the sergeant entered and screamed at them for being too slow. "I am giving you mother fuckers exactly 5 minutes to report for roll call outside. Move your asses." Fear can do wonders during pandemonium. Roll call was in five minutes and miraculously, all recruits were lined up. The names bellowed out were a mix of America's melting pot. The age span was 19-25. College students, high school graduates, working class tradesmen, Africans, Latinos, Asians and few white males like Eric with college degrees and beyond. The draft did produce a healthy cross section of American society. Eric was now in the mix and it was an eye opener for him. He recently celebrated his 25th birthday.

The sergeant called out names during roll call. Aaron, Bates, Cumerford, Davies. Recruits who did not respond with enough vigor were reprimanded. When O'Reilly was called out, Eric responded with a firm "here". The sergeant walked over to Eric. "O'Reilly, do you want to be here?" Eric was unnerved. He hesitated but then quickly blurted out. "Yes sir." The sergeant got into his face and said, 'don't bullshit me O'Reilly, do you want to be here?" Eric could smell the tobacco breath of Sergeant Tobal whose nose almost touched Eric's. "I'm not finished with you O'Reilly, but when I am you're going to regret being here. Do you understand me O'Reilly?" "Yes sir" "Yes sir who?" "Yes sir Sergeant Tobal." Eric's mind was racing. Was the sergeant trying to break him? Why was he singled out? When the men were dismissed they were assigned bunks, lockers, and told to make themselves presentable for inspection. That meant their barracks better be neat, presentable with beds made to perfection. Nothing out of place. Not one item. "You have one hour before I visit your home away from home. You better be properly shaved, cleaned, shined and dressed for your first inspection. Then you all will have your first Army haircut. I can't wait."

The recruits stood at attention when sergeant Tobal entered their barracks in exactly one hour. All men were at attention standing at the foot of their bunks. Tobal walked slowly between them and looked to see their facial hair was neatly and completely shaved. "What's that on your face, Germain?" Pfc Robert Germain responded. "I cut myself shaving sergeant Tobal." "That's too bad Germain because now your chums are going to take ten laps for your mistake, but after you get scalped. The army will show you what a clean shave looks like. Report to building B10 for proper hair removal. After your hair is removed return to your barracks. At eleven hundred everybody line up for some exercise thanks to pfc Germain." After the haircut the recruits looked like pow's and at eleven hundred, out they went, lined up in their assigned place. "O'Reilly, front and center." Eric who was toward the backside of formation quickly moved to the front. "Yes sergeant Tobal." "O'Reilly you are going to lead these men to ten laps around that track. All of you follow O'Reilly who will follow me. Stragglers beware." The sergeant then proceeded to yell out an army mantra while running. This was picked up by the recruits. Off they went in sync and looking better with each lap. Eric could not help but feel a bond with total strangers. The sergeant lead by example. "Hidi, hidi, hidi ho..."

Chapter 15

Basic training made Eric realize what Benjamin Franklin meant by "e plurabis unum" out of many one. He could see how his unit was bonding with every day of training. The men in his platoon became friends who shared experiences during the course of training and worked to overshadow unknown factors of their personalities. The concept of WE was hammered with every exercise. "I" was not important; it was all about WE. After eight weeks, Eric lost seven pounds but gained muscle and his body was hard as a rock. Most other recruits noticed similar changes in their body frames. Their new dress uniforms accentuated their new shapes. When training ended with a marching ceremony, they felt Sergeant Tobal's pride in their progress. Before they left for more training in a variety of disciplines, Sergeant Tobal would bid them farewell. They were in their barracks gathering their belongings when the sergeant entered. Pfc Simmons who saw him first barked out, "Ten hut." The platoon stopped their activity and stood straight as light posts with their uniforms and bodies sharp and crisp. Sergeant Tobal walked through their ranks also looking like a block of wood chiseled to perfection. "Well you men have shown me more than I ever imagined I would get from you. Your hard work has made you soldiers that the United States army can be proud of. However this is only the beginning of our journey together. Our paths will cross again after you complete your selected training that will make your duties more in line with a war being fought 12,000 miles from here. Be prepared for that eventuality. I salute you for your achievements. Next time I see your asses may be in a jungle. You make me proud. Merry Christmas. Platoon dismissed." The sergeant did an about face and walked out. The men stood silently for just a moment because they knew that Sergeant Tobal was largely responsible for their success or failure. His words were sobering as well. They looked at each other, shook hands, patted each other on the back and chattered about their next training exercises in a variety of skills that would precede their deployment and their future destinies. They were given a holiday gift of 8 days of liberty and most would return home to their family and loved ones for the Christmas holidays. Eric did not feel what he thought he should feel at this point. His emotions were all over the place.

There was an envelope in his mail slot and he saw Department of Army Intelligence. He was ordered to report to Captain John Anderson before his leave. He did not share this notice with anyone. After shaking hands with all the men in his barrack, he reported to the officers quarters on base where Captain Anderson was stationed. At the suggestion of the captain's secretary, he left his duffel bag with all his personal items in the waiting room where silence was filled with the sound of typewriters. "Private O'Reilly, you may enter the captain's office now." The voice was that of corporal Susan Martin, a very attractive brunette about Eric's age whose demeanor demonstrated an attraction to Eric. "Thank you corporal." When Eric entered, Captain Anderson had just hung up his telephone. Eric stood at attention, saluted, " Private first class Eric O'Reilly reporting as ordered sir." He told Eric to be seated and opened a file that the captain had read. "Private, I see that you were in training for the priesthood, about two years until being ordained as a Roman Catholic priest, only to be interrupted by the draft. Is that correct?" Eric's response was immediate. "Yes sir, that is correct sir." The captain approached Eric and stared. "How has this change in plans affected you private? Be honest with me." Eric paused. He needed some time to think but realized his response had to be forthcoming. "Well sir I am ready to serve my country and want to perform my duty without any reservations." The captain did not flinch. "You know private I can pull some strings for you, just let me know. Be honest with yourself and with me." Now Eric had to go on overdrive. If he wanted out, he could have it but that would mean making a choice between being a priest, forfeiting an opportunity to be with Michelle, or deceiving the army and maybe himself by simply deferring his relationship after being ordained and in this way assuring him a safe and secure future with or without Michelle. None of those options were clear to him. "Private, I know I have put you on edge so I want you to think about this during your leave. When you return come and see me. I will have my secretary set up a time following your day of return. Merry Christmas to you and your family. That will be all. Dismissed." "Thank you sir." Eric saluted and left the captain's office. Corporal Martin addressed him and asked. "The captain will see you at 1500 on January 3rd." Her smile was very pleasant. "Thank you corporal Martin. Merry Christmas." When Eric boarded a Grey Hound for Ithaca he felt different emotions pulling on him. His parents would first of all want him to bail out but he knew that was not an option for him. He wasn't sure why but something told him to go forward in the army. No one at home needed to be informed. This should be his decision. But then he thought, what about Michelle? Shouldn't he be up front with her. This way she could have options for her future without having obligations and uncertainty. He held that thought in reserve. Too much going on with his emotions. He thought: I need time to process this; eight days and counting. When he arrived in Ithaca, he wanted to do some shopping with the four hundred dollars he had in reserve. He intentionally delayed Michelle's arrival so he could have time to shop along Ithaca's thriving downtown on State Street. It was good to be back where he spent four years of his life. He now reflected what that excellent education had prepared him for: priesthood, military service, marriage, parenthood or something yet to be determined. Eric always related to ideas either taught or learned. He recalled one fundamental of existentialism: that our lives are driven by the choices we make.

Chapter 16

The holiday season was made magical by colorful lights and gentle falling snow on Christmas eve. High school students had gathered along State street and were singing holiday carols.. Eric had bags of gifts and his duffel bag was dragging in the snow. He saw Michelle walking toward him. Her long blond hair was covered by a wool hat that had a ring of fur around the front. His mind now focused on their absence from each other and with the exception of several long distant phone calls, they were disconnected for over twelve weeks. She ran the last few steps. Eric dropped everything and gave her a hug and kissed her in front of the pedestrians who were smiling. His uniform made the shoppers feel the occasion was very special. Snowflakes became larger and more intense. It didn't stop them from their embrace. They exchanged loving words and Michelle gathered some of the bags of gifts and together they walked to her car. No words were exchanged. Eric thought: "Silent waters run deep." Finally Michelle said, "So what lies ahead." Eric almost told her his options then but stopped himself. This time it was he who maintained a mode of silence. Michelle allowed him his space and realized he had a lot on his mind. The snow continued to fall so their drive back would be longer than usual. The extra time would allow them an opportunity to unravel their brief history of love and separation. Eric thought that separation was painful enough, but love can also have a painful face. They seemed to be experiencing similar emotions for different reasons. The more Eric pondered his choices, the more confused he became. Michelle's sensitivity picked up on his mood. She wanted to say something but retreated to her silence for safety, thinking, if you are not sure say nothing. Eric took a deep breath. "How is teaching going?" She smiled and understood their silence served little purpose. "Oh I have some wonderful students and a few may be enlisting. But most will be heading for college somewhere. By the way, your parents and sister are so happy that you will be home for Christmas. They wanted to come with me but your sister convinced them that it would be best if I came alone." Eric was about to speak but was stopped by the thought that at this time silence was the best option. More silence on Eric's part was finally broken by his realization that he had eight days to sort things out. Maybe he thought he should open up and make an attempt to resolve the unknown that faced them by probing her feelings after twelve weeks of not being together. Did she still feel the same? Was there anything that surfaced that would change where they left off? They both knew from their silence that something had changed. Do two people who are deeply in love act this way? Aren't couples in love more joyful, talkative, even sexy with each other? Who's kidding who? Eric knew he had to open up and sooner the better. Being transparent always worked for him in the past. It's just that it was painful. He didn't know where or how to begin. Then he realized that it was not a good idea to open a discussion during a snowstorm on a highway between Ithaca and Oswego. He had to wait. So he resorted to small talk. That always works under these circumstances. So he asked her about her family, her sister and brother and the teaching faculty at school, extra curricular activities etc. It worked. Small talk has its place. It doesn't rattle people. It's not abrasive or intrusive. Route 34 north was filled with snow but with luck, the enormous hills just south of route 104 were conquered by Michelle's skill behind the wheel. They were close to home when they passed Buckland's Grill, a famous watering hole for college students. Every moment of ones life has a purpose if one observes the meaning of circumstances. Eric suddenly realized that he did relish his time alone. It was an important reality check that came to him as he approached his home at 66 Bronson Street.

Chapter 17

Michelle managed to pull her car into the steep driveway. It was mandatory during snow season to keep the streets clear so plows could move mounds of snow. Eric's parents were at the door waiting along with Eric's sister Mary. They had to get through bags of gifts in order to reach Eric. He was smothered with hugs and kisses from all sides. His mother's tears were especially difficult. Her grasp was strong. Finally Eric's father placed his large arms around his wife, daughter and son and they all hugged in unison. It was a beautiful sight for Michelle to behold. They came to the kitchen table where a wonderful Christmas eve meal was waiting to be served. His parents saw his dress uniform and were impressed by his physical shape which made him appear impressive and handsome according to his sister. "Wow Eric, you look so great in your uniform." His father could not have been more proud of his son and Eric could tell he wanted to talk but Eric chimed in: "Later I'll tell you all the details you want to know. It really wasn't as bad as I thought. I've made some wonderful friends, but right now , I'm starved and thirsty. Been waiting for mom's cooking for weeks." His mom glowed and would not let go. Eric hugged her and knew she needed just that. "Everything's OK mom. I love you too." Once she released him from her grip she said: "Go wash up and I will make the finishing touches. Dad will have a cold beer waiting if you like." Michelle observed all the family love and realized how situations like this can create closeness like nothing else. Wartime is not something we wish for to bring families close. All over America she thought there must be similar scenes of jubilation when sons return to their loved ones, and unfortunately sometimes have to leave home again to complete their tour of duty. So as joyous as this occasion was, Michelle knew the anguish of departure would soon be upon the O'Reilly family. However it was time to enjoy the moment and Michelle was good at that.

Eric sat with his dad, Michelle, and Mary around a glowing wood fire. They all glanced at Eric and paused ; he didn't seem ready to speak when suddenly he did just that. "Where do I begin?" Eric looked and felt hesitant. "Maybe with sergeant Tobal who has led by example. I have learned how his type of leadership is unique and very purposeful. He's tough and fair and even funny at times." Eric's father could see a side of his son never seen before; there was a level of confidence and maturity. He seemed more at ease and words just flowed; there was a masculinity that Eric's dad found more gratifying. There were questions that Eric's father wanted to ask in private; he did not want to interfere with the joy and banter his son was relishing. Michelle also saw a side of Eric she had either avoided intentionally or missed entirely. The army changed him, so she thought and she wasn't sure exactly how but there was a difference in Eric; at this point she wasn't sure if it had any significance or not. Eric even confirmed her feelings. "I have really had time to think about life in ways I never thought possible. I see more and know this experience is like no other." He then turned to Michelle and even reached out to her. "Letters from Michelle were very important because she encouraged me to be in the moment and make the most of my situation; thank you Michelle." He looked at Michelle and could see her beautiful blue eyes watering slightly. She felt a strong connection with Eric and her uncertainty seemed to melt away. The conversation returned to boot camp and all the physical demands that shaped Eric's torso and developed his handsome frame. Even his sister Mary repeated how handsome he looked in his uniform and how special he was to his parents. The conversation continued. Eric had shared some of his training experiences with his father, especially at the rifle range where he became quite proficient with his M16. He received a commendation for his rifle expertise. Sergeant Tobal even remarked that his score was the highest he had ever experienced. Basically, Eric was considered a marksman with his rifle which could open opportunities in Special Forces that would require even more training. That decision would have to be made when he returned. Eric's mother entered the room and moved close to her son. She reached out to him and he sensed her need for a hug. She looked up at him and her thoughts were those of a mother whose love for her son was strong and proud. She allowed herself to speak without words. Her strong yet tender embrace revealed all her sentiments. "Come, let's have dinner; you can tell us more at the table."

Chapter 18

The time spent with family recharged Eric and gave him an opportunity to place his life in perspective. Upstairs in his room where he peered at all the memories of his past 25 years hanging on the walls: athletic awards in football, basketball and baseball. Scholarly awards in English, science and history. Photos of his teams, his sister Mary and his mother and father and grandparents. Books that he had read were neatly placed on shelves. All the classic novels of youth. Eric read them all. He loved to read and ponder the meaning of life's trials and tribulations shared by all individuals struggling to find answers to questions.

Eric had a very philosophical perspective which included a variety of factors that shaped his life. Many of the novels read contributed to his outlook; reading about the hardships and choices made by others was an important part of Eric's frame of reference. His life was so sheltered and he realized through his reading that it is best not to live a sheltered life; experiencing hardship, although difficult and challenging can produce character that is strong and meaningful. He realized that hardship had not faced him for twenty four years and reality seemed to beckon him to prepare for its eventuality. Life had to be experienced by a mix of intellectual and experiential moments. From his extensive reading he learned how difficulty faced by many personalities impacted their lives, usually in positive ways. Life was fraught with hardship and Eric sensed that he had to prepare himself. Through literature Eric learned that one had to at times surrender to his choices. After all, life is driven by choices made. Pathways are therefore determined by our choices; our control is therefore limited by parameters of choice. Eric also learned through prayer and meditation to examine and scrutinize carefully. "To sleep on it" was also one of his most used tactics for decision making. His spiritual and rational components would merge after a good nights rest. It was with this frame of mind that Eric fell into a deep sleep. The next morning, sun streaked between the window shade. His eyes opened to a strong beam of light that pierced his consciousness with optimism. He prayed for guidance and wisdom but the smell of his mother's coffee brewing was enough to deter his thoughts . His last day home was finally here. He and Michelle did have time to reconnect but there were restraints they both seemed to understand. Now it was important that he spend some time with his mother; she was waiting for him at the kitchen table, coffee in hand.

Chapter 19

Eric sat for breakfast as his mother served poached eggs, ham, toast, tomato juice and fruit. She gazed at him and without hesitation said: "So tell me what's going on inside, you know, the important stuff we always talk about." Eric expected as much. This is why he loved conversation with mom; she was always direct yet did not judge; she listened more, spoke less. The eggs were perfect. They were cooked in a pan of boiling hot water and mom knew just when to take them out. The toast was made with homemade bread, cut an inch thick. She didn't press him for a response. Her instincts told her to just allow his thoughts to unfold. After all, here was a young man in seminary training for the priesthood, who has since met an attractive woman who apparently has captivated him, and now he's drafted into the army during a raging war in Vietnam. Something had to be going on inside. She waited patiently and he knew she would allow him to enjoy her prepared breakfast and relish in two or three cups of coffee with a large blueberry corn muffin. "Mom, your cooking is so comforting. I really miss it." She smiled. "Well that's always nice to hear. Your sister has a bowl of corn flakes or Cheerios. That's not breakfast." As Eric ate the last bite of his blueberry corn muffin, he confided with his mother. "So what do you think of my three choices. If you're confused, so am I. Any advice for a lost soul, who happens to be your son." Eric's mom was looking out the kitchen window over the sink; her hands submerged in soapy dishwater as she watched bluejays and cardinals feed on sunflower seeds. She had a habit of not looking at Eric directly when discussing serious situations because her emotions were fragile during personal circumstances. What could be more personal and emotional than her son going off to war. Eric understood and respected his mom's feelings so he had to be delicate with his wording. "Well mom, let's take each situation, in chronological order. First, I entered the seminary after graduating from Cornell; a wonderful and spiritual experience. I really believed I was comfortable with it." He paused to allow her to comment but she wisely refrained. "What were your feelings when I decided to become a priest?" She wiped her hands on a dish towel, sat down with Eric and forced herself to look at him directly. "I was happy for you because I knew your heart had a strong spiritual core.

You were always gentle with your family, especially your sister. Your grandmother even said how kind and considerate you were toward her and grandpa too. So your choice for the priesthood seemed very natural; almost a calling." Eric reflected upon her words. She was correct with everything stated so far with maybe one fundamental exception. People change; they evolve. He was sure she understood ; it was going off to war that worried her, nothing else; this was confirmed when she blurted: "My son is going to Vietnam. Was that part included in your plan or am I missing something here?" Now Eric looked down because he couldn't bare to watch his mother's tears roll down her cheeks. "And what about Michelle? She's in love with you from what I can tell. Was that part included in your plan? What is missing in this story Eric? Help your mother understand, please." Eric knew at that moment he had to reveal his inner self in order for his mother to understand and have closure and compassion for his conflicting choices. "Mom, I have some issues to resolve that are private and personal in nature. It's not easy for me, trust me, it's not easy." His mother instinctively and tenderly placed her arms around her son. "You know you can trust me to respect your privacy and that my love for you is unconditional. If you want to share your feelings with me I will love you all the same, no matter what. I will respect your silence as well because I know at some point you would confide in me." It was almost like she knew what was going on inside. She stared at Eric's eyes for clues; motherly instincts are powerful. "Don't carry this weight alone. Share the burden with me, your mother. It will be our secret, forever." A strange feeling enveloped Eric. What secret was she referring to? Was his gentle nature being interpreted by others as something it wasn't. What were his mother's instincts telling her? He decided to redirect the conversation toward Michelle. "You asked me about Michelle and what lies ahead for us. To be honest, I don't know. What I do know is that she means a great deal to me and my feelings for her are real and strong." His mother was direct. "Are you in love with her Eric? She deserves to know your true feeling before you leave, wouldn't you agree?" Eric never imagined how difficult this exchange with his mother would be. He asked himself, (am I in love with Michelle?) He wanted to say yes and knew by that evening he would have to face a similar discussion with Michelle. Was he prepared? His mother didn't press him; she knew when to step back. That is when Eric's father entered unexpectedly. He realized

Eric's last evening was being spent with Michelle. "Well Eric, since you are leaving tonight,I just want you to know how proud I am of you. You have many choices before you. I know you will find your way in the midst of it all." Mother, father and son embraced with watery eyes. Eric's mom had difficulty and broke down. Their only son was off to war; of that she was certain. Hope was that Eric's training and discipline would somehow save him from the horrors of war in the jungles of Vietnam, twelve thousand miles away.

Chapter 20

Eric imagined his final night home would be a special time with Michelle but after the emotional exchange with his mother, he wasn't so sure. Some situations present obstacles that can diminish relationships without warning. This is how Eric felt. Trapped between emotions of love for those special people in his life and his true self; he felt very conflicted and thought this must have special meaning. Most men, he thought, would not have been torn between love for a beautiful woman and other emotional or spiritual needs. How would he discuss this with Michelle? He wanted to be true to her and to himself. There was only one course of action that Eric could take. Be honest with her and allow the aftermath to take shape. Michelle's reaction would also be indicative of Eric's future path, after all Michelle's future was also being determined in part by whatever Eric laid out before her.

When she arrived at his front door, her fur collar shielded her from a cold January wind. Her blond hair and blue eyes glistened under the bright outdoor light and Eric reached out to her as she stepped into the foyer. They embraced and Michelle gave him a sealed envelope. "Please do not read this until you have returned to your base. Promise!" Eric tucked the letter in his lapel pocket and wrapped his long wool army dress coat onto his physical frame; he noticed that he filled it out; it was a loose fit when issued.. Military training had filled his frame with weight and muscle tone. He drew Michelle close and placed his powerful arms around her. "Let's go. Our time is precious." As they walked to her car in snow that was four inches deep, Eric thought of his parents who were probably looking out a window. Their emotions were more than he could handle so he felt leaving now was the best option. Michelle asked. "Where to?" Her smile was a beautiful sight. Eric wondered what destination would offer an appropriate setting for his unknown and uncertain plans, so he said. "Why don't you decide? Whatever you prefer is good with me." There was a detachment in his voice that Michelle picked up but would not reveal in any way. After all, this was not a walk in the park. She sensed his anxiety and even fear while staring at him sitting to her right; she leaned toward him, placing a sensuous kiss onto his lips. Eric's thoughts escaped him for the moment. Her beauty and smell captivated him. For a flashing moment he thought his confidence and certainty had returned, but a beautiful woman can make your mind play tricks on you. "I have a reservation for a room at a lodge. We can get some take-out and just relax. How does that sound to you?" Any other man would have jumped at the opportunity to be with his girlfriend the night before military departure. Michelle drove about a mile before she had a sense that her plans might not materialize. She pulled into a shopping center parking lot and parked at a far corner. "Let's talk Eric. Something is obviously bothering you and I will try to understand. Please share your feelings with me." She left the car running in the bitter cold night. This is not what he thought it would be. Now the question was how does he acknowledge his emotions without disappointing expectations. Eric was looking forward to avoid making eye contact. It wasn't easy. He thought of what his mother had said earlier that day, making reference to his gentleness, kindness and compassion, all required for the priesthood and a celibate life. He turned to Michelle. "You know my feelings for you are special. It's difficult for me to express my uncertainties, knowing they will be interpreted as uncaring but that's not the case." Michelle's eyes were filled with emotion; she stared into Eric's eyes and appeared calm, but it was as if she knew what was going on inside. Her instincts sensed his anxiety. "You know Eric I know you are conflicted about us, but I sense other distressing emotion as well. You have a lot on your plate right now. I want you to know that I understand. If you want to talk about anything, now would be a good time. The only expectation that I have is that you will be honest with me; believe me, we will both feel relieved if you share your discomfort. I will respect your forthrightness and your privacy." Her words were comforting and reasonable and she spoke with serenity. Their personalities were similar in that respect. Two mature adults, a man and a woman whose feelings for each other were genuine. Eric knew from his extensive literature, especially philosophy, that hiding truth, although not a lie, was deception. There were many reasons for revealing his true feelings on all matters and few reasons for concealing them. This was a time for truth telling. Eric realized he owed Michelle all the past chapters of his life that brought him to this particular crossroad. After all she was an important part of that juncture and was worthy of being informed of circumstances that shaped his life. "I think we should continue this discussion in that lodge you reserved for the night. That is, unless you feel otherwise."

The lodge was a half hour drive into the country and was quite isolated. They walked in a foot of snow caring two bags of Chinese take out. The room was very rustic with a fireplace supplied with enough logs for an evening fire which Eric started as Michelle prepared their Chinese potpourri. The stage was set for both of these beautiful adults to share a time in their lives they would always remember.

Chapter 21

There's something about a wood fire that creates an atmosphere of tranquility. This mood was established; Eric and Michelle felt relaxed as they shared a bottle of Cabernet with spicy cuisine that stimulated their appetites. The transition to their discussion was delayed by long embraces on the loveseat directly in front of the fire. Their desires were held in check; the wine soothed their nerves enough to ease their conversation forward. Eric felt liberated from all restraints when he began describing his life from elementary school. He tried to begin his story where his memory recalled important and meaningful dramas in his childhood and beyond. "When I was in elementary school, some boys thought I was too gentle for their liking. The girls didn't seem to mind but I was singled out at times by bullies who called me sissy. My mother had to speak with my teachers because she raised me to be that way. It was Peggy, a classmate who smartened me up. She told me to beat the crap out of this bully and that would solve the problem. Since I was one of the biggest boys in class, it wasn't a problem and that was the end of being bullied. But my gentle way did not vanish in thin air. It would continue to haunt me throughout elementary school. It was also perceived by one male student who had sexual tendencies toward me because of my inherent disposition. That issue would persist throughout high school. I was constantly questioning my sexuality as a result. There was one episode with this student who was a close friend, but I did not initiate it, he did and with force. That was the only episode but it really made me uncertain of my future relationships. I told my guidance counselor that I would like to see a therapist but reluctantly changed my mind. I was ashamed and afraid. Much to my regret, that refusal to get help was a mistake. So I went to my priest whose friendship really helped and basically he told me that my inherent and natural proclivity would eventually emerge. I did not date in high school and as you know I played football and other sports. Looking back now I believe that was all a cover for enhancing my image. Subsequently I realized there was another attraction pulling on me. My parish priest, Father Hall confided in me when I asked him how and why he decided to become a priest." As Michelle listened, Eric could tell she was taking in every word with earnest.. "Are you OK so far?" Michelle was startled by his question. She must have revealed her reaction and wondered whether it was judgmental. Eric did not appear to be concerned. He continued. "So as I thought about what Father Hall had said, I realized that my personality type was very compatible to what he had been describing. He was a Jesuit scholar who before his seminary, was engaged to be married and one day decided to walk away from his fiance and become a priest." Eric paused, looked at Michelle; she was motionless. "Shall I continue?" Michelle moaned. "You mean there's more! Where are you going with this Eric? Are you trying to tell me something?" Eric reached out for her hand but she pulled away. "You said to be honest with you Michelle. I'm trying to do just that." He paused and poured more Cabernet until the bottle was drained. "If you want me to stop, I will. You must keep in mind that my life is evolving. You are a part of that evolution, an important part. But I have to be true to myself before I can be true to you. 'To thine own self be true.' When Michelle stood up, Eric thought she was about to leave. He watched her go into his lapel pocket and remove a letter she had written. "I think it would be better if you read this letter now. It may help both of us clarify where we stand in our relationship." She handed it to Eric and sat down next to him. There was a beautiful smell emitting from the envelope as he removed the letter and began to read her letter for both to hear.

Dear Eric,

Ever since I met you, my thoughts for you have been constant. I still find it difficult to imagine myself attracted to a future priest, but it is made easier by your handsome body and personality. I feel a gentle and soothing calm when I am with you. This is why your decision to serve in the military has confused me; I'm still wondering where your future will lead. Now you're off to Vietnam and only God knows how that will unfold. That is why I have to tell you my feelings now, in writing, so that you can on occasion be reminded how strong my feelings are for you. I want you to know before you leave that I am in love with you and have been for some time. Whether these words make a difference with your future direction in life is out of my sphere of control, but now you know how I feel. I do hope that you will respond to my letter and let me know whether I should maintain my current feelings for you or move on. I realize that our future cannot be determined with any certainty. I won't burden you with any more emotions than you already must feel for a variety of reasons.

Until we meet again.

Love, Michelle

Eric folded the letter into the envelope and placed it on a side table. He looked at Michelle and stared into her eyes. "Eric, please don't say anything now. Reflect and allow life to move forward without any more decisions to ponder. I'm OK with things as they stand. I just had to let you know." He nodded with approval of her understanding. "Thank you Michelle. Let's enjoy the few hours that we have together without thoughts of what the future will bring. You have given me so much to think about; I can't thank you enough." He moved in her direction. She reached out to him. They embraced, kissed and promised to be in the moment without any words that would get in the way. As it turned out their silence was filled with loving memories and passion. The next morning, the wonderful smell of coffee awakened him along with Michelle's voice: "OK soldier boy, rise and shine." Their last few hours had arrived.

Chapter 22

When Eric boarded the bus for his return to Fort Dix, his fatigue from a variety of emotions coaxed him into a natural suspension of consciousness. After one hour of deep rest, his eyes opened when a bright sun reflecting off glistening snow beamed through the window so strongly that Eric had to squint his eyes. To his left was another draftee in uniform. There were no words between them, just blank stares. All of a sudden he felt what his mother must have experienced just yesterday. Fear manifested itself so suddenly that Eric began to hyper ventilate. His training reminded him to cover his nose with cupped hands so as to breathe in some expelled air containing CO_2. It worked but it reminded him of what lies ahead in a war zone where extreme heat and humidity, not a New York winter would take his breath away. He had read of climate conditions in the jungles of Vietnam and heard from those who completed their tour. Jungle warfare drains energy, especially from soldiers foreign to oppressive heat and humidity. Tension was building within Eric; he felt claustrophobic and needed air so he tried to open his window but it was frozen shut. He started to panic but remembered to take deep breaths and cupped his hands again over his nose. It worked. Meditation techniques were also used to bring him back from this brief anxiety attack. Deep breathing. Deep breathing. He kept on reminding himself. Never could he remember a time when he thought he was losing it. Anxiety attacks. Not Eric. He resorted to prayer as a last resort and found that his trepidation subsided. What really bothered Eric was that all of this happened on a bus, not in combat. Was this a reality check? Was reality that frightening? Deep breathing. Deep breathing. His composure returned, but Eric knew he had to see a therapist before his departure for Vietnam. His closet was filled with demons.

Chapter 23

Upon arriving at Fort Dix, Eric was greeted by a few recruits and they decided to stop for a beer before returning to their barracks. The bar and grill was a typical gin mill in a working class neighborhood. When the recruits walked in, several men at the bar looked briefly at them and one older veteran commented to his friend. "These guys are probably going to end up in Vietnam. It's a no win situation." Eric couldn't help but hear his comment but he blew it off and just wanted to refocus on other possibilities. Don't go negative. One recruit, David Bradshaw, was 19 and looked younger. He appeared apprehensive so Eric offered him a look of friendly confidence. He graduated from high school and was not sure of his future plans so his indecision placed him in the pool without a chance for being classified 1-A, college deferment status. Eric saw his trepidation and it gave him reason for neglecting his own uncertainty. He felt their age difference was part of his advantage. Eric was 25 and his four years of college and eighteen months at the seminary had mentally prepared him, or so he thought. Bradshaw's weakness gave Eric strength. He decided right there to use weaknesses found in others as a means for strengthening and sharing his own mental toughness. This was definitely learned behavior from his seminary training. Priests must learn from those around them and to incorporate human inadequacies as a frame of reference for maintaining their own priestly outlook. It turned out to be a healthy and practical method for fighting off a variety of demons and or negativity which haunted him. Eric suddenly felt a surge of confidence by using this tactic. He decided right there in that gin mill with a pint of beer in his hand that he would rise above his fear and uncertainty by using it to give him strength and courage by sharing it with other recruits. For Eric, this was therapy without a therapist. He also realized that his faith had to count for something; how much could never be determined. Eric asked Bradshaw questions about his family back home just to get him to converse and open up. He decided to make Bradshaw, the first of many recruits to follow, a recipient of his humanity. By acting as a mentor and confidant, Eric realized part of his mission in the military, but only after finding comfort zones in men who hid behind walls of fear. Bradshaw loosened up and Eric learned another important instructive example; learn by listening. Fear can be diminished when victims of fear have opportunity to expose or divulge something secret. For Bradshaw the fear was simple: combat frightened him. Even shooting a gun was for him an act of courage. The extreme volume of warfare was in fact frightening. "At the range, I cringe every time I fire my rifle. To think shooting at the enemy would really unnerve me. To kill someone? Do I have the guts to do that Eric? I'm not sure." There was nothing more basic in military psychology, or so Eric thought, than a soldier's fear of being killed in action or killing someone else. Eric allowed Bradshaw to drain himself of fear and uncertainty with more words revealing his fear. Eric now opened the discussion to other recruits who were listening in. "What's your view of this Butch?" Simmons who was older than Bradshaw responded. "We all have fears; it comes with the job of being a soldier. The way I look at it is this. When your number is up, there's not much you can do about it. I'm afraid too. We all are. Ask anyone of us that question and you won't be surprised with our answers. War stinks." All those listening in nodded their heads in agreement. "Well" Eric said, "whenever any of you want to talk about this stuff, I will listen. I don't have a cure, except to say that we must depend upon each other; strength in numbers, and we'll be just fine." In that moment, Eric realized a purpose for his military service; extending his humanity to comfort his brothers; he made a positive impression on these young soldiers and wanted to make his inner strength work for them.

Chapter 24

When Eric and his fellow recruits returned to Fort Dix, there was a sense of comradeship absent just days before. Upon Eric's arrival, Sergeant Tobal gave him a letter from Captain Anderson reminding him of his meeting at 1500. "Sergeant Tobal, would you be available later this afternoon? There are a few issues I would like to discuss with you sir." The sergeant looked puzzled. "Is this about your meeting with Captain Anderson?" Eric thought he may have stirred up something. "No sir. But I think it's important."

"Stop by my office. I'll be here until 5 o'clock."

When Eric entered Captain Anderson's office he was prepared for what he expected.

"Have a seat private O'Reilly. Have you thought about our last conversation?" Eric had in deed thought about his last meeting with the captain and in just the last few days in particular, had realized his military duty had purpose and meaning for his life. "Yes sir I have come to the conclusion that my military obligations should be carried out without any reservations. I want to serve without any preferential treatment sir. I feel very strongly about this sir. I want to stay with my unit sir."

The captain looked somewhat perplexed but tried not to show it. "Are you certain private?"

Without hesitation Eric responded. "Yes sir I am certain." The captain reached for a letter from Monsignor Quaid. "In a letter I received from Monsignor Quaid, I have a request for your dispensation from combat duty. He apparently believes that you will be an excellent priest, private O'Reilly. You will displease the monsignor with your decision." Eric thought about this possibility before. He knew his conversations with Monsignor Quaid were profound and scholarly. There were offers made by Monsignor Quaid that would provide graduate work leading to a PhD at Notre Dame University. It was tempting but Eric made up his mind to be a soldier at this point in his life. "Thank you sir but I want to be in the infantry along side my fellow soldiers,sir." The captain seemed disappointed but also realized Eric's decision was an honorable one. "I think I understand private. Just do me a favor and write the monsignor a letter where you explain to him your reasons for this decision. He may think my intentions were contrary to his request." Eric looked directly at Captain Anderson. "Yes sir I will write him a letter. Thank you sir." The captain approached Eric. "I wish you the best. That is all private. You are dismissed." Eric saluted and walked out. There was no doubt in his mind about his decision. His thinking was now moving forward to a place where he no longer struggled with physical and emotional hardships of being in the infantry during wartime. He embraced his fears and knew he had in such a short time elevated himself closer to the person he wanted to be. As he approached Sergeant Tobal's office he was relieved that his past obligations were placed on hold.

Sergeant Tobal was sitting at his desk when private O'Reilly walked into his office. "At ease private. What's on your mind?" Eric felt comfortable with his sergeant and so he did not hesitate; he went right to the point. "Sergeant Tobal, I have come to know my platoon members socially and personally; they realize I am older than most of them. On several occasions we have discussed personal issues and they seem to look up to me for whatever reason and I enjoy their confidence and respect." The sergeant was not surprised. He smiled. "Private O'Reilly, I am not surprised at your observations; I have overheard your platoon members on occasion. You are like a big brother to them. This is why I am recommending you for the rank of Corporal. Are you willing to accept this responsibility?" Eric was pleased. "Yes sir, I accept. Thank you sir."

"Is there something else on your mind Corporal?"

"Yes sir there is. Some of the men have expressed their fear of combat which is totally understandable. Specifically one member's fears increase with the blast of gunfire so I think we need more time at the range where he and others will learn to cope with the explosive sounds of combat." The sergeant stood and said. "I will see that more time is spent on the range and we'll even increase the volume if you know what I mean. Live ammunition will even add risk so be sure to explain what this means. Keep your body low to the ground. By the way, I have spoken with Captain Anderson and he will visit your barrack where your Corporal stripe will be awarded in front of your platoon. Just so you know, this will happen tomorrow before evening chow. Is there anything else Corporal O'Reilly?" Eric felt confidence like never before. Military discipline and protocol was something he never thought would change his life. Now he realized a major shift in his thinking. How long it would last was another question. "No sir. Thank you sir." Corporal O'Reilly saluted and returned to his barracks. Was his new status just the beginning of more to come or was this just an episode that would diminish with time. Eric thought otherwise.

Chapter 25

The following day was without incident until after morning chow. The platoons were dressed in combat gear and hiked for ten miles with more than 50 pounds of gear on their back. They trekked through the January cold and then returned to the range where more drills were conducted with increased emphasis on maneuvers where live ammunition was being fired over their heads. With ear plugs in place, artillery rounds were blasted within close range and the volume was enormous. Sergeants were screaming at their platoons. "Stay low you motherfuckers or you won't make it back alive. This is live ammunition wizzing by your heads." Sergeant Tobal watched his platoon and had to feel pleased with their progress. After an hour of incredible infantry warfare simulation, the noise subsided. "Everybody up for the march home. REMOVE EAR PLUGS" This order was screamed several times. Only by seeing others comply did the majority know what to do. Now the troops realized why ear plugs were dispensed because even with them, their ears were still ringing. The march back to their barracks was five miles. Today was rough and they knew they were getting closer to the real deal. Standing at attention near their barracks Sergeant Tobal screamed out. "Time to clean up and prepare for inspection at 17:00. Platoon dismissed." They walked to their lockers where their hardware was cleaned and their fatigues were laundered. After showers, they returned to their barracks for inspection which required certain tasks be completed and soon. Floors mopped and waxed. Windows washed. Shoes polished. Clean fatigues worn. Beds made perfect for inspection. The list was on the board for each platoon member to follow. Eric finished waxing the floors and helped others with their chores who were cutting it too close to inspection. When all appeared in order, Sergeant Tobal entered followed by Captain Anderson. Private Butch Simmons screamed. "TEN HUT" The men snapped to attention but wondered about Captain Anderson's presence. Sergeant Tobal's voice rang out. "At ease." Captain Anderson stepped forward. "Men, all platoons who succeed do so because of the quality of their trust for one another. Sergeant Tobal has observed and learned from members of this platoon that one member deserves recognition for his contributions to the success and harmony of your platoon. For this honorable service we recognize him today and promote him to the rank of corporal. Private O'Reilly, front and center." Eric walked with pride and faced the captain. "Private O'Reilly, you are being promoted to the rank of Corporal. Congratulations." There was spontaneous applause from the men who admired Eric for his genuine friendship and guidance. Eric saluted his captain. "Thank you sir." Sergeant Tobal and Captain Anderson were saluted upon their exit from the barracks. For Eric and his fellow soldiers of the 5th platoon, there was a cohesiveness never seen before. For Eric the promotion was a small reminder that his call to serve was gratifying; it was also a test. Shortly after the Sergeant's departure, he returned to the 5th platoon. The men once again snapped to attention. Tobal stood silent for a moment before he said "at ease men." His delay to speak seemed to indicate something special was about to be announced. "I have just been informed that in two months, after we complete our advanced training, we will be transferred to Fort McClellan in Alabama to finalize our training there in jungle warfare. Then most likely we're off to Vietnam. Are there any questions." There was dead silence. Everyone sensed the inevitability of being sent to Vietnam but it was still something they did not want to hear so soon. When the sergeant excused himself, the young anxious soldiers looked down at the floor then slowly raised their fearful heads and looked at one another. Their silence was interrupted when mail call was announced; soldiers waited for their name to be called by the orderly. "Germain, Simmons, O'Reilly,"

Chapter 26

Eric retreated to his bunk to read his letter from Michelle. His feelings were mixed and distant. He felt numb, not excited or emotional and wondered why he was feeling so detached. Was it because he did not want to respond to her knowing what he just heard. Was it that his feelings for her were incomplete and untested? Was it his deeper thoughts of his sexual uncertainty? Was it fear? Was it because he didn't want to mislead her? He remained in his bunk staring at the ceiling and before he could remove the letter from the envelope, he fell into a deep sleep for an hour. He thought it strange that he delayed reading her letter. Was he avoiding something? At this point, events take on a path of their own. Eric surrendered to his fate. Now was a good place to allow his destiny to shape his future and not try to control the ending whatever that might be. Eric decided not to allow himself to lead with his emotions and feelings. When he began reading her letter he found it difficult to adhere to sentimental indifference.

DEAR ERIC,

I THINK OF YOU MORE THAN I KNOW YOU WANT ME TO BUT I CAN'T HELP MYSELF. PLEASE FORGIVE ME FOR MY INABILITY TO DETACH MYSELF FROM YOUR GRASP. I REALIZE I'M NOT PRACTICING WHAT I PREACHED TO YOU. I ALWAYS BELIEVED THAT WE HAVE TO ALLOW LIFE TO HAPPEN, NOT TO FORCE IT IN ANY WAY. YOU MUST HAVE MASTERED THAT IN SEMINARY BUT AS YOU CAN TELL, MY WILLPOWER IS NOT THAT STRONG. ARE MATTERS BETWEEN US BETTER LEFT ALONE RATHER THAN GIVING THEM HOPE FOR A FUTURE? NOW THAT YOU'VE HAD SOME SPACE AND TIME FOR THOUGHT PLEASE SHARE YOUR FEELINGS WITH ME. I CAN AND WILL UNDERSTAND NO MATTER WHAT YOU MAY FEEL AT THIS TIME. IF YOU DECIDE NOT TO WRITE BECAUSE YOU DON'T KNOW HOW TO EXPRESS YOUR TRUE FEELINGS, I UNDERSTAND THAT AS WELL. JUST SEND ME A POSTCARD AND SAY HELLO SO I KNOW YOU HAVE READ MY LETTER. I WILL PRAY FOR YOU EVERY DAY.

YOUR FRIEND WITH LOVE,
MICHELLE

Eric was still with thought. Michelle was a good, kind, generous and beautiful woman but Eric understood that at this point in his life he could not make any commitments. He thought it was good that he met Michelle, if for no other reason than testing his will and determination. He felt he was being tested by a series of events throughout his life that would determine his reality and self identity. There were so many obstacles and decisions before him. Was committing to a relationship wise and fair to him or Michelle? Eric did not think so but he did not want to hurt Michelle either. He decided to write to her right at that moment before he changed his mind. Not writing would be an admittance of retreat and he felt that would be unkind, especially to someone whose goodness was special during a time when he was unsure of himself. He owed her a letter, maybe only one. It would have to communicate, he thought, a finality, so that she could move forward with her life. The time to write was now.

DEAR MICHELLE,
THANK YOU FOR YOUR LETTER. I AM GLAD YOU KEPT IT SHORT AND TO THE POINT. I WILL TRY TO CONVEY TO YOU IN SIMILAR FASHION ONLY AND TRULY BECAUSE I BELIEVE YOU ARE GENUINE AND SINCERE. YOU ARE ALSO A BEAUTIFUL WOMAN WHO WALKED INTO MY LIFE AT A TIME WHEN I BEGAN TO REALIZE HOW FRAGILE AND UNCERTAIN LIFE CAN BE. AS YOU KNOW I HAVE MANY FORCES PULLING ON ME AND THEREFORE MY LACK OF CLARITY CONTINUES. WE WERE MEANT TO CONNECT WHEN WE DID AND ENJOY OUR MOMENTS TOGETHER. THEY WILL ALWAYS BE A BEAUTIFUL PART OF MY ENCHANTING LIFE EXPERIENCE. MY FEELINGS FOR YOU ARE NOT WHAT YOU WANT AND NEED, NOT BECAUSE OF YOU, BUT BECAUSE OF ME. YOU DESERVE ONLY WHAT'S BEST FOR YOUR FUTURE HAPPINESS. ARMY LIFE HAS TAUGHT ME EVEN MORE DISCIPLINE WHICH MAY HELP ME TO FOCUS ON LIFE'S PURPOSE AND SURVIVAL.

IT'S ALL VERY ELUSIVE. WHENEVER A PERSON FEELS THIS WAY, HE SHOULD NOT MAKE DECISIONS THAT CAN HURT SOMEONE HE CARES FOR. THAT WOULD BE UNFAIR AND WRONG.

I WILL ALWAYS HAVE FOND MEMORIES OF OUR TIME SHARED . PLEASE CONTINUE TO PRAY FOR ME.

PEACE,

ERIC

When Eric read his letter he knew it would be painful for Michelle. Giving her false hope would have been a betrayal of his intentions. He could not at this point be one hundred percent with his commitment. Truth hurts us all at various stages of our lives but it is necessary for being able to move forward. Eric felt his letter was honest . Giving up a love relationship before it truly blossomed was painful for Eric but during wartime most options contain agony. He had to release Michelle for her own good; it was the right thing to do.

Chapter 27

The weeks that followed were filled with rigorous training. Recruit's bodies became harder, leaner and stronger. Eric was amazed at his physical strength and endurance. Drill instructors were brutal but the rewards were apparent. In addition to physical training, Sergeant Tobal made sure that Eric assumed more responsibility with his platoon especially in acting as their counselor and mentor. Eric regularly counseled his men whenever they needed guidance, especially as fears escalated. His platoon respected him for his physical toughness and personal consideration. Some of his men were having nightmares and he would have sessions with them privately in Sergeant Tobal's office. On one occasion a recruit from Topeka, Kansas who was having anxiety issues requested a session with Eric. His face looked younger than his 19 years. Eric reviewed his file and noticed that his father was a cattle farmer and his mother a school teacher. He was a good soldier who missed home like so many others.

"Private Henderson, how can I help you?" His light blond hair and deep blue eyes were stunning. However examining his body language, Eric observed fear and emotional stress. Eric was concerned that recruits in his platoon were being traumatized by military training. He also realized the necessity for training exercises that pushed recruits to their limits. Pfc. Henderson was one of several others who experienced psychological trauma. For this reason Sergeant Tobal discussed the problem with Eric and knew his first line of defense was Corporal O'Reilly whose educational training was well suited for this role.

"Tell me about your life back home private. What's it like living in cattle country?"

"Sir I never realized how much I would miss my home and farm life. It's so peaceful and quiet."

Eric noticed that his 20th birthday was tomorrow. He made a mental note. "Well it does sound like a life where one could be very comfortable. I can understand why you miss it so much. Is there a special person back home?" Private Henderson smiled and pulled a photo out of his shirt pocket. "Yes sir. This is Michelle." Eric was caught off guard. The name. He thought he let go but even Pfc. Henderson noticed a look that was unforeseen. "Sir, you look puzzled." Eric smiled and revealed his story. "I too have a good friend whose name is Michelle. I just wrote her a letter requesting her to move on without me because I was not prepared to make a commitment at this time. It was difficult for me." He looked at the photo and saw a pretty young woman whose signature appeared with the words. "With Love, Michelle." Now it appeared that roles were reversed when Pfc.Henderson asked: "I couldn't do that to Michelle, she's too special." Eric realized this subject was diverting Pfc. Henderson from his anxiety; his body language appeared more relaxed when he said, "She gives me hope for my future happiness." Eric was aware their conversation did remind him of pleasant memories. "Well private I want you to know that what you are experiencing is normal and one way to get you through the anxiety is to focus on what lies ahead when you return home in just over a year. Michelle will be there waiting for you. She's very charming." The private did not want to leave just yet. "Sir forgive me for asking but what made you decide to bail out of your relationship." He realized that he may have overstepped his boundary. "Sorry sir, it's none of my business." But Eric did not flinch or appear disturbed by the question. "Private there are times in our lives when we have to sacrifice or delay what may seem to be a proper road to follow. Sometimes it may be best to consider the road less traveled. I want to see where that path will lead me." The session ended when private Henderson smiled and said. "Sir you have really given me some peace of mind. You also made me think about life differently. Thank you sir." Small talk continued for a few more minutes. Eric could tell that by just listening and showing his humanity, Henderson was more relaxed. When private Henderson left, Eric thought about what he advised. He enjoyed his role as confidant and learned that sharing his own personal stories with others was therapeutic for both parties. But he did think of Michelle and wondered how she reacted to his letter. He also ordered a birthday cake from a local bakery for private Henderson's birthday tomorrow.

Chapter 28

Fort McClellan was just a week away. Sergeant Tobal summoned Eric for a meeting to discuss the possibility of another promotion. "Corporal, it's obvious to me that you have skills that must be utilized. Officers have recommended that you be promoted to Sergeant. You have been a natural leader and mentor for your platoon. The officers have been impressed with your training and have even asked men in your platoon for their opinion. They have done this on rare occasions before and believe that rewarding men with your education and leadership skills makes sense." Eric was pleased and did not expect another promotion so soon. "Well Sergeant, you have been a great leader of our unit. I have learned a lot from your example. Are you going to return to Vietnam?" The sergeant smiled. "Hell no. I did a tour of Vietnam and will remain here for the next arrival of new recruits. The draft is in high gear. The army needs trainers. That's what I do best. The army has other plans for you too." Then Sergeant Tobal told him that with his education, training and excellent record the army wanted him to report for a twelve week officer training school at Fort Irwin, California, but he would have to apply for the opening. Sergeant Tobal had all the application papers in his office. "So you understand the army is making an exception for you; this does not happen often so my recommendation is to go for it." Eric wondered what would happen to his platoon. He asked the Sergeant. "Your platoon will go to Alabama for more training at Fort McClellan. You have one more week with them if you decide on officer training." Eric then asked: "Sir if I take the offer, would it be possible to have R&R with my platoon for one night so I can say my farewell. They have been an important reason for my success." Tobal agreed.

"I think that can be arranged. Let's make it this Friday beginning at 13:00. That should give you enough time."

When Eric returned to his barracks, a warm Spring sun warmed the air. His platoon had been scheduled for cleaning detail. They scrubbed the barrack's floors, walls, windows, toilets and all their laundry was washed. The smell of disinfectant permeated the rooms as he entered. He told his men to open windows until the smell dissipated. Then he asked them for his attention for an announcement. They gathered informally around him. "I have been with you men from the beginning. We were all drafted and here we are like brothers. You all have been an important part of my life so this Friday we will have some R&R together beginning at 13:00. We will have a bus take us to the Bowling Bar and Grill to celebrate our friendship." The men cheered and then were silent when Eric held up his hand. "There's more. Tomorrow I will be promoted to Sergeant and subsequently will be heading for Fort Irwin, California for officer training school. So this celebration is my way of saying thank you for your extraordinary achievements and courage. You are an important part of my success and I want to thank you. If and when we are deployed to Vietnam, I will request assignment as your officer, God willing." There was a sad silence. Private Simmons broke the mood with: "THREE CHEERS FOR SERGEANT O'REILLY! Hip Hip....HOORAY! Hip Hip....HOORAY! Hip Hip HOORAY!" The 5th platoon swarmed around Eric to shake his hand and thank him. Eric had to hold back tears of gratitude. These men were his brothers in arms. At that moment he thought more men should experience similar moments at some point in their life. He knew he would never forget the emotion he felt on that sunny afternoon. It would change his future more than he ever imagined. "One more announcement." Eric walked to his bunk where he opened large box of cupcakes to celebrate private Henderson's birthday. "Gather around and take one. Today is Henderson's 20th birthday. Join in with me." The birthday song was sung leading private Henderson to display his emotions for all to see. It was brotherhood at its best.

Chapter 29

The bus ride to the Bowling Bar and Grill was loud and celebratory. Eric had reserved several bowling alleys with tables, and all the food and drink paid for by him in advance. Rather than just sit around a bar, Eric thought bowling and lots of good food would provide some moderation for all the beer that he knew would be consumed. And he was right. He even assigned men to bowling teams for competition. They loved it. After a few hours of bowling, the men milled about the long bar where women congregated, some smoking cigarettes and flirting. The men knew they had until midnight; the bus would be leaving around that time. Sergeant O'Reilly tried to monitor without being intrusive. He noticed how being around women gave his men a feeling of great delight. It was magical to watch. Eric was sipping on a beer at a corner table. He was relaxed and had time to reflect upon recent changes in his life. Sometimes he thought events were going too fast for him to process. He felt he was reacting more than reasoning with the options before him. During many moments of prayer he reflected upon momentous events in his life and where they would lead him. There had to be some larger and consequential meaning for his life experiences. He tried to find a connecting thread. What he concluded was that his humanity was being enriched by the sum total of all of his experiences; he was thankful and felt he was blessed with new friends who expanded his life experiences that allowed him to progress to another stage of life. He knew his faith was a common denominator for much of his strength and success. Did God have a plan for him? He felt a variety of forces pulling on him. There had to be some demons among them. No one is flawless. For Eric, the Army experience was fast forward which did not allow for time to dwell upon unexplained circumstances, good or otherwise. He discovered that military discipline enhanced his life because it was an escape from memories that were not easily suppressed. At times he felt he was being haunted by his past. Was it strange that he found comfort being around men? He wondered. Was he confusing admiration of masculinity with other tendencies that would be considered taboo? Being surrounded by men who respected him diminished the effects of his negative past. Their admiration inspired him to believe in himself. This new recognition would have to be reinforced with behavior consistent with his preferred outcome. Or was Eric just confused about his inherent reality. Maybe whatever was bothering him could be uncovered by therapy. Maybe this emotional preoccupation with his past was caused by a traumatic event for which he was unaware. Was there something in his childhood that he repressed? Could a psychiatrist reveal the source of his dissidence. What was his preferred outcome? He prayed for an answer because he realized his mental health issues had to be resolved sometime before his assignment for officer training.

Eric looked at his watch. It was after midnight. The "happy hour" had to end. He asked private Simmons to gather the troops for their return to base. Many had too much to drink but they all managed with help from their friends to stumble into the bus. The ride home was silent. Eric had bargained with Sergeant Tobal for sleep privileges until late morning. Although he was pleased for his men, Eric's mood was burdened by thoughts from the past he could not identify. He was still struggling with deep emotions that were not going away.

Chapter 30

The final day with his troops arrived on Saturday. He watched as they boarded buses for their ride to Andrews Air Force base in Maryland and was confident with their progress as soldiers; he did his part by serving them to the best of his ability. Now it was time to take care of his own needs. He would have to report to Fort Irwin in California in one week and was granted leave for six days. He arranged his flight to California for departure from Syracuse, New York, so he could utilize his time visiting his parents and seeing a therapist. His first line of business was to contact Father Hall who knew Eric's past and who could recommend a psychiatrist preferrably in Ithaca where he could maintain his privacy. When speaking long distance with Father Hall he told him his schedule and that he would like two or three sessions if possible with a therapist who had at least five years of experience. He was confident that his friend and mentor would be able to accommodate his request. Eric began his journey home and told Father Hall he would call him that evening from Ithaca. He did not bother to call Michelle or his parents because he thought he would stay at an inexpensive accommodation near the therapist's office. He needed space and time alone. This meant his visit with his parents would be brief. Attention to his personal problem had to be addressed first and foremost. If he decided to contact Michelle, it would be a last minute decision.

When Eric spoke with Father Hall that evening, a psychiatrist who fit Eric's needs was available for two, and maybe a third appointment. He lived in college town adjacent to the Cornell campus which made it easy for Eric. He could find a room close by for a few days in one of several homes who boarded guests. Father Hall wanted to visit with Eric so he arranged dinner at THE STATION, a transformed railroad station that had excellent food. Father Hall would drive to Ithaca from Oswego to serve his friend and parishioner of many years. Father Hall was a role model and Eric's admiration for this man was special. When Eric arrived in his uniform, Father Hall was sipping a martini. "Father Hall, it's so good to see you." They embraced like old friends do. Eric sat and ordered a glass of Cabernet. They stared into each others faces and smiled. "You look terrific. So how is life in the army, Sergeant O'Reilly."

Eric looked warn when he spoke. "Well Father, it's certainly different than seminary school. I have made some wonderful friends and will leave for Fort Irwin, California next week for officer training. I was fortunate to be recommended by my superiors. Things are moving fast. Maybe too fast." Father Hall finished his martini and ordered another. "Well let's enjoy a nice dinner. I'm starved." He obviously did not want to press and allowed Eric to take the lead. They shared some small talk about goings on at St. Mary's in Oswego. "You know I'm getting close to retirement so there will be an opening soon in your home parish. That's if you're still interested." There was always a remote chance of that happening if Eric returned to complete his seminary training but there was only one issue on his mind at this time and Father Hall sensed the urgency of the moment. As far as completing his training for the priesthood, Eric had already decided to place that on hold. The evening passed with discussion about the army and other future possibilities including the priesthood. At this point Eric said: "Well Father let me inform you of the latest. The army has been a good experience and the opportunities are there for me. I'm sure the war in Vietnam has and will accelerate many military careers including mine. I have to resolve a few things first. You may be wondering why I requested a therapist. I've had anxiety attacks before my military experience. In fact they have diminished with each week of training.. So it's not the military as far as I can determine.. It's something else." Father Hall listened intently and encouraged Eric to continue. "Please go on. Tell me more." Eric continued. "Well Father it may be that I have issues about my sexuality, although at times I think it's deeper than that." Father Hall twitched which Eric never noticed before. Then he asked Eric. "Have you spoken to your mother about this?" Now why would he ask this question. "Should I." Stumbling for words, Father's response was: "Well I know you and your mother have been close. One usually confides in a parent who is nonjudgmental, wouldn't you agree?" For the first time, Eric felt discomfort with his priest. He did not understand why he felt this but he did. Did his older friend and mentor know something or was Eric fabricating drama out of thin air. Why would he speak with his mother about this? Eric then surmised that Father Hall knew something. Maybe his mother had confided with him about something in Eric's past, however he could not and would not violate her confidentiality. Eric became direct. "Father Hall do you know something that I should know?" It appeared to Eric that Father Hall knew more than he could divulge; it also appeared to Eric that he was suggesting hints, and by doing so was not breaking any promise of silence to his mother, reasoning that Eric was now an adult not a child, and should be informed of his past history. Father Hall exhibited awkward mannerisms throughout their dinner. "You know who I saw in church last Sunday was your Uncle George. He looked quite aged. He lost his wife quite some time ago didn't he?" Why is he mentioning his long lost uncle. Eric's Uncle George, his mother's brother, had a fallout with his mother many years ago and they never contacted one another since. There were other hints too. Maybe that is why Father Hall completed his martini and asked for a third. If Eric's suspicion was correct, he felt compelled to telephone his mother and ask her to meet him somewhere away from home before his appointment tomorrow evening. Eric was concerned with Father Hall's condition after his third martini but he was assured that it was not a problem. He didn't want to push any more than he thought necessary. It was now more apparent that Father Hall was trying to communicate to Eric surreptitiously. When the waiter brought their check, Eric thanked him as he and his mentor priest walked out of THE STATION, arm in arm. The valet retrieved Father Hall's black sedan. They looked into each others eyes again and Eric could see tears rolling down Father Hall cheeks. "If I had a son, I would want him to be like you Eric. Knowing the truth will liberate your soul and free the holy spirit in you." Eric O'Reilly's life drama was finally surfacing with help from Father Hall and three martinis. "Thank you Father. I will respect our privacy, you can be assured." He hugged and thanked his mentor and friend. Eric's eyes too, were filled with tears. As Father Hall drove off, Eric walked to a phone booth outside the restaurant and called his mother. He would hang up if his father answered. Luckily, she answered. Abruptly he told her not to divulge his call. "Mom, it's very important that I speak to you, privately about my past." This was followed by absolute silence and following a very brief conversation , they arranged to meet the following morning at 10 a.m. Before Eric went to bed he prayed that Father Hall would arrive home safely, knowing that his consumption of three martinis was his only way of revealing shreds of Eric's past that continued to haunt him.

Chapter 31

That evening, Eric meditated before his prayers and when he was finished, his mind was the most relaxed he had been for quite some time. The dinner with Father Hall did help and as he lay in bed he allowed peaceful solitude to overwhelm him hoping recollections of his childhood would surface. He breathed deeply and allowed his mind to drift toward his childhood because he believed there may have been trauma hidden somewhere in the past. The tranquility he felt combined with his emotional exhaustion brought him to a deep sleep. When he woke the following morning it was almost eight o'clock. He quickly showered and prepared for his mother's arrival, dressed in civilian clothes. There was a Greek diner within walking distance where he had his coffee and breakfast on many occasions while at Cornell. Since he did not have a car, he told his mother he would be waiting outside the Pavillion Diner on State street. She was there ten minutes early and looked very aged since his last visit home. He embraced his mom and she seemed nervous. She asked him to drive and they decided to go to a town park where they could sit outside in the fresh air and warm sunshine. He told her of his promotion to Sergeant and that in a few days he was flying to California for officer training school. She appeared to be preoccupied and whatever he told her did not seem to register. He parked her Buick and they walked to a bench at the far end of the park. In the distance the sound of children could be heard playing during recess. His mother could not hold back. "I am so sorry you are having problems Eric. What's wrong?" He reached out to her. "Mom you don't have to protect me any more from what happened." She was startled. "What do you mean?" Eric continued, "Mom, I woke up this morning and was in a deep sweat. Do you know why? I vividly recalled in a dream what Uncle George did to me when I was a very young boy. It was terrible and painful. You took me to the doctor because I was bleeding. Now I understand why you cast your brother out of our family forever. I know you tried to protect me but what you should have done instead is bring me to a therapist for help. I apparently repressed the whole sordid incident. My entire life has been trapped in mental and emotional turmoil and I could not understand why until this revelation this morning." His mother was crying out loud and he held her. "It's OK mom. I know you thought you were doing what was best but what you didn't realize is that I have had anxiety issues that have multiplied through the years. On that horrible day I can even hear you screaming hysterically when you walked into my bedroom unexpectedly. This is why I arranged to see a psychiatrist this afternoon. Now I can tell him that I have discovered the reason for my anxiety attacks and traumatic episodes. Now I understand a big part of my emotional past." His mother was still sobbing and he was still holding her when she cried out: "I didn't know what to do or who to reach out to. If I told your father, he would have killed George. What would that accomplish? The only one I could reach out to was Father Hall, bless his heart. He saved me from going insane." He held his mother and let her know that she did what she thought was right. "Eric, you seemed to progress in school and appeared to be OK, so I let it go." Eric continued holding her because he knew she needed his love and compassion more now than ever before. "You know mom, the last time I was home we had a discussion where you asked me if everything was all right. You said, you can tell me your secrets. It will be ours to know, no one else. That apparently unleashed an unconscious reaction in me when riding the bus to New Jersey. I had a panic attack that really frightened me. There are other issues that I have to resolve as well. That is why I am seeing the doctor this afternoon." Eric and his mother walked through the park. He was concerned for her emotional instability because he never saw her so upset before. Once he felt the initial crisis was over, they decided to spend a few hours talking about other things. Eric loved his mother so much because of her tenderness and caring ways throughout his time at home. She always hugged him and loved him and he appreciated the comfort that he felt from her affection and devotion. For a brief moment he thought she may have been compensating for what happened. But that wasn't true because he remembered his mothers loving ways from the very beginning of his childhood. She cried to Eric saying she let him down but Eric assured her that was not the case. "I know you did your best mom." Eric suggested they drive somewhere out in the countryside and find a place for lunch or maybe stop for antiques which she enjoyed. While driving she told Eric that Michelle had stopped by weeks ago but just that once. Eric did not want to discuss his personal matters so he just said they were friends. He held his mother's hand while driving and tried to reassure her that his future looks promising.

Chapter 32

Eric wanted to spend some time with his mother and enjoy memories of good times shared. He was glad her composure returned and when she began describing her garden plans he even felt better. She did ask him whether he planned to return to the seminary and how she was frightened that he would probably be off to war soon. "I still can't believe you were drafted into the Army. Your father seems to think you could have been deferred. Is that true?" Eric wanted to be honest with his mother. "Mom, why should I qualify for a deferment while other men could not. That's not right. I did not want any special treatment."

His mother understood but admitted her fear for Eric would not end until he was safely home. As far as the seminary was concerned, Eric said he wasn't sure. He had time to think it over and needed time to make up his mind. Since neither one was hungry, they skipped lunch. He told his mom when she dropped him off at his boarding house that he would call her at four o'clock to know she returned safely. His mom hugged and kissed him goodbye. They both felt relieved over resolving a crucial part of Eric's life history. Today was a good day, so far. Eric went out for some pizza and beer and anticipated his 4:30 appointment with Dr. Neuberger.

The office was within walking distance from his boarding house. It was a steep walk up to college town. The surroundings brought back memories of his undergraduate days at Cornell. You could not ask for a more beautiful setting "high above Cayuga's waters." The doctor's office was set back from the sidewalk. Eric had to walk through a wrought iron fence then around the side of this old house with cedar shakes. There he saw the doctor's sign. Henry Neuberger, M.D. Psychiatric Therapy.

There was a waiting room with a sofa and chair. He sat and waited at least ten minutes before the doctor appeared. "Good afternoon. Are you Eric O'Reilly?" The doctor was average height and had to look upward to Eric's 6'2" frame. "Yes doctor." He led Eric into his office and asked him to make himself comfortable. "Please fill out this form and I will return in about ten minutes. Be as thorough as you can." The form was one page, front and back and required more information than Eric expected including a brief explanation of his reason for therapy. Eric wrote what he thought was adequate, avoiding particulars until his session began.

When the doctor returned, he asked Eric to sit in a comfortable chair facing him. He read through the paper and asked Eric a direct question with no time lost. "Eric, are you suggesting here that you think you may be a homosexual?" Eric was startled by his direct inquiry. He didn't know how to respond. "Well doctor I think I should give you some background to my most recent discovery today while meeting with my mother. I have finally learned something that I did not know when you were contacted by Father Hall. This morning I learned that I was sexually molested by my uncle when I was a child. I must have been four or five years old. That episode apparently was repressed by me and has haunted me for twenty years. I never received any therapy or guidance because my mother did not want to have my father find out because he would have killed my uncle. Those are her words. So she consulted Father Hall and the entire episode was buried. I needed medical attention at the time; my mother had to take me to the doctor due to rectal bleeding. As I said, the whole disgusting incident was repressed. I don't know if that has anything to do with my sexual uncertainty. But I have had a wonderful relationship with a beautiful woman before I was drafted." The doctor asked: "How wonderful was it?" Eric couldn't help but smile and was amused by the doctor's direct approach without avoidance. "Well doctor we had a sexual relationship if that's what you mean. And we both enjoyed ourselves." The doctor paused and wrote several notations in his pad and then continued to press. "So why are you questioning your sexuality?" Eric had to think about this. He felt there was a reason but did not know himself as well as he thought. "Well doctor I think my personality has something to do with it. I was not a rough child or bully. I was inclined to be gentle, on the quiet side, not the typical hormone driven sort of male. In fact I was called a sissy by my peers on occasion in elementary school. I was easily intimidated and harassed and remember crying to my mother about it." The doctor took more notes and continued. "Tell me more." Eric felt comfortable with this doctor. He seemed to understand his anxiety allowing Eric's words to flow without restraint. "Well doctor, as I got older I grew taller and stronger. I began to take charge of bullying if you know what I mean." The doctor demanded an explanation. "I got into fights and beat the crap out of these boys. That stopped it in its tracks." Eric did not display any emotion but remained calm. "Well Eric did you experience any change in your manliness as a result of this aggressive response or did you maintain your gentle and quiet demeanor?" Eric's response was immediate. "You mean did my aggressive behavior change me. Maybe. But I didn't become hostile or mean. Maybe more assertive and confident but in a quiet way." The doctor moved his hand in a circle signaling: "continue". "Well doctor, as a young child I remember wanting to be a priest. I was an alter boy and was fascinated with the ceremonies, rituals, and music; it all seemed to fit with my personality. Maybe that became something that made me feel disinterested in things other teenagers would consider normal. My interests were elsewhere." More notes were written. "Well, let me ask you this: Do you feel your interest or desire for the priesthood made you feel different in any way, either sexually or otherwise? Did it diminish your interest in girls and sexual urges that teens normally experience?" Eric had to think about these questions. He paused and the doctor patiently waited for a response, then after a period of silence: "Eric I am sure you thought about these questions before, would you agree?" Eric nodded. "Yes I have but I also thought about how a priest must live his life of celibacy and maintain vows of purity in these matters. Maybe I did not find this as difficult as other males." The doctor reached for his pipe and stuffed some tobacco into the bowl, lit it and continued. "Eric tell me about other interests. Were you involved in sports of other activities."

"Yes, I played football, basketball and baseball." The doctor was surprised. "Really! That's interesting Eric. I guess I wouldn't expect your involvement in sports would be so vast." Eric was somewhat annoyed by that comment. "You mean a gentle, mild mannered teenage male with possible ambitions for the priesthood has no business playing team sports. Maybe you are not including my total personality in your evaluation. I happen to be very competitive and love sports. I also am very spiritual, pensive, quiet and gentle with others of both sexes. Yes this is not the stereotypical male you're dealing with. I am still sorting things out for myself and would hope that you would be more impressed with my social diversity and less with your conventional and outmoded thinking." The doctor apologized for what Eric thought was his insensitivity. "Eric, you're right, I'm sorry. You are indeed a unique young man and I do want to help you sort things out. May we proceed?" Eric took a deep breath and nodded in the affirmative. "Tell me Eric, since one issue you are concerned with is your sexuality, have you had any same sex experiences?" Eric was actually relieved with this question because he wanted to get it out in the open so he could understand his mixed emotions. The doctor continued: " I realize that what you learned today about your past may have played a critical part in the confusion you feel. What happened to you was horrific and left you terrified and confused; you have every reason to feel that way." Eric's emotions were starting to show. He took another deep breath and cupped his hands over his nose. When he felt composed he looked directly at the doctor. "Doctor when I was a boy of eleven I was walking in the woods near my home and met a boy my age. We became friends and were close. There was something about him that I was attracted to. Maybe it was his extroverted personality. Opposites attract sort of thing. We were alter boys together, played sports throughout our school days. We were close. We were also two of the tallest, physically fit boys in our class. One day after a movie we went to his house and we had a few beers. His parents were away so he decided to take some liberties with me in my somewhat inebriated condition. He pinned me down and began kissing the back of my neck and ended up having an orgasm on top of me but I did pull away before any penetration. I was so confused by his sudden sexual attack directed at me, his friend, because when he overpowered me he said that I was asking for it. His comment really bothers me to this day. We remained friends but I told him that he was totally out of line with his behavior but he insisted that I lured him into his sexual fury." The doctor allowed Eric to pause and waited for him to continue, but he didn't. "Eric, evidently your friend was having issues with his own sexual orientation when he directed his homosexual desires toward you because he perceived you as weak and too gentle to offer resistance. Your gentle and quiet ways were misconstrued by your friend to mean something they were not, unless you think otherwise. As far as you luring him on, well, was there any truth to that?" The doctor realized that Eric had too much to digest and thought of ending his session. "Maybe we should end our session at this point so you can have time to think things through, maybe in two days." Eric did not want to terminate their session but realized Dr. Neuberger was probably correct. Two days seemed like eternity. "Eric let's make it for Wednesday, say 2pm. Is that good?" After shaking hands and thanking the doctor, Eric walked down the hill from college town. He prayed that he could revisit his past without more anguish and discomfort and was surprised when his thoughts drifted to Michelle. He decided to call her that evening.

Chapter 33

Michelle's phone rang but she did not answer. Eric let it ring for some time when suddenly he thought maybe it was best not to communicate with her for a variety of reasons. He was just about to hang up when Michelle answered. "Hello". Eric did not respond at first. "Hello, is someone there?" Her instincts sensed someone at the other end. "Hello Michelle, it's Eric." There was dead silence. Eric repeated, "Michelle, it's Eric, I'm in Ithaca." He sensed her silence meant something negative so he refrained from further comment. He heard sounds in the background that sounded like someone was there. "Michelle, I'm sorry if I interrupted your evening. Should I try maybe tomorrow" She managed a response that made Eric almost hang up. "Well, please give me one minute." Eric heard Michelle thank someone, then returned to the phone. She sounded out of breath. "Eric, it's so good to hear from you. How are you?" She seemed distant and Eric could understand why and regretted making the call. "How long will you be in Ithaca?" Eric realized at that moment the guilt he felt for leading Michelle out of his life without an explanation. He felt he owed her one but did not know how to approach the subject. She made it easier. "We have a few minor details to discuss, unless you would rather just let it go." Eric was compelled to respond with: "Yes we do, but my time is limited." Before Eric could say another word, Michelle interrupted: "When?" Eric did not have an exact day so he told her Wednesday or Thursday. "Eric, I am only a few minutes away, if you want I'll be there in half an hour." He could not say no without making a tense situation worse. They arranged to meet at ZINCK'S, a watering hole down the hill from Eric's boarding house and frequented by Cornell's students.

Eric's session that afternoon made him so tense that his clothing smelled of perspiration, so he took a quick shower and wore jeans with a light blue collared shirt. Then he walked down the hill to ZINCK'S where he sipped on a draft while waiting for Michelle at the bar. He tried to recall his letter to Michelle but his only recollection was kissing the envelope before dropping it in the U.S. mail box.

Revealing recent details of his past would be difficult and he was reluctant to expose himself to more scrutiny. He wanted closure with

Michelle so they could both move on. He knew it wasn't going to be easy. His body language indicated a somber mood; his head looked down at the floor. At that moment he felt a delicate hand touch him on his left shoulder. It was Michelle. She stared at his sad eyes. "Hi, are you OK?" Eric did his best to put on a pleasant face but it wasn't easy. She sensed distance and placed her hand on his. "Are we still friends?" Michelle's stunning natural beauty elicited a tender response from Eric. His outstretched arms drew her into a warm embrace.

"Michelle, thank you for coming. I owe you..." Michelle placed her index finger on his lip. "Ssssh"

"You don't owe me anything but your friendship." Eric quietly responded. "Thank you." He led her to a corner table where they held hands, waited and wondered about the words that would be exchanged along with emotions attached. Eric felt no need to hide or fear what he knew had to be shared with her. "Where should I begin?" Michelle's silence was inviting. Eric began with his childhood trauma and led Michelle through his session earlier that day that exposed critical information he believed would reveal and explain his chronic anxiety. She listened without comment and looked intently into eyes that were filling with watery emotions. "You must know that I distanced myself for reasons I did not understand then but do now. I did not mean to hurt you and want you to know that my relationship with you was honest; it may not have been what you wanted or expected, but it was all I could give. The reason I called you was to inform you of my latest revelations as a result of speaking with my mentor, Father Hall who led me to discover past horrors which were confirmed when I spoke to my mother yesterday. My abrupt disconnection with you was in part a result of those repressed memories. I wish I could give you more, but at this time in my life it's impossible. And believe me when I say that. Please tell me you understand." Their eyes locked and now both shared tears. As difficult as it was for Michelle, she maintained her composure and dignity. "I understand Eric. Even though this moment is not what I hoped for, I do understand. Thank you for your openness and honesty." Eric reached out and held her hand. "You deserve the best a man has to offer. I wish that man could be me but at this point in my life I would be dishonest to entrap you with my past." Eric held both of her hands and looked straight into her eyes. "I feel God pulling on me and for some reason I'm resisting. Now the army has me for two years and I am sure Vietnam is part of my future, like it or not. And now the most beautiful and kindest woman I have ever met has walked into my life. I hope you know me well enough to realize my feelings for you are sincere and strong; it's not like I have tried dating myself out of our relationship; but the Holy Spirit is also tugging on my heart. My tomorrows are, as of this moment, up in the air. I have shared this with no one but you. Remember our discussion of existentialism and destiny. I realize that I have to make a choice, but I seem to be incapable of doing that at this point in my life. Little did I realize how our lives could become victims of fate." Michelle's body language was detached. She looked distant when she stood up to say good bye. "One final hug and kiss then I better be going." Eric was stunned but seemed to understand. They embraced and kissed with unfulfilled desire. "No need to see me out." She kissed Eric one more time on the lips and walked to her car. If there ever was a woman who was right for Eric, she just walked out of his life.

Chapter 34

The remainder of Eric's night was preoccupied with thoughts of what could have been. He remembered conversations with other men in the seminary who experienced similar dramas with love affairs. Eric's emotions lingered when he sensed Michelle's fragance on his shirt. He stared motionless, just thinking of the unthinkable as he walked back to his room. He knelt by his bed and prayed for wisdom and peace, then he climbed into bed and continued his meditation until he fell asleep. When he awoke the next morning, he was surprised that he had slept so long; he felt refreshed and ready for his next and last session with Dr. Neuberger at 2pm.

The doctor was walking into his office as Eric approached. They both appeared more comfortable with each other. There was open dialogue concerning many issues that were bothering Eric. Eric's relationship with his father and childhood friends through his high school days. There were no issues that seemed problematic. Eric felt his life was fairly normal and the doctor agreed. Their session was moving along for three quarters of an hour when the doctor asked Eric. "You are a very handsome man and there's no question that your lady friend was brokenhearted from your last time together. However your inclination for the priesthood must preclude a romantic relationship. There's no compromise in that situation. Then as we have discussed, there is your uncertainty about your sexual orientation and whether that is a result of childhood trauma or something else. Something tells me you know the answer. And now, the Army has you in their web for at least two years. Tell me Eric, do you think the Army is a road to escape from your past? Let's finish with this." Eric felt the doctor may have hit upon something and also realized that if he was escaping from his past, he may not live long enough to know how it all ends. "I definitely do feel conflicted. When I think of Michelle, I have a longing. When I think of my service to Christ, I feel a calling. And in reference to my sexuality, I believe my desire for Michelle is strong. I don't feel any urges in the other direction. What I have learned most recently has cleared my mind. I think I am just going to allow things to unwind. There's no sense trying to plan anything now. Thousands of soldiers are dying every month in Vietnam. I may be one of them soon, so what's the point of planning." The doctor concurred. "Well Eric I realize this is our last session and we may never meet again so let me give you my personal advice which I rarely do. Focus on staying alive long enough so you can make a choice. They are both honorable choices albeit different. You can find happiness with both and that's what you should keep in mind. Michelle and Christ can fulfill your heart and soul. You have to decide which is most fulfilling and unique to your life. Both will require sacrifice; both can be painful and filled with joy. And lastly Eric, my professional advice. Continue to have therapy until you're on your way with your vocation. Therapy is so important at this stage because you need to bounce ideas around with someone you can confide with in confidence. I have a list of military psychiatrists that I will recommend." He handed Eric a list. "They are all good but I have checked two who I think would be more fitting because of their personal experiences. All were my students here at Cornell. All four are in the Army now. Your paths might cross." At that moment, Eric felt a bond of friendship with a man he hardly knew. But his instincts told him this man's wisdom was vast and worthy to heed in future years. As Eric was about to leave he wanted the doctor to know how much he was helped by his insight and advice. Eric felt relief in probing and learning from his past. Dissonance, guilt and uncertainty were mitigated by discussions with his mother, his mentor, Father Hall, and now Dr. Neuberger; Suddenly life had more clarity. The possibility of his "death wish" by obligating himself for military service during wartime seemed more rational now. "You have been more than a doctor, you have been a friend. I am very grateful for your mindful therapy. Strange but I feel absolved as I would after confession." The doctor was amused by the analogy. "There are similarities." Eric shook hands with him and thanked him again. He felt that his prayers had been answered. He walked back down the hill with his duffel bag to the bus station for his ride back home where his parents were waiting anxiously, knowing he would be off to officer training, then to Vietnam.

Chapter 35

It was almost a three hour ride from Ithaca to Oswego by bus with a stop in Syracuse. Eric had time to reflect on comments made by Dr. Neuberger, especially concerning his relationship with his father. When Eric thought about it, his father was not a hands on type of parent unlike his mother. His father was distant, not very emotional and they didn't spend much time together. It was Eric's mother who was the center force in his upbringing. She was gentle, loving, kind and tolerant, qualities that were passed on to her son. Eric now understood how this feminine/maternal side of his upbringing shaped his personality. There was little paternal input. Eric didn't have the rough edges other boys displayed because of his father's absence. In fact, Eric felt uncomfortable acting "boyish", let alone macho, when he knew it was a sham. Dr. Neuberger encouraged Eric to attempt some self analysis. By probing reasons why some individuals may have misinterpreted his delicate personality traits, Eric began to understand himself. It was his interest in sports that may have spared him from more scrutiny by his peers concerning his masculinity. Eric was keenly sensitive to this as he matured into an outstanding athlete and his friends and coaches respected his athletic prowess. But what about his sexuality. Eric was told by Dr. Neuberger that his awareness and feelings for sexual desires may not have been as strong as other boys. Eric also thought that when he decided on the priesthood, he may have suppressed his interest in girls. This thought, if true, could explain his sexual behavior not his sexual orientation. It only meant that his interest in sex was less and even delayed or self imposed. He felt comfort knowing that his performance with Michelle was more than adequate. So where would this all lead him. His future, at least from his current perspective had more definition but there were still webs that had to be untangled. Nothing unusual, just normal stuff experienced by life's choices surrounding him. Strange as it seemed, Eric thought he should have a discussion with his father whose intelligence he inherited and who did not interfere with Eric's life decisions up to this point. Maybe it was time for a little fatherly advice. It was worth a try.

When he arrived at the bus station in Oswego, he was surprised to see his father, not his mother, waiting for him. The bright sun revealed how his father had gracefully aged, and their similarities were now more apparent to Eric. Their chin, nose and blue eyes were all shared. Eric was a few inches taller and when his father extended his arms for an embrace, Eric was pleasantly surprised. He couldn't remember such a warm reception and wondered if his mother put him up to it even though it seemed genuine. Eric's father told him his mother was out shopping and would be home later that afternoon. He knew nothing about Eric's last few days with Father Hall and his therapist. When his father suggested they drive out to Rudy's for a fish fry or Texas Hot, Eric agreed. He sensed his mother's absence was now planned and that she coached his father to spend some quality time with his son. This time together was meant to be and Eric decided to have that discussion which never seemed to happen during several past opportunities . "Well dad I wanted to ask you about something that has been on my mind for some time. As you know I have wanted to be a priest for some time and was close to completing my training last year when suddenly I was drafted." His dad remained silent for a while before responding. "I think your military decision was questionable only because it's wartime. You could have been deferred but chose military service. I respect your decision; now it's time to make the most of it which I'm confident you will. However your mother and I are both worried about your future safety." Eric knew he had placed an extra burden on his parents. It wasn't exactly planned but Eric made it happen for reasons which were becoming clearer every day. He saw no reason for opening up too much with his father. Assuming he survived his Vietnam experience, Eric wanted his father's opinion on the priesthood, a career in civilian life or maybe even a career in the military. So he asked: "Dad what is your view of my decision for the priesthood?" His father was not a man of absolutes which his response demonstrated. "Well Eric you must follow your instincts. Apparently you have thought about this for some time. I think it would be a wonderful honor to have my son become a priest. And remember, it doesn't have to be a life sentence. You can always decide at some point that your service to Christ and the Church has been satisfied. In other words it doesn't have to be forever." Eric's mind was suddenly opened to a notion he had rarely entertained. Priesthood did not have to be forever unless he felt his commitment was eternal. The thought of being a priest with this proviso was appealing because it lessened his dissonance and motivated his will. Eric had limited himself by black and white thinking; his father just made him aware of that; this was a solution he could live with. Eric was heartened that it was his father who offered a practical and reasonable guiding principle for being a priest or any other vocation. Nothing has to be forever unless you want it to be. His father's wisdom was pragmatic and deeply appreciated. "Thank you dad. I really never thought of it that way." His father smiled. "Well I wish we had more face to face talks like this. I regret my failure in this regard." When Eric looked at his father, he could see his eyes watering with tears. "It's OK dad, you were and are a good father. This isn't unique to us." His father interrupted. "I allowed your mother to overplay parenting when I should have been there for you on many occasions. I'm sorry." Eric tried to understand what prompted his father's sudden emotional display. Did his mother encourage him to open up and share himself with his son? At this point it made no difference. The result was gratifying to both father and son. Eric moved on to his other question. "What about a military career dad. You served. Now I have an opportunity to become an officer and who knows where that could lead. What advice can you offer?" His father's smile indicated an appreciation for moving on and not dwelling on could of/ should of. Before he responded, he took some time to think about the question. "Well Eric, military service is a good thing. I certainly learned a great deal when I was drafted during World War II. Most of the war had ended but I saw enough to make me appreciate so much we are blessed with in America. The military can open many doors for your future, especially if you are high in the pecking order. Business, politics, you name it. Military service is like a big fraternity; brothers who look out for one another. There's a bond like nothing else." His father's tears returned. "It's just not a good time to be in the military, especially in Vietnam. I will pray for you, so will your mother." Eric wanted to change the subject; he could tell that his father was on the verge of breaking down with his emotions and when he did, Eric reached out for his hand and gently squeezed. "I will be OK dad. I'll be OK, don't worry, I'll be careful." Eric realized that his father at that very moment had elevated his fatherhood to a level Eric never expected but deeply longed for. It was as though they were not just father and son, but brothers in arms. After a quiet moment, Eric redirected their focus. "I'm craving for a Texas Hot. Let's eat."

The last hour of discussion with his father was therapeutic for both father and son. Their relationship suddenly became one of substance; their communication was infused with honesty, respect and love. One parent and his son had achieved in one hour what many families never experience. Their gratification was displayed throughout the few days remaining in Eric's visit. His mother sensed a beautiful harmony and her keen sense of knowing what only mothers understand became apparent as well. Eric's sister Mary even sensed something positive she never felt in family gatherings before. It was magical. Father, mother, sister and brother were joined by a rebirth of family bonds. The O'Reilly family had arrived at last.

What transpired during the last days of Eric's time home did more than just deliver peace to his family, it erased psychological barriers affecting Eric's mental health. Eric's only regret was his last meeting with Michelle; now with his goals fairly certain, he concluded there was little sense attempting to reconstruct their last conversation. He had to let go.

Chapter 36

It was Sunday morning, Eric's day of departure. His flight out of Syracuse was scheduled for 3pm so his family had time for attending Mass at 9 o'clock after which Eric's mother prepared his favorite breakfast of eggs sunny side, bacon and toasted buttered English muffins. All four sat around the table for what could be a last family union. No one spoke until Eric asked his younger sister how she was adjusting to her college dorm life at Colgate. Her response was there are men all over the place. "I love it." Eric smiled and wondered about what he might have said if their ages were reversed. Instead he complimented his sister for her beauty and remarked that he could understand why so many Colgate men would seek her out. Mary then asked her brother about Michelle. She told Eric that she called one evening two or three weeks ago and inquired about when Eric would be home. "Have you spoken with her?" Eric hesitated at first, then decided he better inform his family of his status and relationship with Michelle. "Well it's like this. We met in Ithaca and decided that it was premature to lock ourselves into a relationship for the time being. It was difficult for both of us. If we have a future together, it will depend on how our lives evolve. She's a kind and beautiful woman. I really do like her a lot. But for the time being, our status quo hasn't changed. Too many things going on." He wanted to continue but realized he was beginning to babble so he stopped. His mother then brought a homemade apple pie, warm out of the oven. She served it with a slice of cheddar and the combination was mouth watering, especially with a good cup of coffee. Eric's dad had been silent up to this point. But he offered some parental observation that was unexpected. His recent time spent with Eric apparently had altered his relationship with his son and pleasantly so. "Eric, I want to confess that I regret my detachment from your life. You always were in control of things so I saw little cause for me to interfere. But I was wrong to remove myself from your life. I hope we can both learn from my mistake." Eric's mother was silent. She reached for her son's hand followed by father and sister. They all sat around the family table holding hands in silence. Finally his mother spoke. "Nothing in life is certain; everything can change without our knowing when, where or how. So let's pray now as a family and ask God to bless our son and brother." They bowed their heads and she prayed. "Heavenly Father, we pray for Eric, please watch over him, protect him and send your guardian angels to be near his side. Bring him home safely to us. We pray in Jesus' name, Amen." All eyes were teared. They sat silently for a brief moment, then Eric tried to sustain them with his confidence. "I will be OK. We will all be here at this table soon after I return. I promise."

When Eric boarded his nonstop flight to Los Angeles he was in uniform. He prayed again; this time for a safe flight.

Chapter 37

Camp Irwin, located in the Mojave Desert halfway between Las Vegas and Los Angeles has a story involving interesting American pioneers. Eric read with interest how this Army base had cultivated a tradition of training Army officers and was confident that his training would maintain that standard. When he arrived, there were other candidates waiting for transport to the base. The OCS training for college graduates was a 14 week session with graduates commissioned as officers in the US Army. The OCS program was established in 1941 when the Army had to expand the officer corps during WWII. There were also medical doctors who were candidates that just graduated from medical school. The draft was in full swing with the Vietnam war raging. Eric had mixed emotions but feared for the worst; he knew that most candidates had similar sentiments and many in his training class became close friends who commiserated with one another about the increasing death tolls being recorded each week. Every Thursday, Walter Kronkite would deliver the news of American soldiers killed and those wounded. It was very easy to become pessimistic about your chances in a war without an exit strategy. Training included physical , mental, emotional components, and was fairly routine but challenging as well. Eric met some men who would become close friends for life. One, Chuck Vion majored in psychology; he was steadily realizing how this war was imploding with each report of political and military incompetence. Fighting a war with leadership that was blindsided was becoming a topic of conversation among some OCS candidates. Guerrilla warfare in the jungles of Vietnam was no cake walk. Some officers who returned from Vietnam could be overheard on occasion and their perceptions became reasons for skepticism among OCS candidates.

Weeks of training passed and Eric realized that his assignment would be forthcoming. He thought of the conversation with his father whose words of wisdom were ignored; something about avoiding the draft during a raging war undeclared by congress; this was President Johnson's war, continued and expanded by Nixon, under the guidance of General Westmoreland. Eric decided right then not to second guess himself. He accepted his place and would serve his country to the best of his ability. Options were limited unless he wanted to go awol or become a conscientious objector. He knew he would go forward but felt his future was in God's hands. Weeks later, after more training and prayer, Eric had a more positive outlook. His commanding officer, Captain Ryan Morrison was instrumental in his attitude being altered. He served his tour and reported that the mission was an exercise in self discipline, alertness, brotherhood and sacrifice, all concepts that second lieutenant Eric O'Reilly would accept as part of his obligation as an officer. War was many things, including uncertainty of outcome. Life is uncertain without war. War just makes it more challenging to say the least. Vion and Eric discussed the rationale for the war; something concerning the domino theory in southeast Asia. Vietnam, according to this theory was a firewall where communism had to be stopped. Eric recalled meeting students at Cornell who were sons of wealthy Vietnamese families. They were not fighting for their country. Their parents knew better and had the money to get them out of the country where they concealed themselves in Asian Studies at Cornell. In their broken English, they conveyed to Eric that the government was too corrupt and did not have the support of the people. They also believed this war was futile and the United States was making a very large miscalculation about communism. Americans did not understand the international varieties of communism. Americans lumped all communists together which is how they got sucked into this war. Vietnamese communists were anti Chinese. They resented Chinese domination for generations. Vietnamese communists were nationalists more than anything else. Americans failed to realize this and now were bogged down in a guerrilla war in southeast Asia that was going nowhere fast. It's not as though our leaders were not warned by President Eisenhower years earlier. Eric and Vion came to this conclusion but also realized that for them it was too late to back out. So they decided to suck it up and do their tour. There was no sense in spreading their sentiments to the other OCS candidates. Why stir the pot and get court marshaled. They maintained their silence and decided to make the best of a bad situation; translated meant, do your duty and stay alive during your one year tour. When President Johnson announced that he would not seek reelection in 1968, Eric and Vion knew why. Johnson finally realized that he was duped by his military advisers. His Great Society programs were diminished by billions of dollars wasted on war without an exit strategy in sight. Feeling as they did about the political and military incompetence, Eric and Vion realized how they had placed themselves in a circumstance beyond their control. With their successful training as infantry officers, they understood their futures were problematic to say the least. At this point in the war, injured and killed officers were an every day occurrence. In two weeks, they would be deployed and their Vietnam tour would soon begin. The following day, an orderly delivered an unexpected message for Eric to report to Captain Ryan Morrison. When he reported to Captain Morrison's office, Eric was concerned about news from home, thinking, what else could it be. He soon found out. "Lieutenant O'Reilly, I see from your transcript that you attended seminary training after graduating from Cornell. You were close to ordination. What happened?" Eric took a deep breath of relief before responding. "Well Captain, I received a draft notice." The Captain interrupted. "But there's a notation here that states you declined your deferment. Why is that?" Eric wasn't prepared for that question. He wondered now more than ever why he accepted his call to duty when he could have qualified for exemption. Hindsight is 20-20. Eric was bound in his self imposed trap. He tried to respond with an intelligent answer but could not find the words that made much sense. He found it difficult to speak and his ambiguity was apparent. Before he could speak, Captain Morrison said: "Lieutenant, you were rated at the top of your OCS class. But before I assign you to a leadership role, I would offer you a position as chaplain where you would minister to soldiers spiritual and emotional needs in Vietnam. It's no safer or less arduous. In fact it could be even more stressful since you will see death almost on a daily basis along with depression and enemy fire. Your leadership role will not be diminished. I want you to think about this and let me know by this Friday. Your battalion will be deployed Monday."

The first person Eric considered for advice was his father. He found it comforting that his recent connection back home had placed his father in that role. His mother would probably answer the phone if he called before 10pm so he waited. When he called at 10:20 eastern time, he was relieved when his father answered the phone. After some family chatter and news, his father heard coins being dropped into the pay phone. "Give me your number. I'll call you back." Eric thankfully complied. When the phone rang their conversation continued. "Eric, I sense your concern about something. Is everything OK?" It was a nice feeling for Eric to know his father could sense his emotions over the telephone. "Well dad, I need your advice. I successfully completed my OCS training and will be deployed next Monday. My CO called me in and offered me a position as chaplain, seeing that I have had seminary training. I'm conflicted about what I should do." His father also knew what many informed citizens were learning every day. The war was an unfolding disaster with more military and civilian casualties being reported every day. "Son, listen to me. This CO is giving you an opportunity to avoid combat on the front lines. In Vietnam, that may or may not be safer because guerrilla warfare in many instances has no front. But overall it may be safer for you, not to mention that it will remove you from leading troops into combat. My advice, take it son." Eric was amazed in how quick, clear and direct his father's response was. It was as though he knew the question before he even asked. Eric was leaning the other way but he would take his father's advice. "Dad, thanks. I will take your advice." His father chimed in: "Listen son. Use your combat training as well. Defend yourself and your men with weapons, not just prayer and faith. Use all your skills. Be alert always. Promise me." Eric could sense emotion coming from his father. "I promise dad. Thanks. Give mom and Mary my love. I love you dad, bye." "I love you son. Be careful." When his father went to bed that evening, Eric's mom muttered half asleep: "Who called? I heard the phone ring." The dimmed bedroom lighting could not reveal tears rolling down his face. "Just a wrong number. Pleasant dreams."

Chapter 38

Eric boarded a military transport from LA in the Spring of February 3, 1970. The officer sitting next to him had served a tour and was flying to Hawaii to meet his fiance in a few weeks just before his honorable discharge from the Army. He grew to know and like Eric during their training sessions and he wanted to inform Eric of situations that were taboo within the officer corps. He made a point of speaking quietly with Eric. Their seats were close to the rear of the plane where engine noise muffled their conversation. He started with his assessment of the war. "Listen to me Eric because what I tell you now may save your life." Eric was unnerved by his tone and intensity but felt that he was sincere in his intentions. "Let me begin with Walter Kronkite, a man trusted by more Americans than anyone else. He gave his assessment of the war last year and it wasn't good. Basically he said it was a lost cause. What I am going to tell you will only add more credibility; it's information that no one at this point knows too much about unless you've been there. I have, so listen and listen good. Nixon's plan to end this war is going no where. Turning the war over to the Vietnamese government is impossible for a variety of reasons. They are corrupt and inept and lack public support. The Tet offensive has hammered American and Vietnamese troops with multiple attacks on many cities; even though the enemy took many casualties, this was a strategic victory for the north. American forces took a big hit. Many officers have been killed. And here's the part that you have to pay attention to. Many deaths of American officers were inflicted by their own troops. Are you listening Eric? Trust me when I tell you. Why you may ask? It's called fragging in the military. Basically, it's murdering unpopular, ruthless or gun ho officers who want glory for themselves and it's happening because this fucking war has no end in sight. Heard of Hamburger Hill. We were told to double up on our ammo because this was going to be a meat grinder. I was there. I know. I want you to know that this fucking war is lost. Many troops are wacked on booze, heroin and marijuana. There is no moral compass leading them. Survival at any cost is their main goal. And if that means murdering an officer who pushes them into deadly unnecessary combat, it may happen. I've seen it. You may see it too and as a chaplain, you may have to play referee. The deaths of these officers are reported as kia but they were shot by friendly fire which on occasion was intentional because these officers were seen as too ambitious for their unit's safety; they were risking too many lives. That could be dangerous so watch out Eric because your life is worth saving. I survived without a scratch. Don't ask me how that happened because I saw many killed all around me. Why them and not me?" Eric could see Lieutenant Greiner's eyes were filling with tears. "Thanks lieutenant, I will remember your advice." He reached out his hand. They locked hands as brothers. Eric thought of returning a favor to his fellow soldier. He knew post traumatic stress was a real problem and thought his friend could use some help. His role as chaplain began. "Listen Chuck. Let me give you some advice as you prepare for civilian life. I say this from experience, so trust me as I trust you. Get some help. Before or soon after your discharge get some counseling. You want your finance to greet you at your best. I know because I got help when I needed it and believe me, it was time well spent. Trust me." Greiner nodded a yes. Even though Eric had just known Chuck Greiner for a few months, he knew if he survived his tour, they would be friends for life. Exhaustion overpowered Greiner and sleep followed. Not so for Eric. He thought about his friend's advice. Enlisted men killing their officers. He heard about friendly fire; that was accidental? But fragging, that was murder. Now as a chaplain, he knew his role would be even more complicated. He prayed for guidance and wisdom; his instincts told him there is a certain amount of fate at play here. His control was minimal. His faith, he prayed would get him through.

Chapter 39

The landing in Hawaii was at sunset; the sky was a myriad of colors so beautiful it could take you breath away. Lieutenant Greiner smiled when he said, "Two more weeks of life in the United States Army and I'm done. Two fucking weeks." Eric thought he understood emotions expressed by his friend but he knew his experience would present its own reality. An Army bus waited and taxied the men to their quarters. Eric would spend a few weeks in Hawaii where training for special services would be provided by officers who served as Chaplains during their tour. Training for Army Chaplains was usually at Fort Hamilton, New York, but in Eric's case, his seminary training elevated him to a level where his training was more concerned with hands on medical training and saving lives of his men both spiritually and physically, especially, Eric thought, his own life. He was issued and trained with the new M16 and made this gun a part of his everyday equipment. Eric requested extra time on the firing range where he demonstrated his superb marksmanship. That gun became his friend. When he slept that night he could not help to think about how he would handle a fragging possibility. His understanding of the war coincided with what Greiner told him as well as other soldiers he met in hospital care. He provided them with counseling and spiritual comfort before his departure for Vietnam. Some of the men had terrible nightmares and were suffering from traumatic stress caused by what they experienced during their tour. Senior officers had to inform Eric that he should not discuss these traumas with others for obvious reasons. "It is what it is", was the mantra of military commanders. Eric was learning fast how the US military was psychologically losing the war. Kronkite's assessment was accurate. Eric could only pray for those men who were suffering. Many would need professional help for many weeks, months or years. And when Eric was informed that he would be promoted to Captain, he shuddered to think of increased responsibility required by this promotion. He requested a meeting with Major Richard Callahan to inquire what his duties would be, after all, he was a chaplain. It was in this meeting that Eric realized how low morale had become, and this was two weeks before departure.

Major Callahan was a West Point graduate from North Carolina. He did his tour and received a purple heart along with hundreds of others. "I can imagine why you are questioning your promotion Captain O'Reilly. First of all, your record is outstanding. You have received the highest rating of any enlisted soldier I can recall. Your education, training and demeanor have placed you at the top of the list. Basically you will receive orders from high ranking officers who study the terrain, timing, weapons and strategy of the enemy, both regulars and Viet Cong guerrilas. This is why you are getting trained in map coordinates and maneuvers. Take notes. There will be a higher ranking officer in your battalion; you will be second in command." Eric thought about what Greiner had told him. "Can you tell me his name so that I can discuss our MO?" Major Callahan concealed a smile but Eric noticed. "He's a West Point grad, and has volunteered for a second tour. A real Texan." Eric interpreted that as meaning, Gun Ho. The major continued. "Major Roger Wilson has just returned to Vietnam. You'll meet him soon enough."

Chapter 40

Soldiers carried their sixty pounds of equipment onto the transport plane headed for Saigon. Eric was one of the first to board and greet troops, especially those who knew him from counseling and chapel service he provided. Many were between ages 19-24. He wondered how many would make it back in one piece. Word was out that the bloodiest battles were inflicting heavy casualties. Back home, draft cards were being burned and several accounts of men heading for Canada to avoid military service became more frequent. Protests were increasing in number, size and volume. Eric tried to block all that out and display a positive outlook. He knew his men would notice any subtle changes in his demeanor. He was trained over and over again in maintaining a stoic yet compassionate outlook. It proved to be very useful training at a critical time. Eric immersed himself in prayer and meditation to help him fight demons that continued haunting him. His former psychological counseling seemed to surface now and then. He thought of his life as a maze and sometimes felt trapped by pathways that led nowhere. It was a long flight to Vietnam; almost twelve hours later Eric was gathering his bags prior to exiting the large transport.

Several chaplains would meet on occasion to smooth out rough edges they could not conceal from one another. They shared their feelings of the unpopular war and were very skeptical about the absence of any end in sight. They had to collectively avoid negativity so they talked about careers and those they loved. One chaplain had privately expressed to Eric that he was in love with a man back home who was waiting for him. They were friends and lovers for three years. He confided with Eric but no one else. Eric's own sexuality became one of his preoccupations during down time but never a real distraction. It just popped up now and then especially in dreams and nightmares. The cause was still bothering him because he wasn't sure of its origin. He knew he would not have any time for dwelling on his personal anxieties. He was trained to focus on his mission; failure to do so could get him killed and that fear instilled a mental toughness that remained with him.

Suddenly an orderly appeared and gave Captain O'Reilly a written request. A jeep was waiting to taxi Eric to Major Roger Wilson. Eric was

to report to his command center for review of their tactical operations
It was crunch time. As Captain O'Reilly entered the Jeep, the sergeant
snapped a salute. Eric took a deep breath and made himself appear
confident and cordial. When he arrived at headquarters, he entered a
prefab one story building. A tall Texan was standing next to an attractive
army administrative assistant. She looked at Eric and appeared pleasantly
surprised that the Army produced such handsome officers. "Captain Eric
O'Reilly reporting at your request sir." When she left the office, Major
Wilson smiled. "She's worth fighting for, wouldn't you agree Captain?" At
that moment Eric knew what and who he was dealing with. "Yes sir."

Major Wilson was a man driven by his ambition to become a
military superstar.. He was obsessed with military jargon and enjoyed
the masculine nature of war. Eric had read some reports about Major
Wilson just to get what he hoped would be an objective assessment
of his leadership. From the report, Wilson's reputation was filled with
examples of valor and efficiency, but casualties were also very high,
too high. Military evaluations can be whitewashed with pressure and
persuasion. Eric preferred reports of officers under Wilson's command.
Basically they said he's over the top. For Eric this was more frightening
than he expected because now his life and safety were being compromised
by a man driven by obsession with warfare, and this combined with
leadership deficiencies, could easily result in fatal outcomes for Eric and
his subordinates. Eric had been advised by his friend Chuck Greiner that
officers like Wilson had to be feared especially when their orders were
strictly adhered to; the trick was to find ways to obey orders using delay
and circumvention. Greiner advised Eric how to implement orders that
were reckless and unnecessary in jungle warfare. First Greiner advised him
to earn the trust of his subordinates because without their trust, you're
on your own. Consult with them; ask many questions about tactics that
work and those that are too costly. Once your subordinates believe you
have their safety in mind, they will devise ways to throw obstacles into
military plans that if implemented would produce unnecessary deaths
and casualties. These lower ranking officers realized what was at stake
so they were motivated by their own safety concerns. Orders usually
had options attached; these officers used the most credible reasons for
circumventing orders without being insubordinate. Their reasons had
to contain substance so their delay tactics had to be explained down the

chain of command, always keeping in mind their commanding officer's reputation for heavy casualties. Military plans may look good on paper but implementing them was highly dangerous in the jungles of Vietnam, so there was motivation for officers to find ways to block or delay Wilson's orders, or orders from any other officer that only looked good on paper but were needlessly placing soldiers in harms way. These subordinates created logistical reasons for slowing down orders coming down the chain of command. On occasion, shells were fired, grenades launched and rounds of M16 ammunition fired when Wilson barked out orders for aggressive action, even when the enemy was practically nonexistent. Head counts were fudged and some American casualties were self inflicted, all for the appearance of taking it to the enemy. Eric, as second officer in command had to study methods with officers more experienced with the terrain in order to present strategic reasons that were credible and acceptable. Handling his CO without getting anyone court-martialed for infraction of military laws and duties was not an easy task. Going over Wilson's rank would most likely make the situation worse so he decided to discuss his dilemma with other chaplains and officers he could trust when he had the opportunity which fortunately happened during a lull in combat activity. He arranged meetings with three other chaplains and explained the leadership style and deficiencies of Major Wilson whose aggressive reputation was known to needlessly and recklessly place his men in harms way. Now Eric totally understood how fragging came into being. But he wanted to avoid any such incidents under his leadership and became concerned when he overheard a sergeant say he "would take him out" without a trace. Other chaplains related to this problem because they heard from others and even had some experience with fragging themselves. One chaplain, a man in his late thirties, who was a year away from retirement had heard of Major Wilson and knew who and what Eric was up against. He made the following suggestion to Eric and other officers called for a briefing. "Talking to Major Wilson will not work. Captain O'Reilly, you must immediately write a letter to Lieutenant Colonel Robert MacAvoy who as commanding officer has experience with these matters and you must include specific examples and testimony from your subordinates to corroborate your concerns. Include names, logistics, strategies and orders given and any other pertinent information. After you write this letter, let me look at it and I will sign on as a witness to your complaint and concern." Other chaplains agreed to also sign on as witnesses who heard Eric's testimony. Eric never expected a crisis of this magnitude to erupt within two months of his arrival. He thanked all chaplains for their willingness to help and asked them to meet with him in two days. All agreed. He would have the letter written and signed by officers in his company he could trust. That evening he used all his literary skills and composed a letter to Lieutenant Colonel Robert MacAvoy that he hoped would alter an ominous future incident. He decided it would be prudent to limit specific details thinking it better to communicate pertinent information directly, just in case the letter was inadvertently placed in the wrong hands.

Chapter 41

Lieutenant Colonel Robert Mac Avoy
United State Army Command Center
Saigon, Vietnam

Sir:

I am Captain Eric O'Reilly, Company D, Infantry Division, currently stationed in A Shau Valley, and as Chaplain of my company, I am obligated to inform you of concerns arising from problematic leadership that has been brought to my attention by several officers involved in allotting combat assignments delegated from our commanding officer, Major Roger Wilson. I would at this time request that you provide me an opportunity to discuss this issue with you privately in order to avoid opportunities for slander and disreputable comments whose veracity may be questioned. I also request that our meeting be as soon as possible in order to prevent a breakdown of discipline and morale within our units and most importantly, to avoid useless and reckless death or injury to our men in uniform, several of whom have made this urgent appeal to me recently. I trust their judgment and know these men to be upstanding, brave and honest soldiers.

Sir, I plead that you respond soon so this problem can be addressed by qualified and impartial authorities.

Respectfully,

Captain (chaplain) Eric O'Reilly

Eric re-read his letter and made sure the orderly understood the importance of its delivery. Two other chaplains signed on and thought the letter was precise and honest. The envelope was marked, EXTREMELY URGENT. Eric surmised the orderly knew what was going on since soldiers have their own grapevine communication networks. He told Eric that he would make sure delivery would be within three hours and would arrange to have it personally hand delivered by a lieutenant in Captain O'Reilly's company who would board a chopper leaving for Saigon within the hour. Now all that Eric could do was wait it out. In the interim, he met with Major Wilson to implement logistical operations that he hoped would delay operations long enough for a meeting with Lt. Col. Robert MacAvoy. Fortunately the forecast for heavy rain would necessitate delays in aggressive combat assignments. Each hour Eric grew to understand how this was a war going nowhere.

Chapter 42

OPERATION TEXAS STAR took place from April 1- September 5, 1970, in the A Shau Valley and mountains east of the valley. The Battle culminated in the Battle of Fire Support Base Ripcord. The 101st airborne division and ARUN infantry division were involved. Most of the operation took place in the western Quang Tri and Thua provinces of Vietnam. When Eric arrived in late May, several officers introduced themselves to their new captain and chaplain. These combat experienced officers conveyed to Captain O'Reilly their concerns about army commanders experimenting with a variety of maneuvers using helicopters. A LOACH would fly low and make short circles to attract enemy fire, followed by COBRAS equipped with massive fire power including rockets and attack the enemy. WHITE platoons moved with the LOACH followed by RED platoons that worked with COBRA maneuvers. These two fighting units were called the PINK Team. Officers were concerned because these maneuvers were high risk and were not worth the loss of life and injury to many of their men. One experienced officer, Lieutenant Petersen commented: "These Loach pilots are crazy mother fuckers. They are putting themselves and men on the ground in unnecessary danger. This is warfare without regard for our lives; it's fucking crazy. Platoons are also worried about "friendly fire". Troops encircle the enemy and their guns are aimed at one another. Someone has to know what's going on. This has to stop. Some desperate and unstable soldier may refuse to follow orders. I can see and hear their anger and fear. It's not friendly fire when an officer who follows these insane maneuvers is intentionally shot and killed by his own army. That's fucking murder." Eric looked at the other two officers and they concurred. "Sir, this is insanity. Someone has to go up the chain of command and investigate." They looked at Eric who felt their pain and anguish. At this point there were 15 deaths and 62 injuries. He told the officers that he would immediately request a meeting with Major Wilson and discuss their concerns.

Later that same day, Eric wasted no time; his request was honored and his meeting with Major Wilson took place at the Command Post.

When he entered the major's office compound, he sensed the Major must have learned of problems related to his urgent request. Soldiers talk. Anger and fear are emotions that spread up the chain of command. Major Wilson greeted Eric and they sat opposite one another in a room that was barely kept cool with an air conditioner. "Captain O'Reilly, why the urgent request to meet with me?" Major Wilson did not hesitate; his direct question made Eric feel the uneasiness of his task. Eric decided instantly that he had to respond with the same direct response rather than evade or "beat around the bush." "Major, several officers in our company came to me, their captain and chaplain, because they believe our military operations in A Shau Valley are exposing their troops to unnecessary life threatening maneuvers. These are good soldiers. I have confidence in their assessment and judgment. Major, sir, we have a problem." The major stood up, he was over six feet tall and looked fit and polished. "Well captain, war has risk and that means soldiers die for a variety of reasons that we cannot always control." He looked at Eric with what appeared to be scorn. Eric stood his ground. "With all due respect sir, we can control this situation by changing our tactics using artillery and targeted air strikes instead of hueys. Many casualties have been reported as "friendly fire" sir. Pink teams are caught in crossfire. I am afraid of fragging incidents sir. This is a problem we can avoid." The major looked and was irritated by what he heard. This threat of insubordination was for him a cowardly display of duty. His anger could not be controlled. He shouted, "You inform those bastards that these maneuvers have been studied and planned by our war college and they are effective and will continue. That is an order captain. Now if you will excuse me, I have a war to fight and don't have time to spare on any bullshit advice from your subordinates. The ball is in your court captain. I suggest you respect and obey my authority before you proceed. That's an order, Captain O'Reilly." His tirade could be heard by staff in the adjacent office. Eric saluted Major Wilson. "Yes sir, thank you sir." Eric was about to leave when the major said. "Captain O'Reilly, arrange with my secretary a meeting with me two weeks from today. I will mark the 20th of July, (1970) on my calendar. That is all." When Eric saluted he felt his first wound without experiencing live combat. "Yes sir. Thank you major." Upon exiting, the office staff looked at Captain O'Reilly and seemed to understand his dilemma. There were apparently other similar occasions involving questions of Major Wilson's leadership.

Chapter 43

Eric's mind raced through options before him. The situation called for immediate talks with his lieutenants before the next maneuvers were ordered. For Eric, this was a most difficult task because he knew something had to change, but what and how were not immediately clear. He asked his officers for suggestions and their response was: "Speak with pilots who fly these missions. They are taking all kinds of enemy fire. Talk to them." So Eric arranged to meet several pilots as soon as he could to get their perspective of these pink team operations.

Huey pilots were a unique bunch with nerves of steel. Eric arranged to socialize with them two days after his meeting with Major Wilson and could not have been more impressed with their positive attitude and courage. Their exposure to risk was extreme.

He arranged to have some pizza and cold beer available for pilots which they devoured in great quantities. "Thank you Captain O'Reilly. Who says you can't get good fucking pizza in Nam." Eric felt he made a good impression and the fact that he was also a chaplain didn't hurt. He wanted to get a sense of their feelings for flying in pink team maneuvers so he got right to the point with one pilot whose outgoing personality allowed for an easy open question. The question wasn't directed at him but Eric thought he might take the bait. "What's it like flying a loach or cobra in pink team maneuvers?" Pilots looked at one another as if to say: "Are you serious!" The pilot Eric thought would be outspoken was the first to speak. "Well captain O'Reilly, you have to be a crazy motherfucker to even think about it. We're sitting ducks. I think it's fucking insane. There's no long term gain and the short term gains are meaningless.. We've lost some good men. It's like pissing in the wind." Eric wished he could have recorded that comment. It was exactly what he expected to hear. Now that silence was broken, more comments were forthcoming. Other pilots chimed in. "Captain O'Reilly, I have a wife and child waiting for me at home and my tour ends next month. I hope I survive. That's how scared I am. This war has no clear lines. It's jungle war at 360 degrees. The enemy disappears at will and then they emerge out of nowhere." Another pilot who Eric thought was acting strange suddenly exploded with anger. "I hate it. There's no rational explanation why we pilots are being placed in enemy fire along with soldiers in white and red teams on the ground who are being fired at by both friend and foe. It's fucking crazy." His voice was loud and very emotional. The other pilots stared in silence. Eric reached out to the pilot and tried to show him compassion. "I hear you soldier. I will try my best to inform the CO of all comments made here today. Your voices will be heard, I promise you. I will do my best to have these operations grounded until they are reviewed by the company commanders. Meanwhile, please consider expressing your comments in writing so that my attempts to change the status quo will bear fruit. You can address them to me and I will personally deliver them to the proper authorities. Fortunately we are in the rainy season so operations will be on hold until we have favorable conditions. You know when the rain stops the enemy will move into lower grounds. Pray for rain."

Before Eric left he reminded those involved of the importance to keep their thoughts and fears private. Otherwise a discipline problem that already exists could become worse, placing our soldiers in more danger. Instigating or spreading concerns, even legitimate, can be grounds for court martial. He reminded these soldiers that by writing to him, as chaplain, they are being consistent with military protocol. Captain O'Reilly was their go-to guy. Eric reminded the men that his meeting with Major Wilson was in less than two weeks so they should compose their "letters of concern" asap, making sure they were written with accurate information and intelligently composed. "Be forthright, truthful and show your concern for men serving with you." The men were thankful that someone was sticking up for their fears and mistrust. Before Eric left, they all made a point of shaking his hand and thanking him. As Eric was escorted back to his company quarters in heavy rain, he prayed for even more rain. He remembered the tactic suggested by his friend Chuck Greiner: find ways to delay operations that are going to get you and others killed unnecessarily. Other than rain, what could he pray for.

Chapter 44

The rain continued for three days. At times it was so heavy that floods began to immobilize vehicles. Eric thought: "watch out what you wish or pray for." This weather delay however allowed soldiers to think about their compositions and before the rain ended, two letters were delivered to Eric with the signatures of many soldiers involved with controversial maneuvers. Eric read them and was really impressed with both, but one letter in particular made a strong, persuasive and intelligent argument.

It was addressed to Captain/Chaplain Eric O'Reilly. It was brief and directly to the point.

Captain O'Reilly/Chaplain

As senior officer, I believe it is my duty to share with you a serious problem, that if not addressed soon, will result in unnecessary and tragic deaths of soldiers in my platoon as well as those who serve in pink teams. In fact, we have already lost several men and have taken on many casualties without any logistical gains to justify maneuvers that we believe violate military codes for confronting the enemy. My subordinates question the judgment and strategy of these maneuvers and consider themselves pawns in the line of both enemy fire and friendly fire. We strongly believe that our commanders must be made aware of these anomalies before more of our brave soldiers are killed or wounded. We will share with you our specific concerns asap. We hope our testimony will lead to reexamination of our military strategy and maneuvers. I will personally hand deliver complaints of my unit to you.

You are an important link to our chain of command and we strongly request that you become our advocate so our voices can be heard. We are truly grateful.

Respectfully yours.
Lieutenant Frank Nostramo
23rd Infantry Division

Below Nostramo's name were the signatures of all the men in his platoon as well as several others who overheard the discussion at the command post. Signing ones name was in itself an act of courage but Eric would provide the cover they needed because he would take this up the chain of command, consistent with military law. Their stand was made during a time when war weariness was creeping into army discipline. One year tours in Vietnam seemed endless and with more skepticism, staying alive was now the reality because winning seemed out of sight. The danger however was increasing because now the North Vietnamese sensed the end. A trend was now apparent. Winning a jungle war in southeast Asia was unattainable. Eric would have to tread carefully because commanders had egos and strong convictions to reinforce their thinking. It would not be easy. Eric thought he should be certain that these men did not violate any military laws so he read manuals on the subject before going forward with his meeting with Major Wilson. With little time to spare, Eric knew that he had to intervene in some way to protect his men and others from unnecessary death or injury. The war was now being viewed negatively not just by soldiers on the field of combat, but news of the war traveled home to the States where anti-war protests were now very common. For his first time, Eric had difficulty sleeping. He was counting days.

Chapter 45

The military has a grapevine communication. It's a secret that everyone knows but does not openly talk about. All that it takes is for one soldier to pass along information to another and before you know it, what started as an accurate account of the controversy in question becomes a twisted, and sometimes slanderous form of story telling. Eric soon became aware of this when some of his men heard rumors that Major Wilson was pissed off that his leadership was being questioned and wanted to know where and who fabricated a scenario that could destroy his military career. Another week of rain delayed maneuvers and gave Eric time to investigate laws of combat and military law in general. He requested a meeting with a military lawyer to prevent any court martial or demotion of rank for members of his unit, including himself. The soldier he finally met was Captain Michael Shanley who Eric was told, was a skilled military lawyer who could determine whether the code for initiating combat operations was being violated. Captain Shanley was subsequently contacted by Eric and when Eric returned to his compound, he found a letter addressed to him and was surprised that Captain Shanley responded to his inquiry so soon. In his response, Shanley wrote:

"There are always threats when planning combat operations but when men, either in helicopters or on the ground are KIA, investigations follow. Based upon decisions coming from the upper brass, usually Lieutenant Colonels or Field Generals, assessments follow to determine whether combat goals are being met and whether the cost in lives is justified. In the case of Pink Team Operations, no final decision has been made but as of this letter, future operations will be carefully scrutinized before combat operations are approved. In other words, the status quo has not changed. However that being said, future operations may desist. Keep me informed."

Captain Michael Shanley, military attorney for combat operations, Saigon.

Eric felt a surge of positive energy until he opened another letter from Major Wilson, ordering him to report for an important staff review. Now Eric knew that his investigation was being questioned by Wilson and that his rank was being threatened. The meeting was in three days and there was no way he could think of to prepare himself since Pink Team Operations were still the order of the day. This is when an act of fate intervened. The North Vietnamese had moved into positions that threatened American operations in the A Shau Valley. This was a total surprise since the only way they could have made their attack successful was by transporting artillery in pieces in underground bunkers, then assembling them for a massive attack at relatively close range. Enemy artillery destroyed several compounds where several high ranking officers were housed including Major Wilson. The major was fatally wounded. When Eric found out, he felt a gruesome sensation in his stomach. The enemy had taken the life of one man who could have made Eric's military life unbearable. Eric did not believe he would have been successful taking on Major Wilson whose record was admired by powerful officials in the pentagon. The explosion and fire that followed destroyed all records kept on file. Everything was incinerated. Eric never received any written documents that singled him out for insubordination or possibly undermining military operations. It was now more feasible that Pink Team operations would be halted. Whatever strategic value gained by Pink Team Operations were never ascertained, but the consensus among many officers and pilots was negative. American military operations would soon be withdrawn from the A Shau Valley where 36 American troops were killed, and 117 wounded. South Vietnamese killed totaled 370. United States Army claimed 539 North Vietnamese killed, and 1139 wounded, 5 were captured. Eric was told the only numbers that were accurate were American KIA and wounded. The remaining stats were not verified as was the case in many combat operations. The Battle of Fire Support Base Ripcord began March 12 and lasted to July 23, 1970, when the operations were terminated Eric and his division were relocated closer to Saigon where he thought his final days of duty in Vietnam would be relatively uneventful. He realized military bureaucracy had lost touch with ground operations; it was very easy to direct a war from the Pentagon with maps and charts but when confronted with tropical terrain, planning was literally lost to the jungles of southeast

Asia. The war in part became a victim of tropical heat, humidity and an enemy who would not quit. The Viet Cong and North Vietnamese were fighting on their turf and could adapt to conditions and literally dig their way into war zones with underground bunkers where entire armies moved beneath the mightiest army in the world. You can't fight what you can't see. The enemy had devised tunnels where soldiers and equipment could be efficiently transported without notice. Their attacks became so deadly because they could conceal their proximity to American divisions, inflict massive damage and carnage, then escape into bunkers that were practically impossible to detect. When bunkers were discovered, American soldiers found tunnels stocked with all kinds of equipment, even hospitals underground. When this information was discovered and shared among officers and troops, the war effort became a lost cause. Eric was confident that his country had been sucked into a real quagmire. Our foreign policy was misguided and our politicians and generals led us into a war that was a losing proposition from the start. It's not as though our leaders were not warned; their egos just refused to accept defeat even after more than 58,000 American soldiers sacrificed their lives. Our military was being overwhelmed by an enemy that was determined to force the United States to leave Vietnam without any trace of victory. It was just a matter of when and where. For Eric, the end could not come fast enough; his only positive thought was knowing his tour had two months remaining before he could return to the States. Eric missed home and was looking forward to that day of redemption, sixty days and counting.

Chapter 46

Saigon was sweltering when Eric arrived September 3, 1970. The streets were cluttered with bicycles and cart vendors selling produce, live chickens, seafood and many varieties of crafts. Eric was assigned to meet with incoming troops and more specifically those designated as chaplains. Saigon was on occasion targeted by Viet Cong who would terrorize the population with sporadic attacks but lately there had been no incidents.

Eric had thoughts of his latest episode with Pink Teams and realized that his military career, short as it would be, was not tarnished by insubordination and even a possible court martial for questioning his superior commander, Major Wilson who was a victim of his own decision to fight an enemy without regard for the safety of his subordinates and who unfortunately was killed by an enemy who penetrated and outsmarted his flawed Pink Team maneuvers. There was a certain irony in what transpired and Eric felt that he was spared more than a reprimand but maybe even his life. The maneuvers had since been terminated for a variety of reasons and Eric did not follow up with his inquiry; his work was done in that regard and he continued to receive favorable calls and written commentaries from men in his division who knew that he "stuck his neck out" for their safety. Now it was time to move on and stay alive until his tour ended. The chaplains who arrived were taken from several religious and ethnic backgrounds. There were several African and Latino draftees who were assigned the role of chaplain and Eric found them to be fearful but willing to learn what infantrymen needed most, a belief in survival under dangerous odds. It wasn't easy for them at first because they knew what most Americans read in the papers every day. Death counts were high and increasing every week. They understood that the war was a lost cause and watched the antiwar demonstrations before they left the States. Eric opened his chaplain meeting with a prayer.

HEAVANLY FATHER. WE ASK FOR YOUR GUIDANCE AND BLESSING FOR THESE MEN WHO WILL SERVE UNDER YOUR GIFT OF ETERNAL LIFE FOR ALL MEN OF GOD. BLESS THEM WITH YOUR HOLY SPIRIT AND DELIVER THEM FROM DANGER. AMEN

Some men made the sign of the cross. Others merely voiced AMEN. When the chaplains were seated, Eric continued. "You have been chosen for the important role as chaplain for a variety of reasons. Some higher ranking officer recommended you for this honorable position. They observed in you certain qualities they believe are vital for your success. The importance of chaplains cannot be overstated. Your roles are several: spiritual and psychological guidance, mentor, friend, parent, brother, medic and any other life saving therapy you can offer. Follow your instincts; often your gut feelings are on target. If you have any questions now I will do my best to answer them. (Eric paused.) Well if you think of anything come to my office down the hall and we can discuss matters privately if you prefer." Eric knew they were frightened because combat operations outside of Saigon were now escalating. The United States was making a strong effort to stop enemy attacks with mixed results. There were good days and very bad days. It appeared the enemy was closing in little by little and every so often artillery guns could be heard from the distance and Eric did not want to unnerve these new arrivals with too much intensity so he kept the session brief. Experience was their best teacher. Doing their job would give them more skill and confidence.

Eric didn't have to wait long for a new chaplain to visit his office. It was barely an hour after they broke for chow. His name was Emille Rodriguez. He was a handsome Porto Rican from the Bronx. When he entered the room, Eric could see fear in his face. "Please be seated Emille." His body language did not project any confidence or calm. He took a deep breath and began to speak. "Captain O'Reilly, I have nightmares and my nerves are shot." Eric waited so Rodriguez could finish but he froze in silence. Before Eric responded he made sure Emille was looking at him. When they made eye contact Eric said: "You want to know how I felt when I was assigned. I was scared too and could not sleep very well. I found however that when I kept busy helping infantrymen who were even more frightened than I, it made a difference. My advice, get into your role as chaplain by making an effort to speak with the young men in your division. Believe me they need you more than you know. By helping them cope, you will gain confidence and strength in your ability to serve them and this will give your role meaning and purpose. Helping others is the antidote you need." Rodriguez nodded his head and whatever Eric said seemed to take hold. "Thank you Captain

O'Reilly. I will take your advice." He stood and saluted his captain. Eric placed his arms on Emille's shoulders. "You're going to be fine corporal; just fine. Project your confidence and sense of humor to your fellow soldiers. They will appreciate your effort. Now get out there and do your job." Shortly after Emille left Eric's office, sounds of artillery could be heard in the distance. Saigon was no longer a place of safety. Each day, sounds of artillery could be heard closing in on a frightened population, occupied by a foreign army whose effectiveness was slipping each day. More heavy artillery and armored helicopters were now in place around the city's perimeter to maintain security. At some point in the future, Saigon would be Vietnam's last stand.

Chapter 47

The realization that your nation's plunge into a jungle war in southeast Asia was for Eric an incredible miscalculation by the United States military. The terrain, climate and determination of the enemy were all factors that could only lead to an eventual retreat and withdrawal. It was just a matter of time and many officers shared this in common along with their fear, frustration and anger. Eric was no exception. However, his main concern was to accomplish whatever he could to spare as many unnecessary deaths and injuries of men under his command. He constantly reminded them to be alert and to avoid careless interactions with local populations, especially women who collaborated with our enemies and were known to plant explosives in compounds and roads traveled by Americans. He intentionally instilled fear in them hoping that would increase their vigilance and spare them a careless injury or death. He also prayed with them regularly and he could tell from their reactions some tranquility resulted if only temporary. Suddenly and unexpectedly it was during a prayer session that all hell broke loose. Their compound was being attacked by Viet Cong and North Vietnamese soldiers. Fortunately an alert soldier sensed a problem and immediately activated an alarm that mobilized all hands. Explosions and gun fire surrounded them and Americans responded with brutal force. There were few places of safety under the circumstances and the possibility of being killed by friendly fire was also a real possibility. Eric embraced his M16 and knew he would probably have to use it for the first time to defend himself and other soldiers whose weapons were placed in the rear of the chapel. As soldiers crawled for their weapons, Eric took aim through a window in preparation when suddenly Viet Cong raced by an alley that separated the chapel from a compound housing hundreds of soldiers. They were only thirty yards in front of him carrying explosives. He aimed and began to fire relentlessly killing several and wounding even more. Suddenly their explosives consumed part of an adjacent compound that fortunately was vacated moments earlier. It ended as suddenly as it started. Three Americans were killed who were sleeping when their building was attacked. Enemy attackers were killed and Eric's M16 was responsible for all ten assailants. When an investigation was conducted shortly after the attack to determine how enemy forces were able to penetrate the compound, it was discovered that two soldiers on guard duty were strangled and the other was pierced with a bayonet but he managed to sound the alarm before he died. Eric just happened to be at the right place for taking out enemy combatants who were setting charges near a compound housing several hundred soldiers. Of the eleven combatants, ten were killed by Eric. The eleventh died from a self inflicted wound. Eric's platoon paused and looked at each other with faces that were totally bewildered by what had just happened. Before they could even get a shot at the enemy, it was all over and their captain had totally finished the battle swiftly and accurately.. The fact the incident followed their prayer session led by Captain O'Reilly made the experience feel more intense. No one spoke but they did pause and bow their heads thankfully. The man they respected most had protected them from a certain death. Explosive devices thankfully did not detonate and were subsequently deactivated by bomb specialist teams. The other compounds were not so fortunate. Sirens sounded and medics poured out of ambulances to attend to soldiers injured in the massive explosion. Legs and arms were blown off. The proximity of medical crews and hospitals made it possible to save many soldiers from certain death. Saigon would never be the same. Bases were reinforced. After an extensive investigation it was apparent that Eric would be honored for his skill and bravery in the line of fire. Eric was wounded by a bullet in his right shoulder but continued to empty his gun on attackers then added another clip until it too was emptied. This was a near death experience for Eric with less than 45 days left in his tour. He was grateful for his hours spent on the firing range where he practiced his reloading and marksmanship. Eric's father's words also came to mind. "Be prepared to defend yourself." He retreated to his compound after being treated for his wound; his arm was wrapped in a sling. He thought of the men he killed and asked God for forgiveness not ever imagining he could follow through with deadly force. Later that evening he learned one chaplain was killed; it was Sergeant Emille Rodriguez. He had been honored and promoted post-mortem for his bravery in making sure barracks were emptied just before explosions leveled them.

Chapter 48

The next day Eric received a large envelope sent from New York. It was a letter with several administrative papers from his seminary. Monsignor Quaid had written to determine when and whether Eric planned to complete his training upon return and to complete forms enclosed so he could be reinstated for his planned ordination. Eric found himself in a state of indecision and confusion. His sense of duty and obligation told him to complete his training and he did recall his rare discussion with his father who wisely told him that being a priest does not have to be forever. You can serve Christ and then move on; life has a variety of paths to follow. That advice stuck with Eric and he knew it was his father's wisdom that made his decision easier. Follow through with plans to be a priest and see how it goes before choosing to move forward with a vocation that as of yet is still unknown. Eric completed all the forms required and mailed them the next day. He took an important step forward. With only 38 days remaining, his task was simple. Stay alive.

When word spread of Eric's act of combat bravery he could not help feeling very thankful just to be alive. The Commanding Officer of his division, General Lemay Thomas ordered Eric to his compound to hear firsthand Eric's version of what happened. The General had already listened to and read accounts by soldiers who witnessed the act of skill and courage during those moments of explosive combat. Eric merely confirmed that he emptied his M-16 on enemy forces, reloading and emptying his gun twice. "Where did you learn to shoot like that Captain O'Reilly?" Eric had Sergeant Tobal to thank for his skill with his M-16 and he made a point of mentioning Tobal's name more than once. Tobal always said to Eric, "make this gun your best friend; it may save your life." Lemay was impressed and took note of Tobal's name and rank. "Well captain, I have news for you. The president of the United States has just heard about your story and wants you to report to Washington after your tour to receive the Congressional Medal of Honor. You have been recommended for that honor by our staff who have confirmed your act of bravery by written and spoken testimony. Congratulations captain." This was too much information for Eric to digest. "Do you have anything to say, Captain O'Reilly? Eric's mind was racing with emotion and disbelief.

The only thing he could mutter was: "Thank you sir. I am honored. But I only did what any soldier would do under the circumstances." General Thomas's response was direct: "Captain, what you did was flawless and immediate. You saved hundreds of lives because the enemy was destroyed before activating their explosives. Those who observed your actions spoke of your courage under fire. Not too many soldiers could have pulled this off captain." The general noticed Eric's arm in a sling and added. "You can add a purple heart as well captain. I want you to know how proud I am to be your commanding officer. Your tour of duty will be terminated in three weeks due to your wound. Prepare for departure captain. You're going home." Eric was silent and could not think of words that described his emotions. General Thomas apparently understood and allowed Eric's silence to fill the room. Eric eventually responded with: "Thank you General. This has all happened without time for me to comprehend. I am grateful and appreciate your kind words." At that moment the general's phone rang; his secretary informed him that President Nixon was on the telephone and requested time to speak with Captain O'Reilly. The general handed the phone to Eric. "It's for you captain, the president of the United States."

Saigon was now heavily fortified with artillery, barbed wire and combat preparedness like never before. When Eric returned to his compound, his staff applauded as he entered and the compound filled with soldiers who cheered their captain. Eric waved his left arm and realized the wound of his right shoulder was more painful from 42 stitches that held his skin in place. The men quieted down and waited for Eric to speak. He turned and observed as soldiers gathered in front of him. "My experiences with you will always be an important part of my life. I can't thank you enough for your courage, service and friendship. As your chaplain I would like to offer a prayer of thanksgiving." The men all bowed their heads and a solemn quiet filled the crowded room. "Heavenly Father. We pray for your blessing and ask that you watch over these brave men who honor their country with their loyal service. Watch over them and we pray their service to you will continue throughout their lives. We ask for these blessings in the name of the father, the son and the holy spirit. Amen." Eric smiled when he looked up. He continued. "In Ireland after church services, the congregation usually moves into a different type of spiritual domain. The pub. Follow me men. The spirits are calling." The soldiers cheered as Captain O'Reilly led them to a chow hall that was stocked with ice cold beer and hot dogs, all provided at his request. It was a beautiful day in Vietnam.

Chapter 49

Eric had to have his wound tended to because a few stitches did not close his wound properly. This time a surgeon was called in to redress the wound and stop it from bleeding. Luckily for Eric, no bone was broken but muscle tissue was damaged and he would need some therapy to regain his arm strength. There wasn't much to pack for his return to the states. In his office with two weeks remaining he discovered mail from home. He read his father's letter first.

"Dear Son,

We are so thankful that you will be returning soon. Our community is so proud of their native son and many have greeted our family with loving gratitude. When you return to Washington, we will be there to greet you along with a long list of dignitaries including the president of the United States. It's going to be a very joyous occasion for our family and friends. Your sister Mary prayed every day for your safe return. In fact she is in church now with your mother saying the rosary. There wasn't a day that went by without your family praying for your safe return. Monsignor Quaid called me and was pleased to receive your decision to return to seminary training. We are pleased with your decision and know you have thought it through. Your military photo appeared in several newspapers with a description of your combat experience and performance. I must confess many were surprised that you were a chaplain as well as a captain in the infantry. How you defended and protected soldiers that fateful day will always be remembered. Parents of soldiers in your unit have called to thank me for having such a brave s son. I have received letters as well from complete strangers from all over the country thanking me and wishing you well. There is so much more to tell you but I would rather save it until I speak with you in person. I will say however that Michelle has called and inquired about your status and well being. We invited her over for dinner one evening and we had a wonderful time. We can't wait to give you a big hug. Be safe.

Love, dad

Eric saved letters from his dad. There were only a few so he cherished them and kept them in a box under his bed back home. He would add this to the rest. Eric reflected on what he was feeling at this moment in his life. He realized what he felt can only be experienced when you are placed in a situation where personal and unique emotions are merged with relationships shared with very special people. Eric thought of how his parents had raised him. They were not judgmental or condescending. He was allowed to thrive in a learning environment of books, reading, and many cultural enjoyments that many of his peers did not experience. But he remembered how his mother would take him to homes where poverty was the norm. Many of his toys were given to poor children and his clothing as well. He was exposed to class and cultural differences by his parents who wanted him to understand humility and tolerance. Maybe he thought, these exposures early in his life made him kinder, gentler and quieter than most. In fact he realized that personalities similar to his were attractive because they were not focused on self. Instead his personality type invited others to actively participate. His quiet and genuine humanity drew others to him. He had charisma without bravado. Eric realized that his life had taken the "road less traveled" where unique experiences and people enriched his world view. He did not have material ambitions and did not crave for pleasures many others were looking for. He knew his love for public service and helping others was high on his list so being a priest may fit his persona after all. He was glad he decided to complete his training and ordination. He also realized that he did not want to get too far ahead of himself because situations can change ones plans. But for the immediate future his life plan would go forward. Then of course there were friends throughout his life that added to his overall personality. Several friends and mentors who enriched his life. Father Hall had to be at or near the top of his list. Professors like Dr. Dreyfus and Dr. Neuberger who walked him through moments of doubt and anxiety. And of course there was Michelle who made him understand his ability for loving a woman during his quest for understanding his sexuality. Letting her go still bothered him. He prayed for wisdom to guide him forward.

Eric had over the past two months made contact with children who were orphans of war. A brother. Minh, age 6 and his younger sister, Bian, age 4, became part of his everyday routine. He made sure they had their meals and clothing. Any free time he had was spent with these two children. They grew to love Eric and his love for them was known by soldiers who knew him. He found an elderly widow and paid her to care for them and when his departure was imminent, he set up an account for her to use for the children. He took photos and created a folder with information regarding their status and in the future planned to bring them to the States. It was a tedious process so he devoted his last month gathering a variety of documents that would be necessary to bring them home to the States. In letters to his mother he asked if she could find room in their home for them so they could be together. He really loved these children and they gravitated to Eric as if he was their parent. Every morning they appeared in front of his compound entry waiting for him. He never let them down and they would enjoy some small snacks routinely delivered to their open arms. He explained to them in Vietnamese that he was leaving Vietnam and they began to cry, whether out of love or fear. Eric suspected both emotions were in play. He hugged them and spoke to them in their language which he had studied throughout his tour. He also taught them some English, thinking of their eventual move to America. Eric now appreciated love that only parents can feel and this experience made him reexamine and question his immediate future. These two children became an important part of his day and when he realized their impact on his emotions, he knew somethings may have to change; the exact nature was uncertain. He made sure the children were enjoying toys he bought for them. He couldn't bear the sight of them crying and pleading for him not to leave so Eric became acquainted with an American nurse who he introduced to the children days before his departure and arranged for her to monitor the situation until he could bring them home. He promised them they would be together soon. They understood but still cried out of love and fear. Eric realized they viewed him as their parent; they were his children; he was their father and became overwhelmed with emotions never experienced as he hugged and kissed them before leaving Vietnam.

Chapter 50

Eric slept soundly on his flight to Hawaii where he would have a week of R&R that would allow him time to experience civilian life and decompress. After sleeping twelve hours he telephoned his parents. His mom was relieved to hear his voice and safe return to the States. The next phone call was to immigration specialists regarding his Vietnamese children. The Army also arranged a meeting where Eric could meet with General Alan Davies who was informed of Eric's plans to adopt Vietnamese children. The General had successfully adopted children from Vietnam months earlier and offered his assistance for expediting required paper work. Eric's emotions churned inside him; he felt compelled to finalize the process without delay. It would not be easy to adopt Vietnamese children who had living family in Vietnam so attempts were being made to seek out family members to determine whether immigration was even a possibility. Their family name was Trung, which in Vietnamese is defined as loyalty to one's country or king. Minh was the older brother whose name meant bright; and Eric thought it fit him perfectly. Bian, his younger sister's name meant hidden or secretive and she was exactly that. Upon Eric's last contact with them, her emotions were fragile and she cried out for her mother when Eric spoke to her; it broke Eric's heart to think of that moment. Now the task was to find their relatives. General Davies had contacts that could investigate for Eric and knew it would take valuable time. As much as Eric loved these children, he did not want to deny them their family's love and attachment. General Davies' experience with adoption procedures was very crucial to the process because of his contacts in Vietnam that began a process for finding members of the Trung family, cousins of Minh and Bian. When they were found and informed of Captain O'Reilly's interest in adopting Minh and Bian, they did not protest; in fact they were overjoyed because they would no longer have to feed and care for their cousins. Papers were signed by the oldest member of the Trung clan and a small donation was made to family elders to distribute among related families. General Davies then made arrangements for the children to be flown out in three weeks time. When Eric was informed of the General's timely and efficient assistance he was overjoyed. Three weeks time seemed perfect because he would be home where he could investigate all options for housing and caring for the children. Before Eric left his hotel room, an MP informed him that members of the press were milling about in the lobby waiting to ask the war hero questions and take photos. Eric requested privacy so they escorted him from the hotel through a back exit to avoid publicity.

Eric spent the remaining days in Hawaii counseling soldiers who were experiencing post traumatic stress and many resorted to drugs in order to relieve their emotional confusion. Rehab facilities had to be set up to treat soldiers before they were sent home but many returned with minimal counseling and rehabilitation. The army was not really prepared for the psychological fallout experienced by thousands of vets who returned home with emotional scars of war. A large number of soldiers were suffering from the affects of agent orange. It was devastating. On the last day in Hawaii which was a Sunday, Eric held mass for over two hundred soldiers going home. He looked for verses in the Bible that he thought were appropriate for the occasion. He began his biblical sermon dressed in the habits of a priest.

Eric began his service. "In the name of the father, son and holy spirit. To my brothers and sisters who have endured and suffered the tragedy of war. Hopefully these words from our holy Bible will enlighten you, encourage you and bring you closer to our father in heaven. Through his son, Jesus Christ we may learn to appreciate the wisdom of holy scripture. I have printed the scripture for you to follow. Please listen and feel the holy spirit's presence in these expressions from our holy father. I begin with words of wisdom from spiritual contributors of our holy bible." The men and women present followed as their chaplain read the verses. Eric began with: "Here are some notations of love and wisdom from our Father in heaven."

DELIGHT IN ME AND I WILL GIVE YOU THE DESIRES OF YOUR HEART. Psalm 37:4

FOR IT IS I WHO GAVE YOU THOSE DESIRES. Philippians 2:13

I AM ABLE TO DO MORE FOR YOU THAN YOU COULD POSSIBLY IMAGINE. Ephesians 3:20

FOR I AM YOUR GREATEST ENCOURAGER. 2Thessalonians 2:16-17

I AM ALSO THE FATHER WHO COMFORTS YOU IN ALL YOUR TROUBLES. 2 Corinthians 1:3-4

WHEN YOU ARE BROKENHEARTED, I AM CLOSE TO YOU. Psalm 34:18

AS A SHEPHERD CARRIES A LAMB, I HAVE CARRIED YOU CLOSE TO MY HEART. Isaiah 40:11

ONE DAY I WILL WIPE AWAY EVERY TEAR FROM YOUR EYES. Revelation 21:3-4

AND I WILL TAKE AWAY ALL THE PAIN YOU HAVE SUFFERED ON THIS EARTH. Revelation 21:3-4

I AM YOUR FATHER AND I LOVE YOU EVEN AS I LOVE MY SON, JESUS. John 17;23

FOR IN JESUS, MY LOVE FOR YOU IS REVEALED. John 17:26

HE IS THE EXACT REPRESENTATION OF MY BEING. Hebrews 1:3

HE CAME TO DEMONSTRATE THAT I AM FOR YOU, NOT AGAINST YOU. Romans 8:31

AND TO TELL YOU THAT I AM NOT COUNTING YOUR SINS. 2 Corinthians 5:18-19

JESUS DIED SO THAT YOU AND I COULD BE RECONCILED. 2 Corinthians 5:18-19

HIS DEATH WAS THE ULTIMATE EXPRESSION OF MY LOVE FOR YOU. 1 John 4:10

I GAVE UP EVERYTHING I LOVED THAT I MIGHT GAIN YOUR LOVE. Romans 8:31-32

IF YOU RECEIVE THE GIFT OF MY SON JESUS, YOU RECEIVE ME. 1 John 2:23

AND NOTHING WILL EVER SEPARATE YOU FROM MY
LOVE AGAIN. Romans 8:38-39

COME HOME AND I'LL THROW THE BIGGEST PARTY
HEAVEN HAS EVER SEEN. Luke 15:7

I HAVE ALWAYS BEEN FATHER AND WILL ALWAYS BE
FATHER. Ephesians 3:14-15

MY QUESTION IS WILL YOU BE MY CHILD? John 1:12-13

I AM WAITING FOR YOU. Luke 15:11-32

Then Eric added:
"With love, your father,
Almighty God"

Printed below, Eric included the following notation.

"I have printed these words for you to read from time to time when
you have lost your way or recline into a state of emotional turmoil. Please
lean on God's love for you to keep you from falling into despair. Become
a son of our father and a brother or sister of his son Jesus. Allow the
holy spirit to guide you and enlighten you toward a life of worthiness.
Suffering is not reserved for us alone. Many of our mothers and fathers,
sisters and brothers back home also suffer from the emotional stress and
anxieties of war. You must comfort them when you return and your love
for them will invigorate your being as well.

One of the verses reads: I AM ABLE TO DO MORE FOR YOU
THAN YOU COULD POSSIBLY IMAGINE. If you have faith in God's
almighty power, you will find peace. Another reads: WHEN YOU ARE
BROKEN HEARTED, I AM CLOSE TO YOU. You must believe in
God's power. AND I'LL TAKE AWAY ALL THE PAIN YOU HAVE
SUFFERED ON THIS EARTH. And he will if you believe. And please
remember: IF YOU RECEIVE THE GIFT OF MY SON JESUS, YOU
RECEIVE ME. Jesus is God's gift to us because through Jesus, God
is demonstrating his sacrifice for us. AND NOTHING WILL EVER
SEPARATE YOU FROM MY LOVE AGAIN. COME HOME AND
I'LL THROW THE BIGGEST PARTY HEAVEN HAS EVER SEEN.
But before you go home, I want to invite you to my party this evening.

Food and drinks are my gift to you. WILL YOU BE MY GUEST?" Eric could not extend his right arm in a sling, so he extended his left arm and beckoned with his hand that he wanted an answer. He repeated. "Will you be my guest?" The men and women realized his intent, stood up and cheered, many with tears in their eyes. Eric ended his sermon with the Lord's prayer. Then he made the sign of the cross. "In the name of the father, son and holy spirit, Amen. Peace be with you and with your spirit. Amen!"

Then he added: "Festivities begin at 7pm."

As Eric returned to his hotel room, he thought of the spiritual service he had offered to soldiers in need. The thought of being a priest seemed natural at that moment; Eric believed his decision to complete his seminary training was a worthy goal. The holy spirit was with him.

Chapter 51

At the party later that last evening in Hawaii, Eric arranged to have food and drinks that his father agreed to pay for as a farewell tribute for his friends who served with him as well as others who were preparing for their return home. Eric's reputation was well known. He was always greeting soldiers, visiting them for counseling, and helping them in any way he could including spiritual guidance. Many of the soldiers present had made contact with Eric during their tour. Because most arrived in Vietnam around the same time, their tours were on similar time schedules. Some were on R&R leave but most were now going home as was Eric. Music was provided by the hotel and the mood was a combination of levity and gratitude. A line of soldiers formed along a back wall near Eric; soldiers wanted to shake his hand, thank him and hug him. Some had tears in their eyes and expressed their appreciation for a variety of reasons. Many asked for his address so that they could maintain contact with him.

No one seemed to notice but media personnel had somehow got wind of this event and entered the party with video cameras and television journalists interviewing soldiers. A CBS reporter asked one soldier the following question. "What's the occasion?" The soldier responded with many listening in.

"Captain O'Reilly, our chaplain and mentor has arranged this party for all the men and woman here who are returning home after our tour. He is the most remarkable leader I have ever known and we all love him." Soldiers surrounding the reporter all chimed in their comments as well. "He saved my life in more ways than one." Another stated: "He is truly a man of God." Another said. "We need a president with the character of this man." Another: "He's our hero and has made us proud to serve with him under his leadership." Another said: "He rightfully deserves the Congressional Medal of Honor and I for one will be there when he receives this highest honor." When this video was played back home, Eric's father broke down and cried, holding on to Eric's mother who also was in tears. Later that evening when Eric returned to his hotel room, there was an MP waiting at his door with an envelope.

"Captain O'Reilly, this correspondence is for you. Could you please sign sir?" The soldier saluted Eric and left while Eric opened the door to his room. Inside he read the following.

CAPTAIN O'REILLY.
WE HAVE JUST VERIFIED THAT ON FRIDAY, MAY 1, 1971, MINH AND BIAN TRUNG WERE FATALLY WOUNDED BY AN ENEMY ATTACK ON THE AMERICAN COMPOUND WHERE THEY WERE STAYING PRIOR TO THEIR DEPARTURE TO THE UNITED STATES. WE OFFER OUR DEEPEST SYMPATHY.
GENERAL ALAN DAVIES

Eric collapsed to his knees as though he was just punched in the stomach. His eyes filled with tears and he shouted out. "Why God! Why God!"

There were letters from home that were slipped under his door. One from his mother. Eric opened it while still on his knees; he turned and rested his body on the floor and began to read his mother's letter.

"My dearest son Eric,

How I miss you and can't wait for your return. I am thrilled and overwhelmed by recent news of your spectacular homecoming. We are so thankful that you were spared by our Lord and will be home soon. Your sister Mary has prayed for you every day. She really misses her big brother. We are also so happy to house Minh and Bian in our home where they will be blessed with our love and care. As you said, they feel like your children and we want them to be part of our family." Eric could not read any more. He dropped the letter and laid on the floor where he cried himself to sleep. When he woke at 5am, he shaved, showered, packed what clothing he had and was driven to the airport. He was going home filled with emotional pain and with one arm in a sling. He reflected upon recent events and wondered about its meaning for him. Eric knew at that moment that something had changed inside him; he wasn't certain what it was but he realized he had to allow the unknown emotion to play itself out.

Eric was anxious to leave his hotel room just to remove himself from a place where sadness was delivered to him; he had to get out so he called for a taxi to the airport where he thought he could wait and be surrounded by travelers. He wanted to see some semblance of normality; mothers, fathers, children- he did not want to be alone. He also realized that he should call his parents and inform them of the tragic news and found a phone booth where active military personnel could make free calls to home. It was around ten o'clock in New York when his mother answered the phone. "Hello." She sounded happy and when she heard his voice; she was thrilled. "Hi Eric. Where are you?" He paused briefly because the voice transmission appeared to be off a little. "I'm in Honolulu mom. My flight leaves in about two hours. I have some sad news mom." He had to get it out. Holding his emotions in was painful and he knew his mother would find some words for his sadness. He heard her tense voice respond. "What happened. Are you alright." He responded quickly. "Yes mom, I'm OK. It's the children, Minh and Bian. I was informed last night they were fatally wounded by a North Vietnamese attack on the American compound where they were sleeping." There was silence. "Mom, did you hear what I said?" She indeed heard and thankfully her husband was near by and held on to her when she fainted. "Mom, are you there. Mom can you hear me." When Eric's father responded he said. "Eric, mom fainted. Is everything OK?" He repeated to his father what happened and said that he would call him from LA because the phone connection was not clear. He did not want to talk anymore and hung up.

Meanwhile his father comforted his mother who was slowly regaining consciousness. He told her that Eric would call from LA ; she cried and held on.

Chapter 52

When Eric arrived in LA his stomach was bothering him so he went to the military hospital where he was admitted. He had contracted a stomach virus and his shoulder also needed to be redressed. He called his parents from his hospital bed to inform them that his arrival in Washington would be delayed until he was released from the hospital. His official discharge from the Army was scheduled for June 9, 1972. Eric was exhausted and his body craved sleep. In two days he slept a total of 24 hours. After four days in the hospital, he felt weak but well enough to be released and was fortunate to catch a flight to Andrews Air Force Base in Maryland. He arrived by military transport at the D.C. Hilton at 5 pm on Monday, May 21st. where his parents had booked three nights. Their reuniting was very emotional, especially for Eric's mother. They embraced their son whose arm was still in a sling and tears of joy and thankfulness were spilled by all. Their warm greeting was short lived because a presidential aide then introduced himself in the lobby and informed Eric that President Nixon requested a brief meeting with him at the White House and welcomed his family as well. Apparently the president had been informed of the death of his two Vietnamese children and wanted to meet Captain O'Reilly whose reputation was getting more press and fame. The drive to the White House for the O'Reilly family was somewhat surreal. They were totally unprepared for such an honor and memorable occasion. As Eric exited the limousine in military attire the marine guard saluted him as he entered the White House. President Nixon appeared, greeted Eric and his family and introduced them to his wife Pat. Eric and his family were escorted on a tour of the White House. President Nixon requested a private conversation with Captain O'Reilly who was directed to the oval office. The president was cordial and offered some commentary of the setting where momentous decisions were made throughout our dramatic national history. Eric was surprised but pleased when the president asked him about the war and how it was being conducted. "Mr. President. Thank you for this honor. I will respond to your question this way. Fellow officers and I have discussed our war policy and strongly believe that jungle warfare in southeast Asia is a logistical mistake. Our men are being slaughtered by a determined enemy who are gaining strength every day. The South Vietnamese army lacks the will to overcome North Vietnam. I would recommend a calculated withdrawal because our death toll is excessive and unnecessary. I realize you inherited this war but now that it's yours, I strongly believe the time has arrived to leave Vietnam to the Vietnamese people. They will have to sort it out for themselves as we did with our civil war." Eric looked at the president's body language which was not showing any indications one way or other. It appeared to Eric that his words were not received at all; Nixon heard Eric's words but was not really listening. The president then changed topics to the award ceremony where Eric would receive the Medal of Honor. He revealed how proud he was as his commander-in-chief. Now Eric heard the president but was not really listening himself. It was all very strange. When he left the White House, Eric thought that meeting Nixon was disappointing because the gravity of war had not been apparent. He believed his visit to the White House was all for media consumption and politics. Nixon's bid for a second term was in November. Eric had voted for Hubert Humphrey four years earlier and wondered whether any president could have altered our nation's path. Like many Americans he believed the war would go on until public opinion swayed our political leaders to withdraw and cut our losses. Vietnam was now Nixon's war, never declared by congress. A national tragedy was unfolding while Americans died for a lost cause.

Upon returning to their hotel, Eric remained silent while his mother held his hand. He was thankful his family appreciated how silence was at times all the communication necessary. The O'Reilly's always allowed each other quiet space for personal moments; this was such a moment. There was no need or interest for words and they all sensed it. Eric was thankful and exhausted; peaceful sleep was inviting. He had been offered counseling by medical personnel but declined choosing instead to immerse himself in meditation and prayer. The next morning he was prepared for an honor that is reserved for a special few.

Chapter 53

Shortly after Eric showered his telephone rang. His father offered
to help him get dressed since his right arm remained in a sling and still
caused him pain. The White House chief of staff called and wanted to
make sure that arrangements made for the ceremony would be conducted
in a timely and memorable display of presidential power and leadership.
Eric was aware of the hyper political activity surrounding the days events
and was powerless to alter what he thought was too much ceremony
for something that happened 12,000 miles away several weeks earlier.
He was a prisoner of his own fame and knew media hounds would be
following him taking photos and asking questions. He was offered an
escort from the hotel to the White House and realized how public fame
reduced his privacy in a way nothing else could duplicate. Eric's parents
were driven to the White House with his sister Mary; they were seated
among dignitaries from New York State and Pentagon military hierarchy.
Eric was seated on a staging area with a podium where he was engaging
in small talk with senators and the governor of New York. The Army
band was playing patriotic songs while dignitaries filled the room in the
east wing that was decorated for this rare patriotic occasion. Eric looked
into the audience and observed a familiar and beautiful woman; it was
Michelle who was entering behind Eric's parents; they had requested a
seat on her behalf. She looked radiant and several photographer's cameras
clicked away at her before she sat next to Father Hall whose presence
pleased Eric as well. As the president entered, the band played "Hail
to the Chief"; the president walked to Eric's parents and shook hands
with them before returning to the podium. Silence gradually filled the
room when president Nixon was introduced by his press secretary. The
president walked to the podium and the ceremony began.

"Ladies and gentlemen. Today we honor our military for their
unselfish contributions to our country. In particular, we are honoring
Captain Eric O'Reilly whose act of bravery saved the lives of dozens of
men on that fateful day in Vietnam. The details of that momentous event
will now be read to you by a spokesman for the Army, Captain Ryan
Rightmire who was an eye witness during this event.

Captain Rightmire approached the podium, paused and began reading the following statement.

"Thank you Mr. President. Good morning ladies and gentlemen and distinguished guests. It is not an every day experience for a soldier to witness an act of bravery where many lives are saved from certain death or injury. On April 3, 1971, I witnessed such an act in Saigon where one of our largest compounds was attacked by north Vietnamese soldiers who had penetrated our base disguised in American uniforms. As a medic I was on the scene quickly and saw an incredible act of bravery by Captain O'Reilly who single-handedly eliminated enemy fire even after being wounded. He somehow managed to continue a barrage of rounds until the enemy was stopped in their tracks. Ten enemy combatants were equipped with explosive devices that were about to be discharged had it not been for Captain O'Reilly's alert and immediate action. All ten enemy intruders were killed before their bombs could be detonated. Captain O'Reilly's split second action made the difference. The compound housed hundreds of soldiers who were sleeping when this happened; they would have been killed or severely wounded had Captain O'Reilly not used deadly force even after being wounded. Today many of those soldiers who were there also have testified to his bravery over and above the call of duty. They and many of their brethren have expressed gratitude to Captain O'Reilly for his unselfish act of bravery while under attack." Captain Rightmire then turned and handed to president Nixon the Congressional Medal of Honor; the president took it and draped it around Eric's large upper torso. "Congratulations Captain O'Reilly,and thank you from all the military families who celebrate your courage today and we all wish you God's blessings for many years ahead." The audience followed with a standing ovation. Eric's family could not hold back their tears of joy. The president escorted them to the podium for a photo. Cameras clicked from many angles. A hero was recognized by his president and country. Eric was asked to speak. He chose to be brief. "Thank you Mr. President. I am grateful for this honor and thank God for being there with me. To all my military brothers still in Vietnam, I salute you for your supreme sacrifice and will pray for your safe return." He patted his left hand over his heart as a sign of kinship with his military brethren. "I want to thank my mom, dad, sister and all my friends for their prayers. It's good to be home. Thank you." The audience once again stood and gave him a standing ovation led by the president.

Chapter 54

Eric was exhausted when he returned to his hotel room that evening. He enjoyed being alone after all the hoopla and just wanted to sleep. He asked an army doctor for a sleeping pill so he could have an uninterrupted deep sleep which he craved. When he woke, eleven hours later, he felt rested and looked forward to going home with his parents and sister. He needed time alone to think through all his options. Before he left his room the phone rang. It was the chairman of New York State's Democratic Party who congratulated him and wanted him to speak at the Democratic National Convention. He told them his interest now was to return home and take some time to reflect upon his future plans. They were not really satisfied with that answer and Eric surmised their real interest was getting to him before the opposition. His parents were registered Democrats so maybe that was another reason he was called and of course anyone who wins the congressional medal of honor was not to be ignored in politics. Eric suddenly thought politics could be another possibility for his future plans. Life was getting more complicated. One thing Eric knew for sure; he was thankful for how things turned out. Now if he could only make up his mind. He reminded himself what his father had said to him over a year ago. "Nothing has to be forever unless you want it to be." It was good advice then and especially now that his options had expanded; all were attractive for different reasons. Moments like this were rare in anyone's life and Eric felt energized as well as confused. One step at a time. As many times before he prayed for wisdom and knew that in the peaceful setting of his home upstate in Oswego, a decision would be made that he could accept and live with for his immediate future.

His mother had painted his room a soothing light green and it was nice to see that she had also maintained his collection of awards, trophies and photos as they were when he left. There was a new and larger bed, queen size that his mother insisted would suit him better than his single bed of his teen years. It was perfect. His parents were counseled by army psychologists to allow Eric time to decompress from his combat experience in Vietnam. Eric was thankful for the space he was allowed and each day he regained more of his inner peace and strength. The silence of his home was in deep contrast with the burst of cannon shells and bombs exploding in the distance. Each evening his family gathered for dinner and he savored the love he felt from all of them. His sister Mary in particular had become a remarkable adult. She was attractive, intelligent, mature and the kindest person Eric had ever met. One evening after dinner she and Eric happened to find a moment of time where they could share their thoughts about where their lives would take them. "You know Eric, we were so worried for you and I prayed for you every chance I had." Her eyes teared up and Eric embraced her. "Thank you Mary. I could feel your prayers and visualize you praying with mom. Thank you so much." Mary wiped her cheeks with a tissue. She looked straight into her brother's eyes. "Tell me Eric. What's next for you. Are you going to complete your seminary? You have inspired me in so many ways." Eric wondered about what his sister was thinking by her comment. He allowed her to explain herself.

"What would you like to do after college Mary?" His sister's facial expression seemed to indicate uncertainty but her response surprised Eric. "Well Eric I've been thinking how you have directed your life toward unselfish goals and it has inspired me. First I thought of the Peace Corps as one possibility then I thought of serving God as you have chosen. Do you think your sister would be a good candidate for living in a convent and serving humanity?" Eric was somewhat surprised with her response. He did not want to dampen her joy so he said. "Well Mary I'm sure you have prayed about this. Is there anything you can think of that would dissuade you?" Mary's face turned red with what looked like embarrassment. "Yes there's one thing that I need to ask you because you may have an answer for me. I am somewhat confused about my feelings. When you dated Michelle for a while I saw how happy you were together. Michelle and I have spoken about the attraction and love between the two of you. But apparently you let her know that you have decided not to move forward with your relationship. I can understand the conflict you experienced because I am having a similar conflict. My relationship with someone I have been dating and who has made me feel emotions that are difficult to shake. He's a former high school classmate and we have been friends for many years but suddenly we fell in love and we realize now our lives must move forward but you know it is difficult to terminate something that was so wonderful, especially because we have known each other for several years. He's off to Williams College and I will return to Colgate. We realized our feelings for each other are so genuine and sincere. At summer's end we will go our separate ways. We both understand why our personal growth should not be cut short. I thought of myself as living and working for my spiritual aspirations until I came to know other feelings, and now my emotions have taken over. You have experienced a similar situation with Michelle. Can you share with your sister how you resolved your predicament? How did you end your relationship with Michelle without feeling empty inside. Please, I need your advice." Eric could see how his sister was really conflicted and how she wanted her older brother to appease her. "First of all Mary it is not easy. I prayed and meditated often. I even had a discussion with dad over becoming a priest and it was his advice that I will pass on to you. Nothing has to be forever unless you want it to be. So go off to college and you will find new friends and if this relationship is genuine as you believe, it won't end. I had to say that to myself as well. So I am going to complete my seminary training and will be ordained. Where and how this ends is still an unknown. I am twenty six, you are eighteen. We both have time to allow our lives to move beyond the here and now. Does that make sense?" Mary gave her brother a big hug and he could tell he got through to her. "Thank you Eric. You have given me a perspective I needed to hear, especially from someone I love and respect and who has been there. You're right, I just needed more perspective. Thank you." She hugged her brother and left feeling more composed.

An hour passed when Mary's suitor rang the door bell. His name was Brian. Eric's first impression was positive. He noticed how they held hands as they walked out on the porch. Suddenly the phone rang. When Eric said hello he heard her voice. "Eric, it's Michelle." Their conversation lasted about an hour. It was a friendly and honest exchange because Eric knew where his feelings remained. Their conversation ended on a positive note when Eric said: "Michelle, I am twenty six, you are twenty three. Let's both take a step back and know how we feel with one another. Time is on our side. My feelings for you are genuine but give me space and I promise that I will always be honest with you concerning my future intentions. One thing I know for sure. Those beautiful children I loved and who are now gone have left a big void in my life that I feel must be filled. Parenthood was not something I considered until I learned to love those children as my own. That reality may become a major part of my future, maybe our future. Let's allow each other time and space to explore future options. No strings. I will not keep you in the dark, I promise, and I hope you will do the same." Michelle's response was measured but polite. "That's fair Eric. I can use this time and space to complete my graduate degree in English." Eric realized the very good possibility that Michelle's natural beauty would not go unnoticed by many suitors who would seek her out. He did not want to go there; that possibility was mutually understood and he knew he was taking the risk of losing her along the way. Her last words were: "Good bye Eric, I hope we both find what we are looking for."

Chapter 55

When Eric returned to seminary training, his remaining two years were filled with interesting discussions with other men who like Eric had questions about their past and future life experiences. One evening two seminarians joined Eric after dinner on the veranda of the main building. Their conversation started with usual recollections about family, friends and led to their decisions for becoming priests. Even after all the training, meditation and prayer, these men opened up to their realization of what lies ahead. The conversation began when Tom Connelly, a mid western native asked an open ended question for both Eric and Joe Bosco, a man in his late thirties, who appeared reserved but who welcomed the conversation knowing there would be last minute unknowns. "What are your uncertainties?" Joe lit a cigarette and waited, thinking for some reason that Eric would respond first. There was silence while three men peered at one another. Eric thought silence could be an indication of fear, doubt, conflict or all three. So his comment was, "Is our silence concealing something?" Joe smiled. "I was thinking the same thought. Well allow me to start since my seniority must count for something. My decision was made after my wife died. We had no children but were trying. Then while going through all the mourning that one has to endure, I thought about how my employment as a banker was not fulfilling and how my wife reminded me on occasion to find some purpose in my vocation. In mass one Sunday morning I realized that maybe the priesthood could fill a void within. Well I'm about to find out. I must confess that I do regret we were not blessed with children. If that would have happened, I would not be here. Maybe God has other plans for me. I'm not certain what His plan is for me. Had I not made this decision, I would be thinking about it too much so here I am. I'm still not one hundred percent certain but how sure can one be. Either way, I would be thinking similar thoughts had I not made this decision." Eric found Joe to be a very genuine and sincere man and followed his comments with: "Joe, you would be a wonderful parent. I experienced something that also made me think being a parent would be part of my future. In Vietnam, I met two orphans who I grew to love as my own family. They brought me so much joy. Before my tour ended I had plans to bring them to the states and make them part of my life. Had that happened, I wonder whether I would be here today. But tragedy struck and they were killed by an attack at the base where they were staying just before documents were in order for their immigration to America. I still grieve for them. Then there was another experience. I also have spent some time with a woman who is very special and she would make a wonderful wife and mother but I chose to delay that decision until I know where my heart and soul leads me." Joe remarked that Eric's age allowed him time. "You know Eric, your future can be filled with exciting opportunities, especially with the honor that you have received. Everyone knows. In some ways you are making a bigger sacrifice because your options are numerous. Many doors can open for you. You must really be conflicted. You are in my prayers." Eric thanked Joe and knew what he said was true; being reminded by someone with Joe's life experience made Eric think how fleeting life can be and to also appreciate his situation. Eric also knew something was driving him from within and he had to allow time to play itself out. He could live with his decision even though he received a variety of offers on a daily basis, letters from corporate leaders, members of congress, university presidents and the military academy at West Point. There were countless others as well. Eric spent quite a lot of time responding to all of them with brief but meaningful thank you notes. He wanted and needed space to sort out his life ambition. He looked at Tom who had not said a word. "What about you Tom? Where do you find yourself during the prelude of ordination." Tom finished his undergraduate work at Hamilton College, a small liberal arts gem in upstate New York. "Well my situation is nowhere near what you two have experienced. I did teach for a year and found that was missing something. I wasn't sure what it was so I joined the Peace Corps and worked in poor villages in Nigeria building schools and teaching English. That's where I found my pathway to the priesthood. Poverty surrounded me but I realized the native populations were happy nevertheless. Their joy and optimism were inspirational. It appeared to me that with few material comforts, their Christian spirituality became more important and meaningful. Spiritual fulfillment raised their awareness of what's important. From the simplicity of sharing their lives with family, friends and community came joy and fulfillment. Living among them transformed me from materialism to minimalism. Poverty gave them an appreciation of what Jesus preached. I found it truly liberating. I too have experienced pleasures of the flesh and knew the love of a woman. That too was a beautiful experience. However it would be premature of me to appreciate my transformation until I can endure its trials and tribulations; I must allow time for it to permeate my being. Even though our experiences are different, all three of us are feeling and thinking similar emotions. It would be interesting to know how we all turn out. Why don't we agree to meet in three years to see where and how our lives play out?" Joe smiled. "I think that's a great idea." Eric added. "Let's do it. It will be sometime in 1977. Great idea Tom." Their conversation continued but was more directed toward having a celebration to honor their favorite instructor and mentor, Father Robert Hall.

Six weeks before his ordination, Eric sent out invitations to his family and friends. It was similar to wedding invitations he thought. Eric would be ordained a priest along with five other men on Friday, August 1, 1974 at St. Augustine's Cathedral in Syracuse, N.Y. The Bishop of the Arch Diocese of Syracuse, James McCann would preside.

Chapter 56

The ceremony of ordination for Roman Catholic priesthood was
a spiritual experience for the congregation, at least that is what Eric
imagined while he lie prostrate on the alter floor adjacent to four other
candidates. His devotion to Christ was paramount throughout the
ceremony and his thoughts were not too focused on the ritual itself; he
felt liberated when the final blessing of holy orders was administered
by the Bishop of Syracuse. With the ceremony now complete, his mind
raced over his life experiences which made it all seem incredible. He
was now Father Eric O'Reilly, Roman Catholic priest. The congregation
applauded after all names were announced. Many dignitaries were present
including the governor of New York, along with two U.S. Senators from
New York, several political consultants for the Democrat Party, two
CEO's of major corporations and several military officers of high rank.
Eric's parents were beaming, especially his mother. His sister Mary also
had tears of joy when she approached her brother and embraced. The four
other new priests understood the fame factor; their families and friends
meandered toward another lobby of the large cathedral. Eric's entourage
was substantial; cameras flashed and videos were spinning. A recipient
of the Congressional Medal of Honor is ordained a Roman Catholic
priest. Many attendees flocked to congratulate Eric and wished him well.
When the crowd began to thin, Eric noticed out of the corner of his
eye a beautiful silhouette clearly appear on the wall to his right; it was
Michelle. She looked stunningly beautiful as she slowly walked toward
Eric, waiting for the crowd to mingle with one another in the distance so
as not to make a scene. The bright lights only enhanced her beauty as she
reached out to Eric to wish him well. It was awkward for both of them.
How does a man and woman who shared a loving history react under
these circumstances? She was gracious and dignified in her demeanor. So
was Eric. He felt as though he let her down and knew he would have to
at some point talk with her and attempt to ameliorate their relationship.
She seemed to understand by his gaze which if expressed verbally would
approximate: "please try to understand; there may be a tomorrow."
Eric's sister could sense her brother's dissonance and knew his emotional
sentiments as she peered at their detached connection which for Mary

was very unnatural; she knew her brother's heart but would keep Eric's unspoken secret.

Chapter 57

One of the political consultants present was a friend of Eric's from Cornell. The festivities that followed the ordination ceremony were held in a large catering hall near the Cathedral. Political consultant, Dave Dwyer walked over to his friend and colleague to congratulate him. Dave and Eric were fraternity brothers and were involved with political demonstrations at Cornell. In fact both protested against the war in Vietnam and now of course both understood the irony of recent events. Eric liked Dave because he was fun to be with but more than that, he was honest, intelligent and had proven successful with his work as a political consultant after his graduate degree from Georgetown. Dave was also a practicing catholic. When Dwyer approached Eric he was smiling and drinking a gin and tonic. "Eric, (he paused and smiled), I mean Father O'Reilly; I can honestly say that I am happy for you, really, however with one exception." He paused before he said: " You have a political future. There's no doubt in my mind. This is my business; I know what I'm talking about. You are very popular with today's electorate. Your zeal to work for Christ is honorable but could also be done in Washington where social policy can be your mission. Your work for Christ can also be in elected office where your impact could be widespread. You would reach millions. God is beckoning you to serve the public good. I'm serious Eric. Trust me." Eric knew Dave to be serious and this bothered him because he heard the logic of his advice but did not feel he had the instincts for politics. Dave sensed he came on too strong but would not concede defeat. "Eric, OK, fulfill your obligations and duties to Christ and his church, but your larger mission is elsewhere. You have leadership potential. I know. I have spoken with your military friends and know many details of your brave and distinguished service to them and your country. God has blessed you with many natural skills of leadership. Our country needs men like you now. Post Vietnam will prove to be a time when Americans lose faith in their government. Look at Nixon. He will resign his office for the very reason that his leadership had no moral compass. He abused his power. Watergate has made Americans cynical about their government. You fit the needs of our country and you must consider my recommendation sometime in the future. Call me when you're ready to serve God and your country again. God bless brother." He gave Eric a big hug with one final comment. "Your public humility is admirable. Don't allow it to limit your usefulness to society." Dwyer's direct approach caught Eric off guard. Eric's immediate goal was to lead a congregation and instruct Christian values to children. He thought of his lost Vietnamese children and wanted to devote much of his life to educating children in their memory. They loved school and Eric was looking forward to expanding their learning with a good catholic education. Before Dave walked away, he handed Eric his business card. Once again Eric was confronted with another choice. Dwyer was very persuasive and his words made sense but at this point, Eric felt he needed a peaceful retreat where his mind could be emptied and cleared of violence and turmoil. He would be Father Eric O'Reilly, pastor at St. Mary's in Oswego, New York.

When the celebration ended, Eric was relieved. Corporate CEO's, high ranking military officers, politicians and many friends had offered their praise and congratulations to Eric. He was truly honored but he thought the sanctity of his ordination had in some way been violated by all the attention to matters that were secular not spiritual. After all he was now an ordained catholic priest, nothing else. He was disappointed by conversation throughout the evening that he thought inappropriate. But he also realized that the Roman Catholic Church had a strong political history as well. He clearly understood the individuals involved had plans for him that presently, he was not prepared to entertain. When his parents left, Eric walked to his new car purchased for him by his father. As he opened his car door another car approached him with window rolled down; he heard a voice say. "Father O'Reilly, will you hear my confession." Eric turned to face Michelle. "I confess that I still love you but I also promise that I will release you from my heart over time and will not in any way interfere with your love of Christ. When my heart is healed and ready, I will love again." She blew him a kiss and drove away. Eric froze, stunned. While driving to his new home, the rectory at St. Mary's, he prayed for wisdom and forbearance. Deep in his heart and soul he could feel a lost love.

Chapter 58

His first morning at the rectory was spent getting unpacked and sorting out books and relics of his past that would bring him positive thoughts and memories. There were books from high school, college and seminary and Eric enjoyed giving some of them a second read; he believed on some occasions that his first read missed something the author was hiding in his language. However, all of his psychology, philosophy and theology books were most important. He hadn't really scrutinized their contents sufficiently in college and seminary. Books that were historical reading, especially books of Teddy Roosevelt and Lincoln were his favorites. There were also letters from his parents, college friends, and letters from men he served with in the army. Some were killed in Vietnam. He thought of saving these letters for their families. Then of course there were several letters from Michelle. They had special meaning. Eric realized the importance of his personal history with his life experiences being what they were. He stopped sorting and organizing because he did not want to keep Father Hall waiting. Knowing he would be having breakfast with Father Hall was comforting and knowing of his imminent retirement, Eric wanted to spend as much time as possible in his counsel. When Eric walked into the dining room, Father Hall was there drinking his coffee and eating a hardy breakfast. He sensed some dissonance with Eric and imagined many reasons for his uneasiness. "Well Eric, you are assigned the nine o'clock mass this Sunday. I am excited for you." Father Hall's happiness was glowing as he patted Eric's hand. "Thank you father, I'll be ready, but I wanted to ask you for spiritual guidance in reference to my sermon. Any thoughts?" Father Hall understood very well what Eric must be feeling. "Well Eric, I find sharing a life experience that has a spiritual lesson to be a good starting point. Be yourself. You'll come up with something. Ask the holy spirit to guide you through and then let it happen." Father Hall looked into Eric's eyes and could sense that something was wrong. Here was a man who returned from Vietnam with a purple heart and the Congressional Medal of Honor. He was overwhelmed by many outside the church who craved his service, stature, credentials, good looks, and intelligence that could benefit their special interests. Father Hall understood how multiple choices were pulling on him; his instincts told him something was wrong. "Why don't we have a talk in my office after breakfast. The breakfast meal, any meal, is sacred and should be a time for inner peace, relaxation and enjoyment." Eric agreed but felt panic consuming him. Somehow he restrained his anxiety and was thankful when Father Hall was summoned to the telephone. When he returned he sat quietly eating and talked about sports, his favorite pass time. When Father Hall finished his meal, he stood up. "I have to meet with the catholic chaplain at the college at eleven this morning. "I'll be in my office if you want to take the time. Say in a half hour." Eric agreed. He no longer wondered how his mentor could sense his anxiety all too well. Usually ravenous during breakfast, he barely ate anything.

At 9:45 Eric knocked on Father Hall's office door. When it opened his mentor was there with a friendly hello. "Please have a seat Eric. We haven't had a good talk since our meal together in Ithaca. Remember we were at THE STATION." Eric remembered that moment well. Now he felt more relaxed and was assured his conversation with his mentor would be private when Father Hall asked his secretary to hold all calls and to please close the door. They sat facing one another near a window looking out to the courtyard. "So Eric where do we begin? I sense discomfort, dissonance, am I correct?" Eric could not lie to his priest and confidant. "Well Father I'm not sure what it is exactly because my life was interrupted at a critical time. When I completed a little more than half of my seminary training I was drafted into the army. I think I took my eye off the ball and am having some difficulty refocusing." Father Hall then asked. "Is there anything else? Think and be honest with yourself." Father Hall did not say be "honest with me" but with yourself. Eric stared at the wall. "Look at me Eric. I'm over here. Is there anything else? I am not going to judge you. I am here to help you." Eric responded. "Well there were all these offers made to me by a variety of people, one of them my good friend from Cornell. He wants me to get involved in politics because he believes I can make a difference and would reach millions of Americans by reviving a new and necessary social policy. He said my work for Christ can be accomplished outside the church and with more impact." Father Hall just listened. He asked again. "Is there anything else?" Eric paused. "Well there were several high stake business offers from big corporate CEO's and also from the Pentagon and even

Amerigo Merenda

a teaching position at a university with my graduate PH.D, included. I don't really have a desire for excessive material gain." Eric thought he satisfied Father Hall who asked the same question. "Is there anything else Eric? It appears to me that you are leaving something out." Eric covered his eyes with his left hand and looked down at the floor. Father Hall allowed his silence to fill the room. He waited for over a minute before Eric responded. "Yes father, you know my childhood issues and how my innocence was compromised by my uncle. Every so often that episode gives me anxiety. It still makes me shudder and I try to block it out by over compensating in other areas. I feel driven to exceed all expectations that my family, friends and others have of me. I think that is why I excelled; it was my way of overcoming my grief." Father Hall listened intently because he knew Eric's family very well, more than anyone else. The trauma experienced by Eric still haunted him but he was surprised when Eric continued by revealing one more factor. "Father there is one more reason." More silence. Father Hall walked over to Eric and placed his hand on his shoulder. "And what would that be?" More silence. There was no way Father Hall would say a word. Everything had to come from Eric. He waited. Finally when Eric looked up, there were tears in his eyes. He looked at Father Hall's gentle glance and took a deep breath. "It's a woman I met Father. I can't seem to get her out of my life. I didn't know her in high school because she was two years younger. Now she teaches English. She is very kind, intelligent and a very beautiful woman. Her name is Michelle, and she more than anyone can relieve my anxiety and grief. She has a calming effect on me and when I was with her I never felt better. She told me she loves me and I must be having strong feelings for her but now my life is on a different path." Father Hall smiled. "Look at me Eric. Are you in love with this woman?" Eric responded with what he believed was an honest answer. "I don't know what I truly feel. That is the truth. But I do think of her more than I should." Father Hall smiled again. "You know Eric I seem to remember telling you about a woman in my life before I was a priest. I thought we would be married but I bailed out at the last moment when her father got too pushy with me. Your situation is somewhat different but it's not without a solution. Many new priests have second thoughts; their mistake is they deny themselves their true feelings. Remember: 'To thine own self be true.'" You have time now to reflect upon your life's future. The priesthood is not prison. There are no bars containing you. You are free. In fact what Christ wants for you is happiness, joy and fulfillment. The important thing to remember is, don't try to live two lives, one as a priest and the other as a man. Although we are both, priests have a different calling. You have time to reflect and with time you will arrive at your choice. Both are good choices, but only one is for you. God has given us free will. Use this gift and with time your choice will come to you. Don't be ashamed of your feelings. Who knows, maybe someday the church will allow priests to marry and have a family." Eric then explained in detail his experience with the two Vietnamese children. "I loved those children as if they were my own. Their parents were killed by Viet Cong. My future plans included them. They were my responsibility, my children. I truly loved them. I became their guardian and when they were killed I felt parental loss and pain. Had I not gone to Vietnam I may have never thought of children the way I do now. I believe my thoughts have been altered in favor of having a family. You see where this is going? Vietnam changed my life but not in the way one would think. So what do I do father? I need your advice." Father Hall sat down, looked at Eric and said. "Here's one idea. Tell me what you think. Commit to one year in the priesthood. If you think it's a good idea, let Michelle know your uncertainty and that you want to give it your best until such time that you realize and decide your calling. Devote yourself to our parish and congregation, including our K-6 elementary school. Keep busy. Pray, meditate and talk to me whenever you think necessary. The situation will resolve itself. Remember, when you're not sure, it may be best to do nothing out of the ordinary." His mentor's calm and logic was comforting. Eric thought. "The situation will resolve itself." Why couldn't he have thought of that. Eric realized he had panicked, thinking a decision had to be made immediately. Now he took a deep breath of relief. "Thank you father. I was allowing my emotions to prevail, not my rational side. I hope you are not disappointed with me. I will do as you recommend because it makes sense. Thank you." Father Hall walked over to Eric, a man he knew from early childhood. He hugged him and said. "Remember, I am here for you. I would ask you one request. At some point, I would like to meet Michelle. Is that something you would feel comfortable with. Think about it and then you can let me know." Then kidding Eric he continued. "It can be here or at the alter, or both." He smiled and gave Eric a big hug.

Chapter 59

As Eric prepared for his first mass at St. Mary's, he felt excitement and relief knowing his future would unfold one way or another. Many people were informed of his nine o'clock service on Sunday; a large audience was expected. The pressure was on; Eric had become something of a celebrity with all his Vietnam history and famed publicity. Several friends from Cornell and members of the military who were close to Eric arrived in Oswego just to be there. His family and local friends and throngs of city residents who never met Eric, now Father O'Reilly, would be present. His sermon preparation was extensive and he hoped he didn't over prepare. He wanted his message to flow naturally and also wanted a theme that would be part of his mission as a priest at St. Mary's. That theme would be protecting and loving our children. He spent many hours looking for scripture that would connect with his message. Finally he came across several passages in the bible that flowed with his theme. He felt prepared when his time finally arrived. The mass began with a packed church. Father Hall would assist with the service and was thrilled for his protege.

The procession began with two alter boys, one carrying a candle, the other the crucifix, followed by Father Hall and last by Father O'Reilly. The men's choir was singing in Latin under the direction of Richard Lally, outstanding choir director for many years. His excellence in choral directing was well known throughout the community. Non Catholics would attend when his men's choir was singing because of the inspiration and quality of the music. St. Mary's was a large English Gothic church with classical appeal. The packed congregation directed their attention to Eric, who was smiling and acknowledging their friendly reception. His mother's eyes were filled with tears of joy, along with his sister Mary. Seated next to Mary was Michelle whose emotions were also felt by Eric's sister when her hand was squeezed by Michelle as Eric walked by. The procession proceeded to the alter, turned to face the congregation, and the mass began.

The catholic mass is filled with rituals that many non catholics do not understand. Each ritual symbolizes an act of Christ and his teaching. The mass proceeded as usual with the choir adding inspired music. What everyone was waiting for was the homily. Eric's preparation was going to be discerned not only by Father Hall but also by several hundred listeners. When he walked up to the pulpit, an elegant structure elevated on the front left side of the alter, he towered above the congregation. His handsome face and frame were apparent to all. He had typed his sermon, double spaced. He began with the sign of the cross. The congregation followed with Amen. Then Father O'Reilly delivered his first sermon to his congregation.

"I want to thank all of you for your gracious welcome. It wasn't too long ago when I was seated where you are looking up at Father Hall, my friend and mentor." Father Hall acknowledged with a smile and nod. "Today I celebrate my first mass in St. Mary's and I want to devote today's homily to our children and briefly explain why and how my life has been altered by two children I met in Vietnam not that long ago. They were a six year old boy Minh and his four year old sister Bian. Their parents were killed by an attack of their village. When I met them, I looked into their eyes and knew right then we belonged together so after a few weeks, I began the process of bringing them home to America. I spent every spare minute with them and we bonded in some magical, spiritual way. They knew how much I cared for them and I was thrilled they would soon be arriving in the States. I never experienced such love for children. Maybe it was their tragic circumstances but whatever it was, I wanted them to be a part of my life." Eric paused to gather his composure. "The paper work for their admittance to the United States took a few days too long as I was anxiously waiting for them in Hawaii. Then I was informed of another tragic event. Minh and Bian were killed by an attack by North Vietnamese soldiers at the compound where they were waiting before their departure and deliverance. As their guardian I felt parental pain; I can't imagine a parent experiencing the loss of a child. Their lives and tragic death transformed my life. I long for them and will dedicate today's sermon to them and to children all over the world, especially those who crave for peace, security and happiness. Children are God's examples of humble faith. Let me begin with holy scripture. In the name of the father, son and holy spirit. Amen." Eric then opened his notes containing scripture from the holy bible that he found could relate to God's love for children. He felt more relaxed as he continued.

"The apostle Mathew, in verse 18: 2-6, refers to Jesus speaking one day to a crowd where many children were present, 'He called to one child and placed him in the midst of all the other children.' Jesus said to the crowd. 'Truly I say to you, unless you turn and become like children, you will never enter the kingdom of heaven. Whoever humbles himself like this child is the greatest in the kingdom of heaven.... Whoever receives one such child in my name receives me, but whoever causes one of these little ones who believe in me to sin, it would be better for him to have a great millstone fastened around his neck and to be drowned in the depth of the sea." Eric paused and looked at his congregation. "Jesus was very clear when it came to children. We must treasure our children. They are truly gifts from above. God would consider harming innocent children a great sin of malice. The apostle Mark in chapter 10:13-16 refers to an incident where children and infants were brought to Jesus by gathering crowds who wanted Jesus to touch them but the disciples rebuked them. But when Jesus noticed this he was indignant and said to them, 'Let the children come to me, do not hinder them, for to such belongs the kingdom of God. Truly, I say to you whoever does not receive the kingdom of God like a child shall not enter it....'And he took them in his arms and blessed them, laying his hands on them.' " With these instances of His love for children, Jesus is teaching us by his example by accepting the innocent love for our children. The apostle Mathew in chapter 18:12-14 refers to another time when Jesus was speaking with a large crowd. Jesus says: 'If a man has a hundred sheep and one of them has gone astray, does he not leave the ninety-nine on the mountain and go in search of the one that went astray? And if he finds it, truly, I say to you, he rejoices over it more (than) the ninety-nine that never went astray.' Jesus then confirms His Father's love for children. 'So it is the will of my Father who is in heaven that (if) one of these little ones should be lost." we should rejoice when he is found. "When a child goes astray, we must extend our love and concern for their well being so they will know our love is unconditional. We must remember this lesson when our children go astray and to use such instances to demonstrate our love and devotion to them. In proverbs 22:6 the Bible reads: 'Train up a child in the way he should go; even when he is old he will not depart from it.' "Jesus is mentoring all parents to bring your children to God, Christ and church while they are young so they will be exposed to his teachings. Many catholic adults return to their christian faith after years of going astray just as sheep on the mountain side. There are members of our congregation and others who have returned to their flock here at St. Mary's and other religious institutions. It's never too late to find our faith. It is best to introduce our children while they are young. If and when they walk away, later in life they may return as lost sheep."

"Jesus also asks children to respect parents, grandparents, and elders and to practice humility. So parenting children has mutual responsibilities and rewards. We must all practice humility so that our children understand its meaning which simply is to control our pride and self interest. Children live the life we teach them. Let's direct our Christian love to all of our children so our love becomes their security and strength. We must also lead by example so that our children will learn to become servants of Christ." Eric paused again. He thought he was going to break down. "Now that I have personally experienced the love and joy of two innocent children, I wanted to share these lessons with parents, future parents, grandparents and children, taught to us by our lord Jesus Christ. Our children are our future. We must protect them from evil that surrounds us, even from people we know and trust." Recently there were reported incidents of child abuse throughout the United States. Eric felt an obligation to make a statement that might lead people to wonder. His intent was to suggest we must never assume innocence, even from our friends and family. He thought about how his innocence as a young boy was violated and how his loving mother suffered for years thinking she was responsible for what happened. Informing and reminding people, he thought, was very important.

"As I begin my priestly journey here at St. Mary's, I ask for your prayers that almighty God will guide me and give me the strength and wisdom to serve you well. I have received many cards of congratulations from many members of our parish and from total strangers. I sincerely thank you. I also want to inform you that our school here at St. Mary's will be conducting classes for parents and future parents to learn and share parenting skills that produce healthy and happy children. Please join us. The information is in the bulletin." He paused again. " And now let us pray." The congregation knelt on the rolled out padded boards used for prayer. He prayed slowly and with feeling. "Heavenly Father. We pray that You will enlighten us to become the best we can be with our children. Bless them with parental love and guide all adults to respect and protect their innocence and encourage their humility. These requests are made because we love our children and want what's best for their future success. We thank you, in the name of the father, and of the son, and the holy spirit. Amen."

Thus ended Eric's first sermon at St. Mary's. He intentionally kept it short and focused on a subject dear to his heart. Mary and Michelle looked at each other. Both had tears in their eyes.

Later, during the afternoon hours, Eric reflected upon his sermon and how its origin was in part connected to his childhood trauma. He realized how therapeutic it was to release and utilize personal emotions for the benefit of innocent children.

Chapter 60

Almost a year later the rigors of priestly work increased as Eric became more connected with his congregation and elementary school. He preferred keeping busy because he would not have time to reflect upon any dissonance which would creep in during lulls in his work schedule. Children loved him because of his youthful exuberance. His athletic skills were used to encourage physical activity he knew was important for children. He made physical education a major component of St. Mary's curriculum. Active children are healthy children. Basketball in particular became a favorite sport for boys and girls at St. Mary's.

Eric understood that leisure could not be confused with idleness. His leisure was spent reading scripture, theological essays, philosophy and psychology. Idleness for him, was preoccupation with personal issues that stirred desires especially for the outside world. Father Hall was very perceptive and felt there were moments where Eric was grasping for even more responsibility so he requested a meeting with Eric to discuss his progress and other issues that only he was privy to. They convened in Father Hall's office where his mentor and friend sensed Eric's behavior was anxiety ridden. He over scheduled his days with enough work for two priests. "I get tired just watching you. I didn't realize you were a workaholic. Were you always this way or am I missing something?" Eric was honest. "If I keep busy I feel less anxiety. It's a defense mechanism. I know it's not normal but I believe it helps me work through thoughts that take me places I want to avoid." Father Hall sensed his discomfort. "Like what?" Father Hall wasn't certain but he felt that maybe therapy would help. After all Eric was a priest for almost a year. His anxiety did not seem to diminish. "Do you want some professional help? I think we would both agree this behavior must be addressed." Father Hall then reached into a cabinet where his aged Irish whiskey was stored and poured freely into two glasses. "Here, I prefer not to drink alone." They clicked their glasses and drank a healthy mouthful. "Are you happy Eric? It's important that I know how you feel. Something is obviously bothering you. You must share with me if I'm to help you." Eric felt the smooth aged whiskey slide down his throat and was pleased with the taste. Father Hall refilled his glass. The alcohol did have a relaxing affect and Eric gradually felt his tension ease. Father Hall watched and waited and before long Eric opened up. "I don't know what I feel. I've had nightmares where explosions and screaming children would waken me. I've also felt emotions about my childhood haunting me. It's like it's a different episode each night of the week. I need a good nights rest." Father Hall heard of post traumatic stress from other vets but Eric's problems were more complicated. "Why don't we arrange for you to see the psychiatrist at Cornell; the one you met last time in Ithaca. Dr. Neuberger, wasn't that his name. Why don't we do that? No one has to know." Eric's eyes were starting to close but he could still hear and responded. "Maybe I should do that." He yawned and continued. "I haven't been this relaxed in a long time. This stuff works." Father Hall enjoyed his libation as well and remarked. "I will call him tomorrow and make an appointment. Clear your schedule so I can fit you into his work week. We have to get help so that you can clear your head. You will have difficulty moving forward until these issues are resolved. Would you agree?" Eric agreed and added. "I will call Dr. Neuberger father. I still have his card. I know you are concerned and so am I. Each day my emotions are not what they should be, after all as a priest, my mind should not be experiencing this turbulance." Father Hall listened without comment; he sensed a problem but thought it would be best if Dr. Neuberger completed his session with Eric before he arrived at his own assessment. "You know father, maybe I should call him now while I have some time. May I use your phone?" Father Hall responded: "Of course." Father Hall thought this poor soul had so much baggage that his decision-making ability was impeded by doubt. The question was, what caused this doubt. There was also the fear of coming to grips with Eric's reality. However he also thought Eric's problems were coming to a head sooner rather than later; maybe this was positive. Eric dialed Dr. Neuberger's number and to his pleasant surprise he answered, not his secretary. "Dr. Neuberger, this is Eric O'Reilly. I hope you remember me." Eric hoped he didn't sound inebriated. "Of course Eric, how are you?" Before responding Eric had to think of what to say. He stumbled for words. Maybe he had too much to drink but he managed to respond with: "Well Dr. Neuberger, I've had better days in Vietnam than I'm having here. I need to see you and was hoping you could squeeze me in soon." Father Hall was listening and something told him his instincts were right. "Well Eric, it's good that you called when you did because I am leaving in four days for a conference in Denver. Are you free tomorrow?" Eric didn't hesitate. "Yes, absolutely. What time?" He couldn't believe his relief when he hung up the telephone. "You won't believe this. He can see me tomorrow." Father Hall then added. "Take a few days, you've earned it. I will have your schedule canceled until Wednesday." Eric turned to Father Hall and said: "Good night father. Thank you for your help and for the whiskey." Father Hall was sitting in his chair perusing an article in TIME magazine entitled: THE VIETNAM QUAGMIRE. "Good night Eric. Sleep well." When Eric slipped into his bed he had his best sleep in months.

Chapter 61

Eric's appointment with Dr. Neuberger was Monday at 1 pm at his office in college town. He also informed Father Hall that he arranged to meet with a fellow seminarian afterward who was currently a priest serving Catholic students at Cornell and would return the following day. Eric thought they could share notes about their work as priests. When he arrived at Dr. Neuberger's office, his secretary, a rather attractive woman, remembered him except now Eric was dressed appropriately as a priest which surprised her. "Are you...." Eric smiled and answered her incompleted question. "Yes, I am Eric O'Reilly, now Father O'Reilly." She remembered his handsome face from his earlier visit and appeared rather disappointed viewing him as a priest. And why is a priest seeing a psychiatrist? Maybe she thought it was a friendly call. Eric read her look and said. "Yes, I'm in Ithaca visiting friends and wanted to say hello to Dr. Neuberger." Just then Dr. Neuberger opened the door. "Eric", he paused. " I mean Father O'Reilly, good to see you. Please come in." He handed his secretary some papers to be copied and told her to take the rest of the afternoon off when she completed her work. She was very pleased and left but not before smiling at Eric and wishing him well. The scent of her perfume was familiar. Eric remembered he had given it to Michelle as a Christmas gift two years ago.

They sat in a refurbished office now made more attractive with walnut bookshelves and a handsome desk. The carpeting was also thick and comfortable. Dr. Neuberger joked with Eric that the new surroundings softened the acoustics so more privacy could be possible. "You never know who's listening." He nodded toward the door. "Sometimes I think she is listening so I have now piped in soft music in the waiting room. So how can I help you Eric? You seemed anxious when you called. Is everything alright?" Eric took a deep breath. Now more than ever he wanted to feel he could come to the bottom of his dilemma. He sat quietly before he spoke. Dr. Neuberger patiently waited for him to craft his thoughts and words. "Where should I begin doctor? There's so much to tell you." Eric felt like he was in confession and had to ask for forgiveness even though he had done nothing wrong. He realized he lost control somewhere in the past but did not know where. His decision-making was somehow flawed, so he thought. "Doctor Neuberger, the strange thing is I waited too long before I addressed my problems the way I should have." Neuberger was reading through notes he had in Eric's file and got right to the point. "You know Eric I have studied your past history so I have some knowledge of your problems. Because of my schedule, your time with me is limited to today and tomorrow if you can make it. So it would be best if you let it all out and allow me the opportunity to sift through all of your confusion and anxiety. I like millions of other Americans know your Vietnam story and the honors you received. Of course I am not aware of your total experience there. Maybe we should begin with what happened in Vietnam." Eric suddenly wondered if he was experiencing what other vets had reported, post traumatic stress from combat. He told Dr. Neuberger how on many nights in Vietnam he could not sleep because of imminent threats of shells exploding in the distance, some too close for comfort. Many soldiers came to him as he provided them with counseling, and faith through prayer as their chaplain. Eric heard many stories of fear and anxiety from soldiers who flocked to his compound when they had a chance to meet with Eric, who was well known for his ability to appease fears many soldiers were experiencing. "You know Eric, as a psychiatrist, I also hear many sad and emotional stories from my patients and I have to go to my friends who are therapists in order to get relief. Even a psychiatrist needs help from all the stress exposed to him from patients. You are no different. So coming to me for help was the right thing to do. I meet with my therapist regularly to recharge my mind set. That's a good thing. Of course if your pre-Vietnam past is resurfacing, that is something quite different. Life resolutions require the element of time to allow for natural healing to occur. I can understand your concerns now that you are a priest. Am I making myself clear?" Eric nodded. "Absolutely doctor." Eric took another deep breath and began. "You know Dr. Neuberger, what happened before Vietnam is not central to what I believe is troubling me. In Vietnam I met two orphaned children whose parents were killed in an attack of their village. When I met these children they were quite distressed. I held them in my arms and tried to comfort them as best I could with food, toys and lots of love and attention. My skill with their language was enough for us to communicate. I made a point of seeing them every day unless my duties prevented that from happening. I grew to love them as my own and my intentions were to bring them to America. My plans were tragically interrupted when they were killed by north Vietnamese soldiers in a brazen attack on the compound where they were waiting before being sent to me in Hawaii. These children made me feel whole and gave my life real meaning and purpose. I feel empty, sad and depressed. I have tried to work around these emotions before I was ordained but apparently without success. My duties as a priest have not been able to distract me from the loss I feel. I now see having children as part of my life; that does not coincide with my life at present. I strongly feel a need to be a parent more than a priest; this is all a result of that brief but beautiful time spent with them." Dr. Neuberger chewed on the stem of his pipe before giving his response. "Eric, I thought of what I am about to say after you left last time you were here. Basically I concluded your decision to be a priest was based on guilt caused by your traumatic experiences with your uncle. That perverse episode, so I thought, created extreme anxiety in your childhood; that in turn precipitated your decision for being a priest because you may have thought it would cleanse your soul from sin and guilt. It's the old catholic guilt concept which does have some application here. Haste, however, is problematic. Making a decision to be a priest involves great fortitude. I think you would agree." Eric nodded his head. "In my view, you may have repressed what happened during your childhood and presently have arrived at your current state of mind for reasons which you have just explained; by the way, they make sense. But all along, your priestly intentions may have been a ruse. It's totally understandable. I am not judging you, in fact I feel for you. Now in my view, unless you have withheld any pertinent information from me, I believe your life as a priest will have to continue under pretenses that must be addressed. You fought the good fight in Vietnam and before that experienced childhood trauma. Now your life must address your natural desires that bring you true fulfillment. Have I made sense or do you find reasons to challenge my assessment?" Eric felt tension one feels when truth has been spoken. It was in one way refreshing for him to hear a sensible explanation. However on the other hand Eric felt his decision for choosing priesthood must not be discarded without thoughtful deliberation. The doctor seemed to sense his uneasiness and offered the following. "Eric, please understand that your future decision has plenty of time to consider all of your options. Most of all I want you to consider my analysis of the situation you find yourself in. Please challenge me if I'm off the mark. I do want you to know that I have been thinking about you for some time and my conclusion is based on a thorough study of your life history. I have also consulted with other psychiatrists who have come to the same assessment. You also realize that your experience with the two orphans was a confirmation of my judgment because that experience gave you cause to question limitations attached to celibacy and priesthood in general. It's truly a noble profession but as your friends have advised, there are many careers where your life can perform Christ's work. There also seems to be a strong desire on your part for parenthood. There's always room for future parents who have this quality. So you see Eric, there are a variety of reasons why I arrived at my conclusion. Have I left something out? If so please let me know." Neuberger puffed on his pipe and walked over to a window; distancing himself from Eric for a reason. He learned from his years of practice that giving space, actual physical space can allow his patient to be more forthcoming. He waited for Eric to respond. Then after a long moment of silence he realized his patient was frozen in time. He offered a favorable scenerio. "Eric, there are several positive aspects of your situation that I also want to highlight. First, no decision has to be made with haste; patience, deliberation and prayer are recommended. You have a rich full life ahead of you. Be mindful, that is, be in the moment; don't get ahead of yourself. The only reason you should act with immediate action is if you are really uncomfortable with what life is offering you at this moment of time in your life's journey. Because it is a journey. I'm sure you realize this to be the case. You are just starting out and must expect that life presents many challenges and opportunities. Consider yourself very fortunate. It's not a bad situation to be in." Eric took in all the words with great interest; his comfort level improved and he began to place all of his challenges and questions in perspective. He had to believe time was on his side. He realized the wisdom offered by the doctor was persuasive. "Thank you doctor, everything you said does make sense. My anxiety was not allowing me to think clearly. I was for some reason cramming everything together and lost my bearing. I know I have to take one step at a time; I guess I'm having difficulty doing that. I must be patient and allow myself more time." The doctor smiled. "Believe me Eric; no one is saying this is easy.

But, you will know when to throw in the towel. That decision can be made without my advice. You own that decision. However when in doubt, sometimes it's best to do nothing until that moment of truth is revealed. For now, be in the moment and enjoy being a priest. Not too many men have the wonderful options facing you. Be mindful. Be in the moment." Dr. Neuberger once again walked away toward the window, distancing himself again. He asked Eric. "Is there any other issue that could be giving you anxiety?" He waited and this time Eric did respond. "Yes doctor, there's a woman I had an intimate relationship with who I think about more than I should." The doctor smiled and even laughed. "Forgive me Eric, but many men would love to have this problem. Are you in love or infatuated? The difference is critical." Eric did not answer right away and the doctor waited again for an answer. Finally Eric admitted that his feelings for her were genuine but that he placed restraint on his actions due to his vows as a priest. The doctor understood. "Time must pass before you know the answer. Don't rush it. If it's meant to be, it will happen. Either way you will find a resolution. Both are good choices." Eric once again heard a similar refrain involving the element of time. The only problem foreseen was whether Michelle would wait until he knew what his mind and heart was telling him. When Eric left Dr. Neuberger he did feel better but still had unanswered questions that did not require therapy, just time. Eric would have to be patient and allow for his life experiences to reveal his future pathway. He chose not to make another appointment with the doctor but instead to take his advice and wait for circumstances to unfold that would lead him to where he wanted to be.

Chapter 62

When Eric left Dr. Neuberger he called a friend from the seminary who was the new catholic chaplain at the Newman center on Cornell's campus. He had been ordained a year before Eric and both had some catching up to do. John Morley was someone Eric admired because of his quiet deliberation when confronted with unsettling situations. He was honest and sincere when asked questions that could transgress the comfort zone for priests. Eric needed to know certain things that priest's talk about time to time, especially concerning young and handsome men of the cloth. What Eric didn't know was what John had planned for that evening. They met on campus, had a beer and sandwich together and caught up on their latest work. What type of conversation do two young handsome priests have with one another? Eric was thinking about this before they met. "You know John, I had a session with Dr. Neuberger earlier today. I've been having some anxiety lately. I'm not sure of the reasons; it could possibly be post traumatic stress or other issues that maybe you can help me with. I respect your honesty." John could see that Eric was very serious. "I want to ask you several questions John. Is that OK with you." John didn't know what to expect from Eric. He sensed his discomfort. "Of course Eric." The restaurant offered a good place for their conversation being they were situated along a corner in the back. "Have you any regrets or doubts about your decision John? I'm sure you have been told by someone that you are too handsome to be a priest. You know what I'm getting at." John did not hesitate with his response. "I'm more certain you have been told the same Eric so why don't we begin with you." John preferred to hear Eric's experience only because it was Eric who had a problem. When Eric did not respond, the silence between them made John pause. So John offered his response. "Yes Eric, I was dating an attractive woman before I entered the seminary. I thought we were an item and one day I received a letter from her that broke my heart. For me, a "dear John letter" has real meaning. It was not too long after that incident that I decided women were too complicated, at least that was my rationale. My therapist thankfully made me see my shortcomings which were possible causes of her leaving. The priesthood offered me a retreat from mainstream life and I've found that if I keep myself busy, my life has fulfillment. I'm sorry to hear of your predicament. What's going on Eric?" Eric was somewhat relieved to learn of John's romantic episode. "I too was involved with a beautiful woman who I really cared for. I was never one to date much in high school or college. I was at times wondering about my sexuality. Have you ever thought of that? You said your therapist revealed some shortcomings. Were any of your problems related to your sexuality?" John's response was silence which was used to craft his honest and direct response. "Matter of fact, yes Eric. I am homosexual although I do not engage in any sexual relationship. But if it's any consolation, I can tell you straight forward that you are not homosexual. Trust me. Men like me know other men like me and you are not one of us. You're straight as can be. Is that what's bothering you Eric?" A feeling of relief did settle on Eric's mood. "You know John I was sexually abused by my uncle as a child. I never told anyone let alone discuss it, except with my therapist. I've been ..." John interrupted. "Eric, listen to me, that does not make a man homosexual. Homosexuals are born that way. You may not appreciate what I am saying but I can tell you I knew something was different about me as a child. I quickly realized that I had to disguise my behavior because of social pressure, so I did. The woman I was dating seemed to know what I was all about but did not have the heart to discuss it with me. I was in denial. She did tell me in her letter that she would always love me but that her instincts told her our relationship wouldn't work. She was right. I thank her for that. I'm in the closet and practice abstinence for a variety of reasons. There are priests who use their position and status to abuse young boys. If I ever leave the priesthood it would be caused by abuses of this kind in the church. If and when I report such an incident and nothing is done by my bishop, that's the day I leave. Children are innocent and must be protected." It was now even more apparent to Eric that his inclination of his friend was validated by his direct and honest response. "You know Eric, the day may come when we both leave the priesthood, me for a man I meet and love and you for the woman you know and love. Life's a bitch isn't it?" They both laughed out loud and clicked their beer glasses. "I hope you feel better Eric. Do you?" Eric hadn't felt this good for some time. "Yes. Thank you John. Apparently, that was a big part of my angst. The rest I can deal with." They clicked glasses again and drank to each other.

When they walked to Eric's office many students said hello to Father Morley. Female students in particular appeared very interested and several came up to greet them and were pleasantly surprised by their levity and friendliness. "Hi Father Morley. Who's your friend?" Eric was caught off guard. He greeted a flock of students gathering around them. "Hello, I'm Father O'Reilly." John chimed in. "Yes this is my good friend who will be speaking tonight about his experience in Vietnam. I am sure you will want to be there." Eric was stunned. Then a co-ed then asked Eric. "Are you the soldier who received the Congressional Medal of Honor and now you're a priest?" Eric looked at John with displeasure. "I'm afraid so. In fact I was not aware of my speaking engagement until now." Eric looked at John who was laughing. "Well, I for one love spontaneity. I'm confident that Father O'Reilly will present an interesting evening. Spread the word." Another female student responded. "Don't worry, we will be there along with many more." John had announced Eric's presentation at the last minute not knowing whether Eric would be available. "Why wasn't I informed John?" He seemed annoyed but John quickly responded. "Eric, you have been the topic of lively conversation on campus. Students asked me if I knew you and when I told them we were friends they pleaded to have you come and speak. When I was assured of your visit to Ithaca, I posted your presentation on the campus board of events which quickly spread to campus and local papers, radio and television news. Expect a good crowd." When Eric was informed his presentation would be at 7:30 that evening at the Newman chapel; he asked John for some time to prepare a few notes and plan his presentation. John looked at his watch. It was four o'clock. "Absolutely. You can use my office; it's very quiet; we will have dinner around six o'clock. Follow me."

At this moment in time Eric's mind was cleared of uncertainties that were mounting from his lurid past, especially his childhood; his confidence returned and he wondered if it was temporary. Father John Morley had done more for Eric's inner strength in one afternoon discussion than anyone could have imagined. Father Morley's gut wrenching admission and explanation of his personal life was an epiphany for Eric. It re-energized his intellectual and moral authority that up to this point had been held in check. Eric crossed a threshold that released him from past psychological barriers. Suddenly he was mindful that his future was open to many possibilities. As he prepared his presentation for that evening he knew he had to craft a meaningful and relevant speech ; Eric's new and exciting chapter had commenced without any time or desire to retreat. Morley had also arranged for a cocktail party at his residence after Eric's presentation where local professionals could savor good conversation. He called Father Hall and informed him of his overnight stay with Father Morley and that he would return the following morning.

Chapter 63

Eric used the remainder of the afternoon to prepare his presentation which he was told would be followed by some questions from the audience. The word had spread and large crowds lined up outside the Newman chapel. It was apparent by six o'clock that the chapel was not large enough to accommodate over a thousand students cramming the grounds. Father Morley asked campus police if they could request administration authorities to transfer to a larger auditorium a block away. This required some last minute rearrangements and more security was called to maintain order. Students were becoming agitated by all the police which now included police from the city of Ithaca. Father Morley used a portable loudspeaker to inform students that the evenings program would be held in the student union that had a large auditorium suitable for the overwhelming crowd. Students would have to present their student ID to get in. Father Morley assured students they would be accommodated and requested they maintain their composure so no one gets hurt or arrested. Miraculously the students organized in cues and order was restored.

Meanwhile Eric was organizing his presentation; he focused on how the United States was drawn into the jungles of southeast Asia by political and ideological friction connected to the cold war. He had to talk about war and how it can destroy a soldier's humanity, especially when placed in life and death drama that penetrates ones core values. He also provided a very brief story of Vietnam's recent history. Vietnam was a war of liberation inspired by native opposition to French colonialism. With the withdrawal of French forces the political vacuum created was filled by the United States who feared communist expansion in southeast Asia.

Eric was skeptical that his preparation was sufficient when Father John Morley began introducing his friend as guest speaker. He asked John not to include his congressional medal of honor in his introduction because he did not want to focus on valor. His focus would be on policy. Father Morley began his introduction. "Good evening ladies and gentlemen. Spontaneity has managed to bring us together this evening. Tonight we have a fellow alumni who not too many years ago was sitting where you are at this moment. With almost two years left in seminary school, he was drafted into the Army. He was offered an opportunity to qualify for deferment but refused. The rest is history. It is my great honor to introduce to you, one of Cornell's alumni, Father Eric O'Reilly." The crowd was very receptive; there were a few shouts of "war monger", "shame on you", but the crowd was silenced by Eric's steadfast composure. He waited until the crowd's silence filled the room. Then he began. "Thank you Father Morley. Good evening students of Cornell. First of all I want you all to know that I really did not want to go to Vietnam but at that time I felt my personal safety and obligation could not be transferred to someone else; my number was up. Literally speaking my lottery number was seventeen which guaranteed that I would be drafted. I believe in numbers. Seventeen is my lucky number. I was born on the 17th at 9:17pm. If you add nine, one and seven, it adds up to seventeen. I received my draft notice on the 17th day of the month. (he paused) None of this information is relevant. Numbers are just that, numbers. What I really was feeling back then was a need to embrace my fear and live to talk about it. The Vietnam war gave me an opportunity to overcome many fears; the army taught me how to work with others who were about your age. I was fortunate learning to know some of the best and bravest men in my life. We all shared our fears and knew the importance of protecting each others back. But the Vietnam war also taught me how our country was overwhelmed by the cold war's political and ideological divisions. History will demonstrate this to be true.

We were drawn into the jungles of southeast Asia because we failed to realize what the Vietnamese wanted was what we Americans also wanted almost two hundred years ago, self determination. When the French were defeated at Dien Bien Phu, in 1954, the United States political and military leaders believed that our great military could control the destiny of a third world developing nation. The fear of communism expanding throughout southeast Asia was our reality. Our mantra was the domino theory. Communism was presented as a monolithic model, sweeping the Soviet Union, China, Vietnam and other nations into a one size communism fits all. However it was nationalism, not communism that was the real force behind our military defeat. We Americans should have known better. When he left office, President Eisenhower warned us not to entangle ourselves in a jungle war in southeast Asia. We Americans seemed to forget how during our war for independence, we defeated the mighty British Empire. With help from our friends, geographical advantages, outstanding leadership, and our small but brave military force we were triumphant. Now the Vietnamese with help from their friends, knowledge of their terrain and jungle and with determined warriors have handed the United States a costly withdrawal and defeat. The force of Vietnamese nationalism overwhelmed America's preoccupation with communist expansion. Our judgment and decision-making was flawed. We committed a terrible mistake. Over 58,000 Americans were killed, many thousands crippled with physical wounds, some suffering from agent orange and others with emotional scars for life. All of this amounted to over 100 billion dollars and we lost. Now let's hope we have learned from our mistakes. Many of my fellow soldiers are suffering from post traumatic stress. Shell shock. War is hell on earth. Our national nightmare is over and must not be repeated. Our military must never be expected to fight a war that does not threaten our national security. Vietnamese also want their independence from foreign powers including China and the Soviet Union. Our foreign policy and relationship with Vietnam must be implemented with our economic power not our military power." The student body stood and gave Eric a standing ovation. When they quieted down he continued. "While in Vietnam, I met two young children whose parents were killed by north Vietnamese soldiers during the last stages of war. I grew to love these two children and we became inseparable. They also felt a bond with me. Minh and his younger sister Bien were brother and sister. They did not want to be separated from each other or from me so I made arrangements to bring them to America where they could grow and live in peace and security. I planned to adopt them as my own children. Days before their departure to Hawaii where I was waiting for them, they were killed along with many others. The compound where they were staying was attacked by North Vietnamese soldiers. They became casualties of war like thousands of others. What you may not realize is how soldiers pay a price for their service, especially during war time, and now my burden is amplified by this personal tragedy. I humbly ask for your thoughts and if so inclined, your prayers. Today I am a priest. Many of you may be wondering why I chose this vocation. When I was a young boy I remember thinking about the meaning behind the rituals of religion so I began to read and study the bible and Catholicism. I'll spare you the theological details.

So here I am speaking to you and also wondering where my life choices will lead me. Existentialism stresses self determination and what I like to believe is moral responsibility. Our lives are driven by the choices we make. I do hope that you will on occasion remind yourself what your mission in life will or can be. Situations change like the wind and our lives must be prepared for what Margaret Meade believed was the most difficult challenge we all must face at some point in our lives; that being change. We all must be prepared for change. Look at change as a gift that keeps giving so you can expand your horizons. And finally I will leave you with a philosopher who was educated by Jesuits. During his twenties he experienced a time of skepticism as may also be the case with some of you. Descartes believed in God because his reason concluded such a being existed and that scientific thinking could support it regardless of the limitations of papal doctrines. Descartes would truly believe that "a mind is a terrible thing to waste." Our thinking is our being. "I think therefore I am." For him, God was part of the reality he chose. I will leave you with another great philosopher whose thinking on occasion was off the beaten path. That would be baseball's great Yogi Berra who some believe said, "When you see a fork in the road, take it." (students roared) "Peace be with you. Thank you students and thank you Cornell."

Students stood and applauded with loud enthusiasm.. Local journalists who observed, listened and wrote the story of Eric's presentation. In their notes were passages that revealed a connection made between Father O'Reilly and his audience of mainly undergraduates. The political nature of his speech following the Vietnam era was very critical of our foreign policy and utilization of military power. The television and print media were quick to record it all for the next days news. Standing in the rear of the auditorium was an attractive English teacher who quietly observed the auditorium. Her feelings were sprinkled with notions of optimism.

Chapter 64

The crowd of students remained and worked their way closer to Father O'Reilly who was being interviewed by local media; students wanted to see the priest who made them take notice of issues facing them; their questions were directed at him from all directions. Father Morley had to assume the role of moderator and prefaced the moment by saying. "We have time for a few questions but please allow me to select one student at a time. Please.... Thank you. OK this young woman in the third row."

An attractive woman then asked Father O'Reilly. "Father O'Reilly, what is your view of celibacy?" Eric smiled and student murmurs could be heard. It appeared obvious that students were thinking about how a very attractive man could abstain from his sexuality. Eric's response was direct. "If you have ever fasted or dieted you know how difficult it can be. Abstinence requires discipline, prayer and a devotion to serve Christ, not self indulgence. The Church believes that marriage would distract men from serving Christ with total commitment. It would be difficult but I believe that some day this policy which is not biblical, may be changed as other faiths have done. Obviously, I have chosen my commitment and will and must abide by it." Another student chimed in when Father Morley pointed toward her. "You spoke of two children that you were going to bring to America. Had they not been tragically killed, would you have reconsidered being a priest?" Eric nodded. "I have asked myself the same question. Maybe, as some would believe, God had a different plan for me. But to answer your question. Maybe not because I would feel obligated to parent and provide for those children. This of course demonstrates how and why the church maintains their policy of celibacy. Parenthood and priesthood may present challenges that are difficult to reconcile. I see that more clearly now." Father Morley then interrupted with. "OK, three more questions. This gentleman on the end wearing the white jacket." The student seemed shy and struggled with his question. "You are a Jesuit. Why did you select that order?" Eric was pleased that he was asked this question. It gave him an opportunity to praise his brethren who were responsible for his superior education in liberal arts and philosophy. Eric responded: "Jesuits were and are responsible for some of the finest educational institutions in Europe and America. They examined their conscience through meditation and prayer and were intellectual reformers who inspired learning and discipline wherever they lived and worked. In fact, besides my degree from Cornell, my Jesuit training made my military experience more meaningful and productive. In some ways it may have saved me on the battlefield. When I read about Ignatius Loyola, the founder of the Society of Jesus, I knew it was for me. In fact, I was about your age." Father Morley interrupted again, "OK, two more questions." The young man over here with the red hat." The student was poised and direct. "If you were not a priest, what other vocations would have you considered." Eric smiled and said. "First of all, I don't like to play should of/would of, but in order to answer your question I will simply say, work that in some way attempts to uplift people and society. There are many possibilities for this type of work and I hope that all of you will take the time to reflect upon the many ways you can do good things. Being a priest is one of many ways to serve your community. Teaching, social work, psychology, and good parenting are just a few of many choices facing you." Father Morley looked at his watch, then said. "OK one final question." He pointed to a student who had raised his hand throughout with determination. Father Morley had noticed and said. "Alright this student who has been trying to get my attention, yes you." The student was pleased and excited to be selected. "Father O'Reilly, what is your opinion about birth control and divorce. The church accepts annulments but not divorce which many regard as hypocrisy. In other words if you pay the church a fee, in some cases your marriage can be annulled." Father O'Reilly was really put on the spot. He looked at Father Morley, smiled and said. "I will answer the second question and allow Father Morley to answer the first question." Father Morley did not respond but agreed by his nodding his head. Then Eric responded. "Divorce happens more today than ever before. One of the most difficult decisions that you will make in your life is deciding upon the person to marry. There's nothing more important for the success of your future marriage. Too many couples give up their commitment to one another. That could mean they really didn't know each other well enough. Some have said that our laws should make it more difficult to get married. Mandate more counseling for men and women who want to marry. Ask them the difficult questions that married couples have to live with that will make them think more rationally about their decision. If all the right steps are taken and the marriage still fails, then divorce may be the only way out. Of course the Church does not agree but maybe over time they will see things differently, especially if divorce rates continue to rise." Eric then looked at Father Morley who was assigned the second question.

Father Morley then interjected with: "Thank you Father O'Reilly. I must admit you all have asked excellent questions. Concerning birth control, let me say this. First of all married couples should know they both want children. God has given us a mind to think and make decisions. It's called free will. If you are married and either couple practice a method of birth control you are exhibiting your decision based on free will, a gift from God. The decision of practicing birth control should be made for moral and personal reasons; for every individual that is different. Religion and science must merge on this question. At one point in history, the Church believed the earth was flat and was the center of the universe. Galileo proved otherwise. So you see, over time our religious institutions realign themselves with our scientific knowledge. The two need not be incompatible." The students were impressed by Father Morley's response and applauded loudly. Father Morley then thanked the students again and said: "Let's give Father O'Reilly another round of applause to thank him for his work in war and peace." Students responded with a very loud applause. "Thank you for coming this evening. See you Sunday morning. First mass is 9:30am." The two priests then were directed to a car because crowds had surrounded them. They were escorted to a security vehicle and driven to Father Morley's residence. For Eric, today was another day where his future options were front and center. Students' questions had opened his mind for self examination. However he hoped that his comments were not too inflammatory for the church he knew to be still very rigid and dogmatic. He feared that Father John Morley may have opened a "can of worms" for both of them.

Before arriving at Father Morley's residence, Eric was informed to expect a crowd of guests invited by his friend. When they arrived, a caterer and bartender were present serving food and drinks and after an hour and a half, Father Morley excused them, paid them and thanked them for their delicious food and friendly service. Eric was not aware of what was in store for him but as soon as the caterers left, Father Morley formally introduced his friend to his guests who included men and women of the homosexual community at Cornell who were professors, local teachers, lawyers and other professionals. When Eric realized what was going on he understood why the caterers were dismissed early. When Father Morley introduced his friend he said. "Good evening my friends. Many of you have spoken with my friend Eric who attended seminary with me. I wanted him to meet you for a number of reasons. First of all he is in my view a genuine hero; I'm sure you would agree. I have discretely informed Eric of our sexual orientation and am pleased that many of you had the opportunity to speak with him . Ladies and gentlemen, Father Eric O'Reilly." There followed a loud round of applause. While everyone waited, Eric realized he had to greet these people, but exactly what to say was not forthcoming. He began with. "Thank you for your warm welcome. I have spoken with some of you and am impressed with your fine work here in this dynamic community. I realize that your lifestyle is stifled by cultural and social customs, but I pray that your community will, with time, be accepted as Christ would want. We are all God's children and I for one will always work to support justice and equality no matter who you love." They applauded with warmth. Eric then added. "But unfortunately, in the world we live in, hatred, prejudice and discrimination are common practice directed against homosexuals and other minorities." One woman present waved her hand to be recognized. Eric said. "Yes, please," She was an attractive woman who wanted to raise an issue being discussed among homosexual communities. "I have read extensively about pejorative reactions to the word homosexual. We have in our community, prominent spokesmen who want to introduce a new semantic to American society for the purpose of softening and hopefully altering reactions. That word is "Gay" which has not been widespread as of this date but I would encourage all of us to utilize this word because in my view it may be less confrontational. Would you agree?" Eric smiled and said. "Well to be honest, I have never heard that term but would not oppose its use. Yes I agree. Words do have powerful meanings attached to them, so yes, a softer semantic would be appropriate." This same woman then asked. "Please forgive me for asking father, but are you gay?" Eric felt trapped. But his military composure came into play. There was absolute silence in the room. "You know at one time I was not sure until I went to therapy and was informed by a prominent therapist that I am not, to use the new term, gay. He clearly explained to me how my childhood experiences traumatized my self esteem and altered my sexual proclivities until well into my twenties. Then I met a very beautiful and wonderful woman who swept me off my feet. It was during that relationship that I began to recognize and accept my heterosexual attractions. For the time being I have forfeited romantic love for my love for Christ's work and I do hope that those of you who pray, will pray for my divine guidance. I have found that when I surrender to God's will, changes that result are best followed." Another guest then asked. "Father O'Reilly, there has been some talk of you running for political office. Are you interested?" More silence filled the room. But Eric's response was honest and direct. "Up to this point in my life I have allowed the holy spirit to guide me through many decisions. I have to remain in the present and not get too far ahead of myself. I am honored by those who feel that way but at this time it would be imprudent for me to comment on what lies ahead. I am a priest and will move forward with God's help and blessing. The end is not in sight." Father Morley then interrupted and recognized that the discussion had gone far enough. He actually felt sorry for his friend after all he put him through in one day. Many present also recognized that their discussion should now continue on a one to one basis. After another hour, the guests began filtering out but not before thanking Father O'Reilly for his encouragement and blessing. When everyone left, Father Morley looked at Eric. "Are you upset with me? I didn't mean to..." Eric interrupted. "No apology required. Your intentions were good for everyone, me included. In fact I want to thank you for the teaching moments you exposed me to. I have benefited from the experience. Of course you realize our comments....well you know, all hell may break loose, for both of us."

The next morning before Eric returned to Oswego, he and Father Morley watched morning television news that included videos of his speech. News media carried the story and Father O'Reilly now had national exposure. Father Morley poked fun at Eric. "I think you have a political future. Can I be your campaign manager?" Eric responded. "That would be a violation of church and state." They laughed themselves silly as Eric headed for his car. There were throngs of reporters approaching him along with video cameras. "Father O'Reilly, your speech last night was very well received by many in congress. Would you ever consider a run for office?" Eric looked at John who was standing behind him. They both chuckled. Another reporter asked. "Father O'Reilly, the U.S. Senate seat in New York is open next year. There's talk of getting you to run. Are you interested?" Eric's response was: "Ask Father Morley. I think he would be a great senator." Eric then excused himself as he approached his car and drove off. He realized his public exposure was problematic and his instincts told him there would be repercussions. National exposure of yesterday's publicity expanded his recognition and options. Nothing that happened in the last twenty four hours was planned. However Eric experienced a strange feeling about how his life had been altered; he did not know what it meant or where it would lead. Eric's personal experiences seemed to occur as his control over them vanished. Rather than resist this reality, he embraced it thinking of how his future was becoming more interesting and exciting.

Chapter 65

In the rectory, Father Hall was waiting to hear how much Eric had achieved during his visit to Ithaca initially for his therapy session with Dr. Neuberger. But it was all the extra curricular activities that became the topic of their discussion. "You know Eric, Bishop McCann called this morning to talk with you and would like to meet with you at some future date. He sounded adamant." The bishop of Syracuse diocese was considered a conservative by most standards and Eric wondered how disturbed he really was with his news making. "He wants you to call and arrange a meeting. I suggest you take care of that this morning." Father Hall smiled but Eric could tell it was bordering on cynicism. He chose not to respond immediately and began sipping his coffee and eating his eggs and toast. Just then their secretary Mrs. Davis came into the dining room and said there were a number of calls within the last half hour. First was a local reporter who wanted to interview Father O'Reilly. This was followed by Father Elwood, Catholic chaplin at the Newman Center at Oswego College who called asking if Father O'Reilly would speak on campus. Several other calls were received and Eric could tell that he had definitely stirred the pot. Eric waited for silence to fill the room and when it was restored he asked Father Hall: "And what does my friend and mentor think of these developments?" Father Hall sipped his third cup of coffee, carefully placed the cup on the saucer, folded his hands, took a deep breath and said. "Well Eric, I don't know what to think at this point. But you have made a name for yourself and in some ways have managed to divide public opinion in a number of areas. This would not be a problem if you were just a civilian but as a priest it places you and our church in a questionable position. I do however agree with you on the war. I think even a majority of public opinion will also see it your way. The bishop may of course find matters too political, especially your comments on other issues facing the church. That includes Father Morley's comments as well." Then he paused and smiled. "You are a true Jesuit." And continuing said: "You know Eric there is a Chinese proverb: 'Nothing can stop an idea whose time has come.' The problem is, in my view you and Father Morley are too far ahead of the church. You may want to lay low for a while and allow things to settle. Just be pastoral." He said that with a grin. Eric remained silent. Allowed the moment to sink in. "You know Father Hall, this was not something that I planned. I was asked to speak by the pastor of Cornell's Newman Center at the spare of the moment. I kept it short but students asked many questions afterward and it took a life of its own. In retrospect, it was meant to be. I spoke the truth as I see it and cannot look back with regret. But I hear you and will abide by your advice. Time to be pastoral not political." Their day was now filled with tasks that had to be addressed. Father Hall excused himself and Eric remained and poured another cup of coffee. He began to assess all the variety of events and emotions that continued to mount. There appeared to be a message contained in all of these matters for consideration but Eric did not want to get ahead of himself and decided to take Father Hall's advice and enjoy the peace, solitude and joy of being pastoral. He decided to turn down all requests and demands made for him and directed Mrs. Davis to make the necessary calls on his behalf. He then went to a small chapel in the church and prayed for guidance and wisdom. When he returned, he called Bishop McCann and arranged to meet with him later that week.

When Eric made his appointment with Bishop McCann he did not speak with him personally. Whether that was usual or not was unknown. However, if the response of the secretary he spoke with was to be taken at face value, he was not in for a pleasant reception. That was his gut instinct at work and when in doubt, go with your gut. Maybe she was privy to some private conversation between the bishop and others. And maybe it was nothing but his imagination. He would prepare for the worst. Time would tell.

Chapter 66

The bishop's residence was located in an impressive structure which personified the hierarchy of a long established institution such as the Roman Catholic Church. The architecture exuded authority, beauty and strength. It was magnificent and Eric could not help but feel humble in the surroundings. The church, he thought, possessed control over others in so many ways; architecture was definitely one of them. Eric had to walk a very long distance from where he parked his car. He wondered why the gatekeeper would not allow him to drive closer to the bishop's residence. The long walk however allowed him time to imagine the gravity of what could be waiting for him. Then he thought of Vietnam. Nothing could be that bad, not even close. He gained his strength and composure by placing himself in his former military frame of mind. For the time being, he was Captain O'Reilly, not Father O'Reilly. That worked for a while but he soon realized when he saw his reflection in a large window as he approached the entrance that he was a man of the cloth. The arched doors were massive oak with large brass hinges. He rang a door bell and waited longer than he thought was necessary, so he rang a second time. He could hear the chimes inside, muffled by the solid structure. Then an intercom sounded. "Please state your name." Eric was now getting annoyed but he responded and within seconds, the door was electronically unlocked. He walked into a grand foyer when the woman greeting him was interrupted by an assistant. "Father O'Reilly, welcome. Would you please follow me." They walked through a grand hallway into a waiting room. "His eminence will see you shortly. Please make yourself comfortable." Eric sat in a comfortable leather chair and gathered his thoughts for what could be an interesting day. His mind wandered toward all the possibilities that faced him and he was genuinely amazed at how events that unfolded had a life of their own. He realized he had very little control over his predicament; it certainly was not planned but only happened as a chain reaction from what Father Morley had initiated. Destiny has few limitations.

While Eric waited he began to imagine his life ten years down the road. Where would he be? Where would he want to be? His daydream was gravitating toward what he imagined would make him happiest when suddenly he was interrupted by the assistant who returned. "The bishop will see you now." Although he heard the assistant, his thoughts were elsewhere because he was in the midst of his wonderful unfulfilled dream and wanted to allow himself time to finalize the succession of images his mind projected. Like most dreams they remained incomplete but meaningful in some mysterious way.

When Eric walked into bishop McCann's office, the bishop was reading one of many pieces of mail that cluttered his desk. He stood and greeted Eric warmly. "Well Father O'Reilly. I have been waiting to meet with you privately since your return from Vietnam. We are all very pleased with your safe homecoming and commend you for your distinguished service and honors. I have just returned from Rome and must inform you that the Holy Father sends you his prayers." He directed Eric to be seated at a table far removed from Bishop McCann's massive desk. Eric thought it strange and imagined his status in the hierarchy ladder was at the lowest rung. He waited for the fireworks to begin. "Well Father O'Reilly, you must have wondered why I requested this meeting with you. After reading, hearing and viewing your performance at Cornell last week I thought it important to discuss matters of propriety. I'm certain you can understand why." Eric remained silent and nodded affirmatively. The bishop continued. "You know Father O'Reilly, it is important for church dogma and policy to be properly vetted before it becomes overcharged with emotion and libertarian theology or ideology. Our flock must be led not stirred. Proper deliberation of controversy must be maintained so when and if change is to occur, it is through proper channels. Controversy over catholic doctrine concerning marriage, divorce, celibacy, birth control and other social issues must be guided by our principles of faith, not haphazardly introduced in public forums. Our formal decorum is in place for a reason and good reason. To promote our catholic faith and principles. I believe you may have opened us up to controversy which can divide Catholics; that is counter productive. Would you agree?" Eric didn't know what to think or how to respond. Obviously the bishop was well schooled in rhetorical devices. He was stunned by the insinuations and inflexibility of his bishop and began to feel a kinship with other dissidents. Martin Luther was excommunicated and the Bohemian, John Huss, was burned at the stake for questioning transubstantiation. Eric controlled his displeasure and anger. The bishop was waiting for his response so he felt he had to say something. Was contrition expected because if so he did not feel contrite. He responded by saying: "Some your eminence would argue that healthy discourse will make our church stronger and more democratic. Discussion and debate can be therapeutic and create teaching moments. You should not fear healthy debate; it will make our church stronger through transparent and reasonable dialogue. History has taught us that important lesson. Would you agree?" Eric could tell that Bishop McCann was not pleased with his response but rather than pursue his argument the bishop responded by saying: "Well you do make a good point; that much I give you but we must in the future conform to procedures in place; I hope you will comply." Eric pleasantly agreed. His frustration was for the time, being subdued. Then the bishop had another involuntary offer for Eric. "Father O'Reilly, the Holy Father has asked me about you and is very interested in meeting with you. He like millions of others has heard and read about you and is also impressed with your academic record as am I. During my most recent correspondence with him I suggested that you be offered an opportunity to study in the Vatican where you could be schooled in reform initiatives introduced by Pope John during his much too brief tenure. The Holy Father was amenable to this suggestion so you will be assigned to Rome for at least one year of study at THE PONTIFICAL LATERAN UNIVERSITY. Ironically this university was established by Pope Clement XIV after he had suppressed the Society of Jesus, the founding institution of Jesuits. It is also known as THE POPE'S UNIVERSITY. I hope this opportunity will allow you to experience the totality of our faith and to expose you to ramifications of political and cultural movements currently experienced by our church in a changing world. In this envelope is a brochure with information that you should read." Eric was amazed at the ingenious manipulation by the bishop of recent events. He was being ostracized; of this he was certain, but in a way that offered a positive outcome for him as well. Sort of a win/win. Now the media could not approach Father O'Reilly because he would be isolated within the walls of the Vatican. This was a clever maneuver by the bishop, Eric had to admit but it was also a once in a lifetime opportunity to study and learn, two interests highly regarded by Eric. "So what do you have to say about this new assignment?" Eric could not help but smile and offered a bit of humor in his response. "Your eminence, if this is punishment, I willfully accept. If this is a commendation, I humbly accept. My only question is, which is it?" Bishop McCann enjoyed Eric's humor and laughed heartily. He approached Eric. "You know Father O'Reilly, now that I have met you I can honestly say it is a little of both. I congratulate you for your wit and curiosity. I must admit that I am very impressed with your academic and intellectual success, both at Cornell and in seminary training. I've heard nothing but praise. That alone speaks volumes. Add to that your exemplary military record, topped off by the Congressional Medal of Honor and a Purple Heart, well, it doesn't get any better than that." These praiseworthy comments altered any ill feelings Eric may have had of Bishop McCann. The remaining time was spent talking about Syracuse Orange football and how they would compete. They both enjoyed distractions sports offered. Before leaving, Eric told Bishop McCann the story of one of his fellow seminarians who quit his training when Monsignor Quaid turned off the television during the seventh game of the world series. Laughing aloud, the bishop asked: "And what is this man doing currently, do you know?" Eric did know because he had a conversation with this particular friend recently after Sunday mass. "He's happily married, has a child and another on the way." The bishop smiled and patted Eric on the shoulder. "My best regards to your friend. For him, that was the right choice." They walked toward the exit. "I will have all the necessary papers mailed to you. Apply for your passport and I will have the procedure expedited. I would estimate that you will be heading for Rome as soon as all required papers are complete. Meanwhile avoid the press and controversy." He gave Eric that look of concern. "It has been a pleasure meeting you Father O'Reilly. You will have to excuse me. A bishop's day never seems to end. God bless you." Eric thanked him and began the long walk to his car. Words spoken earlier by the bishop were recalled. "For him that was the right choice." Eric wondered, had he made the right choice. He tried in vain to complete his earlier dream cut short; his current state of mind could not reconstruct images of happiness felt less than an hour earlier. Apparently this formidable assignment was an opportunity that altered his primal instincts.

The drive to Oswego allowed Eric time to reconstruct his future plans. After over a year of devoted service to his home parish, he was being reassigned to the Vatican for enrichment of his intellect. Most citizens were not well informed of the caliber of education provided by the Vatican hierarchy. As a Jesuit, Eric thought he could pursue through his study, the true meaning and purpose of Christ's church. There were after all theological transgressions made by dogmatic, ultra conservative and inflexible autocrats who Eric believed misinterpreted and misrepresented original texts in Greek biblical liturgy. He wanted to research the bible and this meant he would have to advance his skill of Greek. He did study some Greek at Cornell and Seminary but now became focused on improving his reading proficiency. The Greek language, he believed, held the secrets of Christ's teaching and theology. It was the language of scholars during the life of Christ. Eric believed translation from Greek to Latin corrupted the integrity of original authors, scholars and the apostles.. He felt compelled to investigate; to seek truth and accuracy through scholarly corroboration of biblical scripture. His interest in this subject was motivated by Descartes, a man noted for his noble and intellectual qualities. Descartes believed that God's greatest gift to humanity was our intellect and it was no secret that Descartes wanted our minds to explore and learn using rational processes. What is important is truth. Eric felt the church was not being truthful with its mainstream theology. His goal would be to find the true meaning of Christ's message. He would also have to explore Buddhism and Hinduism because within their tenets were references that connected to Christ's teaching. The Church discarded and discredited those schools of thought; Eric wanted to find answers. He had a year in Rome and wondered if he could uncover the true and fundamental core of Christianity in that time.. He also wondered whether his mission would even be permitted. Jesuits were still known for their intellectual audacity so Eric would have to plan his strategy when he completed his application.

There are four faculties at the Lateran University, theology, philosophy, Canon Law and Civil Law. Eric wasn't sure if he would be assigned to one or whether he would be able to make his own choice. He preferred philosophy and would make that his preference. He also realized being in Rome would isolate him from pressures he was feeling from many sources as a parish priest. In the Vatican he would not be distracted by duties required at St. Mary's. No press or publicity. He really didn't like to be hounded by media sources, politicians and other special interests. Michelle was his only exception. Bishop McCann had served him well. Eric thought he had misjudged him. But then Eric realized, Bishop McCann was after all a Jesuit.

Chapter 67

When Eric returned to the rectory, television and newspaper reporters approached him seeking interviews. Magazines like TIME, NEWSWEEK and a variety of others also were hoping to get a story. There were cars and television crews parked in front of the rectory; Eric could barely work his way through. This was exactly what Bishop McCann feared. He managed to enter the rectory where Father Hall stood warding off crowds of media journalists. When he saw Eric approach, he suddenly ended his conversation and with the help of local police, quickly led him into the rectory avoiding a barrage of questions shouted by reporters. "It's been like this since 8 o'clock this morning." Father Hall seemed upset but realized that he had to maintain his composure. He looked at Eric and grinned. "Well, any ideas?" He peered out a window and saw two police cars; officers were asking media crews to withdraw to their vehicles because the sidewalk was being blocked while inside their secretary, Mrs Davis, was busy answering telephone calls and had a long list of messages received for Father O'Reilly. It was the next call that created even more tension. Mrs. Davis walked to Father Hall who was having a conversation with Eric. "Father, the telephone call is for you. It's Bishop McCann." Father Hall did not know what to expect. Bishop McCann did however have a plan. "Good morning Father Hall. I have been informed by the Syracuse Post Standard that you have a large crowd of media journalists and television crews outside the rectory. Here's what I want you to do. Read them the following statement. Have your secretary take this down." Father Hall handed the phone to Mrs. Davis whose shorthand would be necessary. After a few minutes she confirmed that she had every word exactly as spoken by the bishop. She handed the phone back to Father Hall. "Now listen Father Hall, after my message is typed by Mrs. Davis, proof read it to me and then I want you to read it to the media. At this time, my press secretary is driving to Oswego; he should be there within the hour." Mrs. Davis's efficiency impressed Eric as she typed the message and handed it to Father Hall who read it over the phone to Bishop McCann. It read as follows:

"Father O'Reilly will not take any questions from the media. All questions however can be addressed to Bishop McCann's press secretary who will arrive in Oswego within the hour. Arrangements have been made with Hotel Pontiac on 1st Street. Refreshments will be served. I will not answer any questions. Thank you. This announcement is made at the direction of Bishop McCann, Diocese of Syracuse." Within minutes of proof reading, Father Hall in a very composed manner addressed the media with the Bishop's directive. The gathering media reluctantly dispersed. The bishop also informed Father Hall that a priest would be sent to St. Mary's to fill Father O'Reilly's position.

Bishop McCann directed Father O'Reilly to return to Syracuse where he would reside in isolation from public scrutiny at the bishop's residence. He was directed to pack all his clothing for his eventual departure to Rome. He gave Eric five days to terminate his duties at St. Mary's and was not to conduct mass or speak in public. Once again Eric marveled at how events were taking over his life. He realized that he no longer had control of events. The tail was wagging the dog. Of course he could take control and refuse, leave the priesthood and begin a new life at that very moment but something told him to hold on and surrender to circumstances before him. This was without doubt another fork in the road. He asked himself: "How would his situation be different if this never happened?" When he thought about this possibility he concluded that opportunity presented itself once again but his other options were there for the taking, so Eric decided to consult with his mentor Father Hall for advice. They adjourned to his office where they could exchange ideas for Eric to consider. Mrs. Davis was told, no calls or interruptions.

Eric felt pressured. "Father, what should I do? I'm torn and confused." Father Hall opened his bottom drawer and removed a bottle of Bushmill's Irish Whiskey that was half full. He poured two glasses, and without saying a word he clicked his glass with Eric's. "Drink up. This is going to be a long and interesting conversation. "You first." Eric sensed that Father Hall was getting pleasure out of this predicament. In fact Eric imagined his mentor would love to be in his shoes. Eric began with: "Like most options, there are positives and negatives." Father Hall suddenly stopped Eric. "Hold on Eric. Before you go any further answer one question. Be honest because it's very important. Are you in love with Michelle?" Eric finished his drink before he answered. "And don't tell me you're not sure. It's either yes or no!" He poured Eric another drink. Eric became flush with the sudden jolt of whiskey, but he was relaxed when he answered.

"Yes I am, but I would prefer to delay any plans with her until I give myself more time and distance. Is that fair? Is that reasonable?" Father Hall nodded his head and confessed it was. He also confessed that one early morning as he walked into church from the rectory, he noticed a beautiful woman praying in the last pew. It was Michelle. He waited for her to finish and as she was leaving greeted her. He wanted to share their conversation with Eric. "She told me that her promise to you was not to interfere with you in any way. She wanted to assure me that her wish was for your personal and professional happiness. I asked her what I just asked you. Her answer was yes, very much so, but what's important is for Eric to make this decision." Eric noticed Father Hall's emotion surfacing before he spoke. "I hope you understand the reason for my involvement. I have known you since your birth and anguished over the pain and suffering you endured as an innocent child. I know how you have suffered through your adulthood. My heart ached for you throughout. I felt your pain. You are like family to me." Tears dripped down his mentor's face. Eric reached out to grasp his hand. "Now all that I wish for is your happiness. Go to her and let her know so that she can and will wait for you." Eric felt such admiration for his friend and mentor. His assessment was correct; Eric should visit with Michelle; he did love her and should tell her so; his plans included her, but not now. Would she wait for him until he could find the will to release himself? He was twenty seven, she was twenty five. Would she wait two more years? Suddenly Eric remembered the dream cut short while waiting for Bishop McCann in Syracuse. The happiness he felt was Michelle giving birth to their first child. He would have to share his blissful dream with her.

Chapter 68

Eric knew eventually his congregation would learn of his departure and some would figure out the reasons. He could not be too concerned because there was very little control on his part. Father Hall would announce that the Holy Father called him to Rome in recognition of his academic achievements and to teach and study at the Lateran University which was true. As for Father Morley, he was also reassigned to a small church in the mid west. In retrospect, his comments on birth control proved to be more controversial. The two exiled priests spoke with one another before their departure and each promised to write as well to ascertain their different situations. A telephone call between them revealed their sentiments. The call came to the rectory on Eric's last night there before moving to his parents for the last four days in Oswego. Mrs. Davis had left and Father Hall had not returned from his weekly class with couples prior to their matrimonial vows.. Eric was surprised when he answered the phone and it was John Morley. "Hello, this is Father O'Reilly." John Morley was pleased Eric answered. "Hello Eric, this is John Morley, remember me." They both chuckled almost as a reaction to their anxiety. "Yes John what's the latest? Have you been chilled into silence or is it worse." John responded with: "I've been deported to a small church in Madison, Wisconsin. I leave in two days. I will still be serving students so that makes it easier. How about you.?" Their discussion centered on making the most of what happened. "Who knows where this will lead us Eric but I insist we keep in touch." They exchanged their addresses and would have mail forwarded by their parents.

"Eric remember what I said about the possibility for leaving the church. Something tells me that's in our future." Their conversation ended when Eric heard Father Hall entering in the distance. "I will keep you informed; do likewise John. Good luck." When Eric went to his room to finish packing his belongings he realized how his time with John changed his life. Now he wanted to try his best to control events, not the other way around.

His few belonging were packed in his car which had fewer than three thousand miles; the car was barely broken in. He planned on having dinner with his parents and looked forward to his mother's cooking but first had to see Father Hall to say farewell to his closest ally. He didn't want to depart on a sad note. When Father Hall came to his room they moved to the parlor where they sat and wondered how quickly Eric's situation evolved. "You know Eric it is amazing how your life plans changed so quickly. There are positive and some unknown reasons for this; we don't have a clue what they are. Do You?" Eric thought for a moment and said. "Whatever it is Father, I just want you to know that you have always been there for me; many thanks. I will write to you and keep you posted. I will also take your advice about my personal life before I leave." They embraced and Eric walked to his car dressed in slacks and a collared shirt. He drove to a gas station that had a telephone booth on the outside wall. He called Michelle. When she answered he told her he would like to meet with her; they drove to a secluded area on the lake shore in her car. He would be direct and forthright and decided to disclose his past history so she could make an informed decision. When he looked at her he knew their future would depend more on her forbearance than anything else.

"Michelle, I called so I could personally let you know what I would like to happen between us. Please listen and allow me to tell you everything before you respond." She looked at Eric and felt his priestly tone but managed to accept his preconditions. "That's reasonable, all I ask for is your honesty." Eric concurred. He began: "First of all Michelle I want you to know that I am in love with you and do want us to have a future together, but first and foremost I want to explain my personal history. When I was four years old I was sexually molested. My mother walked into my bedroom when this happened to me and screamed. It was her brother, my uncle. The impact on my life has remained with me; I repressed this ugly experience that created anxiety and made me question my sexuality and relationships with men and women. I want you to know my personal history so you can make an informed decision and understand why my relationship with you was mitigated by my psychological history. You know Michelle, I may be damaged merchandise; you should know this. I have been told by my therapist that choosing priesthood offered me an escape from my guilt and shame. I blamed myself and was filled with guilt until Father Hall and my therapist rescued me. I was told by my therapist this gruesome episode may explain why I gravitated toward priesthood; to wash away the filth and guilt. I have lived with chronic emotional discomfort but I became a priest with good and noble intentions and now feel an obligation to my church because in some strange way, it has given me the time and space to know my true self. When we met I realized something was not right. Your love changed my life. However I still feel I need closure with my priesthood and church. I have recently been informed that I have an opportunity to teach and study in Rome. I cannot walk away from this opportunity and my vocation, just yet. Before I leave the priesthood I want to hopefully enlighten the church I love by uncovering true biblical teachings and interpretations that have been covered up by theological imposters. All institutions have good and bad elements. The church is no different. Now I have a unique opportunity to at least try to make the church more original and transparent so Christ's true message is known. I am asking you to wait for me until I return from Rome where I will have the opportunity to research original transcripts in Greek and Sanskrit. I understand your concerns because I have disappeared from your life more than once so I will not demand any absolutes. I just want you to know I need this time, probably two years, to do work that for me, has to be done. You asked me to be honest and I have been. Now I will expect the same from you." Michelle was lost for words. She had to digest an assortment of unexpected information. For the first time in their relationship Eric sensed her disappointment; she appeared confused and lost for words. When she regained her composure her response made Eric lose hope. "Well it's not every day that I have to relegate myself to the status of lady in waiting, all for what appears to be your preoccupation with religious purity displayed by your sanctimonious obsession. I cannot honestly say that I am willing to wait two years but I will agree to one. I have to draw a line somewhere and if you learn that your feelings for me change, I would expect to be immediately informed. You have placed limits on my capacity for loving you and as you have said, you may be damaged merchandise. I don't believe you are. In one years time I want to be assured that your love for me is as strong as my love for you. You may have to abbreviate your mission for the woman you love. That would prove to me your true feelings and intentions. If you said to me you wanted to complete a PH.D, I would expect to be with you as your wife. Why not that option instead. I would teach and support you and we could be together. I want what you want Eric; being a wife and mother are core values of mine and for our future. You have to know this now before you leave me again. Maybe your therapist was right. You became a priest for reasons that were honorable but not intellectually honest. God understands your pain and so do I. Sorry if your feelings are hurt but I have to be real with you. It hurts me to be real Eric." Michelle's eyes were filled with tears. Eric realized he miscalculated her response. He didn't want to lose her and told her so. "Michelle, I do love you and will agree to one year." Then impulsively he asked her. "Will you marry me when I return?" She broke down and cried out: "Yes, yes I will. Do you really mean it?" He embraced her and knew without a doubt that his feelings were sincere. Then he looked at her and she intuitively sensed that Eric was not finished. "You mean there's more." Eric waited for a moment to respond. "Michelle, there is one more thing you should know. I am being given this opportunity to study in Rome because of what happened in Ithaca. The bishop was upset when the national media exposed the contents of that evening. He strongly believes I would be hounded by media and journalists who want more information of catholic social policies that are controversial. So his solution was to get me out of sight for a while; I am being exiled to Rome, if you know what I mean. He fears these issues could explode and lead to negative publicity the church cannot afford. Her response surprised Eric. "I know, I was there in Ithaca when you gave that talk and knew you were in trouble. I'm glad you told me this because now I can clearly understand your situation."

Eric had one more thing on his mind. He wanted to return to the rectory with Michelle before Father Hall retired for the evening. Eric wanted him to know his plans, formally introduce Michelle and reveal their plans in the year ahead. He was fortunate that he still had his keys when they arrived at the rectory. When they entered, Father Hall heard the door and walked to the hallway. Eric called his name and he appeared holding a book with his finger marking the page. "Eric, is everything alright." Eric turned as Michelle walked in behind him. "Father, I want to introduce you to Michelle. When I return from Rome we would like to know if you will marry us here in St. Mary's." Father Hall approached and extended his arms around them. "That is the best news I've heard in a long time. I would be honored. You of course explained to Michelle your reasons for leaving the scene of the crime." The three of them rolled their eyes and held back their laughter.

Chapter 69

The next day Eric awoke to greet his parents who were sitting at the kitchen table enjoying their morning coffee. Eric had come home too late to inform them of his latest news. "Good morning mom and dad." His cheerful mood came through and his mother could not help but notice his state of happiness. "Well you sound cheerful this morning. You must have a good reason." There was an expectation on her part for Eric to share his good mood. "Well mom and dad, are you ready." He paused and let them wait just for a moment before he announced: " Next year, when I return from Rome, Michelle and I will be married by Father Hall at St. Mary's." Both his parents moved close enough to embrace their son. They were thrilled. Eric explained all details and his parents were satisfied with his decision. They also realized how his name recognition was being spread throughout the media. His parent's telephone did not stop ringing all day. "One man called three times and asked me to have you contact him in Washington." Eric knew who it must be. And before he could blurt out his name, his father said: "It was Dave Dwyer. He said it was very important that you speak with him. What's this about Eric?" Eric thought about how to explain what he thought Dwyer's phone call concerned. "Well dad, Dave is a college friend, currently a political consultant in Washington. He wants me to run for office here in New York. How does representative O'Reilly sound?" His father was stunned. "You mean the U.S. congress?" Eric could tell his parents were getting overwhelmed by what could be waiting for him. "Mom, dad, first things first. I am going to Rome as I explained but I promised Michelle, at her request, actually at her demand, for only one year. She understands what's going on and knows the repercussions if I remain. You must keep this information private until things quiet down with the media. Just tell them I've been reassigned. As far as politics are concerned, that is something I will have to think about and even ask Michelle what she thinks." His mom hugged him and said. "Come, I want to make your breakfast. You're only here for two more days." Just then the phone rang. His mother answered. It was Dave Dwyer. She cupped the phone. "It's that man, your friend from college." Eric decided to take the call in the other room. When he picked up the phone his mother did hang up.

"Hello Dave. You are a determined man. What's up?" Dave was not one to mince for words. He got right to the point. "Eric, listen to me. I have spoken with the state and national chairmen of the Democratic party. They both agree you easily could win the election for congress in your district next year. Are you interested? Please say yes. I can and will get things in motion." Eric realized the political fallout from his recent public speaking event at Cornell had taken hold of public opinion. Dwyer then added. " I know all the details from your public debut in Ithaca. That's nothing to worry about. In fact, that event even adds more appeal to your political future." Eric then interrupted. "Listen Dave before you go any further you must know that I have been reassigned to Rome where I will teach and study at The Lateran University. I will be gone for a year." There was silence. Finally Dwyer responded. "Then what? Are you even interested in a political future? If not let me know because opportunities like this are rare and after two years in congress, we have you pegged for governor and beyond. You could be a political rock star Eric. Please don't drop the ball. This is big, really big. I will be with you all the way." Eric had to admit. "Well Dave I'm flattered with your offer, really, but it would be difficult for me to fully commit to this offer at this time." Dave interrupted. "Listen to me Eric. I am your point man. If you want I can get things in motion; whether your a priest doesn't matter. The timing is perfect because when you return there would still be time to run for congress. What I will do is make your interest known and allow you to make your decision, as long as it's before August 1st of next year. Does that sound reasonable? Think about it and I will be in communication with you. In fact, I'm visiting Rome with my fiance next spring and you can tell me at that time. Believe me, the timing is right for you." Eric was impressed with Dave's persuasive ability. "OK Dave, I need time to process; I will seriously think about it." He almost said, "and ask Michelle."

When he hung up the phone, both of his parents were waiting in the kitchen with open ears. They waited to be informed and did not pressure their son. He had enough on his plate so they were surprised when he asked them. "What do you think I should do. Dave wants me to run for congress next year. I must inform him next year, before August 1st." His parents sat down, looked at one another and could not believe what was transpiring with their son's life. His father was concerned about everything moving so fast. "Maybe this is too much, too fast. Maybe you need a break and allow your time to be spent with Michelle when you return. Of course, I'm sure you will run this by her." Once again, Eric heard wisdom coming from his dad. He nodded a yes. "I was thinking the same thing dad. Thanks."

Michelle and Eric had to be discrete about their relationship so they waited for late evening before they would see one another, usually at Eric's home. Eric was anxious to hear Michelle's reaction. When she appeared in the dark of night, his parents were in bed. They knew she would be visiting and wanted Eric to have complete privacy. She understood his status as a priest and humored Eric when she entered. "Father O'Reilly, will you please hear my confession." They seemed to understand their relationship was somewhat tenuous but Eric wanted to hug her so he did in a very romantic way. She understood their situation and was graceful. "Well you are not going to believe the latest." Her reaction was: "How much you want to bet? With you there's never a dull moment." He laughed and squeezed her hand and opened a bottle of her favorite red. When he looked at her he felt desire and she could tell he was holding back; so was she. He sat in a comfortable chair and she sat on the sofa close enough to hold his hand. Then she raised her glass of wine. "What should we drink to?" Eric thought to reply with a typical yet personal reply. "Michelle, here's to our love and happiness with God's blessing." She smiled. "That's a perfect and a beautiful toast. So what's the good news; I'm being optimistic." Eric held her hand. "Michelle, my friend from Cornell, Dave Dwyer who apparently is a well connected political consultant in Washington called today and asked if I would be interested in running for Congress next year. Apparently the timing is good and I have to inform him by next August. I've been approached before but this is a definite offer. I need and want your opinion." She inhaled deeply. "Well Eric what would you like to do. I think this is your call. How did you leave it with Dwyer?"

"I told him my plans in Rome beginning in May and that my intentions were to teach and study for one year. He said that's fine as long as I let him know by August 1st. In fact, next spring, he and his fiance are vacationing in Italy and he will meet with me there to discuss details. I haven't revealed our plans for obvious reasons; you understand. I would like you to come to Rome the week before I return so we can enjoy the sights. We'll return together, sometime in June or early July." Michelle was thrilled that Eric included her in his plans. "Eric, I am so happy for us. I will be there for you no matter what you decide. I just want to be with you, that's all that matters." They looked at each other and the force of their attraction was too strong for them to resist. They passionately embraced then gradually realized their limits had been reached. Eric was relieved he had taken control of one important part of his life. When Michelle said good night he knew her love would sustain him during the year ahead. He decided not to reveal his future plan to run for congress. Too many unknowns have turned his life upside down.

Chapter 70

Eric wisely hesitated exposing Michelle to media attention so they decided to refrain from seeing one another the last few days. They would say their goodbyes via telephone conversation and through letters. Michelle was also concerned for her teaching position; avoiding Eric's company was difficult but necessary for both of them. Eric's father drove him to the bishop's residence. His mother wanted Eric and his father to have some private time as she knew it may strengthen their relationship.. She realized after her discussions with Eric that her husband was instrumental in helping Eric make some difficult decisions. Father and son once again found themselves together prior to another fork in the road for Eric. "You know dad, your advice during and after Vietnam helped me a great deal. You offered me a perspective I needed." His father was grateful for the compliment. "Eric, the important thing now is for you to find happiness, set your goal and always present your best image. Be genuine, honest and stick with your moral and ethical standards because the media will still be looking, listening and taking notes of your every move; you want to avoid mistakes; your image is important whether you are a priest or politician. You know what I mean." It was critical for Eric to hear his father's advice; he listened, knowing and appreciating the wisdom and emotion attached to every word. When his father drove away after a warm embrace, Eric had grown to love his father as never before. He also thought of his mother who had suffered during his childhood trauma and now as an adult, understood her good judgment of keeping her husband, Eric's father, separated from the tragic episode. It would have destroyed their family and changed everything. He endured his suffering and now knew he was a stronger person for it.

The bishop had informed his staff of the importance of maintaining silence in regard to Father O'Reilly's fortnightly visit. Eric had a very private room on the second floor where he could plan his teaching lectures on philosophy, a subject he enjoyed and one he felt was relevant to his political status. His lectures would have self imposed limitations to prevent any breach in canon law. He was not looking for trouble. He did not want to create any unnecessay challenges. His students would mostly be young men preparing themselves for ministering rites and theological tenets of Roman Catholic congregations in Europe and America. He was looking forward to being a professor and often wondered about teaching opportunities he declined; everything happened for a reason and he learned to accept how his life situations unfolded. His approach to teaching philosophy was to use a combination of classical and modern thinkers whose writings presented rational and theological arguments for believing in spiritual authority and embracing God's grace. Eric could read Greek and some Hebrew; it was this skill that would be used to challenge the Vulgate bible which humanist scholars centuries earlier had challenged for its inaccurate translation from Greek to Latin. Eric's scholarly interest in accuracy introduced him to past scholars who questioned the Vulgate translations and interpretations. Eric wanted to introduce his students to readings that might inspire them to reexamine canon laws that have been institutionalized by the Holy See, which maintains ecclesiastical jurisdiction of Roman Catholicism. Erasmus, a Dutch priest made this his mission during the 16th century and even though his work was negligible he resorted to satire when challenging errors so as to avoid prosecution from church authorities. Satire was a rhetorical device used by scholars who could humor their readers by playing with words. This was indirect criticism which was acceptable; direct, straight forward criticism was not. Erasmus also realized centuries ago that one error leads to others. The result was a perpetuation of scribal errors in the New Testament. One of Eric's goals was to detect any theological errors caused by careless translation or even intentional misinterpretation of scripture. Eric would need to inspire and mentor one or more young men to continue his quest for theological and biblical veracity. Knowing he would be leaving the church the following year, Eric wanted someone to carry on his concealed mission for reforming church doctrines. Certainly, he thought, there would be one student he could inspire to pursue a scholarly translation of the New Testament from ancient Greek scripture with truth at its core. Eric believed that Christ would have encouraged philosophers to seek truth through corroboration with other scholars. In fact this work had been started by 16th century scholars, Ambrose, Augustine and Jerome. Had Pope John 23rd lived there may have been a window of opportunity for revisiting holy scripture. Agents for change may be hidden within the walls of the Vatican and Eric decided at that moment to make it his mission to find them. It became quite apparent to Eric that he was a 20th century version of a scholarly dissident priest seeking to reform catholic liturgy, a common thread shared by few catholic scholars. Certainly he thought there were at least two young intellects studying for priesthood who shared his quest for reform by reexamining scripture.

Eric knew his confinement at the bishop's residence would pass more quickly if he maintained a busy schedule researching for his lectures. Bishop McCann supported his efforts which released Eric of any responsibilities that could possibly detract him. If the bishop had known Eric's true mission there would certainly be repercussions so Eric protected himself and made certain his notes were hidden in a secret pocket within his valise. His last evening before his departure was spent writing a letter to Michelle which he would mail at JFK. He realized this letter was in fact his first love letter to the woman who would one day be his wife. He kept it short, yet romantic.

DEAR MICHELLE,

I AM ABOUT TO BOARD MY FLIGHT AND WANT YOU TO KNOW HOW MUCH I LOVE YOU AND HOW I LOOK FORWARD TO OUR REUNION NEXT YEAR. PRAY FOR ME, BE STRONG AND BE ASSURED MY LOVE FOR YOU IS ETERNAL. PEACE AND LOVE, ERIC.

When Eric arrived in Rome dressed in his priestly attire, he received pleasant salutations from complete strangers. He was looking for a Vatican courier holding a sign with his name and found him standing behind a roped off area. Eric pointed to the sign and then pointed to himself. The courier was very accommodating and immediately took charge. Eric asked if he would drive by a few important sites before arriving at his destination. He was very happy to do so and artfully conveyed to Eric a story for each historic location. Eric wanted a preview of this marvelous city and was impressed how traffic moved with the assistance of traffic police blowing their whistles and waving their arms almost as though they were conducting an orchestra.

When he arrived at his resident hall, he was greeted by a Lateran University official who escorted him to his room on the third floor. The elevator was just large enough to handle the two men with Eric's luggage. The official was a student from Ireland who was completing research on his doctorate and worked as a resident assistant to defray costs. Eric sensed he was friendly and asked him a few questions. "How long have you been studying here?" Eric learned he had completed two years of research and was planning on returning to Ireland for the summer but would return in late August and submit his dissertation for review; if approved, he would apply for teaching assignments at several universities. "Then what?" Eric was just trying to be social and was surprised at his response. "Then I will be engaged to my sweetheart, get married and have a family. She has strong maternal instincts." If only Eric could have shared his plans and sentiments. His emotions were trapped inside.

The evening was spent with other priests who were familiar with routines that Eric would soon learn. Students were scheduled to arrive in late June and would have one week to arrange their housing, schedule, faculty adviser and orientation for class requirements. All were men who were in training for the priesthood and Eric was given a list of over 40 seminarians from all over the world. His search for profiling a future priest willing to devote himself to research that would possibly transform church liturgy and dogma began in earnest.

Chapter 71

Eric slept late on the day his official duties began. His morning coffee was what motivated him to move quickly, it was that good. Italians love their coffee and now Eric could understood why. They made American style coffee better than Americans and Eric would in one years time attempt to find the secret technique. The dining room was filled with students eating breakfast and perusing their course catalogs. There were required classes that were part of a priest's core curriculum but there was also room for a few electives. Eric was assigned to teach one of each and the remainder of his time could be devoted to research. In the dining hall he made a point of visiting each table and was surprised to hear his name mentioned as he passed. His fame had been revealed throughout the Vatican community; he had to expect some exposure and hoped it would work for him. As it turned out this particular morning he became a person of interest as the word spread. He joined a group of four young men at the far end of the dining room. There was one chair available. "May I join you?" The young men stood and bowed their heads in respect. "Thank you, but there's no need for that. Please be seated. I just want to meet the incoming recruits and your table had an empty chair. Welcome! Does everyone speak English?" One young man responded. "Yes, but with a Polish accent." The others laughed and volunteered their origins. Canada, Nigeria, Mexico were represented and the Austrian candidate commented. "Father if you can understand our English dialect, then all is good." The French Canadian followed: "How is your French, father?" Eric was impressed. "Well, I can see that you all arrived with a good sense of humor and I expect you will find it very useful here for a variety of reasons. My name is Father Eric O'Reilly and it is a pleasure to meet you. I will be teaching Canon Law and Philosophy. I am also researching New Testament scripture in Greek and will recruit at least two students as my assistants." Eric lost no time in spreading his research plans. Specific objectives would not be discussed until he had time to explain what he was looking for in original Greek scripture. He knew where to begin but needed time to allow the research to motivate questions in the minds of students, which he knew was the sign of someone who questioned authority. The Polish seminarian then said. "I can read and speak Greek. My mother is Greek. She married outside her culture and was abandoned by her parents for doing so. She has since reconciled with her family after years of living in Krakow. I have lived in Greece as well during holiday visits." Eric could not imagine a better candidate. Even though Eric also read Greek, his familiarity with linguistic nuances was very limited. "And what is your name?" Eric could not believe that at his very first meeting with students he found a candidate that offered him an unexpected advantage. Now if only his personality conformed with Eric's historical and theological agenda.

"My name is Joseph Rebelowski." The three other men then introduced themselves and Eric used his remaining time with them for casual conversation. When he excused himself, he discretely wrote down a name in his note pad. "Joseph Rebelowski" was now a student of interest. He thought it would be difficult finding another candidate with credentials so critical. As Eric walked through the dining hall to the exit door, young seminarians followed him with their eyes.

Each morning until classes began Father O'Reilly made the breakfast scene and word circulated concerning classes he would be teaching and his research intentions. Three days remaining were not wasted. On the last day before classes, Eric had met with all students with the exception of three who sat at a smaller table near the exit. When he approached their table they were aware of his plans to join them so one student stood up, offered Eric his chair and dragged a chair from an adjacent table. They were pleased to finally meet the celebrity priest whose fame had by now circulated throughout the entire campus. By this time, Eric had two names recorded in his notes as real possibilities, the Polish student he met the first day, and an Argentine of Italian descent. Eric's gut instincts led him to conclude they would be able and willing but he wanted one more. His thinking was for them to corroborate with one another; three heads are better than two. The three he was about to meet appeared more reserved and shy. After introducing himself, Eric asked a few questions about how their orientation was proceeding followed by where they called home. One was from Prague, a city with historical significance when it came to dissidents and protest. Eric's instincts led him to believe that the other two were not suited for academic research. He made that conclusion after considerable discussion with them and wanted to focus on the Czech; this young man was a possibility for a number of reasons that Eric read from his application and resume. His father was arrested for protesting against Soviet occupation which introduced his son to the horrors of living in a police state. He seemed to have a healthy dose of civil disobedience attached to his family history; his last name, Palacky, was a 19th century Czech " historian and statesman " who stimulated a revival of Czech culture. Eric asked Palacky to come to his office for a meeting to discuss an opportunity for doing research. He had already informed the other two candidates of his meeting of the minds. Palacky was interested and accepted Eric's offer. So now Father Eric O'Reilly had established what he hoped would be an intellectual exploration of the New Testament. Three young men would have to be coached to the subtleties and repercussions of research they were undertaking. Francis Palacky, Joseph Rebelowski and Giovanni Brogoglio were about to convene for a most interesting rendevous.

Classes finally began and Eric was thrilled to be teaching; as a child he remembered all his elementary teachers while attending Castle school in Oswego; they were fond memories. Teaching was something he always considered as a future possibility. And now he was involuntarily assigned to practice what he loved. Students create energy if teachers know how to tap into it and Eric's Socratic method worked wonders. He provoked students in his philosophy classes to challenge their conventional thinking of Christianity and Catholicism in particular. He was in fact setting them up to comprehend the mystery of faith; there will always be a gap between rational/logical contemplation and religion. Some would contend they are polar opposites; Eric believed they were not opposite, just different. Many Christian intellectuals had faith in God and Christ. The Enlightenment authors were conflicted. Some were deists including a few American forefathers. It was with this historical background that Eric framed his research objectives with his three confidants. He conveyed the politics of researching topics that questioned church dogma; he explained by referencing catholic intellectuals whose status was threatened by their transparency with original texts or their scientific discoveries such as Galileo. In fact Eric offered these young men the choice of withdrawing from their assigned task if they felt it was inappropriate or unethical. Joseph Rebelowski's response to that choice was: "Since when is truth unethical." The other two seminarians agreed. This understanding was important to establish from the beginning. Eric did not want to place these young scholars in compromising positions that could impact their future unless they chose to embrace intellectual dissidence. He would soon find out how far they wanted to go.

Eric realized his course outline could not reveal, in print, his intentions. He wrote a very general objective that would not draw attention or scrutiny. He required any written work submitted had to be taken from original sources or from secondary sources approved by him. Eric asked students to write their objectives without making any reference to questioning authority. His friend John Morley had advised him of this as a precaution. Eric did not want his students to be too specific in print hoping this would reduce the risk of a paper trail that could lead to problems. They understood and it was strange how this approach to research seemed to motivate them to look for information they may never have thought provocative. The three students were privately assigned topics by Eric; topics that reconfirmed or advanced Catholic teaching during the counter reformation, a time when church prelates made attempts to regain lost souls who drifted from Rome. He reminded his students of Catholic scholars, John Calvin, Martin Luther and others, who had through their research, discovered inconsistencies that were not well received by the Papacy. Eric conveyed the importance of encouraging students to research viewpoints that supported church doctrines as a hedge against a possible breach in his overall agenda, which ultimately was to ascertain the accuracy, validity and transparency of canon law and church doctrines. He had to be careful not to cross the line that church authorities over centuries had established. Students, on their own, without Eric's direction, would discover inconsistencies with church teachings and dogma. Eric's strategy, again, at the suggestion of John Morley, was to protect himself and his students from dogmatic autocrats who might become suspicious of any inquiry from an American priest with ambition. Eric saw the irony here. On the one hand he was asking students to document Catholic authority while at the same time asking them to uncover inconsistencies or malfeasance in established biblical interpretations. His plan seemed reasonable; both arguments were represented, but there was always the chance his true intentions could be inadvertently disclosed by his students. They were reminded of this problem. Being exposed for revealing truth was a chance Eric was willing to take. He realized when starting this project, a year was not going to be enough time to examine doctrines long established and agreed upon by the Curia. Before Eric left Vatican City the following year, his wish was for his students to become personally captivated by their own intellectual curiosity and continue pursuing what Eric believed were long established inaccuracies.

Chapter 72

Eric was amazed at how quickly time passed. He was enjoying himself because he was doing things he loved, teaching, mentoring, and research. Students found Father O'Reilly one of the most dynamic and accessible priests at Lateran University. His lectures were praised by his students and word spread that his superb teaching was provocative. He was however cautioned by the hierarchy to remain uncontroversial as word spread through administrative authorities that his capacity for creating controversy was a real possibility. But Eric understood the ground rules established for him so he avoided any outside attempts to lure him into a media event he would regret. When he received a package from his parents with their letters and with sealed letters from Michelle and one from his fellow seminarian, John Morley, Eric's uneasiness was soothed. When Michelle and Morley called his parents for Eric's address, they were told to correspond with Eric through them for obvious reasons. Of course this secrecy bothered Eric. The total disregard for his privacy fueled his antagonism with church authorities and justified his future intentions to leave the church and expose any historical and theological misinterpretations of holy scripture. One of his research strategies was to have his Greek scholar, Joseph Rebelowski, compare the liturgy of Greek Christians and Coptic Christians with Roman Catholics. Eric sensed he was being monitored so he always maintained his poise by projecting very pleasant relationships with his colleagues, but nevertheless thought it a good idea to purchase a small lock box where he could store personal items including letters and photos as well as documents that were controversial. He managed to find a small storage box that had a combination lock that was also designed for a lock and key which he purchased separately. He kept this item in his suitcase concealed in a compartment that he covered with casual clothing and underwear. The suitcase was also locked. The worse case scenario was he would be exposed by someone who managed to find his private correspondence so he included in his lock box a note that was readily exposed upon opening his lock box. It read: "Upon any violation of my privacy by the individual who has opened this box, your actions will be immediately exposed to the media for scrutiny." Followed by his signature. All of these measures were taken after he read a letter from John Morley who offered security precautions which Eric implemented. Morley also informed Eric to make every effort to meet a former priest living in Rome whose departure from priesthood was motivated by his affinity for Buddhism. He included his name but had no knowledge of his address. Morley also told Eric that life in the mid west was very pleasant. The college community offered him a social network that brought him in contact with a variety of cultures including one similar to the one he enjoyed in Ithaca, but was forced to leave when reassigned. He also informed Eric that the word "gay" was being used more in homosexual circles. Eric felt that it was just a matter of time before Father Morley would reject his current status for a lifestyle suited to his personality and needs. When Eric opened his parents letter, enclosed within the envelope was another sealed letter from Michelle. His emotions stirred as he reclined in a chair next to a window where natural light allowed for easy reading.

"My dearest Eric,

How I miss you and pray for your return every day. I have never told you that upon meeting you the first time I had a strong feeling of our future together. I become overjoyed knowing and feeling your love for me is now a reality and will lead to fulfillment of our dreams together. You must tell me about your new adventure and whether you are enjoying daily tasks before you. I attend mass every Sunday and Father Hall and I speak on occasion. He is truly a man of God.

My teaching manages to keep me busy. I am constantly grading essays and have been asked to assist my colleague with the Players Group which conducts drama activities. I am finding theater a wonderful escape from my daily teaching routines.

Your parents and sister have taken me into your family. I feel so welcome and our times together have brought us closer. Your sister Mary and I have also shared some fun time shopping and going to movies together. Your mother and I have had some discussions that I will share with you when we are together; I hope that is sooner rather than later. Please continue to write because it warms my heart to know your thoughts. I feel so much happiness knowing our love has guided us through our search for what is natural and beautiful between a man and woman. Please know that my love for you grows stronger every day. I will pray that your future and mine will continue to expand around God's gift of love we now share. I will save my best words of expressing my love for you in person when I arrive in Rome. Pray for us.

Love, Michelle

Eric was always impressed with Michelle's ability to say and do what was mature and very adult. In this letter he sensed how her writing skill conveyed love without overstating her message. She was saving that for a special future moment.

Eric now considered what Morley had communicated concerning a man who left the priesthood and was now a Buddhist. His name was Christopher Berdan. Eric had an interest in learning more about Buddhism because he had read papers by scholars who wrote about Christ's eastern sojourn during his twenties where he was exposed to Hindu and Buddhist teachings. Upon his return, scholars concluded, Buddhist concepts were incorporated into his sermons to vast crowds who learned of his message and supernatural power. Jesus had turned into a super star among thousands of masses who listened to his words and who experienced another face of humanity. According to some scholars his preaching revealed subtle rhetorical devices associated with a mind set that was foreign, more specifically, eastern. Eric always sensed the spoken words of Christ included several expressions tinged with an eastern paradigm. If this former priest, Berdan, converted to a Buddhist life, he would have knowledge of Christ's exposure to eastern culture. Eric wanted to find this man and introduce him to his research coalition. He could not explain a sudden trepidation he felt but it was real. Was Berdan, personna non grata within church circles. He did not want to create suspicion searching for this Buddhist intellect. There were directories in the library containing names of priests who attended, lectured and studied at Lateran University.

He decided at that moment to walk to the vast university library and investigate past directories that may include his name. Eric asked the attendent working at the library entrance desk about the whereabouts of directories of former scholars. She asked, "What year are you looking for? Do you have a name?" Eric realized he could not reveal a name so he said: "Actually there are several names all during the last five years. Would that work?" That seemed to satisfy her and she directed Eric to the area located on the third floor. When he approached tall stacks of shelves filled with books at the very end of the isle near the wall, he located directories there in front of him. He placed his hands on each and used his index finger to stop at the year 1973. Eric noticed that included with each name was place of residence, phone numbers and concise descriptions of their research. Using his hands and fingers he gingerly turned pages to the last name, Berdan, and was startled to see a name was neatly didacted. He could not decipher any identification. He looked in the 1972 and 1974 directories; there was no listing of Berdan. Eric concluded his name had been purged along with a brief description of his research. Now the trepidation he felt earlier was more apparent. His interest in pursuing this man's whereabouts was not deterred but rather intensified by his association with scholars whose ideas were considered heresy during past encounters with church hierarchy. Eric looked over his shoulder and noticed another priest had been staring through a book he was holding. He turned away and walked out as Eric noticed his stare. Once again Eric felt the arm of his powerful church imposing itself without justification. His military discipline took over and energized him; he used his anger to determine whether his gut reaction was on target. If his thinking was accurate, he had to move quickly. Eric immediately opened the purged directory to the title page and wrote down the publisher's name, address and phone number in Rome. Maybe the publisher might have a copy that included Berdan's name with vital information. It was worth a try.

Chapter 73

Eric's instincts reminded him that his exit from the library should not appear urgent. He stopped to chat with students so as to appear serene for anyone who might be watching. He then walked out and hailed a taxi and directed him to the Visconti Publishing House in the vicinity of the Fountain of Trevi. He requested to be dropped off near the popular site and walk the final two blocks in case he was being followed. He stopped and purchased an item from a vendor that he thought Michelle would appreciate. It was at that moment when the same priest appeared within close proximity. Eric then hailed another taxi and had him drive him several blocks before exiting. He did not notice being followed so he back tracked to the publishing house which he quickly entered. The woman at the desk was surprised to see a handsome priest walk up to her with his request. "Maybe you can help me. I need the directory listing former scholars who studied or taught at The Lateran school. Could you help me find that. I have limited time." He was surprised how his skill with Italian had improved over the last four months. She was very accommodating and sensed his urgency. "Please follow me." She lead Eric to the hidden staircase and directed him to the second floor. "Turn right and directories would be located on the first isle to your left." Eric quickly proceeded, found the directory for 1973, opened it and there it was: Christopher Berdan, professor of Philosophy and Religious Studies. Eric wrote down his phone number and address first. Then he read the anecdote included. "Father Berdan's studies include an in depth analysis of Christ's experiences with Buddhist teaching and how his sermons incorporated concepts taken from eastern philosophies." Eric was not just stunned by this information but was somewhat puzzled by the reaction of the church. What were the reasons behind suppressing Berdan's research? As Eric began his exit from the publisher, he noticed a public phone in the lobby. He hoped his luck would continue when he dialed Father Christopher Berdan. He answered on the fourth ring with a cheerful Roman greeting. "Buongiorno! Mi chiamo Berdan." Eric decided his English would be more pertinent. "Hello, I am Father Eric O'Reilly from the United States. I am currently studying and teaching in Rome and would like to meet with you to discuss a research project." Eric waited for his message to be processed, heard Berdan clear his throat followed by: "Well, what took you so long Eric? I have read about your most recent history and it is I who want to meet with you." It was then when Eric noticed the priest who followed him earlier. "I'm sorry but I am being followed. I will take a cab to your residence, ciao." Fortunately the telephone was hidden in an corner so Eric was not noticed. The priest who entered immediately walked up the stairs followed by Eric's hasty exit. At the closest corner he located a taxi and as he entered his heart was pounding when he thought about confronting this priest. That would have to wait. Berdan's residence was on the outskirts of Rome, a beautiful setting where he settled after meeting a former nun who left the church after meeting Berdan who resigned his priesthood rather than recant his research. They married late and had two children who were not only their pride and joy but also adored by maternal grandparents who often wondered why their daughter became a nun in the first place; she was and is a beautiful woman who was sought after by several suitors but her spiritual nature directed her toward a life of faith and service. When she met Berdan who would have been defrocked had he not resigned, the attraction was immediate for both. Berdan's wife's family were wealthy from their wine brokerage which provided a very comfortable life for their daughter, husband and children. When Eric approached the entrance of their country home he noticed a large vineyard in the foothills surrounded with beautiful grounds. Two dogs and a cat greeted Eric when Berdan opened the massive oak door. His wife Estelle and her parents were standing in the background holding two beautiful children. Eric imagined a future with similar circumstances. The loving atmosphere completely distracted him from tensions he was experiencing. Eric was led to an open veranda shaded with grapes on the vine that weaved through a massive arbor. Berdan was studying the art of making good wine. He not only enjoyed learning about new wines but also indulged in dark red spirits displayed throughout the tastefully decorated villa. Life was good for Berdan; he had a charming wife and beautiful children but Eric sensed his strong Jesuit principles were still in tact. Berdan's attractive wife Estelle brought a tray filled with cheese, bread, olives, figs, dates, almonds and a few bottles of their wines, both white and red. The scene could not have been more beautiful and relaxing. Eric thought, Italians know how to live; family, food, wine and friendship were all part of their world. The three of them sat and proceeded with small talk related to Berdan's classmates at seminary school. Berdan informed Eric with news that made him feel better. "I am one of sixteen men who completed their training; as of this day, not one remained in the priesthood. That must have significance but the church doesn't see it. Static institutions refuse to acknowledge problems that directly impact their credibility. It's true in our corporate world, government and the catholic church. I could go on but I know you are here for a reason so let's get started." Eric indulged in the bread, wine and cheese which made his taste buds explode with pleasure. He also indulged in figs and roasted almonds. Seeing he was not prepared to speak, Berdan interjected. "By the way, please call me Chris." Eric was finally satisfied with his food and wine indulgence which made Estelle comment. "You have a healthy appetite." Chris nodded in agreement. "Yes I do love good food and must admit I really haven't experienced such delightful tastes. I wish I could say I was here for these wonderful treats, they are delicious. However I'm here for matters of conscience and truth in research. I believe Chris and I share this in common. My research and that of my students has confirmed your conclusion as far as I can tell. That must be one reason for your sudden departure from Vatican autocracy. Am I correct?" Berdan smiled because he had nothing to hide. "Well Father O'Reilly, when I met and fell in love with Estelle everything changed including my faith. I am now a Buddhist and I believe Christ was also. This was too much for the church to fathom; of course you can see why. The ramifications would be a disaster. They want people like me to disappear, so I did for my own security. My family is most important now. They are my main focus, although I continue to write my thoughts and continue my research, not here in Rome but in Austria and Switzerland where my whereabouts is not scrutinized. When I visit there it is for matters of commerce, marketing our wine products. However, I manage to also visit libraries in other countries where my research assistants, who I compensate for their work, compile copies of manuscripts that I cannot find in Rome. My publication will be forthcoming several years down the road. I could use your assistance." Eric immediately wondered: "How brilliant!" Eric thought of his students and whether their research was also being restricted by censorship of historical documents. "Am I to conclude that my students cannot find information because it is not available to them. I have noticed volumes of material are absent from library shelves." Berdan's red smiling face broke out with laughter. "Absolutely. The Vatican has become a monolithic institution." Eric sat silently, while sipping his red wine. "You asked for assistance. I have one student who is fluent in Greek. Others are also very capable of accurately interpreting data. I have read what little they have written thus far and they are on to something but as you have said, the material they need is not available. If you could provide my students with original documents, they could assist you. Is that something you would find useful?" Berdan refilled their glasses with wine. "Let's have a toast to our partnership." They clicked their glasses filled with good red wine and agreed to a partnership of truth and friendship. Berdan added, "Of course we have to maintain our absolute confidentiality along with your students. Only if that is possible, will I agree to work with you. You realize, this is a double edged sword for both of us and especially your students. Removing students from this dangerous mission of probing Vatican dogma would protect them from being expelled. I would recommend caution if it appears you are suspect of something that could cause you or your students harm. The arm of the Vatican has more reach than you know. Even if your students research in secrecy, it's just a matter of time before they are exposed and expelled; you as their adviser would follow them. In either case their future would be jeopardized. I am certain of that. But there may be another way for us to work together. I always believe the more minds that engross themselves in seeking truth, the better. Research requires collaboration and corroboration. It's always good to evaluate documents by incorporating a larger frame of reference. Come to my library and I will explain what I think would work."

They walked through large rooms tastefully decorated with art and Italian country furniture both made more spectacular by natural light emitted through sky lights. Tile floors were covered in part with hand woven carpets and walls were draped with artistic tapestry to silence the acoustics. The center of the library had a majestic stone fireplace who Estelle had stocked with fruit woods that filled the room with a wonderful fragrance. They sat near the fire and Berdan poured from a new bottle. "This is one of my favorites. It's a blend of our finest reds with a tinge of berries. I think you will like it." Eric felt the relaxation that wine induced. He knew this would have to be his last glass. "Here is a plan that might work. I would like your reaction; please be honest.

I have a friend, also a former Jesuit, now a Buddhist, who lives in Florence. He is a publisher and has offered this idea. He would act as a middle man and collect all material from my research teams throughout Europe. Copies would be shipped to him via postage. Since he receives vast amounts of publishing material, this would not appear any different. Here's where we would have to determine the best method of retrieving them; either he forwards them to us at our address or we take the train to Florence every five to six weeks and take possession. He recommends we change our method of pick-up each time. For example we could rent a box at the post office. He could arrange to have a courier deliver packages to us in different locations. You get the idea." Eric now realized that his current mode of operation was too dangerous so he wanted to communicate his urgency to his students. "Could you please allow me to call one of my students to advise him to immediately terminate the research I've assigned. I am worried that based on your experience I must act now." Berdan could see Eric's concern. He pointed to a telephone on his desk. "Please do." Eric called Rebelowski, the Polish scholar who could read Greek and who recently concluded translations into Latin were very careless and quite contrary to their original text in Greek. Eric was fortunate to find him just before he left his room for the library. "Hello Joseph, this is Father O'Reilly. Listen very carefully. You must immediately stop all research and destroy any material gathered. You must also immediately inform the others to do the same. This is urgent. Do you understand me Joseph?" There was silence. Then Joseph responded. "Yes Father I understand. But why?"

"I will meet with all three of you tomorrow after class. Now please act quickly and very discretely."

Chapter 74

Berdan and Eric discussed the issue of Vatican interpretation of scripture and both agreed there were errors in several areas. Christ's sojourn to the east was supported in various sources and his exposure to Buddhist principles were later demonstrated by similarities found in basic rules of ethics and morality preached by Christ upon his return. Berdan used this analogy. When a young man leaves home, goes off to college to study and does not return for over ten years time, that in itself would alter his world view. In today's academic world, being away from home for over ten years is enough time for a young scholar to achieve a doctorate. In a similar way, Christ was a student whose inherent spiritual and worldly knowledge was enhanced by Buddhist philosophy whose existence predated Christianity by 500 years. Why is this so difficult to accept? It does not degrade or refute Christ's deity; what it does say is that as a man, Jesus adopted principles for living that predated Christianity by 500 years. Emulating beliefs is a sign of their recognition that Christ believed coincided with his concept of morality, compassion, tolerance, equality and love for one another, all which are basic tenets of the golden rule. There was no reason to refute Buddhism, so Christ embraced it and continued to expand upon its precepts. So why would this upset Vatican scholars? The answer could be that religious institutions, such as the Roman Catholic Church, refuses to unravel their theology to align itself with historical accuracy after almost two thousand years of misinterpreting holy scripture. The Vatican would come undone; it would be considered an imposter, a hoax perpetrated upon humanity by autocrats who legitimized inaccuracies of scripture and superimposed the powerful Roman hierarchy as their template. As the Roman empire declined, political and cultural vacuums followed that were gradually replaced by the Roman Universal Church. With science, truth can logically lead to reconsideration and adjustment of religious beliefs. When science gets it wrong, truth can correct it. We know the sun is the center of our universe even though Galileo was almost excommunicated for this scientific confirmation of Copernicus, a priest who made this discovery earlier. The church ultimately conceded. With religion, seeking truth can be elusive. It's the nature of institutionalized thinking. Buddhism was accepted by Christ because it comports with his philosophy that our thinking and meditating can alter our lives and bring us closer to God. Thinking, meditation and rationalism are central components of Buddhism. The ancient Greeks evolved to understand this synthesis of God and science. Greek culture became the rational, intellectual and scientific foundation of western civilization, which includes the Catholic church. Now the question for Eric was should he, Berdan and other intellectuals challenge the church's outmoded mentality or work to reform the church from within. Both men believed that sharing Buddhist principles with Christians would enhance Christ's message of love and humility. Both Eric and Berdan agreed that reforming the church from within was the route to follow. They also agreed that all institutions suffer from rot or dead wood caused by feeble leadership, immorality, corruption and loss of purpose. During eras when weak leadership prevailed, the church lost its integrity and became an institution flawed by complacency and immoral leaders. What would Christ think of the enormity and nature of an institution created in his honor? Would he be pleased? What policies, practices and fundamental beliefs would Christ want to reexamine or discard due to their inaccurate interpretation of his intentions? These are questions where Buddhism could offer an honest and open examination of holy scripture. It would eventually necessitate recantation of some catholic doctrines. Many catholic intellects believed that had Pope John 23rd lived, much of this mental fixation would have been reexamined and reassessed. Reexamination of the Roman Catholic Church will require a paradigm shift within the minds of its leaders, many of whom suffer from institutional paralysis. Eric and Berdan realized the enormity of their task and why this transformation would require slow but steady progress. It was at this point when Eric realized he must in his last year as a priest do his best to educate young men to become intellects first and priests second. Their minds must be sharpened to think and lead by example. Introducing them to Buddhism was a good place to start. In fact priests who gravitate toward Buddhism do so because it has done just that for them personally; through meditation, mental and physical rigors of priesthood are mitigated. Before he left Berdan, Eric wanted to make something very clear. Destroying the church he loved was not even a consideration. When Martin Luther attempted reform in 1517, his actions were considered heresy and he was ultimately excommunicated. Eric did not want to parallel that historical movement. Berdan understood. An important reason why he left the church was because he wanted to separate himself from any conflict of interest and any feeling of betrayal. He felt the church had betrayed Christ's simplicity of purpose. His spiritual mission was to integrate Buddhist philosophy and thought into catholic theology. Literature was his vehicle for persuading the church to reconnect with Christ's true intentions. Eric decided that his students would be given the opportunity to work with Berdan if they felt it was something they believed in and was important for their spiritual growth. He would have to reexamine his teaching goals and recalculate where his lectures would have to be modified.

Based on his reading of original Greek scripture, Eric believed that Christ's exposure to Buddhism was significant and did not diminish his intellectual and spiritual teachings. The philosophical nature of Buddhism emphasized eight noble truths which are pathways to what Christians would call eternal life. Buddhism includes all people irrespective of their differences; so did Christ. Christ appreciated the wisdom of Buddhism and emulated and incorporated its most important concepts. His contribution to western culture was how he integrated the wisdom of eastern philosophy with western Judeo-Christian ethics. Christ also may have simplified his sermons since his audiences were the poor and downtrodden. By placing a face on Christianity, both literally and figuratively, Jesus introduced a faith that both rich and poor could understand. Apostles, using Christ's sermons as guidelines, spread the gospel throughout the Roman empire. Jesus may have borrowed Buddhist noble truths but his gift to humanity was how he translated them in a context that made faith more accessible and spiritual, unembellished for commoners. On top of all this was the influence of Greek philosophy with its intellectual foundation which offered Christianity both a spiritual and rational foundation. This is one reason why reading scripture in original Greek was so critical for maintaining integrity and accuracy.

When Eric was about to leave, Berdan gave him two bottles of wine and arranged to have someone drive him home. "Share this with your students when you explain their opportunity to work with me and not against our church. I am with you in spirit. Our goals and intentions are similar, you can rest assured. I hope you will return for a visit one day. It has truly been a pleasure." Eric had such a wonderful feeling of gratitude for acquainting himself with this man of God. "Meeting you was an important part of my mission. Before I relinquish my holy orders, I would like to leave in place a cadre of young priests whose future intentions are discovering truth in holy scripture. You have made my future departure easier by diminishing my uncertainty. Thank you." As he walked to a car waiting for him, Eric thought about Michelle and how she would love the tranquility offered by the beauty that surrounded him. Each day Eric was more attracted to living a simple common life with his future wife and children.

The following morning Eric walked to a nearby chapel for morning prayers and meditation. The church did accept meditation as an important spiritual tool. His goal was to incorporate other non traditional practices with his students that would enhance their control of natural desires. His experience with meditation was very affective in calming his own desire and he understood that he learned this from studying Buddhism's right thought, right mindfulness and right concentration. He would make a point of sharing these concepts with his students and explain how many priests resort to meditation for maintaining their vows and purity. Human impulses can be strong; meditation can alter physical reactions. The more one practices meditation, the easier it is to control desire. Eric prayed that he would be able to reorient his students who volunteered for his research project. After meeting with Berdan, Eric feared he was placing them in situations that could jeopardize their future careers. He did not want to be responsible for their expulsion. If someday they chose to leave priestly life, it would be a decision they could make on their own, as would he the following year.

When his philosophy class ended at three o'clock, his three proteges remained and knew some changes were imminent. Eric said to them. "Follow me to my residence. I have a treat for you." They walked together and wondered what Father O'Reilly had in store. Eric had prepared a small feast of bread, figs, nuts and olives on a tray that were covered at room temperature. Two bottles of red wine with four glasses were arranged at a small table where they would sit and feast. Food and wine was a soothing way of disarming tension and misunderstanding prior to his forthcoming announcement. He allowed them time to enjoy the delicious afternoon snack which in Italian is referred to as a merenda. When he thought the time was right he began. "I know you have all worked on your research and I do appreciate your efforts. However I have been informed by a former priest that I am placing your future careers in jeopardy because of the nature of our research. Therefore, I am asking, maybe I should say, demanding that you terminate all work henceforth. At a future time, currently unknown, you will be offered an opportunity to collaborate with this former priest, if you so wish, on vast quantities of original documents that have to be deciphered. He prefers transparency rather than our current mode of operation. Transparency will protect you from reprisals stemming from the appearance of complicity. His goal is to work with biblical scholars, including you, using documents from a variety of sources. Frame of references from a diversity of intellects, he believes, can and will lead to logical, and rational corroboration of scripture. He does not believe the church at this moment in history is prepared for truth telling and therefore has wisely advised me to protect you from being scrutinized and possibly expelled for your research. Therefore you must abandon your work and at a future date, as of yet unknown, he will contact you. He wants to work in harmony with church scholars to unravel biblical ambiguity. Incidentally, he still considers himself a Christian who practices Buddhism. I have given him your names and place of residence. He would like to meet with all three of you at some point soon. I will inform you when I here from him." When Eric completed his announcement, one seminarian appeared rather upset.. Eric thought he was disappointed that research would not continue. So Eric asked Palacky, the young Czech. "It appears you are not happy with my announcement. Eventually you will see the wisdom of brother Berdan's thinking." Palacky looked at his two friends who now also appeared troubled. "That's not what's troubling me." He paused and looked at Brogoglio and Rebelowski. "Maybe I should say us." Eric's experience with therapy told him something very serious was about to be revealed. They barely finished one small glass of wine and ate very sparingly for young men with appetites. "Please tell me what's bothering you. All three of you look like you've seen a ghost." Eric knew he had to wait so he kept his silence. They looked at one another and finally Palacky broke his silence. "Father O'Reilly. All three of us have experienced behavior from priests that have made us reexamine our future status. I was sexually attacked by a priest who lured me into his residence after class; he tried to rape me but I fought him off and broke his nose in the process." Palacky removed his jacket and showed scratches on his arm where he was held. "He told me not to report this or he would have me expelled for academic dishonesty. I may leave anyway." Eric looked at Palacky. "Francis, this really upsets me and I will personally make sure this priest is exposed and removed." The other two then chimed in. "Father, this almost happened to me but I too had to physically remove myself. It wasn't easy. I'm afraid." Brogoglio was very upset. Tears appeared rolling down his face. Rebelowski then added. "Nothing has happened to me yet but I may just pack up and leave based upon how this makes me feel. We are living among a ring of predators, disguised as priests, hiding within the confines of the Vatican." Eric thought how these young men who sacrificed their lives to serve Christ, were now being victimized by a homosexual ring that he had learned about just days before. Then Eric said out of anger. "I will get to the bottom of this but please, before you make any decision, give me a few days to investigate. I will inform you after class before the end of this week. Is that OK with you?" They looked at one another and agreed to wait for information that Father O'Reilly would uncover. Eric wrote down the names of priests involved. When they ended their session, Eric went right to work. For the first time he could remember, his anger peaked.

Chapter 75

Eric lost no time. He went directly to a senior administrator to expose the priests involved; one from Rome, the other from Bavaria. Both had taught at Lateran for years. Monsignor Olivetti tried to appear calm, seeing that Eric was noticeably angry. "This is a disgrace. My students have every right to be upset and may leave the university. They told me they would go public with their outrage unless both priests were immediately dismissed." Eric couldn't remember getting this angry before. He thought it could have been triggered by what happened to him as a child or teenager when his ability to ward off sexual assaults was minimal at best. As a grown man with his maturity now established, his reaction was more than assertive, it was aggressive. Monsignor Olivetti was taken back and reacted with: "Father O'Reilly, I would like to speak with these two young men. Could you arrange that?" Eric regained his composure. "Yes, how about this afternoon, before they decide to totally withdraw. If they go public, I want you to know that I will support them." Olivetti agreed. Eric thanked him and went straight to the library where he usually found them. They were not there. He waited, hoping they would arrive later than usual. When he realized time was being wasted, he quickly paced to their residence hall and asked the attendant whether he knew them and if so had he seen them recently. "Yes father, both Francis and Giovanni signed out. They were headed for the railroad station. They just left five minutes ago." Eric raced out and noticed someone getting out of a taxi. He was lucky that the cab driver saw him waving. He stopped. "Please take me to the rail station quickly. I'm late." The driver sensed the urgency and raced out faster than even Eric expected. "I will take a short cut through the residential area. I know the way but only take it when I'm alone; it's much shorter." Sure enough, the route taken bypassed much of the heavy traffic, cut through narrow roads and Eric was at the station before they arrived. When he paid his fee and thanked the driver, he saw Francis and Giovanni walking toward the platform. He approached them with words of support. "I totally understand your reasons for leaving. However I do have another option to offer you." They did not appear to be interested. Palacky commented. "You know father, we were happy doing research you originally assigned and now we both have good reason to continue on our own. We don't need the church, in fact we are better off being independent of church censorship." That is what Eric had in mind and he offered them exactly what they wanted; he had no choice. "How would you like to work for a man who is no longer a priest and who shares your same goals? I will take you to him right now. You can do original research. Maybe eventually, Joseph will want to join you." They looked puzzled but interested. "If you are interested I am prepared to take you to visit with him at this very moment." They looked at one another and Palacky said. "Father we know and trust you. I for one would be willing to learn more then decide. Brogoglio agreed. "Come, we'll take a cab. I'll explain on the way. It's only a twenty minute ride." The three of them packed into a taxi. Three suitcases in the trunk and Eric held one on his lap. If this plan worked, the timing could not have been better. Eric was confident that Berdan would also be interested. As they drove to Berdan's villa, silence filled the car. All three were thinking and planning their next move. Eric explained what Berdan had suggested at their first meeting but he wasn't sure his three students would be interested. When they entered the villa, Eric sensed their change of mood.

When they arrived at Berdan's elegant country estate, Palacky and Brogoglio discretely informed Eric about two handwritten letters addressed to daily newspapers in Rome which they signed. In these letters, they revealed names of two priests and provided specific information which became even more convincing when other seminarians also revealed similar vial acts directed against them by the same two priests. Their letters were graphic and truthful. Their final statement was. "As a result of the sexual assaults we experienced, we are both leaving Rome and the priesthood. We could never serve an institution that harbors such evil men." After learning this information Eric knew there was no turning back. Publication would be sometime this week. Newspapers would most likely visit their residence to confirm alleged criminal acts. Their friend and fellow researcher, Joseph Rebelowski was given copies of their letters in the event originals were conveniently destroyed. Joseph would also confirm their story. The Italian press was now obligated to print these stories after listening to corroborated testimony. When the taxi stopped in front of Berdan's main entrance, Eric approached the front door leaving the other two waiting near the road. Berdan opened the door and saw Eric. "You have returned sooner than I imagined." Then he saw the others with valises standing on the side of the driveway. "Do they belong to you?" Eric smiled and nodded yes. He motioned to the young men to approach. "These young scholars no longer want to be priests, but they do want to work doing research for you. I will allow them to inform you of recent events." Berdan walked up to them and introduced himself. "I've been told you have a story to tell. Your arrival may have answered my prayers. Welcome to my home; please follow me." The next hour was spent inside, relaxing around a table filled with a variety of fruits, nuts, cheese, bread and cold beer. Their story was revealed in detail; Berdan was horrified. He understood their emotions because he knew about such behavior and could never understand why it continued. "The horror you experienced which somehow directed you to my home must now be used for positive actions on our part; our research must move forward without delay. I have plenty of work for you. I will pay you and house you in a small cottage on the estate where volumes of material must be deciphered. Does that sound amenable?" After a nightmare scenario, these two young scholars believed that whatever the reason, God had looked after them. Eric felt as though a miracle had happened. They were allowed to call home and inform their families. Berdan estimated the time required would be at least one year or more but they could have time to return home on occasion. Eric mentioned Joseph Rebelowski to Berdan. Joseph could read Greek which Berdan praised as extremely valuable. Berdan wanted to call their attention to a few important details and requirements. "We all must keep a low profile. That means avoiding unnecessary exposure to outsiders especially now, knowing what happened to both of you. Let's not make a spectacle. You both should have a prepared statement and stick with it. Hopefully we will have you isolated long enough to make progress with volumes of original research I have received from my research teams scattered around Europe. When we organize this material for public consumption we will make it available to media outlets, universities, theologians, including the Vatican. Our work must be open for all, historically validated. That means translations from original manuscripts must be accurate, collaborated, corroborated and written in language that speaks truth in meaning and intent. It is the most important theological undertaking for Christians and people of all faith. When scholars from all over the world have an opportunity to evaluate our conclusions they will be convened to revisit holy scripture. Word by word we will enunciate the holy bible.. There's an old saying: LET THE CHIPS FALL WHERE THEY MAY. Christ would want his true message revealed. He is with us."

Eric was relieved when he returned to his Vatican residence because the research goal he originally planned was now being assumed by another Jesuit. He was gratified to let go of past intentions since they no longer fit into his new reality. He wanted instead to focus on secular goals, especially after noticing a letter from Michelle, one of three letters in a package. His parents and John Morley had also written. Eric wanted to quietly and discretely complete his final months in Rome. His teaching and visiting historical sites became his daily routines. He also had to decide when and how to announce his resignation of priestly vows by composing a letter to his bishop in New York and believed reading Michelle's letter would motivate him.

Dear Eric,

"I miss you more each day and pray for our reunion to occur as soon as possible. Your parents have taken me in like a daughter. They told me you had written to them about our plans. That has made me feel closer to you. I have never felt so happy in my life knowing that our future holds many wonderful possibilities. I cannot wait to hold you in my arms and feel your love. I long for you more than you could imagine."

That much of the letter was enough for Eric to realize he would no longer delay writing to Bishop McCann. The remainder of Michelle's letter was filled with news of her teaching and how her parents were helping her plan a wedding for their daughter. It was all positive. Eric realized how her happiness was now an integral part of his future. It was a beautiful feeling.

The following morning Eric checked his mail; there was a note from Chancellor Crisifulli, head of academic studies at the college, who wanted to meet with him that afternoon after his philosophy class.

Eric surmised the reason for the meeting and was prepared, especially knowing he was leaving sometime in July after he and Michelle toured Rome and surroundings together. The meeting was cordial until the Chancellor made reference to three students who left the university after charges of sexual misconduct had been made against predator priests. "Father O'Reilly, what do you know about these three young men who have left our university." Eric stood firm. "I know what you know. Two were attacked by the same priests who were pardoned earlier for similar crimes. The third young man simply felt he no longer wanted to be associated with this institution. He told me he was leaving because of blatant disregard of moral standards. I will share with you that I too am leaving the church. I have notified my bishop of my plans effective June 30th. I share their sentiments, even though my plan to leave was made soon after I arrived." The chancellor was shocked with Eric's response. Eric continued. "I do not and cannot understand why you are so surprised by the sordid culture that exists here. It's shameful. Now if you will please excuse me, I have another appointment at the library with my students." Eric turned and walked out.

Had Eric demonstrated the type of reaction he displayed with the chancellor while in the army, he would have been court-martialed. Knowing he had liberty to act with impunity encouraged his departure from the priesthood and diminished his dissonance. He did feel obligated to compose a letter to Father Hall as soon as he returned to his room.

Dear Father Hall,

I have written my letter of resignation to Bishop McCann and want you to know that my decision is based upon many factors we shared. You know me better than any adult, with the exception of my mother. Your friendship, comfort and guidance throughout my life has sustained my humanity and ability to cope with all the trauma I experienced. I now understand repression and how it can affect ones mental and emotional stability. Thank you for being there for me when I needed you most. My respect and admiration for you were factors behind my choice to become a priest. I think we both know that and realize there must be more profound inspirations when making such a momentous decision. The holy spirit has guided me and I have always relied on wisdom you imparted, especially prayer and meditation. Thank you.

Michelle and I are looking forward to that special day at St. Mary's. She will be in Rome July 1st when we will enjoy touring the eternal city. Wish you could be here with us. God bless you. We are so thankful that you are part of our lives.

Peace be with you always,

Eric

When Eric mailed the letter the following morning, he felt a surge of joy knowing his life was moving in a direction filled with new possibilities.

Chapter 76

The last two months passed quickly for Eric. He visited his students who were researching ancient manuscripts for Berdan. They appeared to be content with their surroundings and work. Berdan became their father figure and thanked Eric for connecting them to his research. "Having young bright minds whose skills are suited for this work is so remarkable. I cannot thank you enough." Eric was thrilled to hear that. After all, this project was his intention until he realized how that pursuit would take him away from the woman he loved. However Eric made a point of consulting with his students. He wanted to be assured of their willingness to continue and Berdan understood his concern. The cottage where they lived was a fair distance from the main estate. Eric walked there followed by Berdan's dog Bella. One student must have seen him approach because he motioned for the others to greet their former professor. Three young scholars waited with smiles on their faces as they greeted Eric. "Caio! I'm glad all of you are here because I wanted to be reassured of your situation. How is everything going for you?" They appeared happy with their work and even made comments indicating some major findings. "Professor, we are fine. Progress is being made and we are learning so much we would never have learned had you not introduced us to Christopher." Joseph also revealed that his Greek language skills have exposed some interesting findings. "We are starting to see interesting connections between Christianity and eastern philosophies. Boethesius has demonstrated how Greek philosophy elevates our faith with rational and intellectual components. It has for us been a confirmation that Christ utilized several eastern teachings." Eric was pleased that his research, although different, came to similar conclusions. He knew he would have to leave it to other scholars to convince the Curia. "My only advice to you when you complete your research is this. Use all of your intellectual and marketing skills to persuade church scholars of your findings. Your research could dramatically alter the future direction of church doctrines. Your future presentation of this important information must be presented with documentation that is persuasively presented. Joseph understood totally. "We know how important this will be and must spend several years of deliberation. We plan on releasing our findings in piecemeal for scholars to discuss and debate. Fortunately our research demonstrates how the church has many ideas that are solid, but misinterpretations of original scripture is very clear. We must expose discrepancies first and allow scholars to prove us incorrect. We think our interpretations are accurate." Eric was pleased for his students and was curious about their future. "How much time do you want to devote to this project? Berdan tells me how pleased he is with your work." Joseph looked at the others before he spoke. "I can only speak for myself. I will commit no more than two years. There's a lovely woman in waiting." Eric was pleased to hear that and felt comfortable telling them about his imminent engagement. They were all very congratulatory and before Eric left, Giovanni and Francis said they would only commit for a year. They both decided to return home and pursue their graduate work hoping it would lead to university teaching. Eric could not have felt better when he left. He wished them well and gave them his home address. "Please keep me informed. Let's all agree to pray for one another." He embraced them and repeated his congratulation. He thought the likelihood of seeing them after leaving Rome was remote.

Eric returned to Berdan's home to inform him of his future engagement and to inquire about a ring. Berdan was sipping a glass of wine while looking at some of the research completed by his three scholars. Eric interrupted him. "Do you know a jeweler? I need to purchase an engagement ring before Michelle arrives." Berdan placed his arm on Eric's shoulder. "Matter of fact, I do. Estelle's uncle is a jeweler. Come, let me call him for you." Berdan communicated with Estelle's uncle, an Italian-American who opened his shop at 10am. His name was Pat Moretti who lived with his Italian wife just a short drive from Rome. His shop in Rome was Via Ignazio Giorgi, 67. After a cup of espresso with his friend, Eric was on his way, but not before Berdan insisted upon having Eric and Michelle over for dinner before they returned to the states. Eric had rented a Fiat for his remaining time in Rome so he could visit sites during his free time. He wanted to familiarize himself with the city before Michelle arrived and was preoccupied with thoughts of being with her and loving her as never before. He had suppressed his sexual fulfillment throughout his priesthood and it baffled him to think how unnatural that was for men, especially of his age.

The jewelry shop was tucked away in an alley set back from the street. When Eric approached, a man in his thirties was opening the entrance. It was Pat Moretti, a former teacher from upstate New York who after his first marriage failed, left teaching and trained to learn the trade he always found interesting. His success expanded when he met a beautiful woman in Florence at a trade show. They fell in love, married and shortly afterward he became one of thousands of American ex patriots who reside in the eternal city. When Eric said good morning with his upstate accent, the man quickly turned his head. "You must be from upstate New York." Eric smiled a big yes. Eric's confidence in Berdan's connection proved to be beneficial. An assortment of rings were presented and when Eric found the one he liked most, he was charged a very reasonable price. It was that easy. They sat and talked about upstate New York where their lives began. The connection was strong and Moretti wanted his first child to be born there; his wife was four months pregnant and agreed to his wish. That way the child could have dual citizenship. Moretti was raised in the Mohawk valley, foothills of the Adirondack mountains, filled with natural beauty that he loved and missed. It was a hard sell to convince his wife to move permanently. Time would tell. Before Eric left, Moretti told him they would meet again at Berdan's for dinner.

Michelle's flight was in two days. Eric had arranged to rent a small studio for two weeks close to several Roman attractions. They would have walking access to a variety of Rome's shops and historic sites. It would be a honeymoon before their marriage. The last night at Lateran, Eric received a letter from Bishop McCann confirming his resignation from holy orders. It was official. While he lay on his bed that last evening, Eric reconstructed his life beginning with elementary school when his emotional anxiety emerged without explanation. He cringed when thinking how his innocent childhood was violated by his uncle and how he repressed the vile act throughout his youth until it emerged in a vivid dream several years later. Throughout his early childhood and into his twenties, this nightmare scenario crippled him and produced guilt and shame. Father Hall's nurturing saved him and it was through his mature love that Eric embraced the idea of becoming a priest. Now he realized life's compensation and for good reason. It was God's plan for Eric to conquer shame, guilt, and fear by serving his church and his country in Vietnam. Both served to strengthen his confidence, discipline and self esteem. Now in Rome, where his spiritual journey would formally end, Eric knew his faith in Christ would sustain him toward his next challenge. He also knew changes in church doctrines would not be altered in the foreseeable future. The Roman Catholic Church had established and ingrained doctrines over generations and even though they were not based on accurate interpretation of holy scripture, they would continue to be believed and practiced until young dedicated scholars exposed the truth which would emerge in stages taking several more generations. Eric wanted to experience Roman Catholic revival and reform during his lifetime but realized that it would not happen unless a remarkable pope emerged. It was now time for him to utilize his talents on secular issues, especially in America's political arena. He seemed to gravitate to the new challenge before him. Politics would offer him the opportunity to make public policy that would open new opportunities for forgotten citizens while allowing more fortunate citizens to see how upward mobility benefits millions which ultimately trickles upward as well. Never before had Eric realized how instrumental leadership could be in pointing America in the right direction. He was amazed at how suddenly he understood the opportunity before him and realized how his college friend made it possible by recognizing Eric's potential. He told Eric during their last conversation. "You have the right stuff." It was for this reason that Eric decided to contact his friend and political consultant, Dave Dwyer, in Washington to inform him of his interest in running for congress. Election day could change his life.

Chapter 77

When Eric saw her walking through the arrival concourse of Leonardo da Vinci airport, he marveled at her beauty and grace. She saw Eric waving and began to walk faster. Their embrace was in total disregard of all strangers who cared to observe their strong attraction. For the first time she could feel Eric's emotion and commitment; it was reassuring and made her love flow even more. "You are a beautiful sight. What a lucky guy I am." She blushed with joy. "Oh Eric, I have never been so happy to see anyone in my life. How are you?" While they walked holding hands, Eric listened to news from home. They retrieved her luggage and were soon in the Fiat. Michelle preferred stopping at his studio so she could unpack and freshen up. They were both too excited to think of food. That would come later. "Father Hall sends his love and was informed by bishop McCann of your letter. He's very happy for us. Your mom and dad also want you to know how much they miss you. They are wonderful. I got to know them and your sister Mary quite well." Eric loved hearing her voice. "Tell me more." She squeezed his hand. "I will but please share with me your experience in Rome. What's the latest with your research?" There were other things on Eric's mind right at the moment. He was thinking of the best time and place to propose to her and offer the engagement ring. She could tell he was preoccupied and did not force conversation. However, Eric did respond. "My research is now being completed by a group of scholars, three of whom were my students and the other a former Jesuit. It's a good team for a project that will require years of research and translation. That is now part of my past. Our future is what's important now." He left it there and she understood. When they arrived at the studio Eric had prepared some fruit, cheese, roasted almonds and crusted bread along with wine. He had learned to appreciate what his friend Berdan had offered. They sat with a glass of wine and shared delights. "I'm impressed. You're quite the host." Their discussion continued on a more comfortable sofa where after devouring snacks and wine, they moved to the bedroom where their bodies were close and emotionally charged for lovemaking followed by two hours of needed sleep.

When Eric wakened, he quietly moved to the kitchen area and made fresh coffee, an addiction he looked forward to in Italy. He had mapped out a walking tour that included the Trevi Fountain where he imagined he would ask Michelle for her hand in marriage and offer her an engagement ring. He thought of his former life where he was married to the church he loved, only to exit and now marry the woman he loved, and as much as he wanted this, it made his mind race. He sensed joy with a trace of disappointment and realized this moment is not an every day experience with traditional relationships between men and women. He thought of his Vietnamese children and how they may have rescued him from the void he felt after meeting them. He thought of the moment he met Michelle and how his emotions stirred when seeing her beauty and grace. He thought of the men he served with in Vietnam whose fears he shared but who gave him strength and a strong willingness to survive. He thought of his students who left the priesthood after betrayal by immoral and corrupt priests. He thought of his mentor, Father Hall who throughout his life was more than a priest to him and now he understood why. He thought of his mother and how she must have suffered for her son's psychological pain. He thought of the father he hardly knew until recent years when his wisdom and love surfaced out of mutual need. As Eric processed all these important individuals and events, warm hands of Michelle surrounded him from behind. She kissed the nape of his neck and whispered, "I love you." He turned and hugged her closely. "Thank you. You're my love and joy." He thought of beautiful children they would create and shared this with her. She smiled and agreed that would be something special to look forward to. They sat and chatted over delicious coffee that Eric had perfected over the past few months. " I thought we would walk to some sites and later have dinner. At this time most stores are closed until six o'clock. Can you be ready in about an hour?" She looked at him and smiled. "You must realize that living with a woman requires adjusting to a different time frame. How about giving me thirty minutes more?" They moved toward one another and kissed. Eric held her close. "Take all the time you need. There are more clean towels stacked in the bedroom closet." Her sexuality was then expressed with: "We could save water if you shower with me."

Then she disrobed and walked to the shower. Eric followed with desire and was not disappointed.

They walked along narrow alleys that meandered through Roman neighborhoods. Children were playing in the streets and their joyfulness did not go unnoticed by Eric. He felt his life was finally leading to some very special experiences with Michelle and beyond. He couldn't remember feeling so free and happy. When they approached the Trevi Fountain, Michelle walked faster with excitement, holding Eric's hand. They gazed into the water and observed other tourists and lovers enjoying the moment, some throwing coins into the water signifying they would some day return to Rome. Eric slowly reached into his sport jacket pocket and pulled out a small box. He was nervous but determined to maintain his composure. He moved in front of her and placed a small silver box in her hand. "Michelle, you have made me a very happy man. I have one simple question, will you marry me?" She looked at Eric with watering eyes. They kissed while other tourists could sense what was happening. She opened the small box and removed an elegant one carat diamond ring with small diamonds embossed on both sides. She placed it on her finger while several bystanders glanced and applauded, congratulating them. The spontaneity of the moment made it even more special followed by throwing coins over their heads into the fountain pool. At that moment Eric felt his life would once again be placed in God's hands which he acknowledged with silent prayer as they walked hand in hand toward other sites along the way.

Sharing experiences with Michelle was magical for Eric because she was pleasant, patient, intelligent and fun to be with. Days passed and the intensity of their love was apparent. In two days their flight to JFK was scheduled on American Air Lines so Eric utilized every moment driving to many sites including the Vatican, Sistine Chapel, Colessium, Pantheon, Roman Forum, and Trajans market where Michelle spent time purchasing items for their families. The last stop at Michelle's request was The Lateran University where Eric spent his last year as a priest. It had special significance to her because while back in the states she imagined he might change his mind and maintain his priestly vows. As they approached the entrance, Michelle was impressed with its charm. "So this is where you taught and did research." She turned to face Eric. "Any regrets?" Eric took a deep breath. He wasn't certain how to answer. "Before I answer, allow me time to think about it." She understood and respected his reluctance to respond immediately; knowing Eric she knew eventually he would provide her with an appropriate response. However Eric did remind Michelle that on the following day at Berdan's dinner party, she could ascertain answers to her questions and be informed of imminent changes Eric believed were necessary for the church to move forward. For the time being, that seemed to satisfy her curiosity.

Chapter 78

While driving to Berdan's villa north of Rome Eric thought of Michelle's question about "any regrets."

He wanted to respond honestly but did not want to appear unsure of his decision by introducing notions that could be discomforting. Her question really made him evaluate not only their future together but his personal and professional goals. In part his decision to become a priest was based upon serving the spiritual void that many people of all faiths have for a variety of reasons. Studying meditation and Buddhism exposed Eric to profound philosophical and rational components of life, death and beyond. He believed Michelle would be amenable to his beliefs and also be an excellent partner for applying them to their lives. Eric came to the conclusion that Christ was a Buddhist convert who merged that philosophy with those of his own making. He believed Christ's eastern sojourn happened for a reason. It was part of God's plan for his only begotten son to experience gifts that other wise men had perfected. Buddhism was a good fit for merging the spiritual with the philosophical. They were not incompatible and this is why many priests continue to rely on meditation and other aspects of Buddhist philosophy. The convergence of Eastern and Western cultures could have been bridged with Christ's words and acts of faith synthesized with Buddhism's words of wisdom. Eric believed Americans in general were religious people but they were not philosophical in nature. He used this as a starting point to explain his response to her "any regrets" question.

"You know Michelle, I have thought of your "any regrets" question and appreciate your patience in allowing me time to respond, after all this is a major life changer for both of us. First I want to preface everything by telling you that I am truly in love with you and look forward to sharing my life with you. If I have any regrets for my decision to leave the priesthood it's related to ending spiritual and meaningful assistance to those who need it. But the imperfections in the church also have a part to play in my decision. These imperfections are found in several areas: liturgy, misinterpretation of scripture, close mindedness of church leaders, financial and immoral corruption. When I met you I was not familiar with these imperfections but over the last four years I have been made aware of them from a variety of sources. So loving you became easier because the pull of priestly obligations were diminished by what I have learned and experienced. I believe God has another plan for both of us. You will not only be my wife, you will be my partner and together we can serve millions more than I ever could have served as a priest. I hope that answers your question; does it?" Michelle was silent for a moment, then said. "Could you please pull over to the side of the road for a moment?" Eric's pulse began to beat faster, but he complied. The car came to a stop overlooking a beautiful meadow. Michelle turned to him and pulled him as close to her as that small Fiat would allow. She kissed him passionately and held him close and whispered. "Yes that answers my question." He smiled and drove a few miles to Berdan's villa thinking how actions speak louder than words.

Michelle was very impressed with the entrance to Berdan's villa. "This man was a Jesuit priest and now all this. Could you explain how?" Eric really did not have time to respond because Berdan was in the yard with his dog Bella waiting for their arrival. He was standing along the drivers side of the car when Eric came to a stop. Eric had brought a gift he purchased because it was the latest tool for pruning vines. Berdan was very pleased. "I would never think of something so practical because our tools are good but these I've been told are much better. Made in California." When he glanced over the Fiat and saw how beautiful Michelle looked, he was stunned. "Please introduce me Eric." Michelle immediately sensed a good connection with this man. His wife Estelle approached while Eric introduced Michelle to Berdan. Then Estelle introduced herself, in English, to Michelle with a warm welcome. The women walked into the home and left Eric and Berdan who were busy talking about variety of grapes and how the climate thus far proved to be a positive factor in their maturity and flavor. "Eric, your lady is very charming. I am so happy for you. Congratulations on your engagement. We have something to celebrate." Eric smiled and thanked his friend; knowing they shared a common past was certainly comforting for Eric's transition to a secular life he was now anticipating. They walked into the ancient home where the scent of fresh flowers released a pleasing fragrance. As they moved to the backyard patio overlooking vineyards, Eric noticed outdoor dining tables tastefully displayed under a wooden canopy filled with grape vines that provided an elegant setting for evening dinner. A trio of string instruments played classical music making the ambiance even more spectacular. There were several people Eric did not know sipping wine and eating a variety of fruits, cheeses, nuts and a large seafood platter of appetizers. There were servers dressed in black and white who offered trays of food that made ones pallet explode. Estelle had introduced Michelle to women guests who were impressed with her beauty and charm. Eric watched from a distance and slowly walked toward Michelle who reached out for his hand. She looked at the women guests and introduced Eric. "This is my finance Eric O'Reilly." Eric's Italian was good enough to explain his connection to Berdan. One woman responded in English. "Your Italian is very good. You even have a Roman flair." The conversation moved into their life work and other typical exchanges. Although it was a very pleasant social gathering, from the nature of conversation, Eric felt a disconnection between their lives and those less fortunate. He could not validate his feeling but it was something he strongly sensed. The waiters followed with trays of champagne for everyone. Berdan then took charge. First in Italian then in English. "Could I please have your attention." His voice was loud enough to draw the crowds silence. "It is my pleasure to announce that my good friend Eric and his lady Michelle were recently engaged. We offer you our best wishes for a wonderful life together. Salute." The crowd sipped champagne followed by applause. Eric and Michelle were surprised and flattered by this kind expression. They were a very attractive couple and all eyes centered on them as they toasted one another followed by a tender kiss. The crowd then milled about for an hour, walked about the vineyard; the aroma of lamb and veal roasted on wood fire was tantalizing.

The dinner table was lit with candles and guests were directed to their chair with prearranged seating. Eric and Michelle sat close to Berdan at one end and his wife Estelle at the other end. Michelle whispered to Eric. "Our last evening in Rome will be one I never forget. Your friends Berdan and Estelle are wonderful people. I am so happy we met." Eric could not believe how his life had evolved into such a beautiful moment. He kissed Michelle and said. "God has blessed us with gifts of love, family and friendship." Then Berdan chimed his wine glass again getting everyone's attention. "Ladies and gentlemen. Let us pray and thank God for this wonderful gift of family, friends and food we will now enjoy. Heavenly

Father we thank you for all the blessings we share. Remind us of our duty to each other and to all those in need of our service and generosity. In the name of the father, son and holy spirit. Amen".

After dinner, Eric had some time to spend with his three students who left their seminary training but who now appeared even more determined to research for truth written in holy scripture. Their goal was simple as Francis Pulacky and Joseph Rebelowski verbalized. "We want only to find the truth, if that is possible. We must not force our views of Christ's life upon others; we want evidence and truth to speak for itself." Eric was pleased to hear them speak with such enthusiasm which reaffirmed a goal he would have pursued had he remained a priest. Eric sensed that his farewell to Berdan and his students was a termination of one part of his life that would not end with closure because the end was not in sight.

The following morning sunrise was their last in Rome. When they returned the Fiat, Eric and Michelle wheeled their luggage to American Airline Flight 967 to JFK. They were finally going home to a new life. Eric had set his future in motion weeks before. The political arena would be his next challenge.

The long flight home provided Eric time for reflection but after one hour of flight, he dozed into a deep sleep. It was during this time when his dreams recalled events in his life that he either forgot or repressed. He saw his uncle's face turn when his mother opened his bedroom door to discover the sexual assault inflicted upon her son just moments before. She screamed and struck her brother with her fists and hands and scratched his face. She grabbed Eric who was bleeding and took him into the bathroom to attend to his needs, crying and holding him close to her as she began attending to his bleeding. As a four year old child he did not understand but sensed his mother's terror. Moments later she called Father Hall to inform him while crying to him almost in panic mode. Father Hall arrived and comforted his mother who was still emotionally unstable. Her horror brought tears to Eric's eyes as he clutched her arms. He remembered crying and Father Hall holding him while saying, "everything will be alright now Eric." The three of them sat together holding hands and when he looked at Father Hall he saw tears in his eyes as well. Suddenly Eric felt someone holding his hand and gently touching his temple. It was Michelle who sensed his trauma but wasn't aware of its source. Was it wartime trauma overwhelming him or something closer to home. When she heard Eric's faint whisper call out "mommy" she realized the possibility of his childhood horror had resurfaced. She kissed his cheek and whispered, "We'll be home soon. Everything will be alright."

When they arrived at JFK, Michelle had to wake Eric who slept most of the way. He told Michelle that her presence made him feel secure enough to sleep. Here was a man with military experience, recipient of the Congressional Medal of Honor and former priest who realized that even with all his strengths, his childhood anxiety could unravel him. Eric realized his military combat experience was traumatic and would have to be dealt with, however he knew that his childhood trauma was his Achilles' moment. He also believed Michelle understood his past; this state of affairs would be their unspoken secret.

When they exited with their luggage, Eric heard his name being called out. It was Dave Dwyer who had flown to New York for a political event that unknown to Eric, was about congressional elections that November and Eric was being selected by the New York State Democratic delegation. "Eric, welcome home."

He noticed Michelle and introduced himself. Eric introduced Michelle and asked. "Dave, what are you doing here?" Dave seemed out of breath. "I ran to your gate to meet you before your flight to Syracuse. How much time do you have?" When Dwyer was informed their flight was in two hours, he looked at Eric and said. "Your next job will be as a member of the congress of the United States. You did receive my letter in Rome?" Eric did receive his letter but was unaware of how quickly events were moving. "You must understand Eric. In politics as in many professions, timing is very important. Your name recognition is everywhere. In fact, Republicans will be asking you to also run. This is your time. I have papers with me from the New York Democratic delegation. They want to know soon because the deadline is just two days from now. If you sign, we will make the announcement and you will begin your campaign in two weeks." Michelle was silent, mostly out of shock. Eric looked at her and asked. "Michelle, is this something you would want for us. Please tell me your thoughts. I can't make this decision without your blessing." Michelle whispered in Eric's ear. "As long as we get married after your victory in November." Eric looked at Dwyer. "The answer is yes. Where do I sign?" Dwyer took papers out of his briefcase and Eric signed his name. It was that fast. Dwyer then excused himself. "I have a meeting in Manhattan in just over an hour. Have to run. Nice meeting you Michelle. I will call you later this evening Eric. Congratulations."

In Syracuse, Eric's parents were waiting. The occasion could not have been happier. Michelle was smiling as Eric's sister Mary hugged her brother with tears of joy. She turned to Michelle and said. "You have made my brother the happiest man in the world. Thank you Michelle." Eric's mom and dad looked on with joy and everyone embraced. Michelle displayed her beautiful diamond ring. There were no dry eyes.

Chapter 79

Once the news about Eric's run for congress was announced along with their November wedding, the excitement for Eric's mother was overwhelming. Displaying her baking skills was her way of celebrating joy and she knew her children would reap the benefits so she planned on making Irish soda bread, lemon meringue pie and homemade tapioca pudding which she knew Father Hall enjoyed. She told Eric that Father Hall apparently had been informed of Eric's plans for marriage and that several members of St. Mary's Church were inquiring about his status with the church. Father Hall requested a meeting with Eric so he could officially respond to their inquiry. Eric decided he would address the congregation; without going into detail, he felt obligated to explain how his life had turned in a new direction after meeting a special woman. His mother thought that was a good idea and Eric went to visit Father Hall the next day to once again show his appreciation for all he had done throughout his years filled with pain and joy. Eric had a strange feeling when he entered the rectory; this was his home away from home for over a year. Father Hall greeted him with a tremendous hug. "Boy am I glad to see you. Your life just keeps moving in new directions; quite remarkable don't you think?" Eric agreed. In fact it was difficult at times for Eric to comprehend his transition from one path to another. "Father, it feels good to be home. My mom made one of your favorite desserts." It was still warm to the touch and rather than wait, Father found a spoon in his desk and savored several mouthfuls. "I would like to address our congregation this Sunday. I don't have much time to spare because my campaign for congress will soon begin and I will be planning with my advisers. Also Michelle and I will be married here at St. Mary's after the election, win or lose." Father Hall was amused. "You will win and win big. You have not only name recognition. You're a military hero, scholar, former priest and now you are marrying a beautiful woman. How can you even think of losing. You have a proven track record. In fact, you're going straight to the white house with those credentials." Funny how words are said by others that have crossed Eric's mind. He was twenty seven years old and doors were opening so fast. He wondered at times if he could maintain his composure and not get too far ahead of himself.

He realized how little control he had over events in his life. They just happened without too much effort on his part. His life was mapped out by others but he didn't seem to mind. When would he hit that proverbial wall? Father Hall could sense Eric was overwhelmed but maintained his silence. After all, Eric paid his dues in more ways than not. He deserved the good fortune and joy that lay ahead. "So what about your research at Lateran. Any progress?" Eric shared how his personal life had altered his research plans but that others were carrying the torch for him. "Father, I believe that in two or more generations, the catholic church will return to its core values. At present, the bureaucracy is corrupt to the core and there's not much that is being done to change anything. Once catholic scholars unveil the hypocrisy and inaccuracy currently guiding our ministry, all hell will break loose." Father Hall nodded in agreement. "I will never live to see it, but you will. We need a Jesuit pope. That could make a difference; we both know that much. In fact, I thought that could have been you one day, but now I can see you have other plans. What are they? Tell me. I'm not going to be around forever. I'll keep your secret." Eric smiled because he knew if anyone understood his instincts, it was Father Hall. Up to this point in Eric's life Father Hall had reserved his opinions about Eric's future. He refrained from offering options for Eric to consider because he did not want to interfere with his personal direction and goals. Suddenly however the silence usually exhibited by his mentor ended. This was Father Hall's time to speak out with words that conveyed strong views never offered before. "You know Eric I'm much older and must convey an important message before I die, especially now that your life has placed you at an important crossroad. So listen carefully. Personally, if I were you Eric I would take this political opportunity all the way to the top and you know where that is. You have always demonstrated a genuine ability to help others in many different ways. Now you are heading for positions of power where you can really create social policies that impact millions." It was important for Eric to hear this from his friend and mentor. Father Hall validated his feelings and gave them meaning. "You know Eric, windows of opportunity usually only come around once in a lifetime. You have a wonderful opportunity to pursue the public good and alter our nation's direction from its current malaise with Watergate and Vietnam to something spectacular, filled with hope for our children. You can make this happen. You are in a position with great potential and must realize you have not only an opportunity but an obligation to serve. Up to this point, your life has been directed by events not of your making. Now it's time for you to become the play maker. Set your goal and take charge. Michelle will be right there at your side." Eric never imagined Father Hall would have presented a call to duty. He was out of character. "You know Eric, I feel it is my obligation to tell you to be all you can be for a reason. I know your character and good intentions. From this point on, you must think of my pleas as part of your destiny. You were meant to lead. That's your calling Eric."

As Eric drove away from the rectory, he was deeply touched by what his mentor had shared with him. Never before had Father Hall been so direct and forthcoming during their discussions. His priest, friend and mentor was pleading with Eric, almost as a dying wish not to avoid his destiny. He recognized Eric's potential for leadership and was practically insisting that Eric make it happen. "Don't pass this up", were his last words before Eric left the rectory.

When Eric returned home his mother told him that the chairman of the New York State Republican party had called to offer the Republican nomination for the congressional district. "Eric, I thanked him and told him you were running as a Democrat. He thanked me and hung up. Maybe you should call to say thank you too. Did Father Hall enjoy the tapioca?" Eric snickered and hugged his mom. "Yes mom, that's all he talked about."

Preparing for Sunday's address to St. Mary's congregation was his next objective. He wrote down some thoughts to convey his appreciation and love for all the church community. His parents, sister, Michelle and her parents were in attendance. Father Hall told the congregation that Eric had a message he would deliver when mass was over. After the benediction, Eric walked up to the dais. The congregation applauded him and he tapped his heart to show his appreciation. Then silence surrounded the church.

"Good morning to all and thank you for your warm reception. We all know how our lives evolve with time and experience. My life is no different and I thank you for the opportunity and experience to serve you as a priest for over a year here at St. Mary's Church. I enjoyed working with you and your children and hope that educational and athletic programs we started will continue to prosper. I remember serving mass with Father Hall as an alter boy not too many years ago. His devotion to our church and community is outstanding." Eric applauded and the congregation joined in. "He was an important part of my reason for becoming a priest. But along the way a war interrupted plans and my obligation to serve in the military pulled me away for a while before I was even ordained. Wars can alter perspectives and ones future, so when I was discharged I delayed any other considerations until I could complete my seminary training and experience life as a priest here at St. Mary's. It was a wonderful experience and I thank you for your love and friendship. But my interest in theology and teaching led me to Rome for a year where I continued my education and research. It was there in the eternal city where I could process my life experiences and conclude that God had different plans for me. I knew that some day I would want a family of my own and along my journey I met a woman who waited for me to decide my fate. She is here today along with our parents. Michelle, would you please stand so everyone can see you." (The congregation applauded, and gave her a standing ovation) " Michelle and I will be married this November here in St. Mary's." (More applause) "I also want you to know that I will be running for congress this November and would like nothing more than to serve you again in a different capacity." (More applause) "Thank you and God bless you."

Eric kept his explanation short but informative. As he and Michelle walked to the exit, followed by their parents, members of the congregation greeted them warmly. It was an exciting reception and a brief taste of what campaigning for office would be like. Eric was glad to have Michelle there with him. Her presence made him view his political plunge with more appeal and conviction. They were a handsome couple. His campaign had begun.

Chapter 80

Dave Dwyer called to inform Eric of an important strategy meeting for the upcoming campaign. Media consultants were hired, campaign stickers, flyers and buttons were printed, all with Eric's name and Dwyer added a slogan to the posters: PROVEN LEADERSHIP! "I did not have time to consult with you because I wanted to have these printed for this week. We need to get your name out there. Hope you like it." Eric thought it was clever and so did Michelle. Eric had the opportunity to meet with Dave's partners who were experienced and successful in running campaigns for congress. When they saw how beautiful Michelle was they told Eric to have her attend as many campaign stops as possible. New York's 23rd congressional district included Oswego, Watertown and surrounding communities. It was mainly Republican based but a military hero could easily win over constituents, so a Democrat like Eric O'Reilly had a very good chance for success. Eric planned to introduce himself to various community organizations and Dwyer had arranged over a dozen meetings for the next ten days. Newspaper articles, television and radio ads were set in motion. Eric was impressed and felt confident that with a team led by Dwyer, victory was assured. The next two weeks were spent meeting all kinds of people, usually in fire houses, high school auditoriums, farmers' markets, public libraries and parks. Eric's charisma was appealing. His good looks dramatically enhanced when public officials were introduced to his fiance. Michelle met many teachers and shared with them her experiences in the classroom. Their energy was dynamic and Eric could sense that his audiences enjoyed hearing him speak, especially with Michelle standing behind him. He conveyed plans to improve funding for needed public projects that would attract industry. He researched all his district to tailor his presentations to community needs. His opponent had an advantage; he was the incumbent, but the economic decline in the 23rd district worked against him. Eric focused on his opponents failure to address problems with conviction and this strategy was working according to polls. Eric put in sixteen hour days campaigning, meeting all kinds of constituents, and making speeches throughout the district. He realized he had good political instincts for selling his candidacy to the public. Days turned to weeks and months of grinding out his campaign strategy. His discipline and competence worked to his advantage. He could tell by comments he heard and read in the press. Military heroes do have an advantage in politics, especially when they are intelligent, good looking and persuasive. Having Michelle tag along on occasion also helped. Dwyer couldn't believe how Eric's political instincts and savvy were so natural. Even Michelle commented to Eric. "If I didn't see you and hear you, I never would have believed you had it in you. This is your calling just as Father Hall had predicted. You're a winner Eric." On election day Eric won an overwhelming majority of votes to be elected a member of congress.

Their wedding plans were set and they were married at St. Mary's church on November 15th. It was a beautiful wedding with many prominent military officers and Vietnam veterans present. Dwyer was his best man and Eric's sister Mary was the maid of honor. The wedding was nationally recognized by media outlets who promoted stories of political theater.

Two years later he was re-elected to congress by even a larger margin. During his four years in office he brought more pork to the 23rd district and his constituents could see the results of his leadership in congress. Eric worked across the isle and with bipartisan cooperation he assured that Camp Drum near Watertown would be an important part of the economic success for his district. Industrial parks were also planned adjacent to the port of Oswego with new rail lines rebuilt to handle growing commerce.

In Congress, Eric had made some very important contacts with powerful members of both houses giving him high name recognition nationally. He was a rising star and New York State's gubernatorial election was just over a year away. His name was being mentioned. When he called his wife Michelle to tell her the news she told him they were expecting their second child. He cried with joy and took the first flight home to be with her and celebrate the good news. Being a parent was very important to Eric. He had a two year old son and was thrilled to be home with him. They purchased a home in Fruit Valley, a suburb just west of Oswego. Michelle was fortunate to have grandparents from her family and Eric's to assist them so she could maintain her teaching position which she loved. Family was very important to both of them and Eric had never been happier with his life. He also made a point of always visiting Father Hall to thank him for all he had done for his family and was informed that he would retire from St. Mary's that fall, 1980. He looked aged and tired and Eric could tell he was feeling his age but his spirit was strong. "I'll reside in a home outside of Syracuse for priests who are waiting to be with the Lord. When you are elected governor, I want an invitation to your inaugural, followed by the White House inaugural, if I'm still alive." He roared that wonderful sound of laughter Eric remembered. They shared memorable moments of joy, talked about Syracuse basketball and the restoration of St. Mary's Church which was in need of structural repair. "I'll be saying my last mass in St. Mary's next month. I hope you can be here for the occasion." Eric promised him he would as he said good bye but not before mentioning that Michelle was expecting their second child. Father Hall beamed with joy. He knew Eric's dream of parenthood was being fulfilled.

That evening Dwyer called with news that Eric's candidacy for governor would be entered in the primary election. His Democratic opponent from downstate was a state legislator, also a veteran, so the race could be more competitive. Dwyer once again took charge and began promoting Eric's name and military history for political videos produced for TV ads. Fortunately his campaign funds were sufficient to make his candidacy well known downstate. Dwyer had also organized political dinners in Westchester, Manhattan and Long Island to get his name recognition out there. Upstate voters were familiar with their native son but Dwyer also flooded the western counties around Buffalo with ads to keep his base support strong. Once again Eric realized Dwyer's political instincts and was confident he would be successful. His opponent did not have the resources to compete. When Eric met his opponent, Randy Pelow, he was impressed with his character and intelligence when he said to Eric: "Let's promise to work together at the end of our campaigns. As veterans we must not let our party labels separate us from our commitment to New York." Eric immediately felt his military comradeship with his opponent. After Eric's victory, he praised Pelow for his service to his country and state and called to thank him for his friendship. Pelow would prove to be a key player in O'Reilly's success with the state legislature.

The election for governor of New York received national attention. A rising star was making his candidacy known nationwide. Eric was elected governor of New York with a large majority of the vote. It wasn't close. His success in politics was based upon many skills. Eric was gifted with remarkable assets and people around him sensed his ability to set reasonable goals, listen to all sides during debate, cooperate, compromise when necessary, work across the isle, use rhetorical skills to persuade and then lead to close the deal. It was a process that worked and both parties appreciated his finesse and leadership instincts. Eric did not come across as partisan. Although his political philosophy was based upon using government power to stimulate ideas and solutions for public benefit, he did not antagonize voters who may have a different view. He understood that purists from the right or left will not be objective and pragmatic. Politics, he believed, had to be practical and persuasive. Eric understood that principle. He was not an ideologue but he did retain his ideals. He had a natural instinct for calming his opponents in the legislature and often invited them to have hands on experience with problems so they could see for themselves that solutions are rarely simple or easily resolved. Whenever possible he gave his political opponents an opportunity to work with him and openly and honestly attempt to solve problems. He reminded supporters and opponents that "solutions do not have to be left or right. Solutions have to be clearly explained, fair to public perception and implemented so that benefits outweigh costs." Eric often used the bully pulpit effectively to promote his political philosophy. In Manhattan, the New York governor spoke to a national audience, dining at the Waldorf. His speech was listened to, printed, read by millions and discussed in the media. His political philosophy was taking shape. "Government is not our enemy; it is and should be our servant. We the people are the government. Our government should not distant itself from serving the public good. Whenever necessary, private and public sectors can and should work as a team to provide citizens with practical and meaningful solutions. Tax revenue must be used intelligently and efficiently for public interests. Free enterprise and private capital are mainstays of our economic future but they must be socially and environmentally responsible to protect public interests." These ideas appealed to moderate voters who were usually reasonable with their demands and Eric believed as a public servant, it was his responsibility to educate citizens in problem solving. After all that is what people want. He would call for public meetings throughout the state where he encouraged citizens to ask private developers how their investment in a region would enhance economic well being without damaging our environment. "What good is development if the environment is destroyed with air, water, noise, or traffic pollution." He insisted on intelligent planning where state and private planners designed future economic development followed by open meetings where local officials and the general public could be involved. Transparency and community involvement were important. He devised strategies such as tax free zones to attract investment from around the country and overseas. He encouraged New York State to showcase its skilled work force, great universities and colleges, transportation network, cheap power and water resources. These ideas became public policies for New York and the results led to steady economic growth, especially upstate where decades of economic decline were forcing residents to leave for opportunities elsewhere. His leadership did not go unnoticed by New Yorkers who reelected him to office. Eight years as governor of the Empire State exposed him to prominent media outlets who referred to him as "another Roosevelt" in his intelligent and persuasive style of politics. When asked which Roosevelt he emulated and admired his response was. "A little of both." He was not branded a liberal or conservative. He was called the "problem solver" by media icons; the national audience found him very attractive. He and his wife Michelle now had three children which enhanced his maturity and appeal. It was just a matter of time when Eric O'Reilly would run for president of the United States. The opportunity came when he was interviewed on prime time by Walter Kronkite on CBS. "Governor, the citizens of New York and around the country are encouraging you to run for president. I have two questions for you. Are you planning to run for president and if so when?" Governor O'Reilly looked into the camera and smiled. "If the American people will not mind supporting a family of five, plus our dog living in the white house at public expense, I will offer them my candidacy today." Kronkite was amused. ""Is that a yes governor?

After that interview, Eric received several invitations to appear on television shows. One invitation was the TONIGHT SHOW with Johnny Carson. Sunday morning it was MEET THE PRESS and FACE THE NATION. The Washington Post, New York Times and Wall Street Journal all had poll numbers with him far ahead of all other prospects. Their editorial pages were filled with accolades for his style of leadership.

The chairman of the Democratic National Party had contacted his political consultant, Dave Dwyer to set up a press conference where he could announce his candidacy. Events were happening so fast that Eric did not have time to think about Michelle and his family. This bothered him so when he was home he asked Michelle to find time for a discussion after the children were in bed. He wanted her to know that their lives would never be the same. "Is this what we want Michelle? We'll live in a bubble. Our kids won't have a normal childhood." Michelle agreed but also understood that he could not reject his destiny. "Eric, you have worked so hard and now the decision is no longer ours. Our country beckons your nonpartisan style of leadership. Your wife knows you better than anyone and I understand your reservations but no one else can lead the way you do. I have never seen you get angry with your opponents. You have a way of persuading them by inclusion. They appreciate this and will work with you. It's an eight year commitment, assuming you win two terms. We are young enough to enjoy our children and our lives after that. Our children will also benefit from the rich experience they will enjoy. I say you run and win." He moved toward her, held her in his arms and said. "Sometimes I'm afraid, especially for you and our children. There are so many unknown events and individuals who can destroy our lives at a whim. I never thought of fear before now." Michelle recognized the look of his face and eyes that she only saw once and that was when he told her about his two Vietnamese children who were killed years ago. She understood his anxiety from that type of tragic loss. And of course there was the Kennedy assassination. His fears were well grounded. Her gentle touch and kiss appeased him. "We must not live with fear. You have always told me there are things we have little if any control over. Our faith is strong. I will be with you every step of the way. Lean on me." At this point it was Michelle's strength and conviction that lead Eric to his decision to run. Had she wavered even one tiny bit he would have called everything off and peacefully retired from politics at age forty.

Chapter 81

The TONIGHT SHOW was first on his list of invitations. Johnny Carson was considered nonpartisan and because Eric had a reputation for practicing that style of politics, Carson did not hesitate during his introduction, to mention that "this man and I have something in common; we both gravitate to being nonpartisan if that's possible in politics. That's probably where the similarity ends. (laughter) Ladies and gentlemen, the governor of New York, Eric O'Reilly." The California audience cheered as if he was one of their own. The governor looked more like a movie star than a politician. He was dressed in a well tailored dark navy suit, white shirt, black shoes and sky blue silk tie. His posture was straight and he looked tanned from playing a round of golf earlier that day. There was no doubt that he made an impression with Carson who also was meticulous with his attire and demeanor. Both could have been models for GENTLEMEN'S QUARTERLY. Carson started with: "You know governor, if you change your mind about running for president, I can get you a gig with a top model agency here in Burbank." The audience roared their approval and even whistled. Carson looked at them with that look that only Carson projects. "It appears this audience is primed for having a president with style." (more applause) Eric was not accustomed to this kind of attention. Flirtation was not something he had experienced much in his personal life or politics. Carson picked up on that and humored the audience with. "Our guest is being overwhelmed by all this attention to appearance. I'm sure he would like to demonstrate his many other assets so please allow me to ask first, how is your wife and family preparing themselves for this daunting task of running for president?" Fortunately Michelle coached Eric in the use of humor. "You know Johnny, it wasn't an easy decision. It's a jungle out there." At that moment the curtain opened and a handsome male lion roared inside a large cage. Carson jumped and laughed hysterically. So did the audience. Dwyer had arranged the whole thing after speaking with Michelle. It was a great stunt and would be a topic of discussion throughout his campaign.

The governor then elaborated upon his nonpartisan approach to politics reminding the audience that President Washington frowned upon factions as divisive and non productive, especially during our formative years. Carson wanted to clear the air. "Why not tell us your political philosophy?" The governor was more than willing to answer. This he thought was a teaching moment. He looked directly into the camera and spoke with conviction. "A president's political philosophy has to be persuasive, but more important, practical and with public interest at the center. National interest over special interest. It's not always clear cut either. Argumentation must maintain reasoned debate which means one side must concede when their reasoning, logic, rationale and persuasion is in some way lacking. One argument has to be favored not because it is popular but because facts point to the best solution. Another important part of this process is not holding on to preconceived notions. Being an ideologue only interferes with objective thinking and processing. Sometimes solutions appear liberal, sometimes not. It doesn't matter. What matters is solving the problem. (The audience applauded their approval) Many politicians have problems seeing that because they lead with their ideology, not with pragmatism. Half a loaf is better than none. There's always time for the other half. Another important feature in politics is to remember that change is inevitable. Each generation introduces a set of new social norms and eventually they will be replace some older traditions. That does not mean we totally discard tradition but we must remember that younger Americans are aware of social injustices and are demanding a level playing field. We must recognize and respect their call for reform throughout our society. Johnny, that is basically my philosophy of government." Johnny Carson applauded and said. "It makes sense to me governor, but if it doesn't sell, remember, I do have a back up gig for you." The audience roared and Carson applauded and thanked the New York governor as he walked off stage. His introduction to late night television was very effective and was highlighted on television news and newspapers the following day. His team of consultants, including his wife, coached him with great skill. However it was the governor's skill in delivering the message that persuaded public opinion. He came across as level headed, moderate and open-minded.

An important message was delivered that first night on Johnny Carson. American politicians must prepare citizens for a changing world where change is constant, especially among younger Americans. Polls taken after a few more talk show appearances were positively reflected in polls taken by the New York Times and CBS news. Governor O'Reilly was leading in the polls.

Subsequent interviews were arranged and O'Reilly's candidacy and message were clearly delivered, some with bipartisan support. Prominent Republican governors endorsed him because they sensed his intelligent and moderate approach which in their words were excellent signs of leadership. Good leaders persuade citizens to follow using ideas that are mainstream but driven by ideals. Michelle even made an ad where she was seen with their three children. The message focused on how we must protect our children by investing in their future. As a public school teacher, Michelle understood how students who have early childhood education before kindergarten have measured advantages with their academic skills. Teachers all over the country rallied for this cause and energized the electorate. "We are what we teach and learn" became her message for parents, teachers, and schools all over America. The campaign for educational investment crossed party lines but the message was won by Democrats which demonstrated how Dwyer's team of political strategists knew how to capitalize on issues that a majority of Americans could support. The entire campaign focused on practical aspects of leadership that believed in common ground and public good. Partisan politics was not mentioned at Eric's insistence. Eric even mentioned to Michelle that if the "honeymoon" lasts and major reforms are instituted during his first term, he would not run for reelection. In this way he would not have to be concerned with playing politics which he discovered was not something he relished even with his proficient skills. As unusual as it seemed, Governor O'Reilly was experiencing a rare moment in American politics where an era of non partisanship had great appeal. For this reason he believed that one successful and productive term would be enough. Then he could hand it over to his running mate, Bill Nelson, governor of California. Michelle liked the idea too. Both realized they had more fish to fry, but they were mindful of their immediate goal: get elected and get to work. Of course if they won, they could change their minds about reelection. They also realized that Americans seemed to prefer governors as president over other elected officials. Executive experience did make a difference.

The Democratic National Convention was the last week in July and the host city was Austin, Texas. Southern politics, in Texas and throughout the south was evolving from a "solid south" that leaned toward Democrats, to conservative politicians of either party. Republicans were making inroads but the New York governor's heroic military record was for southerners a mark of distinction. As he toured southern cities and suburbs he could see and hear patriotic, conservative voters in the audience. They seemed to give him the benefit of their doubts even though he was a northern Democrat and catholic. His military record was a big reason, also the fact that he was white and Christian helped. His catholic background, especially being a former priest, made many southerners skeptical, but with his beautiful wife standing next to him, their skepticism faded.

Eric planned his acceptance speech with Dwyer and Michelle who both had rhetorical skills with political language. Together they made great strides in writing a speech that would appeal across party lines. Eric's Republican opponent resorted to partisan division but Eric did not take the bait. He refrained and even during the presidential debates he managed to expose the foolhardy tactic for what it was, political theater. When his special moment came on the night of July 31st, 1988, Eric was introduced at the Democratic National Convention with references to his proven military and political leadership. The response of the partisan crowd was deafening. After demonstrating his gratitude to political office holders and special guests, Governor O'Reilly began his speech being careful to use language that was non partisan.

"Good evening citizens of the United States. It is my honor and privilege to speak to you tonight from the great city of Austin, Texas, about the America that I envision for our future. It is indeed a great honor that you the citizens of America have bestowed upon me." He continued to provide his audience with many examples of presidents who frowned upon ideological divisions that hampered cooperation. "We are a pluralistic culture and must always remember how important tolerance becomes when moving forward." He continued to point out how America is best when the middle class is capable of moving up the latter of success. Acceptance speeches can be long and meandering. His was not. At the end of his speech he closed his speech this way. "Let me tell you why I want to be your president. History has taught us many lessons about our people and our nation. When our nation acts in defense of social justice, equal opportunity and economic growth that enhances the lives of all of our citizens, we are at our best. When our national wealth is motivated by hard work, personal freedom, and economic justice, we are at our best. When our children are being educated with excellent values and with the necessary resources, led by teachers who put students first, we are at our best. (long applause) When we realize the importance of clean water and clear air and enjoy a quality of life, we are at our best. When nations of the world respect, admire, marvel and emulate our democratic-republic, we are at our best." He was building momentum and the audience responded loudly. "When we lead by example using our rational, scientific and moral compass, we are at our best. (The volume of response increased dramatically) When we demonstrate our compassion, generosity, and humanity, we are at our best." The partisan audience roared. " And when we utilize our military power to defend and protect freedom for reasons that are morally justified after all diplomatic efforts have failed, we are at our best. I want to be your president so I can, working with all political parties, make these goals a reality, so we Americans can be our best. I humbly ask for your support this November. Thank you! Thank you! And may God bless America." Just then balloons dropped from above. The band played popular patriotic songs. Confetti began to cover the roaring crowds with colors of the rainbow. The spectacle was a dynamic presentation of American presidential politics.

On November 4, 1988, Eric O'Reilly became the second Roman Catholic elected president and also the first former priest (Jesuit) elected as well. As discussed with his wife Michelle and Dwyer, if mid year elections in 1990, maintained or expanded his majority in congress, his political agenda could continue without gridlock. If it turned out that his administration would be able to successfully complete his long list of legislation in a variety of areas, both domestic and international in scope, President O'Reilly and his beautiful wife Michelle decided they would limit his presidency to one very successful term. He would make the announcement after he was satisfied that his agenda was successfully completed which meant he would have to wait until his last year in office. In the interim period, the president established a very ambitious set of goals to be accomplished. Among legislative accomplishments were term limits for all members of congress, an energy policy that encouraged new technology, national health care for all citizens, national gun registration, tuition waivers for college graduates who teach in ghetto schools, and new efficiency planning in the pentagon that members of his joint chiefs were encouraging. The pentagon's portion of our national budget was filled with waste so our military would be made much more efficient. The list also included legislation for reforming immigration policies so that illegal immigrants who were hard working members of our society, could become citizens after paying their fines and also pay income taxes like most Americans. Also a highway and infrastructure trust fund that is replenished every five years. Environmental laws that protected our water, air, food supply and wildlife were implemented with future adjustments included. Our scientific research and development was funded in many different areas that would ultimately produce results worth much more than their cost. Banks, Wall Street financial institutions and corporations were regulated to prevent transactions that violated public interest. The new mantra was public interest must always be paramount. Transactions must be transparent and strictly comply with anti trust laws. Our federal tax policies were revised to assure all Americans paid their fair share. Loopholes in our tax system were eliminated so that federal tax policy encouraged wealth in proportion to its merit. Middle income wages increased making the middle class capable of energizing the production and consumption cycle. Government became a practical partner and working with our private sector, promoted national pride which lead to a new national industrial policy that corrected unfair trade policies. Our federal government became a proud steward of national policies that enhanced and unified American spirit. An "era of good feelings" spread across America.

Our military posture was strong but we asked our allies who wanted our protection to contribute resources to assure our collective efforts. Our military was also made more efficient and utilized new technologies that saved lives and resources. Research and development were encouraged in both private and public sectors, for military, space and domestic consumption.

When President O'Reilly felt the time was right to announce he would not serve another term, he would inform his cabinet and political consultants. He did not want to contend with their disappointment longer than he felt necessary. He prepared to deliver the State of the Union Address in January, feeling confident that his goals as president had been achieved and decided to wait until late Spring or summer before making his announcement not to run for a second term. His state of the union address was important because it would act as a statement of fulfilled leadership. He made sure it contained lists of achievements made in three years and that would continue during his fourth year in office. His political audience would not be aware of his momentous decision and he felt if he achieved even more success with his time remaining, Americans would see his rationale and accept his decision. So he decided to make his state of the union speech a teaching moment; it would act as a prelude to his farewell speech, especially in regard to term limits which he believed would reinvigorate our political system. The congress was congratulated for rising above partisan politics and for supporting the wide variety of legislation that rewarded them with their reelection. However he explained the limits of political office by a select few and expressed the distribution of power to larger segments of our democracy so political power could be distributed and assimilated into our national fabric. Congressional terms were limited to two four year terms. There was also a law prohibiting lobbying of any kind after leaving office, with strict penalties for violations. The president's rational was simple, logical and to the point. Politicians are not indispensable. There comes a time when leaders have to bow out and provide leadership opportunities for a wider diversity of our citizens. His state of the union address provided a persuasive argument for what he had in mind. His state of the union address was well received and members of congress who voted for term limits were especially commended for their political courage. Many in fact came to him privately after his speech to say thank you indicating their relief from political posturing and grandstanding. They too had personal lives waiting to be lived but were unaware of the president's imminent decision to step down after his first term in office.

The last year of his term continued to produce wanted and needed legislation. Even retirement packages provided for government service from the president down to the lowest employee of the federal government were adjusted to satisfy fiscal conservative practices. Moderation in spending with budgets kept in line with minimum debt incurred became the law, with exceptions for national emergencies. The national press expressed their satisfaction with congressional leadership but pointed to the president whose ability to work with both sides was exceptional. The results of political harmony were also supported by an expanding economy that set all kinds of records for growth, especially for the middle class whose purchasing power stimulated upper and lower levels of society. Social mobility continued to provide optimism reflected in public opinion polls. Seeing all this progress convinced the president that his work had been accomplished by a combination of his leadership and national desire for progressive politics, not impeded by ideological fixation. President O'Reilly had achieved his goals and it was now time to move on with his life. He was in effect term limiting himself to only four years as a way of highlighting the importance of abbreviated public service. Rumors circulated about what information the public was about to hear. In late August of his last year in office, when congress was recessed during the sweltering heat in the nation's capital, the president was enjoying his visit to the Thousand Islands, on the beautiful St. Lawrence river , in upstate New York. It was at this point one evening on a beautiful house boat where he and Michelle were dining alone when he decided that a second term was not something he wanted. "You know Michelle, we need to spend more time with our family. I want to enjoy my children at this age. It's our only chance." She knew what was coming so waited for him to continue. She knew what she wanted to hear and was not disappointed. "I have decided not to run for a second term. Are you OK with that?" She held his hand and kissed it. "That is wonderful news. I just want to go home and build our beautiful home, raise our kids and be a mom. Maybe even return to teaching some day." They both were tired of Washington and the pressure attached to constant public scrutiny. "I will make the announcement when congress is in session in a few weeks, or do you think I should wait." The president was surprised by her answer. "I think you should wait until Thanksgiving. The children will be returning to school and I would rather not have more attention drawn to them. They will be settled in their classes come November, and I also think the national mood would be more accommodating. You know what I mean, the Thanksgiving feeling is perfect." The president nodded in agreement and once again saw the wisdom of his wife's thinking. She was right.

So one week before Thanksgiving, President O'Reilly would deliver his Farewell Speech crafted after weeks of thinking about what to say. He privately told the house speaker, leaders of committees in both houses and members of his cabinet. He would address the public and both houses of congress on Thursday night, one week before Thanksgiving. As he entered the House of Representatives, and after all standard introductions, he delivered his Farewell Address, speaking to millions watching at home.

"Good evening my fellow Americans. Although I have already informed you in January that our state of the union is strong, and we are at peace with the world, my reason for tonight's speech concerns something that is very important, personal and emotional." Absolute silence filled the chamber. As he continued to deliver his address, the television public noticed some white hair on his temples and even though he had aged, his attractive qualities were not diminished. He enumerated a long list of extensive accomplishments and credited congress for their success. "There were many differences of opinion and we experienced intense debates but in the end, reason prevailed over political gamesmanship. One of our most important pieces of legislation is that involving term limits. Members of congress discussed and debated reasons for voting for what is best for our nation. They admitted that pressure to be reelected often forced members to vote against bills, when deep in their gut they knew it was wrong. They felt pressured to vote against a certain bill because it would not favor them getting reelected. On many occasions, instead of fighting for what they believed was right, they surrendered to political posturing and calculation. Ultimately however they realized it's better to go down swinging rather than caving to self interest. They also decided to labor, persuading their constituents rather than fearing them. Ultimately these brave members of congress felt liberated by their decision, liberated from the pressure of playing election year politics. Together your president and congress have worked very hard with very successful results that I have enumerated on several occasions including this evening. Ladies and gentlemen of the United States Congress, I want to thank you for your cooperation, leadership and devotion to our national interests and common good. Working with both parties, I have been impressed with our ability to compromise intelligently and demonstrate how bipartisanship is suppose to work for our citizens. Therefore it is due to this rare occasion, and knowing that my obligations and responsibilities as your president have been satisfied, that I am announcing I will not seek a second term as your president." There were shouts of disagreement from both sides of the aisle. The president raised his hands over his heart. "Our country is blessed to have such cooperation and harmony and I know our vice president, if he decides to run for president, will continue with the traditions we have established." The congress gave the president a standing ovation. The viewing public had never expected such news from their very popular president.

President O'Reilly's leadership without partisanship proved to be truly transformational. Continuing with his farewell address, he advised all citizens to resort to dialogue, tolerance, compromise, and to always make very effort to follow the true intentions of our forefathers, knowing that our society is constantly evolving. "It is necessary to display flexibility when interpreting our constitution in our changing world." The president reminded his audience that his decision of intentionally limiting himself to one term allowed him to lead by example and without the restraints of reelection politics. His popularity gave him large majorities in both houses of congress for four years making it possible to pass legislation in many areas requiring national leadership. Term limits gave members of congress the will to vote with moral integrity knowing they did not have to constantly concern themselves with reelection. Historians would ultimately label this one term presidency as the golden years of modern American politics.

As for Eric O'Reilly, his tenure as president ended in his 45th year. Many universities offered him their highest office, but he declined. Instead he gravitated to the classroom where he could expand the intellects of young students striving for their own American dream.

In Memory of

A generation of Americans who served in Vietnam must not be forgotten. Our nation's foreign policy mistakes and lack of understanding in regard to the people of Vietnam were major factors leading to this tragic episode where over 58,000 Americans died as well as countless Vietnamese. Today we understand the animosity Vietnamese have for China; it is true now and it was true during the war in Vietnam but our leaders were telling us that all communists are alike. That's like saying all Democrats or all Republicans are alike. They're not. Communism is not and was not a monolithic ideology. The Vietnamese wanted our support and understanding but our mentality was frozen in the Cold war. Part of this novel is therefore dedicated to American soldiers who served in all branches of our military in Vietnam. Their death and suffering were tragic because of our leaders excessive reliance on military power, not on historical facts and diplomacy. These are important lessons that should remind us not to continue with similar policy errors in the post 9/11 era.

Websites/books referenced

the buddhist cntre.com

religion.answers.com/philosophy 10 schools-of-philosophy

unknown years of Jesus- from wikipedia, the free encyclopedia

the zensite:buddhist.christian studies, annual 2005 v25 p 75 (15)

paarsurrey/poweree by wordpress.com

the vietnam center and archive-hosted websites

divisional operation texas star 1 april '70 to 5 sep '70, courtesy terry atkinson

'hunter killer' or 'pink' teams: vietnam war

pontifical lateran university:from wikipedia

vietnam war the bitter end, history press

Lost Years of Jesus Revealed by Charles F. Potter

I woul~~ 12.95 ~~lence
which enl~~ ~~ aka
Operatioı

3/26/15.